Praise for

VICTORINE

Victorine is a compelling rendering of the life of a model working for Édouard Manet in the 1860s, who longed to be a painter in her own right. In this book, you will feel paint flow onto the canvases of Manet, Monet, Degas, Morisot, Stevens, Meurent, and others. You will imagine life on the streets of Paris in all its beauty, harshness, and fragility. And you will see a relationship between painter and model unfold with remarkable clarity and sensitivity. Victorine Meurent's body is the vehicle for Manet's artistic vision, while her robust courage, irreverence and honesty, and her longing for her own agency, shape the painter's vision. The intimate collaboration between two artists creates life-changing revelations on both sides—this dance of color and light complicated, sensuous, and intense.

—ELEANOR MORSE
author of *White Dog Fell from the Sky*

The model for great impressionist artist, Manet, the sassy, sexy, smart and artistic Victorine is as vivid as his best paintings. Yearning to paint herself, she questions Manet and his artist friends closely— annoyingly—about what they paint and how they paint it, treating the reader to a sequence of fascinating exchanges about art, its creation and demands. In a gallery of episodes, narrated in the gaudy, evocative voice of the protagonist, author Drēma Drudge renders Victorine Meurent from flesh to soul. Applying bold strokes of language, Drudge animates the story of a life lived at high intensity—sparkling, inventive, imaginative, ambitious—a totally original life. You can't help but love them both.

— JULIE BRICKMAN
author of *Two Deserts* and *What Birds Can Only Whisper*

VICTORINE

Dear Eleanor,
Here she is!
Thank you so
much for the
beautiful lunch.
Love,
Drema Drudge

VICTORINE

by

Drēma Drudge

Fleur-de-Lis Press 2020

Front cover painting: *Mademoiselle V. . . in the Costume of an Espada* by Édouard Manet (1862)
Back cover painting: *Autoportrait* by Victorine Meurent (circa 1876), with permission from Édouard Ambroselli
Author photo: Barry Drudge
Book design: Jonathan Weinert

Printed in the United States of America
First Edition

Library of Congress Cataloging-in-Publication Data
Drudge, Drēma.
Victorine.
I. Title
Library of Congress Control Number: 2019954342
ISBN 13: 978-0-9960120-3-4

Fleur-de-Lis Press of *The Louisville Review*
Spalding University
851 S. Fourth Street
Louisville, KY 40203
502.873.4398
louisvillereview@spalding.edu
www.louisvillereview.org

Contents

ONE: *Portrait of Victorine Meurent,* Paris, 1862   *3*

TWO: An Earlier Portrait of Victorine Meurent   *29*

THREE: Victorine of the Camera   *39*

FOUR: *Mademoiselle V . . . in the Costume of an Espada*   *65*

FIVE: Victorine's Song   *81*

SIX: *The Picnic (Le Déjeuner sur l'herbe)*   *93*

SEVEN: *Olympia*   *119*

EIGHT: *The Guitar Player*   *145*

NINE: *The Fifer*   *149*

TEN: *Young Lady of 1866*   *167*

ELEVEN: *Le Sphinx Parisien*   *199*

TWELVE: Like a Book   *219*

THIRTEEN: Our Father   *225*

FOURTEEN: The Siege Continues   *237*

FIFTEEN: Perennial Paris   *251*

SIXTEEN: Académie de Julian   *271*

SEVENTEEN: *A Game of Croquet*   *307*

EIGHTEEN: Room M   *331*

NINETEEN: Trials and Errors   *339*

TWENTY: Manet's Funeral, May 5, 1883   *341*

For Sena

and
for Barry

ONE

Portrait of Victorine Meurent, Paris, 1862

I AM CALLED The Shrimp, *La Crevette*, because of my height and because I am as scrappy as those little question-mark-shaped delights that I used to study when my father took me to Les Halles. I would stand before the shrimp tank and watch the wee creatures paw at the water, repeatedly attempting to scale the tank, swimming, sinking, yet always rising again. I hoped eagerly for one to crest the tank, not realizing until later that the lid was there precisely to prevent their escape.

So why am I reminded of that tank today?

Today, while I am giving a guitar lesson in my father's lithography shop, the gifted yet controversial painter, Édouard Manet, enters the shop. He gives me the nod.

I cover the strings of my guitar with my hand to silence them.

Mon père has mentioned Manet's recent patronage of his shop, of course, but I have never been here when the artist has come by.

"M. Manet, this is my daughter, Victorine. I believe you've . . ."

"We've met," I say.

"And where is it we have met, Mademoiselle?" he asks, wincing as he looks in the vicinity of my nose.

Is this a snub? I run my hand over the swollen, crooked lump of flesh on my face.

"I must be mistaken." I turn away, smiling bitterly at my quick temper, at my trying to turn up a nose such as this. Of course he doesn't recognize me.

I motion for my student to put her guitar away: "That's enough for today, dear." Though she looks at the clock with a puzzled brow, she does as I say.

Claiming he loves to hear young musicians learning to play, my father graciously allows me to give lessons in his shop, though I suspect it's more because my mother hates allowing anyone into our house besides her regular millinery clients.

Manet moves toward me, puts his face close to mine; I don't pull away, but only because that is the way painters see. I would have punched another man for standing so close. He snaps his fingers. "*La Crevette?*" he exclaims, backs away.

I raise my chin to regard the posters on my father's wall. One poster is based on a painting which used to hang on the wall. Though it's beautifully done, it's a whisper compared to the vibrant painting that was once there: my father's painting of my mother and me.

In it, we are seated. I am perhaps four. Maman drinks her tea from an eggshell-like cup while I protect my hot chocolate from her vexing dog, Jup. My mother, her hair upswept, a curl upon her forehead, is turned towards me, her arm protectively, lovingly, along the back of my chair. It's before, of course. Before she finds my father painting me alone.

Just after her discovery, the painting of us disappears from the wall of his shop along with any lingering affection she might have had for either of us, as far as I could tell.

I don't think of the poster after this day until much later, after my father's death, when I see an advertisement for *Compagnie Francaise des Chocolats et des Thes* that could only have been a copy of this one. Except the company replaces Jup with a cat on the poster, which pleases me beyond my understanding.

The poster, Père's uncharacteristic, defiant replacement of his painting, declares his fine sense of color, his signature mingling of coral and scarlet. The other posters reveal his repeated twinning of these, his favorite, colors. This is how he paints now.

Manet grasps my hand, startling me from my ruminations with his friendly smile.

"It is you; I've seen you model at Couture's. But what has happened to your nose?"

I rise on my toes, though the height it gives me is minimal. I motion for

Gabrielle to gather her music, and she shuffles the sheets.

I move closer to him while withdrawing my hand from his, take out my emerald green enamel cigarette case (a gift from a wealthy student at Couture's studio), and light a cigarette. I empty my lungs straight at the yellowing ceiling (though my torso is not a foot from his).

My father frowns and waves the smoke away; how many times must I tell him that I am eighteen and I will smoke if I please? He smokes a pipe sometimes. What's the difference?

"I give guitar lessons now. Obviously, I'm no longer a model."

Manet's eyes graze on me. I stand straighter, push my breasts out in my best model's manner without meaning to. When I realize it, I relax.

"I know just how I'll paint you. Shall we say tomorrow at one?"

My father runs his grungy shop cloth through his hands.

I raise my chin, art lust in my eyes.

"We shall say two."

He crooks his eyebrow. "Wear something else, will you? That frock does nothing for your apricot skin tone, much less your eyes. And wear your hair down. . . ." He touches a section of my red hair that flows forward, and I jerk away. "No. Better wear it up."

I glance down at my mud-colored calico dress, pick up my guitar case, and make to lead my young charge out the door.

"*Meurent?*" he says. I smile, erase it before turning back.

"Do you know where my studio is?"

"You may leave your card with my father."

I am well aware of the opportunity I have been offered. If it weren't for this trouble with Willie, I would be ecstatic. As it is, I'm a flicker beyond moved.

My boyfriend, Alphonse, is taking me to my first fight, where I meet Willie.

"There's an Englishman named Willie Something fighting against one of ours tonight," Alphonse says one evening as we are eating supper.

"Boxing? Let's go."

"You know you can't." He waves his hand. I leave the room and return in a suit of his, my hair jammed into one of his hats. Though he doesn't want to take me, he does. Of course he does.

We rush through the gray and black buildings, gleaming in the wet night, to an old theater near Notre Dame, one slated to be torn down. Suits of all shades and qualities mingle. The room smells of liquor and sweat and the pungent scent of men packed together. A heady mix.

I thrust my hands in my pockets and stand astride, occasionally kicking a leg to feel the freedom of wearing pants.

Usually the French do *savate*, kickboxing, but I have heard of this boxing with the hands. That seems like a more honest, intimate way to fight to me—there is nothing distinctive about our limbs, but our faces are unique. It makes the resentment seem real.

An announcer introduces the bare-chested fighters, has them shake hands. The men wear breeches and thin looking shoes. The Frenchman fighting tonight is short and small. The Englishman, Willie, is of medium height and red-haired, with a pale face which will be overlaid with ruddiness when he is fighting. Or, I will discover, while making love.

The bell unleashes Willie. He leaps off the double ropes tied to a wooden frame, coming at his opponent as though he holds an ancient grudge. I lean forward. My heart pounds with each shot he takes, each hooked punch he pushes from himself. Soon his knuckles drip blood, but whose is it? I look to this side, then that.

My right fist bunches and thrusts with his. Sweat dripping from his face, he grins madly and looks our way as his opponent hits the ground and slowly rises. For a moment I fear he has discovered that I am a woman, until I realize he is an automaton who sees no one and nothing.

The two collapse onto one another in an exhausted hug of sorts until, it seems, a secret signal intrudes, and they head to their corners and come out, enemies again.

Delacroix-red blood flows from the Frenchman's forehead, into his eyes, and he shakes his matted mane, flinging the blood. Willie stares at it as if it alone is his enemy and he pounces. One-two-one, go his fists and I rise and shoulder my way up front. Ringside, I watch Willie hit the man as if he must slay him. I cheer with my fingers in my mouth, whistling up something deep. Willie glances my way, and, with a grin, lands one last blow. The Frenchman falls.

Willie waits long enough to see his opponent groggily sit up, and then he runs from one side of the ring to the other, hands raised, before abruptly leaving the ring. The wooden floor shakes and I look down to find I am the one causing the quake; I cannot stop bouncing up and down. I follow Willie into the makeshift dressing room.

"What are you doing?" Alphonse hisses, grabbing my arm. I knock it away and walk straight up to Willie and lick the sweat from his face. He jerks away, cursing, until I take the hat from my head, my hair fireworking down my back. He laughs and pulls me onto his lap. Alphonse makes a noise, but only one.

The moment I sit on Willie's lap, I know I am free. Body and soul. Here is a man who will only take what is given, who will never demand, never want more. He dwells in his body alone.

I look back for Alphonse, but he is gone.

"Leave the suit on," Willie says when we make love an hour later. We combine quietly, harshly, only moving strategic bits of clothing. Under his hands my body and my mind thrum as surely as they do when I play guitar or violin. His touch is more animal than Alphonse's, his lust pure. It nearly matches my fever.

I send an omnibus round to Alphonse's for my things the next day and ask the driver to deliver them to Willie's apartment. When I open the trunk, I find Alphonse has neatly folded my clothing. He has also included a photo of me, one in which I wear a Grecian dress of muslin. I laugh, because of all of the naked photos he has taken of me, he gives me one in which I am clothed. A tiny part of me will miss the man. Willie hugs me from behind and takes the photo from me. "You're so beautiful," he says reverently.

In reply, I burp.

Willie laughs wildly, especially when I do it again, which reveals that I can do it at will. It is a skill which never fails to keep me from being taken too seriously.

Until Willie and I fight, all is bliss. We hike in Fontainebleau, tour the Seine crammed into a *périssoire*, stay up more nights than we sleep. He introduces me to his British and French sporting pals and teaches me that nothing is as important as I have always thought it. My muscles relax; my mind does, too. I eat, drink, fuck, but not in that overwrought manner in which I did with Alphonse. I do it now to declare that I am alive, and that I get to call the shots and right now, I don't want to call any.

Not that Willie calls them either—neither of us does. My soul rests, recovers.

The Day We Fight, we are at Café Margot, drinking absinthe. Drink opens holes of longing in me that no one and nothing can fill, and I know it even as I feel it. Yet it's delicious, this yearning.

Willie glances at a woman walking past us, just for a second.

"She's gorgeous," I say.

He laughs and turns up his glass.

"I'm with *you* now." The way he says it sounds as if he's never moving on, ever.

My life has relied upon comings and goings, beginnings and endings. Father's projects and mother's. A sitting for me here and there. I find this briefness comforting.

A man about my age enters with shy virgin eyes, sits at the bar. As I leave the table, I tell myself not to do it, but I approach him, whisper into his ear.

When I return to a confused-looking Willie, I grin. "He's coming home with us tonight."

"Like bloody hell he is." We argue and I accuse him of many things: fear, worries of impotence. I put my hand heavily on his shoulder and tap it with each accusation. He shrugs his shoulder, but I won't leave him be.

"Fine. I'll just go home with him instead."

Suddenly his fist meets my nose and colors ring my head, and I take a swing at him. We pummel one another over nothing, everything. Violets, pinks, reds, wake me. Mercifully, I see no absinthe green. The blood drips from my nose, dots the dry wooden floor and wildly I think at least my blood will moisten the oak planks.

My labored breathing sounds from a place far away while I fixate on the vivid red running on the floor—it's a pure, costly color. Willie examines his hand, my nose, in apparent horror while I laugh. This isn't the thrill of drinking one too many and dancing in the middle of the street, raising eyebrows and ire with Alphonse, tossing off my clothes at a party. This is better.

The room grows quiet, and a large man stands and comes towards Willie. I leave the café, laughing, and run all the way back to our apartment. I'm packing my bag when Willie enters.

"Victorine. I'm so sorry."

I turn to face him, my chest drumming. "Do it again."

Though my head hurts, and my nose is killing me, my face tingles. Why can't women box?

"What? No. I love you." His eyes apologize, and he reaches a hand towards my face.

"It's okay," I say, clasping him close to my chest, my nose bleeding into his hair. Red, red, not fairy green. We drown in red kisses. His hands tremble. I taste my blood on his lips, on his chest. We slide against one another, onto, into. The sun rises; we go for a swim.

While we dry our naked bodies in the tall green grass on the left bank of the Seine, I stroke his repentant face. In the distance, a train sings. If only . . .

"Willie," I say, kissing his soft cheeks, "I'm sorry, but I have to leave you."

He bows his head. "I won't do it again."

I stroke his cheek. "I know. But I will."

After the fight, after I tell him we can't be together, I put on my grass-stained dress and walk slowly back to my parents' home, hoping they will take me in.

I debate whether or not to tell my mother that Manet wants to paint me. She will only ridicule it, because of my newly broken nose. It won't occur to her that he can paint whatever nose he chooses onto me.

At the door I greet my mother who is sitting on her stool, and I praise the blue roses she has fashioned for the high-brimmed spoon bonnet with its double sets of ties. The utility ties will keep the bonnet on the head, while the pink grosgrain ones are for decoration. She murmurs something; she is on the island of hatting, my father and I call it.

When I was a child I would catch her in that space and sit at her feet and talk to her for hours. She never responded, but I made it enough.

I try to make my news live for me by telling her anyway: "*Maman*, Manet came into *Pére*'s shop today." She murmurs something about thread.

"He asked me to sit for him. He doesn't mind my nose at all." Though I am thrilled on one level, my excitement is manufactured over the catacomb within me. At least now my longing has a name: Willie. The ache of his absence is almost as good as his presence. I don't blame him for hitting me, not when I wanted like anything to feel the force living within those fists upon me. I wanted to excite as much passion in him as boxing does. His physical need for me seems so much tamer than the fury he unleashes when he is boxing.

What I didn't intend was to cause us to part. Without Willie my mind whirls, a flight of questions pecking inside of me, and I am unable to shoo them all away.

I'd like to tell him about Manet, even though he wouldn't appreciate it for its own merit, but because what excites me excites him. But telling him means chancing myself around him. Still, I do need to get my things.

"Have you eaten?" I ask my muttering mother, but she continues to stretch fabric over wire, secures it. I don't begrudge her this, because I have seen the same look on many a young painter's face. How is it that she has found a way to express the tender things in her heart through her hands and never her lips? Why has she allowed herself to be wed to this art once removed?

Art can raise a person, but this colored commerce cannot, this field of flowers on a fussy hat or my father's mosaic of shades printed onto pieces of paper even less permanent than my mother's creations. At least her hats are sometimes made over by the thrifty. My father's posters end up on the ground, sometimes pulled down by ornery schoolchildren, sometimes merely rained upon or loosened by wind.

I once chased one of his posters about town as the bright bird flitted from one street to another. Coral and turquoise, swoops of white and black. I grabbed it up just before a horse trampled it and I held it to my chest, sobbing, unawares.

Is there no way to stop the decay, the inevitable death of all but art? Good, solid, great art. I want to create it because I want to live forever. Me, not a child of mine who carries only the color of my eyes but not how my eyes see. Not a child who will love and hate me and never understand, not really, who I was or am because that is the way between children and parents. That ache of being misunderstood on both sides is all that separates us, and it is necessary. Otherwise we would suspect we were just an endless march of humans being born, wanting, dying, all the same. No, as long as we keep that distance, we are *different,* and the secret is never revealed. And so the cycle continues.

Never mind: I want to understand my mother.

Mother's skin is still smooth, her hair raven. We are similarly shaped, though her extra three inches of height thins her. Her brown eyes echo in mine, though I see with my father's.

Her eyes hide secrets I know I will never be told and am not likely to ask about. Hollow, my mother's soul. Perhaps I inherited that, too.

I fetch a thick slice from a *boule de pain* and motion for her to eat. She picks it up as if she's holding a mouse. I'm quite sure she's eaten nothing since breakfast. For all of our country's love of food, none of us in this house knows how to cook worth anything.

As she nibbles at the bread, I ask her about the bonnet.

"It's for Julianne. She's going to the country for the weekend and wants to take it with her." Always a reason why she must take the latest rush job, when I know the real reason is that she prefers that gentler world she creates with ribbon and straw.

My father distances himself too, though more genially. It doesn't make me less lonely. When I speak of art, he listens.

Once the bread is gone, my mother picks up the bonnet. I retreat to my room to stare at my nose in the mirror. It would ache more if I hadn't landed a few blows of my own. I put up my fists and pretend to box, my hands flying at my reflected image.

I put down my hands, only to raise them again to cover my face. Willie. I miss Willie's urgent, bestial lovemaking that somehow never left me doubting that he loved me. It troubles me, though, that sometimes when he kissed me I thought of Helen, the one who taught me to play guitar when I was thirteen, to have feelings under my tongue that I could not name. Watching her close her eyes in exultation at the sounds her fingers made caused me to lean in, longing to kiss the wedge of tongue that peeked out of the corner of her mouth when she formed a particularly difficult chord.

After she finished a song one afternoon, I hugged her for what she must have thought was a bit too long and she pushed me away.

"We're both girls," she said.

"So? Your music stirred me." I didn't know how else to describe it.

"No, no, that was your soul stirring, not your body."

What does gender have to do with love? Even then I knew my body understood something that my mind did not.

Being with Willie drives doubt from me in part because his maleness—his dense, fungal scent after a bout, the bulk of his solid shoulders, the swollen bulge of his arms—are all so very different from the emaciated painters I typically bed.

I languish in my parents' home. I am miserable in this small wooden bed with its cheerful counterpane. Why does my mother excel at using color and fail at love? Her generosity of hues rivals a bordello madam's.

I don't suffer at her coldness as I would if Paris were not beautiful. In Paris, beauty is everything and everywhere. From every meal to what one wears, appearances are everything. Life's brevity makes beauty necessary.

I dress early the next morning, then sneak a box of rouge out from under the bed and apply it before the mirror with a fluffy brush. I pour a bit of water from my pitcher into my washbasin, just a dab, and add some of the powder. I dip in my paintbrush and begin painting my mirror. The mix is too thin, so I add more red, and soon I have covered my mirror with a sheer layer of scarlet. I make a circle, cheeks, and I attempt to shape it with the tip of the brush's handle. I angrily wipe the smears away with a hand.

After cleaning my mirror with an old scarf, I go out to the small dining room and drink my *café*, eat my *pain au chocolat*. There is nothing I like more than chocolate.

"A day improves immeasurably with chocolate," I say in my best shop girl voice, enunciating the way I was taught. Chocolate can cure nearly any ill, even those of the heart. Or so I tell myself.

My father says *bonjour* to my cheeks. I toss my black shawl about me in reply. My mother glances up only a moment from her work, a black mourning bonnet that will depress her until she finishes it; when she uses color, she hums.

My mother eyes my appearance, my white shirt, my red hair hastily pulled back. "And will Manet dress you then?" she says as her eyes gauge the color of my cheeks. "Where's your hat?" She knows I hate wearing hats.

"Hell, Mother. If he can fix a broken nose, I suppose he can paint whatever clothes he wants to on me. For that matter, since when do I need clothes to model?" I glance at my father as I say this. I regret my outburst as she instantly retreats into her work, as my father steadily drinks his *café*.

"Let me walk you to your shop," I say to my father as I pick up my guitar. I always take my guitar to sittings. Inevitably a wait arises while a painter mixes a color or rearranges the scene. Or even goes to lunch, forgetting that I am flesh and blood and require nourishment too. To prevent starvation I always bring a *mouchoir* with some *pain blanc* in it, maybe some cheese. And always my guitar. Not my violin—never it.

The distance between our home and the shop belongs to my father and me, as it always has. On the way he gently scolds me, says that my mother worries about me. Instead of arguing that criticism isn't concern, I play the game we have always played: that my mother really does care about me. "You don't like it when she picks at you either," I say, and he tries to hide his smile from me, but he cannot. I nudge him with my shoulder. "I love you."

He nods and swallows. I am his only child, and he has treated me as both daughter and son, has taught me his trade, although I don't want his trade, or my mother's. I admire what my parents do, but it is not enough. It only takes care of the common beauty and does not raise a person above the mundane. A woman may wear a hat every day, but when she wears it she cannot see it unless she is before either a glass or a person who acts as a glass.

Lithographing and all of the signage he makes are an art of sorts, but my father only processes what others create.

I want to paint. It's all I really want. I am well aware that it's this roof over my head and food in my stomach that allow me to want more. There are too many starving artists in this city. I should not despise my parents for their practical choices, and yet a part of me does.

I want to make something that is both transient and intransient. Painting, it could be argued, is the same, really, because we are only capturing the now—the ideas, the politics, and the appearances of now, that is, if we don't follow the academy's strict ideas of what subjects art can take, which is what I hear Thomas Couture drill into his students: "Come on, young men, say it with me—historical, portraits, genre, landscapes, and finally," he here always crooks a dark eyebrow and waits for the students to finish it in a grumble: "still life." There is a hierarchy, and if a subject isn't in it, then it is unacceptable. After that, though, he always nearly whispers: "But paint of your time."

It is maddening to watch the rich young students push their paint around on their palettes, muddying the valuable pigment as if it is their birthright to waste it, while the poorer ones skip lunch to afford paint.

Sometimes on breaks I quickly throw on my dressing gown and quiz the teacher about painting. Usually he says he is too busy, or he flits from painting to painting, criticizing, or complimenting. Sometimes he explains why this should be mixed and not that, and what happens if you don't prime a canvas.

Once he even declared to the class that, for a woman, I had a fine artistic mind. I hated him for saying that, hated myself for loving it.

Instead of learning to paint, then, I learned to sing, to play the guitar and the violin. The arts are sisters of the senses.

We arrive at my father's shop without saying another word, until I wish him goodbye. "Tell that soap king you won't do his work on credit if he comes in," I scold. I move to kiss my father on his cheek, but he jerks away. I wave cheerfully and leave.

With hours to go before my appointment with Manet—hours, I tell myself, I have no clue how to fill—my feet reveal what I had already guessed: I am making for Willie's.

If he is not at home (or asleep—a burglar could take everything and Willie would sleep on), I will simply take my things and march them back over to my parents' house, I vow.

I enter the room through the slightly ajar door. A glance tells me that my trunk is at the foot of the bed. Willie's light breathing sounds in the warm room, and his animal scent travels quickly to me. I move to his side and stand over him, watching the sunlight through the door lap across his face.

Gazing at him tells me what I have not been able to admit until now: I haven't come for my trunk at all. For one thing, how could I carry it without hiring someone to haul it? No, I am here because I want nothing more than to sink down onto that bed of forgetfulness. I need not go to Manet's. This could be enough.

I have hours yet before my appointment. I could just lie here beside him; he wouldn't have to know.

He stirs and turns toward me, his mouth wide, his large tongue hanging sideways. I shudder; I am right to allow the better part of me to rise. How can you clamber over the tank's lid if you insist on lying at the bottom, even if the rest does feel so nice, even if just for a moment?

Without opening the trunk, I flee.

I am at Manet's studio at four rue de Saint-Petersbourg half an hour early. I do not knock until a quarter till. Instead, I stay outside and admire our city's stately trees, listen to the guitar music from just down the street. It is always evening in Paris for someone, usually the wealthy. All pastimes must be available at all hours for not only rich Parisians, but also for those tourists (especially those Americans and British) who insist that we must never sleep. Their money ensures it is so.

There are two cities: that for those of us who work here, and that for those who do not. Rarely do the two meet.

A stiff breeze reminds me of the numerous horses that the street cleaners cannot keep up with, as well as the trash and sewage that run in channels on either side of our streets. A new law limits the dumping of garbage from windows too early in the morning and late at night, so one has less chance of being unexpectedly covered in the contents of a slop jar, but it's so new a law I dodge away from the side of a building when I hear a window open. Seconds later: *swoosh*.

Though painters never want you to feel yourself better than they, they do insist that you show the same degree of decorum, so I check my face and hair in a hand mirror I carry in my purse.

Manet answers the door in a black suit jacket, light colored pants, and a tie. The boys at the school never dressed up to paint, but then Manet is a gentleman painter. He ushers me into an airy, multi-windowed room that smells of all of the things I love best: paint, turpentine, linseed oil, old clothes, and the odor of drying canvases.

The rug beneath my feet blends blue with hideous green and yellow flowers. I drag my muddied feet over it, to no improvement, but at least it hides the snarl of colors. Who decorated this place?

A small footstool waits by his ornately scroll-worked beechwood easel equipped with a crank for lowering or raising it. How could one fail to create wondrous art with such a base?

Rolled canvases, like corpses bundled in sheets, people the tables, nearly crowded out by *objets d'art*. Brightly colored shelves of costumes call from crates. Property Master Manet, I nearly say aloud.

It reminds me of my days working at Le Bon Marché, and I long to go through each crate. My eyes tour each corner, and my smile grows. I am sure I could create here.

Sunlight through the windows reveals the cobwebs in the corners, the dust under the tables. It's always the same: artists so busy creating that they can't maintain reality.

After a time: "Welcome," Manet says as he rubs his hands. "Your things."
He gestures to a bench where I pile my shawl and my bag (which holds my
lunch and not much else), smooth my hair again. I place my guitar case carefully on the floor.

"Do you approve of my studio?" he asks.

That curl will not stay behind his ear, and I fight the urge to smooth it back,
but only for artistic reasons. His hair would have to be cut quite short, I imagine, to keep it under control.

I raise my chin. "It will do."

Water stains mar the elegant sideboard; dabs of paint (and now mud) spot
the rug. At least there is a bouquet of fresh flowers—irises and peonies. A wet
bar hugs one wall. Indeed.

He stares me up and down and I turn slowly for him when he gestures, my
shoulders forward, my chin lowered.

"Wash your face over there, please." It was a chance I took; face painting
(called "makeup" by prostitutes) is approved of by some, vilified by others. I
inwardly curse myself for trying. As if I care.

I pour water into the porcelain basin with a much finer pitcher than the one
I handled at home. Its smoothness makes me hold it longer, and I gaze upon
its flowers and its rim of gold as if looking at them is to feel them. I cup water
with my hands and splash myself. He comes over and makes a noise, picks up
a rough white towel, and dips it in the water. "It won't come off easily that
way. You must not be used to wearing it." He briskly wipes my cheeks, drying
them gently with a soft towel. The tender way in which he touches me makes
me want to cry, and something in me opens, just a crack.

"The shirt will do, but the hair . . ."

He indicates that I should take it out of the bun I have wound it into. I
fumble the pins and can't unknot the ribbon I have tied about it. He turns for a
moment and examines the canvas on his easel: a plate of mesmerizing oysters,
a fork thrown down in front of them, half a lemon cut and lying juxtaposed
upon the table. A small crock of pepper stands behind the pepper. Who would
think such a picture worthy of painting? Who else could do it so masterfully?
He almost convinces me.

As if I hear Couture talking, I look at the painting: no midtones, pure colors,
too much black, obvious outlines. I look again. The overturned fork claws its

way to the dish; it's a great, predatory sea monster. The emptied shells to its right testify to its bloodthirstiness. The table housing the tableau is brown, and I coin a word, based on other still lifes of his, for the area in the painting behind the oysters:

"Blackground."

"*Excusez-moi?*" He blinks.

I wave my hand slightly as I let my hair fall and comb it with my fingers. "Nothing. I was just admiring your background." It's not done in the traditional style, yet I do admire the painting, just not that dreadful backdrop.

A tall, thin man with sideburns enters the studio unannounced (as all of Manet's friends do, I discover) and stops right before me, stooping over me, touching my nose gingerly as I jerk away.

"I beg your pardon," I yelp.

"I came as you asked, Manet. This needs setting," he says, shaking his head after glancing again at my nose.

"Bazille, Victorine—that is, Meurent," says Manet. I am grateful that he remembers that I have insisted on being called by my last name, just as the men are.

"I know your work," I say to the man who seems young, even to me. There's something gentle and sweet about his eyes, and he's just as pale as some of his paintings I have seen displayed in shop windows. His work intrigues me, but I'm not yet sure it moves me.

"Hold her, Manet," says Bazille, "while I fix it."

I startle. "Wait. What?"

"I trained to be a doctor," Bazille says.

Manet touches my shoulder and indicates that I should sit. I do, but I brush his hand away. "Go ahead," I say bravely, closing my eyes.

"This may hurt, but you'll breathe better afterwards," says Bazille. I think on his painting, his work that seems as if it's generated by five people, none of them who could possibly be this quiet man, while he grabs my nose. Then pain sparks through me, and it feels as if he is trying to wrench my nose from my face. I know nothing until I feel a wet cloth on my face.

"Thank you," I say, sitting up and holding out the cloth to him. "Why do you not practice if you are a doctor?" I ask, finally breathing deeply, deliciously. The scent of paint heightens now.

He grins shyly and shrugs.

"He failed the exam," says Manet.

We all roar with laughter, but I secretly tug at my nose.

After Manet sees his friend out he stares at me and I am not offended by his steady gaze. "Do you have one of those hair things with you?"

"A snood? No." Le Bon Marché—shelves and shelves of beautiful things in a thoroughly modern building. I do miss the counters full of glory, just not the bowing and scraping, the way those empty women sought to fill themselves repeatedly. It saddened me to watch their desperation, to realize that money wasn't the answer.

It became clear to me that one needed enough money, but that more than enough wasn't necessary or desirable.

He rummages about in crates, among the open shelves. I see more of him here in his props, almost, than on his canvases. Imagined lives thrive in his possessions.

Women's hats from years, decades, past, pile up. I cluck at that. In Paris one would not dare wear a head covering that was out of date, not unless one were trying to make a statement. What would *ma mère* say?

I again wear no hat at all, and she always has plenty to say about that.

"Here." He hands a black velvet snood to me.

"I'm afraid I don't know how to wear one," I say, twirling it on my finger.

He rustles through his wares again and brings out a boar-bristle hairbrush, holding it up to ask permission. I turn around and he brushes my hair awkwardly at first, and then with more assurance.

"From London." The bristles of the brush grab my hair, pulling it authoritatively back, even as his hand falters. My scalp yields to the brush's tenderness, but my shoulders stiffen. It is one thing to give myself to others, but they are unimportant. Everything I do and say here means something.

He gathers my hair into one hand (the black handle of the brush reflects in the mirror) and slips the net over it with his other. He stands back, hunts again until he returns with a green ribbon.

"No." I say.

He ties it around my head, frowns, and fixes it again.

"I don't want to wear that insipid thing."

His hand falls. "Your shirt will do, but we need something around your neck, something black."

He shakes his head at a number of necklaces he removes from a cedar jewelry box and bends over and pulls a thick shoelace from his boot. "It's new," he says as he makes it into a bow gingerly about my throat and echoes it above with a tight knot in the string. He stands back, nods as he fingers my left earring, and confirms that I have one in my right ear.

These moments of intimacy that aren't just preludes to sex make modeling worthwhile. Manet touches me as if he is aware that I have a soul.

"Sit here." He faces me toward the window, his hands gently upon my shoulders. Too soon I will be in place and he will quit touching me.

"I really don't want to wear the hair ribbon."

"I will not ask you why not. The man in me wonders. The artist requires a hair ribbon be used."

I cross my arms but realize I appear to be a pouty child, which will make him more likely to insist upon the ribbon, so I quickly uncross them.

He sighs. "My dear, perhaps if you just hold your objections until I've done some work. You don't know me yet. It's natural you don't trust me, but it's imperative that you do." As he says this, his face reddens slightly, and he breathes heavily.

I let out an exaggerated breath. "I haven't modeled for you yet, so it's natural you don't trust me, but it's imperative that you do." I reach up to remove the hair ribbon.

His hand grabs mine. "I'm afraid I must insist."

"But I'm not twelve."

"Yes, but you're also not twenty-five."

He is certainly not Alphonse. Not Willie. I could be curled in that warm bed with Willie, away from this uncertainty, from this longing.

I look behind me. "What will be in the background?"

"Black," he answers.

Blackground.

I know that Manet is great and will only get better, if for no other reason than that no one else is like him. I've seen so many paintings of me that nothing impresses me, although I do know what does not work, and I know this: I am far too worldly for a child's hair accessory.

"Just look at me when we begin," he says.

"*At* you?"

"Yes." He moves things about while I gape.

"But." Women do not stare directly at the viewer in art. We stare off into space; we stare to the side or above, but not at the viewer. It's considered immodest unless one is posing as a goddess. He objects to face painting, but I may stare outward?

He removes the still life from the easel and replaces it with a blank canvas.

"Now, over here." His brush raises and lowers, adds color to his palette. It dips and waves, then he puts it down, loads another, threads it through the hole in his palette. The dragonfly dance is dizzying. No one speaks of the art of the brush. The flight of the brush is just as instrumental in creating the painting as are the paints. I wish I could paint its path upon a canvas.

There is an art to modeling, as well. It requires being aware of the body, having good posture and correct positioning, combined with a capacity to occupy one's mind while wearing an expression that may be very different from the scene playing out in one's head. Along with scenes that I paint, I tell myself stories or hear music. Hours can go by that I am unaware of. I'm grateful for the time to imagine, and my face does not share my mind's secrets, so I may think of anything I wish.

I choose a neutral expression. Anything else I find contrived or forced. If I am to have a chance at being represented accurately, it's only if I don't ask my face to overplay itself. It has nothing to do, I'm sure, with my father asking me not to smile when he painted me.

Eventually curiosity drives me to lean forward while Manet mixes a color and to peer at what he has so far; I'm eager to assist him in what he seeks to capture. She's a waif, a poor innocent, someone young and inexperienced. I allow my face to show the mix of hope and anxiety, and a distant cousin of longing. I cannot bear to show how I long for things that must be there, somewhere, if I crave them so badly. What if they're not? No. They must be. I tie them all up with my expression that only hints at my thoughts.

A few years ago my mother had a client over, a wealthy woman with the most intriguing purse. "Would you like to hold it, my dear?" she asked when she noticed me staring at it. The bag—decorated with exquisitely shiny green glass beads—had a silver clasp which doubled as the mouth of the frog.

As I put out my hand to touch it, my mother said, "Would you go buy me some black thread?" My mother never ran out of black thread—it was the color she used most often. I went out for the thread, staring back at the woman, Madeline, and her purse, and when I returned, the woman was gone. Occasionally I would encounter her, but my mother had put a barrier between us, one I didn't understand. Madeline said no more than a hurried "*bonjour*" to me after that.

Manet's brush somehow dusts away my usual look and uncovers the longing. Most decidedly, he paints a virgin, and then the wish for a return of my innocence leaks through as well.

Surely he has seen Alphonse's photographs of me? Who has not? My heart thanks him through my eyes, and I use my eyelashes to make me for just a moment *la femme innocent*. The ribbon makes perfect sense now, damn him.

Every so often he gives me breaks, unlike other painters that one has to beg for a moment, though I pride myself on my stillness. He does not mind, either, if I study what he has done, and I do, silently at first.

"What do you think of the background?"

Begrudgingly I admit, "It's perfect."

"Why?"

I know so many things I don't know how to say. Articulate, see, that's the word I should have thought of, but the simpler words came first.

"It will highlight her."

"You speak of the figure as if she's not you."

"She's not." I pull my cigarette case out of my purse, watch him note its expensiveness, light a match, and put it to my cigarette. When he recoils slightly, I blow smoke. I rub my still shoulders.

He washes his hands, squeezes the last out of a tube of white, flattening it repeatedly. As soon as I finish the cigarette, I get back into place. I have hurt his feelings, but how?

The day wears on. Does this other me perhaps exist apart from myself? Maybe he sees someone who is really there that I just can't see. I don't know this waif, this young woman.

Later, I shake my head as I examine the woman who is emerging from the canvas. "You will hate it." It slips out.

His brows raise and his face tightens.

"This isn't what you want to paint. I am not so innocent. I am not so vulnerable. You are painting it for me, not of me, and not because it's what you want to paint. It's deadly for a painter to be so concerned about what others think of his subject or his technique." I have forgotten that I am not sitting in a classroom full of young men who will welcome my words.

He reaches out his hand, almost touches my shoulder, and whispers: "Why don't you play us a song while I rest?"

I sit on one of the striped sofas about his spacious studio, nearly as big as my parents' apartment. Living happens outside of the house, so one does not need much space, and nowadays the new Paris apartments are getting smaller, as the boulevards get larger. We are to worry more for the state than for ourselves, they say. It makes sense, but not for it to be foisted upon us.

I chord a gentle melody, losing myself in the music until Manet sits beside me. Then I play a bawdy bar song. I sing "The Wines of France," and he joins me on the chorus. I follow it with an instrumental piece, my fingers sliding into bar chords.

"I don't recognize that song."

Embarrassed, I shrug. "It's something I made up."

He leans forward and examines my still-swollen nose.

I don't want to say it, but I do: "You don't have to cover it up."

"Is that why you think my painting lacks authenticity?"

See, why can't I think of words like that? I know my vocabulary is just something else that separates me from an educated man like Manet.

Well, if I thought I could catch his sophistication from bedding him, I might. As it is, I find myself wanting him, but on a far-away level, the way I might want a *crêpe* because I know they are good, not because I am hungry. I have a rule: I do not sleep with the artists who paint me, except for the boys at Couture's school. It's bad for art, but their art reeks, as a whole, anyway. Until Manet makes a move on me (he will, they all do), I will not tell him my rule, and his desire will show in the painting. If anything can save this piece, it will be that.

I glance at the canvas. Well, normally it would. I'm not sure this painted girl knows anything of desire. Which means the artist lacks it towards her. I must remedy that, and quickly.

I wouldn't call myself a muse, but, maybe I am *une muse peu*. I have seen young men who don't know green from gray sprout a palette after I whisper into their ears, squeeze their tubes, and tell them to mix; stick figures round and bloom after I offer them air-drawn lines in front of their canvases. I can feel the diagonals, become the horizontal or the vertical. My perspective fades along the same line as that of the painting.

How to tell Manet that more and more the paint lies about me? There is no way I told it to say those things. Afternoon after afternoon the lie grows, and it is too late for him to go elsewhere with it. When he finishes it, he asks what I think. I know what I am supposed to say, and I have said it to other artists, the lesser ones in art school, and the novices. I open my mouth, but.

"This is still not me," I say.

His shoulders stiffen and he gets taller. "What made you think I wanted to paint you?"

I see the truth of what he says, but . . .

"Then why did you paint her alone, with nothing in the background? It seems as if it's meant to be a portrait, but don't people pay for portraits? Artists don't enter them in the *Salon*, do they?"

His face hardens. "They do if they are good enough. Besides, didn't you say the woman in the painting is not you?" He raises his hands, seems to carefully modulate his deep voice: "When I saw you at your father's shop, you were helping that dear child play guitar, your fingers atop hers. There was such tenderness in what you were doing, and the moment you saw me, wariness replaced it." He glances at the painting. "You don't trust me as an artist, and if you don't trust me, well, I can't paint what you won't reveal."

She is so young, so pure, yet her gaze is unrelenting. At least her nose is straight. I need to try to understand.

"You fixed my nose."

He shakes his head. "A nose is a far cry from those qualities you seek to hide."

Maybe there is something to what he says.

"May I look at it alone?"

He frowns. "Suzanne is expecting me for lunch. Just lock the door if you leave." He turns around from putting his jacket on. "You won't touch it, will you?"

The door closes; I am already lost in the portrait.

I stand before the canvas. Thick *café*-and-black cloud about my likeness. Nothing behind "me" matters, just the future. (Maybe if I try to see the painted woman as me I will understand her better.) The net hides my length of hair, and only a tidy expanse of hair is seen coming down from a straight part except on the left-hand side where a tuft of hair has "escaped" (coaxed forward by him with hands that remind me of my father's).

Only one of my earrings is visible. The ribbon on my head seems to shift color—it's either blue-gray or green, and his capturing its two tones is a sign of genius.

I lean forward. The shoelace around my painted neck seems to divide my head from my body. Isn't that exactly what is happening? Art is my head; Willie my body. How can Manet know that? The askew shoelace echoes the hair ribbon in its movement.

Black and white stripe my shoulders, and as I move closer to the painting I note clumps of white paint on the bottom left of the shirt. This piping repeats around the neckline where it becomes something a bit fancier—a scrolling design. Above the design a strip of white, and then a repeated gray. Below the rounded collar two pleated columns with black flowers trail off into infinity.

The shirt itself is too large, as are my dreams. Excess fabric blouses just below the shoulders: I do not fit into my life. Like the "necklace," the shirt also slants. Where are my arms beneath the material?

I do like the painted expanse of the net, and my ear pleases. He only hints at the earring, as if he does not care about it. No, as if he knows I do not.

Lastly I survey "her" face—she is not me, I remind myself. The eyelashes perfectly match the hair and eye color. Yes, I suppose he is right: My eyes *are* like glasses of claret. Something shines on my face, from its width on my forehead tapering down to my chin. My cheeks glow (after he made me wash) a peachiest pink and they make my hair appear even mousier, a timid red.

The nose—I could love him for it. It must have been difficult to paint this nose as if it belongs to a patrician. If only he could give me that in real life. Still, slowly my real nose is returning to me.

My lips press primly, virginally, together.

The chin is crooked, as are my clothes, as if to compensate for his having fixed my nose.

He makes me seem so pure, so prim. So innocent. I have never been innocent. A deep thirst recommences, but I don't know what for. Were he here, I know what I'd try to substitute for this undefined longing.

Without taking my sight from the canvas I eat a slightly stale bit of bread. I shove the remaining piece of it into my mouth to mask a sob.

I am still searching the canvas, searching, when Manet returns. He takes off his jacket and throws it on the sofa.

"How was lunch?" Having him here instantly alters how I see it, and I look away from the canvas and back to clear my gaze.

He clears his throat. "Just fine."

I turn towards him, stare at the ceiling. "What did you have?"

He walks towards the painting, towards me. "Beef, vegetables, *consommé*."

I note he doesn't ask if I have eaten. My handkerchief is now empty; painters do not like to see their models eat. I think it reminds them that we are real.

I turn back towards the painting, and he puts a hand on either of my shoulders from behind.

"What do you see?" he asks. His touch is companionable. I like it until he puts his chin heavily upon my head. It makes me feel weighed down.

From deep within I pull up rusted words of truth: "A portrait, no story."

He withdraws his hands, removes his chin from my head. "Why should there be a story?"

"I'm not a stalk of asparagus. I am not a beautiful woman, so without a story, no one will want to look at me. There must be a story." It hurts to admit that I am no longer physically appealing, not with this nose. Somehow even with the new, painted nose I do not look attractive in this painting.

"You don't know what you're talking about," he says as he turns from me and cleans a brush with a rag dipped in turpentine. "First of all, your brand of attractiveness has much more to do with your inner fire than a nose. If anything, your nose makes you more attractive than you were at Couture's."

"So you do remember me?"

"After I got past your nose, of course I remembered you. There you were on that platform, slumped in a chair with the side of your face in your hand as if daring us to find you attractive. You were the Burning Bush. You didn't blink, didn't move. You were as still as a tree and had twice the depth of one's roots. I couldn't move when I watched you. I don't know how those young men brought themselves to paint. I knew that I would paint you some day."

I blush at his assessment of me, and yet it pulls at something in my stomach, too. "Is that why you came to my father's shop?"

With his hands in his pockets he steps backward. "I sat in the shadows in the back of that class until you finished posing. After you put on your faintly orange dressing gown you went from a *fleur-de-lis* to a rose; I saw your flame. It's not just your red hair, you know. Your skin goes from the palest ivory to the most delicate peach to cheeks ruddier than I've ever seen. Though your face mostly wears no expression," he whispers this and moves closer again, then rocks back on his heels, "sometimes when you think no one is watching I see desire or triumph, and beneath that, longing." He puts his hand back on my shoulder, though I am facing him, and he takes a tour around me. "Most women are like lovely presents, and you know what you will find even before you unclothe them. They have their place. Who doesn't like beef and vegetables now and then? Then there are those women that never do what you expect them to do, and they love you and hate you all at once and make you feel they have done you a favor by giving you the tiniest amount of attention. They make you believe you are the most capable man in the world, and then when you have grown accustomed to drinking of their approval, they" (he pushes me from him) "yank it from you." He orbits me once, twice, more before pulling me close. "Which is it today? Are you going to want to kiss me or kick me? And which do you want of me?"

I hide my indecision quickly by lowering my eyes. Until I know, I don't dare give myself away. The woman in me wants Manet and his artistry, wants his astuteness, wants to play this game. The artist in me knows he will only paint his best if I deny my feelings and urge him to deny his.

My rule.

His breath flutters against my eyelashes, nearly forcing them open. Either way, I win; one way, art loses. Always first and last, art. I can have these other urges filled anywhere, and probably better. Artists are not the best lovers— they are too busy trying to record their impressions or make an impression. The bars crawl with better lovers, men who live in their bodies, who labor with them daily, and who know what they are capable of; men with tensile bodies hardened by the repetitive lifting of barrels of wine or crates of produce.

My voices raises now: "I am not a patron who will pay you for this almost-faithful rendering. You have made no statement, have made no object of beauty, and have told no story." I am trembling.

"I'm not a writer. Leave the storytelling to Zola. I know," he says, coming towards me again, "that I have at the very least made a statement."

I cross my arms over my chest and let them drop.

He turns his back. "The bank is closed. Come back tomorrow for your money."

"Keep your money."

"Tomorrow at ten," he says calmly.

"I won't be back." I gather my jacket, my guitar. I look again at the young girl I am not on the easel. This man doesn't know me at all.

I am in the rear of my father's shop two days later inking a stone to make a print when my father calls to me: "Someone to see you." I wipe my hands, remove my apron, and come to the front.

"Can you sit today?" Manet says as he hands me a fistful of francs, the pay, I assume, for sitting for the painting. I close my hand about them. The rent on my parents' apartment has been raised in hopes of forcing them to leave. Now landlords want their houses bought by Paris to be demolished for the new streets. Money in the hand.

If only I didn't long so for art classes, if I didn't have to help support my family, I would never take the money.

I look at my father, who nods.

"What time?"

"After lunch. And Meurent—please bring your guitar."

"I'm giving a lesson at one." As if I would go anywhere without my guitar.

"Impossible. Tell your students their teacher is going to be much too busy to teach."

My lips lift without permission. "For how long?"

He smiles back. "For a very, very long time."

Slowly, my nose heals. My heart takes its time doing so. I miss Willie, and when I walk home at night, it's all I can do not to travel to the other side of town, go to him.

I needed the distance from art, sometimes, that his fighting gave. In Paris, as lovely as it is, it is easy to feel you are nothing if you are not an artist or wealthy. Some, like Manet, dare combine both, although he is considered more comfortable than rich. In Paris you are funding art, creating art, or material for it—or you are nothing.

The writings of Baudelaire have challenged the Academy's very ideals of beauty. Now writers, artists, and fashion designers claim all women can be beautiful, if only they buy the right clothing, which the department stores capitalize on. Perhaps it was meant to be liberating, but it is anything but. Our unpainted faces are no longer considered attractive. Our bodies in workaday clothing are not enough; we cannot either be or not be beautiful—we must pursue it by buying the most expensive garments we can afford in sprawling department stores that rival the size of our cathedrals. They are our new cathedrals; I can attest to that. Throngs of women rush upon the store at the slightest sign of a sale or a new shipment.

Had Manet painted my nose crooked, I would have respected him more for it.

Manet gives me the painting he did of me without ceremony. Ironically, the more I look at it, the more I like it, because he shows what he wants for me in it, what he imagines I want or maybe deserve. Nothing is true or untrue. There is no truth, only shading.

"Take it home," he says.

The train in the distance rumbles the studio. I long to jump aboard, take the painting with me. I want to protect this not-me, this could-have-been-me.

Nearly as strong is the urge to poke a hole through the canvas.

I bring it home, undamaged, and my parents and I avoid looking at it. It is the only painting in our house.

TWO

An Earlier Portrait of Victorine Meurent

I SURREPTITIOUSLY TAP my left foot back to life as I shiver beneath the ivory brim of a violet sprigged hat, but other than that, I stay as still as a nine-year-old can.

My father's Victorine astonishes me. With his brush "my" skin glows beneath vermillion hair. My father holds the completed paintings up to the light as if he is lifting a baby, and my insides clench.

He never shows my mother these paintings. Years later I realize that the smell of paint is not so easily concealed.

My father's slight frame moves incessantly while he works, his breath quickens; a flush appears on his cheeks followed by a distant smile, and I sit, no matter how long it takes, no matter how painful, no matter that I know it is a betrayal of my mother if only because we do not tell her. I don't want to tell her. I want this time alone with my father, although I wish he would let me wear my clothes on the cold stone floor. I yawn without opening my mouth today while he paints in the quiet morning.

Lovingly he arranges my arms, moves my legs, smoothes my hair. I smell the turpentine on his hands as he tucks a curl behind my ear. The sun gradually pinks the room.

He seldom speaks, but his brown eyes are firmly upon me; I finally feel noticed. But then.

My mother comes through the living room doorway in her white nightgown, her long black hair loose about her reddened face. She's so beautiful that I open my mouth to tell her so, when her face contorts. Siren, I think, from the story my father told me once as we gazed at the *Seine*. The foreign animation of her face, her gnashing teeth, the way her hair gestures as she moves forward, fists clinched, gorgeously angry.

"Victorine Louise. What are you doing?" To my father: "That hat is to be Mme. Marseille's. And why are you wasting what little money we have on paint again?" Her right fist beats her left.

My father stretches his hands out to her, but even I can see that he is taken by her unexpected beauty, that he sees the picture, not her. Paint *her*, see *her*, I want to say. I do not.

When my mother takes in my nakedness with her wild gaze, I quickly cover the spot below that has recently begun sprouting red hair by jerking the hat from my head and hiding that place. With a gasp my mother leaves the room. That is the last time I smell paint in the house, the last I see of that hat.

After my father quits painting me, my childhood passes in sameness and schooling, except for art. I am impatient with learning letters, doing sums. I make change for my father in his shop; my mother makes change for her clients. What other math do I need?

Reading is fine, if I find a particularly intriguing book, but it is an extra step for my mind to paint the picture the words try to form. "I prefer paintings," I tell my teacher when she shakes her head at my lack of interest.

"Fine, then draw the story instead," she says, handing me a pencil, a scrap of paper. I haughtily grab it and scribble upon the newsprint. "Here," I say breezily, my heart tick tacking in my chest.

"Victorine. This is wonderful," she says. "How would you like to be trained to paint porcelain in one of the government's schools for women?"

My face melts with disappointment. I rise, and with some effort, pull my calico dress up and my undergarments down. "How would you like," I say as I struggle, "to teach my ass?"

As she gapes at my bared behind, the other students laughing, I know it's the last I will see of her, of school. I'm twelve. I gather my things and leave without being asked. I don't care, not even when my father blushes when the teacher visits our home that night, not when my mother pulls my hair and calls me names after the teacher leaves, says I will never be anything. I do not contradict my mother, because words are not needed to do so. Just a paintbrush.

◈

I know even then that I am not meant to paint dainty, prissy porcelain. I want to roar at my mother that I will never, ever consent to make flowers for hats that women will merely wear on their heads, bonnets that the wind and rain will ruin, violets that time and dust will fade or that changes in fashion will cause to be tossed into the trash. There's only one thing that lasts, and I see it weekly in the Louvre. I say nothing, but my face must give me away, because she makes as if to slap me; instead she drops her hand and turns from me. Her folding shoulders say that perhaps she has once felt this way, but it is the only indication she ever gives me that she might understand.

I am sent out to find work, pretending to be older than I am, finally landing a job, as I have said, at the largest department store, Le Bon Marché, becoming as glassy eyed over the merchandise, at first, as the other young women working there. Before long I realize this is all just frosting like on top of the gorgeous cakes in *les boulangeries* lining the streets. "Eat, drink, wear, fuck (I don't know quite what that last one means yet, but I have a clue. It has something to do with a man and a woman rubbing bodies) buy, die."

This overheard refrain sings in my head, and the only way I can drive it out is to play my guitar or my violin, as I quickly catch onto my lessons that my mother has insisted upon to help fit me for teaching both. I dutifully show up at each session and practice in between, knowing it is my mother's hats that trade for these lessons.

Of an evening, she asks me to practice the guitar, and it's only when I catch her foot tapping that I realize she enjoys the music from the instrument she has begged from my uncle, her brother. "You never play it," she accuses him when she has him over for dinner on a rare occasion to ask him for it. He impatiently waves his hand. "How can you know that?" but he gives the guitar to her, to me, and when he dies, childless, spouseless, six months later, my mother is smug: "See, he didn't need it after all." Then, though, I tenderly touch the crumpled music inside of the case, old-fashioned songs I hadn't considered playing until his sudden death. It seems then that I hear a melancholy voice whispering through the hollow body of the wooden beast, something of him dwelling in the instrument, and I am glad I can speak for him. Alas, the guitar is stolen right from my arms on the street soon after his death. Though I run after the thief, I don't catch him.

My hands make chords in my sleep. My arms crook like a dancer's, ready to hold the absent guitar, with nothing to fill them.

Though my mother makes her feelings about my "carelessness" abundantly clear, I get another guitar; only, enough time has passed that I fear I have forgotten to play. I don't allow my mother's bitterness about the theft of my previous one to spoil my pleasure in the new one.

My boldness comes upon me in dashes, in flashes, as I realize those around me have not lived what they meant to. I will not, cannot do the same.

That year my father is never home just before Christmas, and I ask him what project he has taken on that keeps him from us, but he is vague. On Christmas morning I have learned to expect nothing much—it's a day to go to church, yet this Christmas a violin tops my breakfast plate and I weep. His extra work has paid for this.

My hands are thrilled as I gratefully relax my chin upon my own violin, though it is not of the best quality, instead of the one borrowed from my teacher. Yet the greedy gleam in my mother's eye tells me she expects a return on this. I don't allow that to diminish my pleasure.

The violin and the guitar are not only what my soul wants and certainly not merely for a profit. My fingers itch, twitch, and these instruments sound some of my soul's notes, but they can't get at what my eyes want to say. "Would you like to learn to paint porcelain?" echoes in my head. She might as well have asked if I wanted to learn to make hats.

"Never." I say to myself. Still, I find myself stroking fabric, cradling linens, silks. My eyes fire at the profusion of colors on the display tables, one new aniline color atop another: mauve, bright purple, magenta, and solferino, all of a stripe.

I even find myself asking my mother how she cuts the wire she uses for her hats so matter-of-factly. When she eyes me thoughtfully, I vow to never show interest in her work again.

Two years pass at the department store. I have also taken on an odd student or so during my off hours. My skills with the guitar and violin are enough to make others want to hear me, and because they enjoy what they hear, they imagine I can teach them what I know.

Knowing how to play is different from knowing how to teach. I am not a great teacher, but younger students who only want a taste of playing don't seem to mind, nor do their parents with their tin ears.

Because of this, however, the store remains necessary employment for me.

"Charles Worth is a wonder," I say to my mother at dinner, having seen him in the store the day before. He is working with the store on a collection. My mother has already lost work to this "English interloper," as she calls the designer.

"Charles Worth is a frustrated painter with a needle," Mother scoffs. But on his command women give up one style, take on another. Some women have even given up hats altogether at his signal.

"Surely wherever a man may find and make art is all right," my father says quietly.

"What do you say to that, Victorine?" my mother asks, leaning forward in her chair.

"No. Art comes from the soul. It is what is inexpressible by words and cannot and should not be worn upon backs, pasted onto lampposts and walls nor worn on heads," I say, my voice rising, tears running down my face. That's when I know there are truths inside that we cannot be dissuaded of, deep beliefs that are ours alone.

I run from the room, but not before seeing my mother hide a smile and my father nod. As I hole up in my tiny room I cry upon my lumpy bed. The roof above my head was spun by my mother's flowers; the walls beside me "pasted" from those very posters my father makes. Yet, yet, yet. I have turned fourteen now, two years of learning to flatter and sell, to handle women who are either too poor or too rich for our store. Squeezing fat women into clothing. Tying skinny women into too-large clothes. Life is too short to do the same to myself. I must find a life that fits, and I have not.

Weekly, I bring home my francs and hand them to my mother who counts them, nods, and puts them in the bottom of her sewing basket. Since I have been working, we have had more meat, less *pain*. We have had more candles and light. My mother doesn't seem quite as worn, although her eyes are exhausted behind the glasses she wears for the fine sewing. She dons a pair of magnifying glasses then that makes the material seem huge indeed, I notice when I walk behind her, and yet she still squints.

The next week I don't withhold the usual two francs to buy my fripperies. My mother doesn't mention it, but she smiles, and I hate how quickly the rare bird flies from her lips.

While many of the women who work with me are housed within the store's attic, my father has insisted I remain at home because of my age. He and Maman argued about it, but this time, he won.

I don't mind coming home, except it's often late and very dark by the time I get my department cleaned up and organized. There are dozens of saleswomen and men, so many I don't really know everyone. I don't wish to know them all, either. I will not be here long, whereas they are not only content but overjoyed. How would this life be any better than painting porcelain? Just thinking that makes me want to drop onto the floor the garments I am so carefully folding. I want to tell everyone that women are not art. We are not meant to be feathered birds. We are meant to experience it all, to make art. Yet who am I to say so?

My fist balls and the velvet cape I am clutching falls to the floor. I am possessed of the urge to do something just as desperate as what I did at school. Yet this is what that act brought: another tiresome existence. And exist here I must; my family needs my help.

The weeks are the same, and I don't mind, not yet, not as long as my father and I take our Sunday walks. The gentle slopes of Montmartre foster art everywhere on the street, and as we walk the weaving lanes with cones of *pommes frites*, my father steers me away from the more salacious sights: prostitutes leaning out of windows, against walls. Drunks (so early) vomiting in the street. Gambling games out in the open, the barkers begging for participants.

Haussmann hasn't demolished all of it, and there are yet a few *moulins à vent* with their gently twirling blades. I am mesmerized by their turning and churning. It's as if they are swirling up some magic for these gentle hills, a spell particular to the area. It's my favorite place in the city, besides Luxembourg Gardens. I don't understand the women in their gay clothes, but they exude a power I want to possess. The way men stop by them as if they are heat sources is not lost on me. My father's face remains grim, even as he stares at them, even though he keeps returning to these same dirty parts of town.

My hands move through the air as I follow the lines of the windmills, trying to capture their motion with my nonexistent paintbrush.

One Sunday a month my father and I go to the Louvre. I long to stroke the marble statues; their translucence causes my heart to ache, the rose of sun permanently etched into the delicately carved ears and the crooked-under pinky toes—just like mine. Their stillness and pale faces remind me of those pale women in the doorways of Montmartre, the "den of sin." Their unself-consciously worn beauty is also the same. As I grow, I compare my bosom to theirs and am pleased to find one day that not only is mine as large, but that it surpasses most. My mother has begun insisting I wear cumbersome undergarments. I have fought her on it, to no avail.

Slowly we trail by works by Turner, Lawrence, Reynolds, and Hogarth. Their size impresses as always. I compare their styles, pointing out the similarities and differences.

We pass rooms filled with men copying the more famous paintings. Always there is someone before The Masters, especially David's work, although I don't understand the attraction.

This Sunday, two men stand before David's *The Oath of the Horatii* and argue its merits and meaning. Many Sundays my father and I have stood in front of this painting. Not only has my father educated me on these works, but I have formed my own opinions as well.

The pedantic man on the left gesticulates: "The man's arm about his partner's waist simply means to show they are bound together in a common cause."

"I agree, but it also opens up the possibility of a sexual relationship. Look at the sensual tightening of the man's hand around the shoulders—pure . . . well . . . what shall I call it?" says the other man.

I laugh and stop before them. My father seizes my hand and pulls, but I shrug him off. "You do know the men in the painting are brothers?" I ask. There's nothing worse than an undereducated painter.

They both glance at their feet, as does my father.

"The painting is from a story based on Livy, where the brothers take an oath to participate in a ritual duel to settle the trouble between Rome and Alba Longa. Notice that the men are shown as strong and straight, and the women as weak and curved because they mourn for their loved ones. It's supposed to tell us to put the good of the state over our personal lives. It's a bit too geometrically composed for me." I want to say so much more. The men say nothing. I laugh again and take my father's hand, lead him away. They don't take art seriously, for all that they have easels and paints before them.

A well-dressed gentleman to the side smiles with amusement upon me. Our eyes meet, and I can tell by the movement of his eyes that he, too, is a painter. He reads my face as if it is a painting.

As we walk, my father glances backwards. How my father's eyes lingered longingly on their palettes full of paint. I want to tell him to paint, that it's not my mother's business; artists cannot help painting any more than they can help breathing. I have tried broaching the subject before, but he will not listen and will certainly not talk about it.

There is a maddening stiffness and formality in my parents that I cannot get beyond. I used to think it meant there was something wrong with me, but I know now it's not me. They are in that odd place between artist and artisan, and they both struggle. If they could surrender on either side, they would be happy. I know which side I will choose, just as soon as I am able.

When I began working at the department store, I told myself it was "for now," to give my parents something for my keep. It was penance for giving up on my schooling. Now I see the sad lines in their faces try to sculpt themselves into the sides of my face.

The tormented face my father makes when he sees those paints decides me even more: Whatever it takes, I will go to art school. It's a prayer almost answered and almost immediately, and in the perverted way my answered prayers seem to be, not exactly what I had hoped for.

My father nods for me to follow him out of the Louvre.

The dark-haired man in the elegant suit who had stood near us earlier stops us before we can walk away and bows to us, hat in hand. "My name is Thomas Couture. I have an art school." His forehead wags upward.

A wild dream in me rises, and I imagine he will ask me to be the first woman to enroll in his school, because he was so impressed with my analysis of the painting.

"Of course," my father says. "One of the finest."

The man bows again. "I frequently need models, and I don't have many red-headed ones. Would your daughter like to sit for us?"

That a man of Couture's talent and renown should approach me and that he would compliment my hair that my mother despises stuns me. Early morning sittings, sun shining just on me. I haven't felt seen in so long.

A pity he didn't mention what I said about the painting.

My father recoils.

"Please?" I grab my father's arm. I haven't been in school for what seems forever, and I have been let go rather unceremoniously from the department store due to a certain customer. Though I have been useful in my father's shop since, my mother says he does not have enough work to justify keeping me there. I wish she would see him strain to lift the limestone by himself.

"Maman won't mind, as long as I make as much as I did at the store. I can still give lessons and sing at cafés on the weekends if it's not enough." I have only recently begun singing in cafés, and while it doesn't yield much money, it satisfies me. I enjoy the praise, the admiration. My violin teacher accompanied me the first couple of times, but then it was judged that I was old enough to take care of myself. At first, I played at *brasseries* during the weekend afternoons, and no one paid much attention to me. Lately I have begun to learn tunes and movements from other performers that have garnered me more notice. I don't mind.

Mon père hesitates, but a glance at my pleading face convinces him.

The next week I start sitting for Couture's school and life blooms in small ways and large, but not in the way it does when I meet Alphonse.

THREE

Victorine of the Camera

M Y FATHER'S lithography shop is the forest of my childhood memories: those huge slabs of stone, so like tombstones, the tuche crayons he let me mark upon the ground stone before sealing the stone with gum arabic, patting it with talc, taking off the excess ink with the acid, wetting the stone with a sponge, inking it with thinly spread pigment, wetting again, repeating. Then the part I love most— he would cover the stone with a piece of paper and roll it through the press. When he took it out, he always smiled and said *"Voilà"* as he motioned for me to take the paper from the stone. There before my eyes was a copy of my artwork.

As I have grown, he allows me to help him. When he needs multiple copies of a poster made, he marks off where I am to duplicate what he has done, and we work on stones side by side. Though an apron is necessary for the work, I don't mind the mess.

Soon he says my drawing is as good as, maybe better, than his. But I always say it is not. What I really mean is that a daughter should not presume to admit that she is better at something than her father, even if she is.

Artists sometimes bring him sketches to copy, and he does, which seems a kind of magic to me: How does he manage to get what they have done onto the stone? It's with ink and acid, with gum arabic and water, then pressure.

He cautioned me from early on to never put my hand in the press and never let me work the press if I was wearing anything with dangling trim.

I have been modeling for Couture for about six months when a man comes into my father's shop. While my father fetches an advertising lithograph for the man's photography services from the back, the man sizes me up. I'm used to being stared at, so I continue cleaning the counter. I know I'm not beautiful, but I've been working on how to use my eyes to say what those naughty painter boys want me to say, and I do it just so they won't touch my body—they're so young they're terrified, maybe more scared of sex than I am. Even though I am intrigued by what I see in the mirror, in the pond in the Luxembourg Gardens.

"I'd like to photograph your daughter," he says as my father returns. The man in the cheap suit pretends to move his thick hair out of his eyes. It is slick and curled and wouldn't move if beaten. I turn my head.

"I would pay," he says. He mentions a rate twice what I make modeling; he stares at me twice as hard. Photography is a relatively new marvel, so I am excited to experience it. Only the rich are photographed, and I love modeling; surely it will be nothing but modeling of a different sort.

"Come back tomorrow," my father says. He will speak with my mother—I know what her answer will be, since she receives most of the money I make modeling for Couture. When she handles money, she seems nearly cheerful.

We are all amazed at what this new eye, the camera, can capture, so similar to ours and yet with the power to stop time, to reproduce exact likenesses, to remind us of what someone who has died looked like. I want to be photographed, but I do not wish to give up modeling at Couture's. Alphonse assures me that photography takes much less time, and that I will still be free to model for anyone else I please. I am pleased to model for Couture's students, and I have been from the beginning.

The first day I model at Couture's I notice that the schoolroom is spacious, with bright walls and plenty of windows. I am awed by the chandelier that hangs in the opulent room, lighting the room even when day recedes. The whitewashed brick casts back perfect light for painting. Velvet green curtains swag from the windows in a typical show of Second Empire excess that I, in my youth, admire. The school is, naturally, only for men.

"Is this the first time you've posed nude?" Couture quietly asks as I come out from behind the screen in my dressing gown.

So many faces wait for me to disrobe, and all of them male.

"No—I mean, yes."

"They have seen many naked women. To them, you are nothing more than that chair." He smiles; I am meant to feel relief.

"Then perhaps they ought to paint the damn chair," I say as I brush past him and throw the slick rainbow of material off me, straddling the chair in a way that makes them all forget a chair is even beneath me.

Couture quickly calls out a more traditional pose, but he's trying to hide a grin.

During breaks I cover myself and circulate among the painters and see row after row of me painted as breasts, as buttocks. Some capture a likeness, some something more, certainly some less. Why are these parts of me so important? The highlighting and shading tell me they are, but they aren't for walking or lifting things. Besides their baser biological uses, I don't know why men should care about them, and since men have similar equipment for voiding, I don't know why they should be mystified by mine, but I can feel their worship of those parts of myself I don't yet value, and yet their valuing them warns me not to treat the parts lightly.

Some nights when I am in bed I touch myself in the areas that seem to fascinate them most, and gradually I understand. Teasing my nipples causes a thirst I do not know how to quench. When my hand touches the plume of hair between my legs, it is pleasant, but so what? Ah, as I continue to explore one night, I find a trigger that sits upright just between the sweet folds. By touching first it, then my breast, I feel a building tension that ultimately sings through me. Instinctively I know to be quiet as I pant with pleasure. Oh. Is that what this is about? Do they desire to give me this gift? Why should I need it given to me, when it is something I can give myself? Gifts come with prices. I may be young, but I know that.

Some of the men at the art school ignore me as socially beneath them. Some share their lunches with me, ask me if I'm cold while I sit. Couture, a decent enough man, always shoos them away if they pay me too much attention. I resent this. I like being surrounded by young men of all nationalities and varied means. Can it be Couture knows I have found that secret place between my legs? He need not worry—I have told no one of it.

A few months after I have begun sitting for Couture's class, Édouard Manet, a promising former student of Couture's, comes into the school. While others crowd about him, I strum my ever-present guitar.

"Who is this?" he asks as I continue playing. His eyes scan the space around me; he peers at the middle of my face, above my head, down at the floor. What does he see? He looks as if he knows more about who I am than I do. After the break, I strip slowly and toss my robe haughtily off the platform. I don't need any covering. I lean my face on my hand. Impress me. Make something of me, if you will.

Couture has not returned from break, but I have been instructed to take my place when it is time. I climb upon the platform raised above the stage.

I would know if Manet had left. He hasn't. The thrill in my middle measures his presence in the rear of the room. If only I could pose with my guitar, I would call out with it all of the things he is thinking in his lurking. There is a man who wouldn't be content with a body (the model's rule—look, don't touch, unless she is unwise). He'd have to have my soul, too, and worse, he'd have to paint it for all to see. Artists can't keep a damn secret. He frightens me; he thrills me.

I recline; I am *The Nude Maja*, regaling, provocative. I invite with the crook of my head. The boys don't complain because even though it may interfere with their previous compositions, I'm giving them more. I can feel them lean in, and I know that even though I don't fully understand this, I am doing what I ought to do to titillate them. They take a collective breath as I push my hair away from my face; my insides tingle.

Couture reenters the room, and I clamp my legs together and follow his barked order to turn sideways. I don't have to look around to see who has left the room when the door closes.

When my father tells my mother about the photographer's interest, she looks sharply at me, at my father. I don't yet understand the look, but I soon will.

At our first photography session, Alphonse slices my clothes from my sixteen-year-old body with a word and a hand motion: "Off." His studio is full of boxes, crates, and mysterious equipment, and I've had to climb three staircases to get to it. Gingerly, I remove my rustling dress, and with a bowed head, my undergarments. He tosses me a pair of satin dance slippers and I cock my head on command. *Slippers. A tile floor. The sun slanting on my young face. My father, brush in hand.*

When Alphonse notes my interest in the equipment, he smiles. "This is a bellows camera. It takes an eighteen-by-twenty-four centimeter plate," he says.

"I'll be using the short-focus lens." He places it on a wooden tripod. Later, when I see the result, I will think he is short-focused indeed. All Alphonse captures is my flesh, plump, fruity. A commodity at the corner market, ready to be taken home and eaten in a fever, or just wiped on one's sleeve and consumed in the street.

The first session is short, over with so quickly that I cannot think it could be satisfying for the artist. Why, he can't even see what he is creating, not really, can he? I certainly cannot tell what he is capturing because I have not yet learned to watch for his breath, for the flash of light and smoke that try to prove what was and now is not.

When I return home, my mother merely holds her hand out, and I place the coins into her palm. She doesn't ask how it went. Neither does my father. I heat water and fill a bath to warm myself after they have gone to bed. For all of the briefness of the event, those stone tiles have left coldness in my bones.

At the next session, Alphonse shows me the prints of the earlier one. Even I can see that they are useless. My image is pale and grim, and I look as if I am cold. Certainly I do not look even as good as the peach I had envisioned myself.

Alphonse is dark-haired and darker-eyed, attractive, a man who wears suits that pretend to be more by their elaborate cut but inferior fabric, much as photography pretends to be better than painting. I fear my lack of respect for the form (for all of my curiosity of the process, I do not find it more than a cheap copy now) shows. Still, there is something to be said for a man who smells as if he's trying to please, who wears deep, dank scents of secrets. He, this camera, they know things I want to know. Things I can take back to Couture's.

"Try sitting like this," Alphonse requests and I laugh to see him bat his eyelashes.

I put my head to my fist and my elbow to my knee. Alphonse asks me to look at the camera in ways I do not understand and talks quietly of desire.

He moves with a jerk away from his camera. "Let me show you," he says as the deadbolt clicks into place and he closes the blinds, and begins disrobing, and I am eager to know, though I am as repelled as I am fascinated.

I force myself to stare unflinchingly at the parts that make him different from me, because I will not have him think me intimidated. The sway of that which lies beneath his penis reminds me of a single breast, although it is covered with dark hair. The penis itself is a bit longer than the ones I have seen in most paintings.

I believe that whatever Alphonse is about to teach me is the key to why men are so fascinated with my body. I see those eyes in my mind as Alphonse's nose comes closer, closer, so close I don't think I've ever seen one so close, and I stare at the black-specked pores, feel warm, absinthe-scented breath on my lips.

So that is a kiss. One moment it's there, and then it's gone. Where does it go? How can Alphonse kiss me in the same way men who love women kiss in books? Are love and this the same?

I sob, but from disappointment, not fear.

He kisses me again, as if to comfort and quiet me, and this time he stays there, kissing longer, deeper. When he takes his lips from mine, I don't want him to. This is a feast of flesh, of warmth, of skin touching mine. I had thought humans must walk alone, but no, this says not.

What happens next opens up a new, glorious vein of longing, and I finally understand it: it is that thirst that remains after I have eaten and drunk, and it is too deep and wide to be filled. I stare at the difference between us that I see between his legs, and as he touches me, magically that member becomes firmer, and he groans and puts my hand upon it. I like the way he sighs when I touch him. Power. Yes, my body is powerful.

He pushes my head downward and tells me to take his penis into my mouth, but I will not. It's alive; for all I know it can move on its own and I don't relish not knowing what it might do; he tastes my breasts and puts his hand between my legs, touching the switch, and oh, now I know why it's better with someone else. How come it's so much better with another?

He takes his hand away and I cry "No," but instead he replaces it with the magic between his legs, and now he's, it's, inside of me. I cry in pain, but it doesn't hurt too badly and now it doesn't hurt at all and I feel his heavy, smooth body on me, and he is panting and sweating, and he grabs my shoulders, my face, kisses me, pushes himself into me and I have never had anyone touch me so thoroughly.

That feeling begins to throb in me again and just before I feel that same explosion I felt alone, he begins to shake and his face squinches and then he's not inside me and before I can ask how I have failed him my front is wet. He falls onto my chest. Wait, I want to say. Wait. But the excitement in me goes away. Does everything go away, eventually?

He laughs at the look of disappointment on my face, rolls off me, and puts his hand back between my legs. "I guess she didn't get enough, did she?" he says. Though I feel raw, I move my body against his hand, back and forth, until I too am shaking, until I feel that moment of joy. "Why would anyone ever do anything but this all day?" I ask as my breathing slows. He laughs again, a wicked laugh that makes me feel wicked too.

"Whatever you do, don't tell your parents," he says.

I think of my mother's outstretched hand, of the coins I will drop into it. This she may not have. "Why would I tell them?" Long ago I learned that all things involving the body were private. Not even when I began bleeding monthly did I trouble my mother with the news. A friend from school explained what I must do to care for myself.

"Why did you wet my front?" I ask.

"To keep you from having a child, of course."

When he says that, bits and pieces of overheard schoolgirl conversation make sense, and I know he tells me the truth.

"You don't want to get sick, either," he says. "Some men can make you sick," he says, holding onto my arms. "Not me," he says when I look worried.

I think of those women my father looks at in Montmartre, and how ill they seem, the whispering about such women I have heard. Ah. That is why they look so feeble.

For a moment my happiness fades as I realize even this is not without a potential price: a child, an illness. Though I am momentarily satiated, it only reminds that it's always there, this hunger, always capable of being stimulated. I fear it; I love it.

After that my appetites grow wildly, and I consume as often as I am consumed. He takes me to nightclubs, to underground parties in the catacombs where I am passed about as if I am a cigarette. Giving pleasure, getting it, yes, this is being alive.

I learn ways to get and give pleasure that do not endanger me, ways to protect with and without those precious condoms so hard for someone like me to get. My better friends warn me against certain men and women who are diseased.

I buy makeup, rouge, pots of lipstick, eyeliner that makes me look Egyptian like the paintings of queens in the Louvre. There is so very much warmth in the world, and I can give it, too. Alcohol, cigarettes, flesh, colors, cards, cameras, fabrics. All it took was opening my eyes, my arms. My legs.

I understand the music I play now, and I make it say what I want said. I fret that guitar, press my fingers upon its strings. I ring out pleasure; I can move a man with notes. My concerts are more than mere accompaniments to meals now—they are meals. The world belongs to the fearless, I remind myself daily. The beautiful (or someone who can convince that she is), the young, and yes, the fearless. I build it in myself, this bravery, by knowing that others do not have it.

Alphonse invites me to a party he says I will enjoy. I know my parents would not approve. So what? I am getting more than enough approval from everyone else; I am even being asked for approval from men, from women. I get to decide who I think is good enough and who is not.

He leads me at dusk one night (my parents believe I am staying late "again" to model for the night class) to a door in an ancient wall and looks about carefully before entering. As soon as we close the heavy iron door, he lights a lantern. We descend into the womb of the damp earth.

The scent of dark, dank death surrounds us. My spine chills as I behold the first ragged line of skulls that soon become art, trails and shapes arranged to please the eye. I pause and pick up one of the hollows, hold it. I touch my cheek, put my finger in the skull's eye socket and wriggle my finger in the blackness. I press the palm of my hand upon my eye, hard.

"How much farther?" I ask as I toss the skull aside.

"You'll hear when we're there."

I cross my goosebump-covered arms.

After what must be another ten minutes, I hear a murmur of the ancient made new, of death resurrecting: moans and music, wind and a wisp of light growing brighter as we walk towards it. We duck a bit and enter a room, taller than the hall we've been walking down. On every side of us is a pile of bones: neatly arranged skulls, walls of femurs and tibias, a memorial to all who have been and who ever will be. A dozen or so lanterns and candles bathe the room in wild, irregular light, and guitars, concertinas, and accordions try to frighten away the remaining dark. Couples dance, men and women, women and women, men and men swirling to the faster and faster music. Skirts and sleeves float—reds, blacks, whites, and blues. Tarlatan, muslin, calico. Organdie. Silk-stockinged legs show, high heels peeping below. Bottles of wine line one wall.

The smell of candles and lanterns mingle with cigarettes, with sweat. Soon I am handed a cigarette, and before it is lit, I am yanked onto the dance floor. I gladly accede.

We do the cancan, both men and women, as they do in the dancehalls. It's too prim for me, so I just let the music lead. It is a mere prelude to sex, and I am the bridge between the two. When one dancer is worn out, I am handed to another, and another. I outlast them all.

As they fall aside the music goes faster and faster. I whirl, turn, remove my scarf, toss it aside to whistles. I stop dancing so quickly the music cannot halt as fast. Then it, too, stops and everyone applauds.

Alphonse has taken from his pack pictures of me, those photos that told so much, and he is selling them. I am anguished; I am bared. What is the difference, I ask myself, in an audience I sit for that I cannot see versus one that I can? There *is* a difference.

I begin to dance again, grabbing hand after hand, until everyone is up. The photos fall like leaves, forgotten on the floor.

Before we leave the caves I gather the trampled prints and secret them in my bosom. I have paid too dear a price, but it is too late. It has, after all, already been paid.

In the early days with Alphonse I believed it was merely him I wanted, and I warded off the others, but I soon discovered that I felt this fire with many other men (and women). Why should I deny myself this onslaught of warmth so easily yielded to my pretty (not beautiful) face, my determined eyes, my firm body?

The albumen prints bloom a me I don't know, fetching, fresh. I want her, too.

These prints make the best nude paintings at the Louvre immature imitations of flesh, strangely angled and oddly imagined women who never existed.

Paintings tell so much more than photos, though. I don't want to think about that, not now.

I am *La Parisienne,* the notion of the representative Parisian woman; I *am* Paris. From the scores of paintings of me to this newest way of showing all a woman is. From fashion to action, I do as I please.

"Take more photos," I whisper, and Alphonse does.

That pulse that has always throbbed just outside of our apartment, the one my mother sought to keep me from, now includes me. When I return to Couture's, I begin feasting on the virgins more from pity than from need.

Men on the street turn their heads and stare at me.

At first Alphonse doesn't mind the attention I receive, and neither do I. Then after a few weeks, he tells me I must live with him so he can "protect me." When pressed, he reveals his concern that my naiveté will get me hurt or used. I'm not afraid, but I take him up on his offer of a home, eager now to leave my parents' where my mother frowns and my father merely sighs when I visit his shop. I can't stop, won't. Better I am away from these pale-souled people who can't possibly understand me. My mother seems relieved when I pack my few things; my father, disappointed, and I don't know how to explain to him why I am leaving. I just say I have had an offer of work that involves my moving into my work place. They know what I mean. Without me, their expenses will go down, so in the end, I'm sure they are secretly relieved.

I have no desire to quit my sexual explorations. Bodies are like faces—all different textures, temperatures. I want to try as many as I can. Men, women. I remember the girl who taught me to play guitar, and it is she I touch when I run my hands across a woman, regardless of the jealousy Alphonse begins displaying. I refuse to rein in my lust at the whim of a man who requires fidelity from me and not himself: I walk in on him with another woman. At first I am upset, but then, realizing what pleasure he would be forgoing to pass up this opportunity, I toss the ridiculous idea of love from me firmly and get into the bed with them.

"What are you doing?" Alphonse asks.

"Don't we want the same thing? The moment of orgasm, the feeling that all of this endless living, this building up, is going to pay off, isn't that one of the ways we transcend? To pretend that we want less than we do, to confine ourselves to one person, is cheating ourselves."

They don't understand my words, so I use my hands and mouth until Alphonse and his tart are weak. Power trumps love. I am a bit scared at my power, at my fearlessness. Is there nothing I would not do? I don't know. Everything is a pleasure and a revelation. From picking out my own produce at a grocery (I like green grapes. I will never again eat soggy *aubergine*, no matter how purple its skin) to sleeping as long as I like, these are the simple freedoms any young adult's life yields. Mine doubly so, as I add the more illicit activities.

At other times I travel to strange places via large amounts of absinthe that my smallness magnifies. Colors dance and I am not weary of being alive. *L'heure verte*, the green hour, begins at five. Many artists call her "the green muse." Soldiers were given it, Alphonse tells me in his all-knowing tones, to protect them against malaria. They enjoyed their "medicine" so much they brought it home with them. I am heartily glad they did. Though I have been given small amounts of wine my whole life, this is something else.

The first night I try it, Alphonse and I go to one of our favorite spots. The taste, the effect, and oh, the presentation of absinthe causes my heart to moan with pleasure: The bartender puts on the counter a larger absinthe fountain, a beautifully clear glass apparatus with silvery tentacles. He puts in equal amounts of water and ice, something I had never seen before outside of winter's icicles. Though there are many plain glasses behind the bar, the man pulls out footed glasses—tantalizingly see-through ones with a reservoir at the bottom to show the correct amount of alcohol to pour.

I watch wide-eyed while the man behind the counter pours goblin green spirits into the glass, just to the fill line. Then he puts the absinthe spoon atop (an ornate affair more like a knife with a slot in it than a spoon) and places a sugar cube onto the spoon.

I lean in. He turns on the fountain's tap and the water melts the sugar cube, which flavors the drink, turning it opaque. After stirring it briefly he presents it to me. I sniff the scent of licorice. The anise-and-citrus flavor annoys my tongue, but soon my mouth is full of my new friend.

"Drink up," Alphonse says. I do.

"So this is art, too?" I ask Alphonse, but he just laughs. "You should see what they do for the tourists—they set it on fire."

After a few minutes, the heat wanders up and down my body, and I stand and sing. Soon everyone sings with me, and I realize that, drink or no drink,

I adore their attention. They need me. The night blurs; the little green fairy's wings brush me, and I welcome her more than once. The next morning I discover, as I hang my head over the slop jar, she has more of flesh than fairy about her.

After the bottle and the bed, my mind spins with barefooted questions: Who is a model? Is she herself playing a part in a painting, or is she the one the painter paints? I did not think to ask myself this question until the photographs. Now it seems terribly important to know, and nearly impossible to find out. I don't know who I am. All I know is who I am not.

I am no longer an innocent. Many of the women in these bars scorn me because I give away what they sell but selling just causes the lie to be bigger: I will not deny my desire, will not accept pay for what I do for sport.

I give lessons, sing, and play in cafés, and continue to model. What else would I want or need? I can think of nothing, at least not during the day.

Hashish, cannabis. We use both infrequently, but when we do, it's at the catacombs, and I become a hot air balloon and, for a time, my questions cease.

Still, I am more than ready to be done with Alphonse when Willie comes along. Willie, my Willie.

Manet's studio becomes another chamber of my soul. When Manet tells me how to pose for a second painting, I agree with him. In it, I am a street singer. I suppose the pose came to him when we talked before one of my concerts. Even if I didn't need the money that comes from performing publicly, I wouldn't stop. It is a different sort of hunger, but it, too, needs feeding, my love of music.

In this painting, Manet and I co-create.

"Street singers are fashionable," I say.

"Yes. . . ." he says doubtfully.

"I mean they are in fashion, not that they dress fashionably. Apparently you agree, judging by the clothing you have me wearing."

He grins and paints on.

We speak of politics and art, of architecture. At the end of each sitting he begins handing me books he says I must read. I take them reluctantly, feeling the unspoken words: I am uneducated, and our conversations have revealed this to him.

Then we begin discussing the books and I agree with his opinions sometimes, but when I don't, I tell him so. His back stiffens when I do this, and his brush moves woodenly up and down. Sometimes I give him an opinion I know is the opposite of his just to see his hackles rise.

This painting continues, and he tells me what he expects: "You are just getting off work; there are patrons still there, but you are, finally, going home. You grab a fistful of cherries and your guitar, and you head out the door. Perhaps you have had a bit too much to drink, but you're accustomed to it."

"Why should I look like that? Is that what you think of singers, that we drink too much?"

He arches his brow and I think of the mornings I have come to him looking, I am sure, a bit green. Well, I had to do something to keep going, didn't I? Back home with my parents, and not even having that entertaining snake Alphonse to turn to. How else to amuse myself?

But I vow to cut down on the alcohol. Then I realize the books he has given me are to substitute for it, and I appreciate him just a bit more, even as I hate him for his constantly condescending attitude. If I thought he hadn't earned it, I would hate him.

So I flick at my skirt. "This outfit . . . it really is homely."

"How could she afford better?"

I eye the paintings around his studio, especially *The Spanish Singer* which won an honorable mention last year at the Salon. The folds on the singer's trousers are so crisp I want to touch them. As I look closer, I see how the diagonal of folds parallel the man's head and guitar. Manet uses the real detail of the man's pants to shape the painting. Clever.

"You're the artist; you could have her wear anything you please."

"That's why she is wearing this, because I please. Besides, would you really like to see her wearing a bustled princess's dress such as Stevens would paint?"

I scoff. "You know my opinion of Stevens's work."

He frowns at me. "Stevens is a very good painter. Very good. Just because someone's work is not to your taste does not mean you should insult it." He strokes the canvas with his brush.

I bow my head. "You're right. It doesn't mean I like his work any better for it, but you are right. And I never want to wear one of those horrid dresses with the protruding hindquarters."

He smiles. We both know I'd give a day's wages to wear one of those dresses, just once. But only once. Overall, I disapprove of the Le Bon Marché misses, as I have dubbed those of the prissy set. While I might covet their clothing, I have had quite enough of them as people.

I don't ask for more direction.

Our talk of fashion leads to a discussion of what a *La Parisienne* is, and why he does not believe I am the one to stand for all of the modern women of France who are both fashionable and liberated. They, he says, are also wealthy and well connected. They have a place in society. His admiration for those things cannot be concealed.

Ah, I say, because I am young and free, because I do what I wish with whom I wish, I see myself as more modern than the women who pretend to a freedom they do not have. I, in my poverty, am freer than they will ever be. And I wear my clothing with so much panache I might as well be in designer clothing. That, I suppose, I get from my mother.

When my guitar begins to slide, he motions for me to put it down as he focuses on another part of the canvas. For all of his talk of painting after nature and not from memory, we don't actually paint it in front of the café that is near his studio. Backgrounds seem exempt from this in his thinking. I try not to think him a hypocrite.

Because my fingers are calloused, they don't hurt anymore when I play. When I was learning the guitar, though the strings were cat gut, after a while the pads of my fingers ached and turned red. Soaking them in water helped.

I carefully learned the chords that tell the tale in ways my mouth will not, cannot. The chords sound—well, everything. I long for as many voices as I can have.

I want something that only exists between the audience and me, a temporal art. I also want to paint to leave a legacy, to say what I have to say, whatever that is. How can I when I don't know how to paint? It takes money; it takes time and a place. So few schools allow women in, and those that do cost beyond anything I can hope to pay. I don't know how, but I know I will learn to paint.

Willie has taken to following me down the street but not speaking after I am finished sitting during the day for Manet. At first he begged me to come back to him, but eventually his words dried up and he simply fell into step with me.

Though I went to his rooms long enough to fetch my things and allow him to bring them to my parents' apartment, I have steered clear since.

"Your nose looks so much better," he says tonight as he falls in with me after I quit posing. His mouth sags as if he is remembering that punch once again.

"How long have you been waiting for me?"

He shrugs. "I've got all day, haven't I?"

I pass up my parents' house and go beyond it, on and on, as if it's my day's work to walk.

"Hold up," says Willie, "I've got to box tonight."

"Then don't follow me." I put my arm in his, slow myself.

Eventually we end up in the Tuileries, the place for promenading.

I'm angry with myself before I even do it, yet I do it. I pull Willie into the tight section of bushes I know to lie right behind me. There is space beneath them, shelter above, and I have often thought of them and Willie when passing by. He grins and before long, it's as if we've never broken up.

"This means nothing, Willie," I warn him, but it does. Surely I can't love this brute, this human pet? Yet I am happier with him than ever I've been with anyone else. I'm at peace with him. As long as I don't egg him on, don't provoke him, I think maybe we will be okay.

"Marry me," Willie whispers, his finger running along my bare side.

"What?" I sit up and quickly gather my clothes.

He rubs his head. "What's wrong with getting married?" Willie asks.

"But we don't love one another."

"Don't you love me?"

I look up, down. "I don't know. I've never said that to anyone."

He shrugs. "You act like you love me."

I want to love him so badly at that moment.

"You said you asked me to marry you because you love me. Can't you love me without marrying me?" I think of my parents' marriage.

"I already do," he says, pulling on his trousers. "I just thought it might be fun to get married; you know, make it official."

I pull on my underthings, hopping from foot to foot to keep my balance.

"Marriage fun?" Almost I am tempted. Crimson disdain on a hardwood floor. No. I must wed art.

I stand and put my hand out to help him up. It occurs to me I have the best excuse of all, though it's not my own. "But Willie, you aren't French."

He refuses my hand and pushes himself to his feet. There is nothing else to be said.

The next day I quickly don again the dress Manet gives me, and the hat, the snood. The heat makes the clothes damp and limp. I pull the dress away from my skin.

Again, he dims my hair to almost brown in the painting. I wear an earring and my ear peeks out of my hair like a frightened mouse. Is he trying to make me more respectable by making my hair color quieter?

While I pose, I think about my time with Willie yesterday. My face flushes with desire and I pretend to admire the floor as I review my pleasure.

"There—what were you thinking just now?" Manet asks.

I quickly make my face assume its desired countenance.

"Manet, how important is it, do you think, that the French marry the French?"

He startles his eyes at me. "Why? What have you heard?"

I shake my head. "I just wondered if you think it's at all important."

He puts down his paintbrush; his eyes grill the ceiling. Finally, "It would depend on the couple, I think."

"And would one's art suffer if one were to marry someone other than a French person? Or if one were to marry at all?"

His brow shows his displeasure. "What are these questions? Have people been gossiping about me?"

I laugh. "No." They have, but I'm not the one to tell him that. Still, he is an artist. Perhaps I can confide in him.

"Someone has proposed to me. He's not French and decidedly not an artist."

Manet laughs, picks up his brush. "Ah, and what does he do, this boy? Does he perhaps work in your father's shop?"

"No indeed. He is a boxer. Willie isn't . . ."

"You mean Willie Wayne?"

"Yes."

"Him? Does your father know you are with such a man?" Manet puts his hands on his hips, nearly getting paint on his suit jacket. He puts down his brush. "I've seen that man fight. There's nothing left of a man when he's through. I've never seen someone box with such exuberant violence."

I rub my nose. "Exuberance. That's right."

I roll my shoulders backwards. "My parents little care who I see. I am a burden upon my parents. To marry would make it easier for them."

His eyes soften. "So you would marry even if you didn't love him?"

I inhale, exhale, touch my toes. "Why is everyone so obsessed with love? Can't I just desire him?" Willie's wild touch on my back, my buttocks.

Manet chuckles and his pupils enlarge. "You can do that without marrying him, certainly."

"Is that right?" He lives with a woman they say has borne him a son she pretends is her brother. Manet has not married her, and yet they say she is nothing to him without the child.

"That's exactly what I told him," I say. "But I'm afraid he's having trouble seeing it my way. I only hope he doesn't go to my parents."

Manet scoffs. "Your parents surely can't make you marry."

"Our parents have a strange way of making us do many things we'd rather not, don't they?" I ask. I raise my arms to the sky. "No. I'm not going to marry him."

He opens his mouth, but I am quicker, picking up my guitar. "Look at how the light shifts, Manet."

His attention is again riveted by the sun's waning rays.

Carefully Manet adds layer after layer of paint. First an indistinct shape, and then a button. Added to that is the cone of tissue that holds the vibrant cherries—always he lavishes his best upon the still life in the painting. Why can't he show the same regard for me? Cherries—are they meant to symbolize purity or a prize from a lover? If the former, what does it mean that I am about to eat them? Does this mean by singing professionally I am giving up my womanliness? My virginity? Too late.

I wear a hat in the painting, a rounded one with a black ribbon of sorts that perches on the top of my head. My right hand is large and fully formed; the left is misshapen, ready to detach itself and play my guitar.

A twist of yellowish gold paper, an open-mouthed golden cornucopia, guilds a bouquet of cherries.

The guitar melts into my dress—part of the headstock embeds into me. He understands how important music is to me.

At every break I stand before the painting.

In it, I am outside of a set of swinging doors: one thrown wide, the other closed. The potential for movement exists, just as there is the possibility that I will begin playing the guitar, that I will open my mouth to eat the cherries. In which direction will I head? Perhaps he asks in which direction he will allow me to head—inside of his world, or will he keep me at arm's length?

Does he deserve to become a true part of my life, or am I to be just a thing for him to paint? My respect for him is growing. He's a decent sort, possessed with the same vices of other men, though at a muted level. While I've seen him drink nearly every evening, never does he drink so much that he stumbles home. I suspect his dignity is too important to him to allow that, but for whatever reason, I admire his restraint and wonder if perhaps I should imitate it until I imagine an evening without a haze on it and I shudder.

Though Manet's a bit hot tempered, I like that in a man. The distance I keep from him is not because we are a man and a woman. It's because of the respect I have for his art. One can either love the man or love his art. One cannot love both effectively. To love someone means having to be able to lie to them when it's necessary, those polite, kind lies that make them feel better about themselves or their work. I will not lie to an artist about art, and so I cannot love an artist. Will not.

Doors opened; doors closed. Sometimes I despair at the simple symbols so overused. Two choices. What does he mean by them? To me they mean art: either I am all in, or all out. Willie or my desire to attend art school.

It's not fair. Manet is allowed his Suzanne. Why am I not allowed one?

Because I cannot balance. My compulsions are darker and deeper than I have allowed myself to admit. Manet merely hints at them in the painting. Oddly, I do not feel judged, just seen.

He creates something even he cannot understand, I think. Those fresh colors bolt from his hand and he beholds his work with a surprised smile. He rounds a cherry as joyfully as if eating it.

While critics wish him to paint "real" works, I've seen the "beautiful" traditional painting he can do, and frankly, it is staid. This new is not done because he can't paint in the way everyone knows and expects but because something unprecedented burbles in him, I'm convinced. If they saw an ounce of the passion with which he approaches the canvas, they'd never doubt. If they heard any of the thought he puts into composition they wouldn't either.

He mottles the two louvered doors with brown and moss among the warmer bluish green. The doors are intentionally, ornamentally painted, versus the weathered, aged wall to the right of the door. He juxtaposes me with the purposefully created and the naturally aged. Artifice versus nature. Is he trying to decide if I am genuine or created? I could tell him, if he asked: We are all both.

This painting says who this wild-haired (though well groomed) Manet is and was and will be, and I want to kiss him as I watch the painting crawl out of his fingers and onto that gorgeously taut canvas, which is ready for the secrets of the world Manet will pull from me and about me and will place there for all to see.

Though there is plenty of quiet in the studio, it is by no means silent. We talk of artists, some of them mere names and paintings viewed in gallery windows and on streets to me. We speak of my father's business and of my mother's.

"From where does your beautiful French come?" he asks.

I pause. He notices, I suppose, that I do not use the careless shopkeeper's French of my father. "I worked at Le Bon Marché when I was younger." The store manager worked studiously on getting me to use language in a way that wouldn't alienate our more affluent customers. I find myself flinching at the casual, low way my father speaks to his customers.

Patiently Manet readjusts my guitar for what must be the tenth time today as it slides down my body, lifts my hand holding the slimy cherries. Their intense scent reminds me of the undertone of sweet rot in the sewer smells outdoors.

He mixes more red and black to create that tantalizing cherry color, and then a bit more red, then a dot of black until it's just the right shade. It's a tone I search for in nature but only rarely find in a deeply hued leaf, the passing wing of a bird I can't identify, in these cherries. Or in a red calla lily.

"How do you know when it's the right color?" I ask, although I think I know.

"When it looks right, of course." He grins and I blush.

"Yes, but how can you be sure that what you are seeing on your palette will translate the same on the canvas?"

"You try it. Either it works or it doesn't."

I don't believe him. The way his fingers confidently take hold of the brush every single time tells me he knows exactly what's at the end of it.

Such peace encompasses him when he paints, even when he paints passionately. It's as if he's hearing from beyond.

As he rearranges me, he plucks one of the cherries from the bouquet and holds it to my mouth. I turn my head, and his thumb grazes my lip.

He smoothes my brow and touches my nose. I flinch, but not with pain. As he repositions himself he finally whispers: "Tell me more about you and this Willie."

I move my head and reposition the cherries.

"Are you entering your work in the Salon this year?"

He grunts. There are things he doesn't wish to talk of, either.

I squeeze my arms to attempt to hold the guitar for just a bit longer, to keep the cherries in place.

"One object at a time," he says, removing the bundle of cherries. Now I must keep my hand away from my left side so it does not interfere with his work there. I hold the fruit.

He doesn't know me, not really. This painted "me" could be eating before my set, or during a break. I could be waiting nervously outside, wishing I had the nerve to duck in. Or I could be finished and exhausted, ready to eat.

The dress is of no help in identifying myself. My painted hem is filthy. Were I wearing this outdoors, it would be as filthy as Paris's streets, so he is correct, but I don't like to be seen this way. The city works at the problem, swabbing sidewalks with wet brooms daily, but it is no match for the horses and the ashes from fireplaces that are everywhere. Gas is beginning to replace coal, but slowly.

Through the open door in the painting there are at least four people: two at a table, two at a bar. A couple of them may be women, but it is hard to tell for sure. It is not an elegant place, and it could be any number of cafés.

Color appears in unexpected places: A patch of peachy red to the left of the door, repeated to the right—the color of the building—with a brighter shade of bluish green, just a small strip that makes up the edge of the door. Color is many a building's redeeming quality in this city. He daubs these spots on towards the end as his eye travels the painting.

"You do know I would never eat cherries near my guitar? Or let it slide down my body while I eat messy fruit."

"But that highlights your exhaustion," he says with a careful, assured tone. While he is terribly insecure over some things, he is quite arrogant about others.

The painted cement beneath my feet flows, a carpet of velvet brown. Again he surrounds me with dark, dun-like colors. He seems to know that beneath the conviviality, the woman who relishes sex and drink and books doesn't know what all of this is for and fears it's just a distraction. She wonders why we are alive at all, and the darkness he surrounds me with says he knows this. Now I am truly naked.

The light diffuses on my skin, whitens my face, my hands, deadens them. Again peach brushes my cheeks that I did not put there.

He allows me to stand in the painting. How often are women permitted to do so? This is a mark of respect.

One afternoon Willie wanders into Manet's studio, saying he just wanted to see where I was keeping myself. When he's nervous, his French is halting. Manet grins and continues painting me, tells Willie to please sit down, stay as long as he likes.

I roll my eyes, but Willie is never moved by such displays. He watches as I stand as still as I can, not looking at anyone or anything, or so it seems. That is, of course, not the truth of the matter at all. My eyes wander between Manet and Willie and back again. The journey is a curious one, full of contradictions. One moment my eyes linger over Manet's well-fed hand holding the paintbrush, the next I glance at Willie sitting so uncharacteristically still.

"I've seen you fight," Manet says to Willie as he holds his palette high. "You're a machine. Do you often get into fights outside of the ring?" Then Manet looks at me and back at Willie, then questioningly at me. I look away quickly. He puts down his palette, his brush, rolls up his sleeves.

Manet strides over to Willie. "Stand up." Manet says quietly.

"No. You don't know what really happened," I say, trying to get between them. Willie stands before Manet, clueless.

"Did you do that to her nose, you animal?" Manet asks.

Willie drops his head and rubs it in anguish. "God help me, I did. I've been trying to get her to forgive me ever since."

I tug at Manet's sleeve. "It wasn't like that. You don't know what I did."

"In my world, there's nothing you could have done." His teeth grind and his face reddens.

"But our worlds are different, aren't they?" I know it more surely now than I ever have.

I put my hands on my hips and stand in front of Willie. "I think it's time we were going."

Manet turns his back on me, fists clenched, and I shiver as Willie and I exit the doors.

When Manet is finished with the painting, he stands before it and calls me to his side. It has taken weeks, and I wonder what it says.

"I like it," he says. He waits for me to say something.

"What's the story?" I ask.

He curses. "Do you dare tell me there is no story?"

"There's a story," I say. "But we have to look for it."

He curses again. "And what is wrong with that?"

"Nothing. Except."

"Except what?" he paces away from me, running his fingers through his thick (yet receding) hair. "I painted what I saw. I added in a scene."

"I know." I don't know how to say what I want to say. He's been to school—there's nothing I can teach him.

"Have you done this with every artist you've modeled for?" he asks.

"No." I rub my forehead. "Yes."

"What is missing?" he asks.

"It's beautiful. The colors are rich; the cherries are luscious, but I want to hear me play guitar and sing."

"You don't hear those things?" he says, his shoulders sagging.

"No one will fault you for it," I say, touching his arm. "It's a lovely painting."

"A lovely painting," he says, picking up his brush. I grab his hand.

"No. You are getting at something, but you haven't completely uncovered it, and maybe that's my fault, but there's nothing else to be done." He will never hire me again, but I have helped an artist, so it will be worth it. Unless he spreads around that I am difficult.

"I'm sorry," I say, remembering that he was patient with me when my nose was heinous.

"No," he says slowly. "I think I understand what you are trying to say. How does one get to that state between real and staged? I can't tell a story if I don't stage it, and you claim I'm not saying enough. This is no portrait. This is a young woman coming out of a seedy bar after a long jag of singing to drunks. She hasn't even had time to eat, and her face isn't that of an insensitive woman who is happy to sing bawdy songs for men and women who throw coins at her. She is exhausted. She doesn't show any emotion because she's been so steeped in it. All she wants is to be alone."

"I see." I've been that street singer so many times and usually what I feel when I come out is exhilaration. I've often had too much to drink, too. And sometimes I am accompanied by someone who is going home with me. He makes me feel the shame of what I do, when I prefer to see the choice of it.

"You've given her a layer of respectability she might neither want nor deserve. Ask yourself why she plays there and what she does after. You've made her noble, Manet, when she may be just what others think her and happily so."

As I gaze at it again, I see what he sees, beyond the bold strokes and the carelessly outlined dress. He tried to get that face into focus, the face that hides behind the cherries. He hides it because . . .

"I cannot see it," he admits finally. "You won't show me. Why did Willie do that to your nose?" he asks. "Did you cheat on him? Did you refuse to have sex with him? What? I must know." He throws his hands up.

I sink down onto the chair.

"Next time," I whisper. I cannot talk about this with the man with his muscular wrists and thumbs hanging out of his pockets who speaks of sex.

He sighs. "Next time, then." He begins cleaning his brushes.

"You haven't signed the painting," I say.

"I never sign them until they are finished." He puts his hands on his hips and frowns at me. I put my hands on my hips and frown right back. I do not owe him my story.

Now I see: The cherries in the painting point to my nose.

After a time he puts his hands down, picks up his brush, applies black, and returns to the painting. I protest, but he is merely dabbing at the bottom of the painting. When he steps back, the woman has shoes.

He glances in my direction and then signs his name in the bottom left-hand side and slices a black line along the left after the "t."

"You are free to go."

Gooseflesh breaks out on my arms. When I am almost out the door, he says, "Please return on Monday." Once outside, I sit on the curb until I stop shaking.

Mercifully, Willie is not waiting.

I spend my day off in my father's shop. Between customers he questions me closely about Manet's methods, his colors. He never asks how I am treated.

We lift a stone onto rollers, and he grunts.

"Père, you really must get some help. Some of these stones are entirely too heavy for you to lift alone."

"I get by, Victorine. Don't worry. Now, what were you saying about how he refuses to layer paint?"

When I describe what Manet and his friends are doing, my father nods as if he sees exactly what I mean. "They are taking a page from Turner's book and even, perhaps, Delacroix's," my father says.

"Certainly Turner."

"These men meet regularly, then, and speak of art?" my father asks hungrily.

"They do. We go to the Guerbois nearly every afternoon, after work. They speak of the new colors and methods that excite them." At first the group seemed reluctant to include me, but when Manet repeatedly brought me in they acquiesced. While those of my class may range freely, if I had been as cultured and well-bred as my voice suggests, I certainly wouldn't have risked being seen in an establishment such as this. Well, most women wouldn't have, anyway. And "my kind" would have been welcome to go home with one of those respectable men, just not to be seen in his company, had I been what they must have thought me initially.

"When I was in school, we did the same," my father says.

"Art school?" I have suspected this, but he has never spoken of it.

We lift the stone again and transfer it to the press, where he pushes it through. I almost wait for the "Voilà" still.

"Of sorts. I worked with a painter who gave classes out of his home. He taught a handful of us. I went for a couple of months before my father died. After he was gone, my mother discovered our family was deeply in debt. So, I apprenticed to a printmaker instead."

Sacrifice. I should have known. My mouth is dry, but I say it anyway: "You were—are—a good artist. That's why so many ask you to make posters—that all comes from you. All they do is tell you their ideas." It costs something to say so, but art first, always: "You should paint again for yourself."

He straightens the things on the counter before him. "A man must have money and time to paint." His head bows.

"As must a woman." We swirl in our own miserable worlds for a moment, until I remind myself that I *will* find a way.

"I'm going to art school sometime, somehow."

He flicks at paint on the stone before him before running water over it, grinding it to erase the image he has just made. "Have you considered marrying someone who could hire you a teacher?"

"No, that has not occurred to me, Père. I will find a way and it will not involve marriage."

He moves his hands. "Is marriage such a terrible thing?"

"Has mother been talking to you? I have no desire to marry. I bring you what money I can; we seem to get along. Isn't that enough?" I fear it is not.

"The rent is being raised again, come next month. We may have to look for different lodgings soon."

The room tilts; I push myself upright. "But we have lived here ever since I can remember." "Remember" seems like a real place all its own, one that ought not to be tampered with.

"I know, Victorine." He wipes at the clean counter. "What of that red-haired man? You seem to like him, and he came looking for you recently."

"Surely you noticed that he is an Englishman, Père?"

"He told me he is part English, part French."

"Since when was half French enough for anyone?" I will not be herded into marrying when I can make my own way. And yet I do not hate the idea of waking with Willie's warmth beside me, feeling his heavy arms about me as if I were just as much his puppy or a friend as a lover.

"Victorine, you cannot live on art alone." My father has successfully removed all traces of the previous image from the stone, and he begins inking it again.

Can't I? My soul answers, not my mouth.

My father stops his work long enough to rub a spot on his back. All of those artists who spend franc after franc at the Guerbois with not a care, and my father who often works until sundown, my mother who works until her fingers are stiff with not a franc to spare, though they make "art" of a sort. If art is for us all and about us all, why isn't it *by* us all? I think that's the very next thing I will ask tomorrow afternoon during The Green Hour. I doubt any of the artists will have an answer. That's okay. There must be a question before there can be an answer.

FOUR

Mademoiselle V . . . in the Costume of an Espada

I DON'T GO straight home after sitting for Manet the next time, nor do I agree to go to the café; I can't bear it, artists with their biggest problem whether to buy a larger canvas or not when my family is threatened with eviction.

That's not fair of me: There are just as many poor artists there, those who would rather be homeless than work in a shop. I can't bear to think of that right now either.

So I wander past the theater where a sign tells me Willie will box tonight. I don't go in, though he is likely to be there warming up. We are still keeping company, though I have made it clear that I cannot marry him. For some reason, I am as faithful to him as I was unfaithful to Alphonse, although I still see plenty of people to desire.

I walk the entire city as if I am trying to trumpet down its walls, past pits of earth where men with wheelbarrows and picks and shovels finish carting off the remains of buildings. For as much beauty as there is in this city, there is an equal amount of destruction that will, they say, end in beauty and better health conditions. Haussmann's renovations.

Medieval Paris is being stamped upon and crushed. The city my grandparents knew is no longer. As Second Empire notions of fashion have affected art, so Second Empire notions of architecture have affected our city. Is nothing to be left untouched by this regime?

Just as advertising posters begin to color our city to make up for the horrible gray stone (however clean) now invading, so ready-made clothing stores have begun overtaking the traditional tailors, even more so than when I worked in one. My mother's hats have competition, the ready-to-wear ones being sold in department stores, sometimes less expensively than she can afford to sell hers.

As much as we women are covered, one would think we are ashamed of ourselves. I forever have to roll up my sleeves and secure my skirt when working my father's press. Why must we women hide and hamper ourselves with fashion?

When I said this once in my frustration to Manet, he laughed. I notice in one of the paintings he does without me, he gives the woman a shorter walking dress, and I bless him aloud for it.

I end up in a garden chair at my beloved Luxembourg Garden by the Medici Fountain, a place where things remain the same, where annuals bloom and water trips down the fountain and back again and again. My parents would bring me here when I was small and pay a few centimes so I could rent a toy boat to launch upon the pond. Watching them together watching me pleased me nearly as much as the boat that, after all, only drifted farther and farther from me. When I was very young, I would cry when my father said I should put it in the water.

"You have to let go if you are to see it sail," said my father.

"But it won't go where I want it to go if I let go," I said, stamping my foot. As long as I guided it with my hands, I knew it was in my control.

My mother laughed, and my father joined in. My brow lowered as I tried to understand their amusement. By then the boat, pried out of my grasp by my father, had made a quarter circuit of the nearby pond. When I turned to insist my parents watch it, they were kissing as I had seen so many other couples in the park do.

"My shoe. My shoe," I insisted, tugging at my mother.

"For shame. It's buttoned just fine," my mother said after glancing down, then laughing up at my father.

That was while my mother still went out, and before my father stopped painting me.

It did indeed please me more to follow the small vessel with my eye, but I was still grateful when it was back in my hands. That afternoon I drew a sailboat on a piece of paper. The next day my father helped me make my very first copy at his shop, and he displayed both the original and the copy proudly on his wall.

When my mother brought him lunch, she insisted on taking the original home.

"But Madame, I do not give up originals—that is why I make copies. See what a fine copy this is—why, you can scarcely see the difference."

"Indeed I can see the difference. I would know my own daughter's choice of colors anywhere. See her strokes here."

"If you insist," he sighed playfully and handed it over.

My drawing remained on the mantle for a few weeks until the paper softened, and it drooped under its own weight. Over three days I watched with fascination as it gradually sank until I couldn't see it anymore.

I watch the pond from my chair, see the children sailing their ships, running from one side of the small pond to the other, and I pull out my sketch pad. There is art everywhere in Paris, absolutely everywhere. I cannot imagine living anywhere else. I, even in my humble position, know so many artists. True they are as a whole poor, dirty, and some of them drink too much. They are not truly poor, though; how could anyone with so much art ever be poor?

The fountain calms me. After I quickly capture the young man who pursues his boat, I close my eyes and allow the sun to warm the parts of me that have grown cold in the studio. I am paler than ever due to the time spent indoors and my muscles hurt from maintaining the constant positions demanded. Manet did let me stand. He did. That has to mean something.

Rather than go back to my parents' home, I relax into the light.

Lunch announces itself with the swell of people in the park, an anonymous mass. A well-dressed woman goes by with a nod, comes back.

"Victorine?" she says.

After we have established that it is me, she asks, "How is your mother?"

Then I recognize her: the woman from my mother's shop, the one with the frog purse. Madeline. I haven't seen her for a couple of years. Reflexively I look at her hands as if she would be carrying the charming purse.

"May I sit down?"

I move my bag that contains my shoes and book and hope she does not get her fur—much too heavy for now—soiled.

"This is one of my favorite spots," she says as she unwraps a *mademoiselle* and offers me half of the sandwich. I am hungry, but I decline.

"Are you sure?" she asks. She watches my eyes follow the food and she hands it to me anyway and shrugs out of her cape.

"*Merci*." I take a bite out of it and I immediately know from the sharply herbed butter that it is from Café Voisin.

"What have you been up to, my dear?" Her eyes long for me.

"I have been modeling." My eyes answer even as they slide over her fur.

"For whom?"

"Manet."

"Ah yes. Such promise. So controversial." Her eyes ask me what, precisely, have I been doing with him as she rubs her ruby pendant.

"You know him?" My eyes tell her she wishes she knew.

"Who doesn't? What was the painting?" I will know.

"I modeled as a street singer." I gaze at her mouth.

"Ah. Is that why you have the guitar with you?"

I have neglected my instrument during the painting. My body was too stiff from holding it to want to play it much, so I ended up leaving it at the studio most days. Only today I took it away with me.

"Yes. I also give lessons and concerts, though."

"Guitar lessons? I would love to have lessons. Might you. . ."

"I am to start sitting Monday for a new painting," I say regretfully.

"We have until Monday. Perhaps we could at least begin? I don't know how much you get paid for modeling, but I could be generous."

My eyes tell her that I imagine she could be. Especially after having sat for Manet, my wish to go to art school has grown to a full-fledged need. "I would love to." My parents need help first—photography threatens my father's trade, and rent threatens their home. If there is any money left, it will go towards art school, I promise myself.

She gives me her address and I agree to show up the next day. Though she is older, she is beautiful, with curves not even aided, I am guessing, by a corset. I watch her leave and suddenly I cannot wait for tomorrow, for the unbridled feast she and I will have in a silken bed complete with hand-formed chocolates and fruit, with wine liberally splashed from dusty bottles fetched from a plentifully stocked wine cellar. I could ask for anything and would be given it.

For a moment I think of Willie, but then I don't. I discard the thought, as I must.

Monday comes too quickly. I do not want to leave Madeline's opulent side, and I haven't much, except to make appearances at home, excuses, really. The news has spread; one of Couture's students whispers eagerly when he stops in at my father's shop. "Everyone knows—she is the widow of someone said to be quite important in the government. The cafés are buzzing with it."

I know who her very-much-alive husband is, not was, and that he is a diplomat assigned to America. That I'm not going to share. Madeline has remained loyal to my mother's trade even when she could have gone to more celebrated milliners. I will return the favor.

"I'm with her because of who she is, not because of who her husband is or was."

The boy's face falls. Before Manet, they didn't care, but now that I am his model, I am an object of speculation. This will help his reputation, as much as it tarnishes mine.

Madeline, sweet, soft, Madeline. She is, of course, not the first woman I have slept with, but she is the first I have slept with for more than one night in the same bed. Her warmth is welcome, but it is not the comfort of Willie. I feel a flicker of something that just might be guilt and remorse, but when she hands me money, I quickly forget.

I hum as I knock at Manet's door.

"How are you?"

"I'm wonderful," I say as I sprawl on the chaise lounge.

He grins. "I had a new idea over the weekend."

When he tells me, I'm once again surprised and then I'm surprised that I'm surprised.

"What will you call it?"

"*Mademoiselle V . . . in the Costume of an Espada.*"

"You're calling me by name? But I'm just a model." My heart warms.

He ignores my implied thanks. "A title is important. It tells what the artist intends as much as the painting does."

"Shouldn't the painting tell us what it is called?"

While a title might be important, to place so much emphasis on it shows a lack of execution and conviction even before the painting is done. It shows a dearth of confidence. My eyes must betray this, but he says nothing, and I say nothing further.

Just like that, the goodwill between us is gone.

He picks up a set of garments and hands them to me. I recognize the coat and the hat—they are from *The Spanish Singer* that he exhibited a couple of years ago. Why would he reuse them? The pants, the shoes, and the shirt, at least, are different ones. Are they meant to bring him more luck?

Wait, *pants*? "You want me to wear pants?"

He laughs. "Dark pants, like a man. It is exactly right, isn't it?" He chuckles. This is his only mention of my weekend's activities.

I stick my tongue out at him, secretly excited not only to wear pants, but to have my name added to the painting. This showcases me as a model, almost as if I were an actress.

The shoes are a mystery to me, too-large ruby-colored affairs with little ribbons.

I pull on the clothes he has chosen. "Paint me as I am," I say. Previously he has hidden me in voluminous fabric. I am short but I am not tiny; I have womanly curves and a belly. I don't want to be depicted as other than who I am.

I am to be a bull fighter, a toreador. What does it mean? I feel his excitement creeping up in him, and this is the best sign I know that art is about to happen.

I eagerly take up my position, holding a coral swath of material in my left hand. Almost I can feel the bull breathing on me. I move my arms into position without being told. He nods.

Perhaps this painting is inspired by my weekend, but I suspect he already had it in mind after learning that I gave as good as I got when it came to Willie punching my nose, or so I have hinted to Manet. Willie is the bull, then? But he is not!

I position my feet. My hair is hidden by the scarf, hidden twice if you count the hat. Manet is trying to keep the lid on his desire. I pity him.

As always, he positions me, fussing, then goes to his canvas as if eager to start. He picks up his brush, returns to me long enough to move my head a fraction. "Hold there." But he hesitates and I can't tell if it's from anticipation or anxiety.

"Shall we begin?" he says as he leans forward and backwards.

"One stroke," I tell him. I have said it to many a young painter. "All you need do is take one quick swipe with your brush and you will have begun."

His chest protrudes. "I was just checking your posture." But he loads his brush.

"There is such a thing as being too careful," I say.

Already my arm aches.

"Do you require my arms first or my legs?"

The brush quickly dives, and just like that, we have begun.

What a strong face he gives me, determined. He does not attempt to make me beautiful. No more shadowed planes. I am almost sad, however, that my nose has mended. Here it might have done nicely.

I don't like wearing the beige-yellow gloves, and he must not like it much either, as he has me cram one into my pocket. A blue cravat peeks from my blouse.

The tassels sway at my knees; I steady myself.

My legs look like two pieces of bone china, bits of white and ivory. That they are revealed is scandalous, and I laugh. He paints other things in the background, figures of huddled men and a rider on horseback. My body is a woman's: plump and curvy. I proudly inhabit every inch of it.

My face is expressionless but beginning to open. Maybe he has been depicting me more faithfully than I believed. He has trouble with the painting, though he doesn't say so. On a break I stand behind him and stretch my neck to one side, wondering what is wrong.

"Why am I in the ring?" I ask. Willie in the boxing ring, taking on life with his fists.

What are those men doing there, in a different life, a different perspective? As if I were a tourist dressing up for a sidewalk souvenir painting.

Again with the added-on hand. It's not that he can't paint hands—I've seen better from him, but this hand is too light, too, yes, *detached*.

"Tell me about Willie," he insists.

He waits with his paintbrush. I stare at the painting.

He is having trouble with the face.

"What of the nose?" he asks with exasperation.

"I gave him a black eye and more." I sit in the nearest chair. "I wanted to make him do something that couldn't be taken back. I wanted a reason to leave him, so I kept hounding him until he hit me. We beat one another so brutally that we're not allowed back at Café Margot."

Manet chuckles and removes a clump of paint from his brush with a white cloth, but he scrutinizes me. He rummages in a box and comes back with a Spanish sword that he puts in my right hand, raises my arm.

"What of this Madeline? If you are with Willie, how does she fit in?"

Pink, peach, and silk.

"I didn't take you for a gossip."

He freezes, and then lifts his brush. The movement of his brush seems to draw the words from me.

"Willie and I have been apart for some time . . . that is, we only get together occasionally." I blink and squirm. Does the painting need to know this?

He paints on. Having my back to him opens something in me, and whether it's for the painting or because I am tired of not speaking, I talk, then, about Willie, about Madeline.

"She wanted me to give her guitar lessons," I say, wilted from the effort of not talking about it. "My parents need the money. The rent, you know, goes up and up and up until one is forced out. The landlord wants to sell his house. And someday, you know, I'd like to get enough ahead to . . ." I bow my head to the inevitability of it, speaking to no one, just my words into the quiet room, nothing but the sound of the scratching of his brush that seems so useless against real life. A brush will not save a family from eviction. It will not love one. A painting is nothing, and I have made it everything because I have had nothing else.

"You'd like to what?"

"Go to art school." It can't hurt to say the words aloud, can it?

He asks me quiet questions and I stumble over my answers. I realize I don't know what I want as much as I say I do.

By the end of my story, Madeline doesn't seem quite so attractive, and when I return to her that night, it is with dissatisfaction. Sadly, she seems to know, but she says nothing, only brings me an extra pillow for my back, as I grumble about my aching body, and fetches me an extra glass of wine, though she disapproves of excessive drink.

Her home is a boudoir of a place, filled with puffy, colorful pillows and flowers, a soft nest. When she touches me, she brushes off the uncertainties, causes my doubts to leave for a moment, but she's not Willie, even if her touch does bring me some mechanical pleasure.

"Madeline." I run my finger along her left side. Her eyes widen in her just-beginning-to-wrinkle forehead. I stroke her hair with its white strands throughout. I, too, will age. I kiss the sagging skin between her breasts. Her body trembles under the power of my finger. She may have money and comfort to give, but I have my youth and sex. Power is not love, but it will do. When she goes to sleep, even her night noises sound silvery, and I find myself longing for Willie's frank snores.

The next morning there is a gift at my place at the breakfast table: the frog purse.

"Do you remember it?" she asks, her face hopeful.

It brings back all of my girlish hopes. I open it as if I will find my younger self's dreams inside. Instead, I find five francs. I hug her as she hands me un café and a croissant.

"It's bad luck to give an empty purse," she shrugs.

"Thank you." I reluctantly close the purse. "I must go, or I'll be late."

"You'll be back this evening?"

I say nothing, just kiss the top of her head. A powdery scent flavors my lips, and I wipe at them as I leave the house.

I am not due at Manet's until the afternoon, so I go by my father's shop.

He is with a customer in his shop, which now seems so small and shabby. My father wipes his nose with his dirty sleeve. I grab a cloth from behind the counter and swipe at the window in the door.

After the customer leaves, my father nods at me.

"What have you been up to?" he asks.

"Everything you've heard about Madeline is true," I say bravely.

"Your mother doesn't understand. . . ."

"Do you?" My eyes beg him to lie.

He hangs his head. "No, I can't say that I do."

"Father, there are things no one can understand about us, not even ourselves.

That doesn't mean we should be loved any less for them." My eyes feel scratched by my tears. I continue to stare at a man who cannot stare at himself. Forgiving someone does not mean they will accept it.

My father examines his blackened fingernails. I upend the purse before him with both the coins Madeline gave me today and those from before. It is all I have.

"Will this allow you to keep the apartment?" I ask frantically.

He glances at the pile and nods. "Your mother said you can't . . ."

He doesn't need to finish his thought. Of course. One of her meddling customers must have told her; he wouldn't have.

"I need to pick up my clothes."

"Best I bring them to you here."

My stomach hurts. "Tomorrow, then?"

"Yes." He shuffles through receipts on the counter. I long to feel the little green fairy's wings flutter in my throat. There is time for a drink before I pose. I wonder if my father even hears the bell as I leave.

One drink at the bar around the corner turns into more.

Absinthe burns away the demons; the green liquid colors everything. By its light I make my way to Willie's apartment where he is still in bed. He never locks his door—why should a boxer? I take off my big fussy dress, heave it to the floor, and crawl into bed with him. He opens his eyes, smiles, and snuggles against me. His red hair glows.

It is dark before I even come around, and then I only wake because Willie nudges me.

"I was supposed to model this afternoon." I look around for my shoes as I hold my head.

"I have a fight," he says. "Go with me?"

I've missed my modeling appointment, been kicked out of my parents' house. Now what?

"Don't forget to bet on me," he says, flexing his arms in the mirror.

I stop in the middle of forcing the shoe onto my foot. "Willie, I will always bet on you." Just not with money. I have seen too many foolish men waste the pittance they do have betting. Even sure things aren't always.

The fight is short and typical. His opponent cannot begin to match Willie's zeal. Punches are rapidly fired, and the other man lies on the mat too soon.

Afterwards, Willie doesn't rejoice.

"Willie?" I ask.

He is surrounded by men who love that they have just made money off him, by sweet-scented, low class women who obviously want him, by fans asking for his autograph. He carries his gloves in one hand and waves them away with the other.

"Come on," he says.

"You don't want to celebrate?"

"No." He slows.

"Are you sad?" I've never seen him sad.

His head lowers. "Don't you think I have normal feelings like everyone else, Victorine? How come you think all I can do is box and fuck?"

"What are you talking about?"

"You don't love me because you think I'm a stupid brute. Truth be told, that's half the reason I hit you anyway, it's because nothing I do will ever be enough for you. If I hit you, you leave, but if I don't hit you, there's nothing you want from me."

If only someday a simple man like this would do.

"Willie, I spent the weekend with a *woman*."

His eyes open wide. He kicks at a rock, and I love that he still just wants to please me more than he cares for his sycophants.

He howls. "Why can't it be enough that I love you? Why do you need more than that? You act like you and that stupid art are all going to live forever, or like just because that painting of you might live after you're dead, that means something. You know what it means, Victorine? It means you might live on ten seconds longer than the rest of us."

He wipes his nose with his hand. "That's right, Victorine, some people think this planet's not going to be here forever. You working so hard to act like it was such a beautiful place isn't going to change the fact that it's gone, and all the records you made of it are too, when it goes."

This is the closest to intellectualism I have heard from Willie.

"You're right. We don't know what might happen. We just keep thinking it's going to go on and on, and maybe what we're doing is for nothing. Maybe every last painting ever painted of me will burn, and to be honest, maybe that would be for the best. But as long as I don't know, I have to prepare for what might be. Maybe I can capture something of now for later, and if I can, I mean to."

I reach for his hand and he gives it to me. We walk, hand in hand, on the quays beside the Seine.

"Is it something I did?" he asks again.

"God, no. You are the best lover I've ever had."

"You don't love her, do you?"

"I don't love anybody." Here, now, I can't understand why I was ever with her.

I want so badly to go home with Willie, to lie down in his dingy-sheeted bed and put my head on his down-stuffed pillow again. I want to allow myself to love no one but him, to forget anything exists outside of him, but it won't be enough and soon I will agitate him until he hits me and next time it might not be just my nose.

Maybe I can control me. Maybe wanting to is enough.

When I was a child, my mother had a box of chocolates in her workbasket. If I were particularly good, she would allow me one on Sunday evenings. The evening I broke a glass at dinner she told me I could not have a chocolate. I waited until she went to bed and got into her workbasket. I opened the chocolates and ate one. As I looked at a second, I thought maybe if I just smelled it, but then I figured one lick wouldn't hurt. I sucked it as if it were a lollipop and then nibbled from the bottom.

Next Sunday I would be sure to lift it so carefully she wouldn't notice the dent, I thought. After I realized what a large dent I put in it, I decided it was best to eat it and be rid of it, so she wouldn't think we had a mouse again. That left only two, not enough for all of us, so it might be fairer if I ate them both, and quickly.

My mother didn't say anything, but she never bought another box of chocolates for Sunday nights, either. Whenever I got extra money, I bought some, but I brought them home to her and Père instead of eating them. Some days, though, I would buy two boxes and eat all of one myself before I even got home.

Trusting myself to behave with Willie seems unwise.

Willie holds me to him before letting go. "You can always come back to our place."

Our. I don't deserve him.

I nod. I wish comfortable was something I could afford to be again. Better I return to Madeline.

The thing I regret most today is missing my modeling session. My mind is muddled.

I go to Madeline and I explain that my parents have kicked me out, and she says I may stay as long as I like. Why does that make me feel queasy?

The next morning I appear at Manet's and his grimace as he returns to his canvas tells me all I need to know.

"I'm sorry," I say.

"Models do not miss work," he says. "They especially do not disappear without a word. Why, I imagined you had returned to that beast and that he had gotten hold of more than just your nose."

"His name is Willie. You know that."

I light a cigarette. Is there nothing Manet's set doesn't know?

"Put that thing out and get into costume."

I don't put it out, but I do put it in an ashtray while I dress.

His painting is hurried, and his posture glum. Manet makes impatient movements with his arm. Is it just me, or is my mouth grimmer? Am I the bullfighter now or a woman pretending?

He sullies (I see at break) the canvas with a puddle of brownish black at the bottom; he does not let us forget this is paint, and I a model. I am being punished. Instead of co-creating, instead of being created, I am being defined and limited. The bastard.

"Blackground," I mutter, and I know it's a remnant of his classical training, but it feels wrong when applied to these brightly lit faces. Still, there is something undeniably different about his work. There is a definite nod to Velázquez and Manet's other beloved Spanish painters.

"Turn." He motions until I am at three quarters; he has me grasp the fabric. My hand clenches on it as if I am afraid. In my other hand is a thin sword and I hold it with a gloved hand, a creepy being of its own. He is careful to have me raise my right hand enough so that my gloved hand and the glove in my pocket are parallel. Anyone who believes paintings are unplanned should sit in on a session with Manet.

He draws my true body, as I have asked. My stomach and my ample back-side mound in opposite directions. My breasts aren't even visible. I approve.

A man on a horse in the background mirrors my stance. The group of men behind him is barely distinguishable and still seem utterly unconnected to me. Is this a comment on men in my life?

He makes my eyes uneven, as they are in real life, allows the tip of my nose to drop, and paints my lips as full, my cheeks ruddy. A suggestion of a dimple tips my chin, which is all I have, a hint of one. The title of the painting makes it clear that I am playing a part, as does my pose. I don't quite understand his message, and I tell him so.

He does not answer. I wait. He paints. I wait. And wait.

Two days later there is a knock at Manet's studio door in the afternoon. I lower my aching arms. When Willie is admitted, he waves his arms and speaks English at me. When I shrug, he switches to French.

"Will you come back to me?"

I pat his shoulder. "We talked about this. I am with Madeline now. I'm sorry."

"Victorine?" Manet says.

"Stay out of this," Willie says. I take Willie by his arm, lead him away from Manet.

"Willie, we can't be together. That's all you need to know."

He shakes his head. "Then why did you come to me?"

Manet dabs at my face in the painting, making it paler.

"I was drunk, Willie."

"You don't love her more than you love me."

Manet jerks his head, curses as if he has made a wrong stroke.

"I'm sorry, Willie," I say, moving toward him, lowering my voice. "You knew I wasn't like other women when we got together."

"You came to me, and then you left me again, and you went back to an old woman, Victorine?"

I pity him and me. "She's not that old, Willie."

"Is it her money?" he asks, looking at me as if I can tell him anything, as if he would understand.

I shove him. Manet backs away from his canvas.

Willie will never understand how I can love him but refuse to be with him because it's too dangerous. Seeing the tears in his eyes, I almost believe I am mistaken. Ah, but there are no tears in my eyes, and that's the problem. I touch his cheek by way of apology.

He leans in and kisses me as only a boxer can, nothing withheld. I jerk away and walk to the door, point "out." Good boy walks through it. Manet laughs behind me.

When I return, I lift my arms. I glance away.

For just a moment, I let my shoulders fall, but then I stiffen. Back in position.

That night I wake from a nightmare to Madeline hovering above me, her breasts sagging under her night gown, her hair standing out from her head. Her breath smells.

"What?" I gasp.

"You were yelling in your sleep."

I rise, pack quickly, and leave before either of us can understand that I am.

"I'm sorry," is all I can manage before I go, and I wish it were true. I want to go to Willie's, but I know not to.

The lights are on at Manet's studio and I let myself in. He is at the easel, carefully adding detail to the men in the background. He hums, something I have never heard him do.

"I like what you've done to it," I say from the door.

I put my bag down on the chaise-lounge.

"Only for tonight," he says.

"Thank you." I smile artfully at him.

"Victorine?"

"Yes?"

"I don't charge rent."

I gladly put my simper away.

FIVE

Victorine's Song

AFTER OUR morning session (Manet thoughtfully brings me a brioche and *un café* in an enameled mug), he leaves me to sort out my affairs, but not before foisting some francs in a monogrammed handkerchief upon me. "An advance," he says.

I take the coins gratefully, offer him back his handkerchief, wishing he had advice to dispense as easily: I have no idea what to do now. The "friends" I had while with Alphonse quickly fell away as Willie and I wrapped our lives as one, two bodies in a bath towel. To return to my former friends would be to return to their hopeless way of life. I will not. To go back to Madeline is quite as impossible.

The room lights up with the sun as if the answer leaks in with it, but it doesn't, not even as I acknowledge that the rosy bits of sky look like Willie's cheeks. I reject the sky's proposal: One does not welcome a tornado into one's room. True, I have survived Willie, but just. My hungers do not scare me, but even I can recognize an unwinnable bout.

I pace the studio, but the room is too quiet, and the sun insists I listen to things I will not. I pick up my worn canvas bag, the one I used to carry my schoolbooks in, now filled with my portable life. Hesitating briefly, I pull the door shut, lock it behind me.

Paris will tell me what to do next, I think, as I promptly stumble over a loose brick. At the time, it doesn't occur to me to be grateful. "Haussmann," I mutter as I grab my ankle.

I've watched the architect ruin our city, block after block, a hungry monster with the sightline of a sugar-crazed toddler, squashing decades, centuries, of our history, obliterating my people, the poor, as if they were a nest of rats.

Poorer Parisians have run from him from quarter to quarter, but no sooner are we safe in one house than Haussmann finds it, has his people give us notice one day, and tears it down the next. We can only watch, hope to rescue a brick from the house where our grandfather was born. I despise him.

There is, however, something euphoric about the planned natural disaster; I love the confused buildings that seemed so stable and secure now shaken. Watching them collapse thrills me. The rubble is a symphony of colors and textures. We see the inside turned out. We see things we are not meant to see. I notice that most people avert their gaze when they pass a worksite. Not me.

His new lines are straight and wide, and though I hate the uniformity of his design and his disregard for history, I do admire his ambition.

The wide boulevards are to aid, it is rumored, in the moving through of troops in case of another uprising. True, but there is such space now that has so often been denied us. I hate the daily cost as I watch the poor get poorer, as they pile into a house twenty thick, disease following them. At least outdoors we have all of the space God created; they cannot take that from us, and Haussmann creates even more as he purges the city of centuries' worth of buildings.

While some have praised his sanitary building of public urinals in the streets, others have been scandalized that men would touch themselves in this manner publicly. Once when I had to go very badly, I lifted my skirts and managed to utilize one as well. Though there were men on either side of me, the cries of protest I heard behind me weren't aimed at them, even though my wide skirts more than covered me.

My stumble provides me with an answer: A nearby sign in a window announces a room for rent. I bend over and kiss the brick before limping over to the soiled tavern.

I have to pay extra rent because the proprietress assumes I am a prostitute. I don't bother to correct her because I don't care what she thinks of me, and the "extra" isn't enough to matter. For the first time I am to live alone, and though it is cold (I have bought no coal yet and it is not equipped for gas) and though it is dirty (I will clean it), it is a space that belongs entirely to me.

I strum the lovely, dove gray rails of my bed in my newly rented room. A few good wallops smooth the worst of the lumps in the horsehair mattress. I must carry my water up at night and my slops down in the morning, but I don't care. It will give me an excuse to buy flowers from the little stand nearby. Flowers trump even night soil, and they certainly help mask the odor.

The first night I create shadow puppets on the walls to ease my loneliness and the slight ache in my ankle, in my heart. I wake to see a melted candle stub—I kept it burning not out of fright but because I adore the way the flame lights the walls.

My clothes hang from stray nails. That is all there is to my room besides the two windows and the cold tiled floor. I need nothing else besides enough dishes for one, possibly two if I invite anyone else over. I don't know that I will. This brand of loneliness instructs, and I mean to surrender to it until I've learned all that I can.

I grab a chair and yank the paint skin from the ceiling in pieces, showering myself with plaster but revealing splotches of pink overhead. I laugh as I walk past the cracked mirror and see my whitened face. I stop and really look, see things now the other artists haven't, like the humor at the corners of my eyes, the content set of my lips.

I'd rather model forever than paint flowers on a cup that someone is going to drink from without seeing. Tiny sips of beauty ruin the deeper thirst for art. Pretty cups and cheerful hats are made to mollify women.

Why can't I paint myself? Create myself? I count the francs left. I may not be able to go to art school, but I can buy some art supplies. I pocket the money. There is next week's rent to consider. Mine, not my parents' rent, because they have decided that my money is not worthy of saving them. I must find a way to get them to accept. They cannot afford their pride, but I don't think they know that yet and they may not before it's too late.

And without a teacher, someone respected by The Academy, no one would take me seriously as an artist anyway. "So what?" begins gently stirring in me, and I crave absinthe. Instead, I carry up some water for a wash. It may have taken God a week to create the earth, but I have gone from homeless to having my own place in one day, which seems an impossible task. Being a woman and so young, I'd say I'm giving Him a run for His money; I think I can do without a drink for one day.

Without meaning to, I cross myself.

◈

Manet's brush slows; his eyes close frequently, signaling the approaching end of a painting session. Finally he waves for me to get my things while he closes up his paint tubes, as if he cannot bear to even hold the brush once the muse has left.

I gratefully release my awkward pose and stretch. As always, I breathe deeply of the paint fumes and chatter on, asking Manet questions about technique, hoping that he will ask me to come along to the café with him. He does this afternoon as he seeks to explain his obsession with black.

"It is a part of everything we see. It's where one object begins and another ends—it delineates things. It tidies and organizes our sight," he says as we walk the short distance.

"So why are your backgrounds so dark? Is it the Dutch influence?"

His eyes darken as he holds the door open for me and my guitar as we enter the café, and I have the distinct impression that he is trying not to say something rude. I am both proud to have piqued him and upset with myself.

We enter the dim room, and I quickly steer him to a corner table, away from the squinting Monet, whose acquaintance I made through Couture, but Manet bristles.

"That's the man who steals my name. He paints 'impressions' of things as if he can't properly see. People are getting us confused," he calls to the young painter, who blanches but does not leave. I smile at the newcomer's bravery.

I pat Manet's arm and signal the bartender to deliver drinks. "How could they confuse your work? He is making his statement, and you yours. Soon no one will confuse you." I don't say that neither of them is favored by the Academy.

The women naturally gather around Manet at the café, as do the men, though these are not bourgeois women; those wouldn't be seen in here. His fiercely wild hair invites ruffling. Beneath the hair, his eyes say wonderful things. He is small and slightly stocky, just the build of many a Frenchman, though his chest is broad and his shoulders proud.

He humors them for a few minutes, but the moment he gets interested in a conversation he ceases accepting their ministrations. Drinks are either taken wordlessly or waved away, and his charisma is directed at his fellow painters.

I question the artists about painting techniques without revealing that I want to try the methods. Their assumed humility quickly falls away; they would talk all day, each of them, about their own work if allowed. It is with mere politeness that they ask of others' painting. They don't seem to see how they build on one another's work, how theirs is better for what they have studied. I will not make that mistake with my own art.

Manet is the undisputed leader of his clan. Renoir, Degas frequent here. Émile Zola enters, his writer friend who treats him as a god, and Monet cannot quit staring at Manet. Manet is witty and well-liked.

"Why do you paint so often with unmixed colors and with such a limited palette?" I venture to ask Manet quietly. Though I am familiar with the work of many of the artists here, I am not privy to their processes and so right now I prefer to quiz Manet because I can relate his words with the strokes I have seen him take.

"I paint *alla prima*," he says carefully, "because it seems right to me."

I grin. "I thought maybe you just didn't like to clean so many brushes."

He blushes.

I often find myself picking up cloths and cleaning his brushes, dusting his furniture. I do this not because I am a woman, but because I consider myself in service to his latest machine, *Mademoiselle V*. I don't find the painting aesthetically pleasing yet, and maybe I won't. It seems more an exercise in light and perspective. Why must he stray so far from the ideal? Unfortunately it makes people listen less to him. I've tried to say this, but he doesn't hear me, or he rages if he does.

I have courage, but it isn't equal to what he did last month that I can't bear to see repeated. He was hard at work on a still life of flowers when I questioned his palette, which is so delicate and sensitive when he does still life compared to the harsh hues he chooses for humans. He had also just started a canvas of Léon, Suzanne's son, and I compared the two canvases. He picked up his walking stick and pointed to the pigments he used on the canvas of the boy.

"Perhaps you don't like this color?" he asked as he pointed to the black around the boy's head, caning the painting repeatedly until the canvas tore. Then he ripped it from its frame and walked to the fireplace.

"No." I raced him there, but I couldn't reach it before it hit the fire. Then he proceeded to choose two more of his paintings, one of them of me reading, one a still life of a peony surrounded by black, and he threw them on the fire, frame and all.

That's when I saw the crumpled blue envelope from the Salon sat atop his mantle. Another refusal.

"I'm sorry," I said as he fell onto the couch, covering his face with his hands. I gave him a limp painter's rag to wipe his face and turned from him as he blew his nose.

"Is it true, Victorine? Am I no good?" he asked, his eyes not flinching from mine.

I sat beside him on the couch and held his head on my chest. "You can't say you will paint what you want and still court their favor." The words came without my knowing I said them, almost. "But Manet, is that why you paint?"

He sat up stiffly. "I am one who paints honest art. I can do no more."

Soon he is up and shaking hands with Monet, inviting the young man to sit at our table, which by now is beginning to overflow with artists of every stripe: painters, writers, and more. Tables abut tables, and the room becomes ours. I wish someone would paint this gathering.

Manet looks up at the man who next enters the bar. "*Zut.* Here comes Stevens."

"*Alfred* Stevens?" I whisper as the large man approaches us. His work is beloved by the Academy, and it seems tailor-made to be so. It's like the hats in department stores: cheap constructions meant to entice rather than quality pieces meant to endure. It doesn't matter that his hats are one of a kind because the intent behind them are the same: commerce. And yet they appeal in the same way a new bonnet appeals (bonnets are not what I would call a hat, and thus I don't mind them). But I wouldn't want to hang a bonnet upon my soul's wall.

"Manet," says the *homme galant* in the dark suit.

They embrace. He has just returned, he says, from visiting his family in Belgium.

Manet introduces us, and I glance first at the Belgian's hands as I do with all artists. They are plump, pampered hands. Typical artists' hands, so unlike my father's. Stevens scans my face.

"You are *that model*," he says. "Those haunted eyes—what do you see? You'd be perfect for the next painting I have in mind."

"Not yet," Manet says.

"Forgive me—are you working on something with her?"

I bristle. "I'm the one you should be asking, not him."

"Artists' courtesy," Stevens and Manet say together.

I stand and sweep the glasses from the table, instantly admiring the diamond-like shards on the floor. "Since when does the courtesy of an artist trump the courtesy of a man to a woman? I am not a pipe to be passed back and forth."

A bar attendant hurries over with a broom and dustpan, and I am sorry to have caused her more work, but I do not stoop to help her.

Instead, I pick up my guitar. "I have a concert at Café Boulogne tonight across town. It's time for me to go." Without looking at either of them, I march out of the room.

The café where I sing belongs to a patron of my father, and I've sung there once a month for over a year. It's early yet, so no one's visibly drunk. Many patrons are outdoors in wrought iron chairs lined with Spanish-inspired, red velvet-covered cushions, watching the promenade of people, chairs facing the street. Conversing that way rather than facing chairs toward one another can be more intimate, can allow a nudge, a wink, a secret pinch on the leg when someone amusing or irritating comes by. In this city of declared and undeclared artists, it is preferable to share a view than to exchange words. Parisians are so fond of using our eyes I am not convinced we require mouths. While facing the street one can see an army of hats, a flotilla of walking sticks, and an armada of large-skirted dresses with swaying bustles floating by.

I tune my guitar in the corner farthest from the bar; the strings yielding to my familiar hands. I do love it.

I finger a scale, warm the catgut with my ivory plectrum, quietly strumming to warn the night I am about to take over. My voice, too, insists on a gentle warming, and I ask for my first glass of whisky, upturn it with a gasp before shaking my shoulders and calling forth the night.

It's a pink Paris evening, and the lamplighter cannot keep up with the dancing in of dusk. I dare it to come faster with my strings, singing the songs to seduce, the songs to call people inside, come to me. Men and women of the lower classes mingle here, and no one cares. They flirt and think of dancing, start to stand but sit. I can command them to dance with my little lilting finger plucking at their desire. They do.

As Cousin Drink comes to my aid, we all get more comfortable, and in a haze, we sing and couples dance and drink and ask for songs I know and songs I don't, and I try them all: "Desiderata," "Le Mot," "Jasette à Notre-Dame," "Si je ne le lui dis pas." Every man wants me because I am every woman right now. Better: I am *La Parisienne.* I want every person within the sound of my voice, and they know it. We seduce one another: my music, the men and women with dangling cigarettes and piercing stares.

The room warms with sweat and swaying, with bodies pressed against one another, crammed into the café as if it is a sanctuary. I sing on, raising my voice above theirs, competing for their love and affection, for their ears and loins, and I win. I will always win because I want it more.

Drinks sent up by patrons cluster about me, and I pause and sip from each. Yes, your goddess has accepted your offering.

Soon the gas lights must be lit, and the light forms a dull patina on the faces that now and then swim by me. I do not allow the music to slip from me the way smooth singers do. I am too aware of the raw nature of the world, the seamy yet pleasurable side of sex. We all need someone to worship and tonight, that someone is me.

I drink from a glass someone puts before me, and I hike my skirt a bit in appreciation, but just a tad. I am already plotting who I will go home with, and I will save the final show for that lucky audience member, the one in the back corner who arrived after I had begun, unmoved by either me or the hubbub. When I take a short break, I meander past the now-weaving drunks and pull out a chair. He puts down his sketch book, rises automatically, and sits when I do.

"Not a music fan?" I ask.

"Music is fine, but silence is better for drawing." He plucks a white handkerchief from his pocket and leans forward, wipes my brow.

I smile. "Should I be offended?"

He continues sketching.

"Such movement. How do you do it?" In chalk—pinks and reds, blues and greens, I see myself with my guitar, surrounded by the drinks which he has made candles. The glow illuminates my face.

He ignores me.

"Will you be here when I'm finished?"

Then he puts down his pastel and meets my gaze head on. "I thought that was the idea."

"Well." I feel almost shy.

When I finish playing, I accept my pay from my father's friend, the bar owner who has allowed me to play, pick up my guitar, and sail right by the arrogant man. I hear the tap of his walking stick on the cobblestones. I know Manet will catch up to me, and within a block, he does.

"Your studio, if you please," I say.

He tries to take my guitar, but I resist, giving him instead my free arm.

When we get to his studio, he lights a gas lamp and opens his sketch pad.

After he finishes the sketch, he waves it before me, and I try to take it from his extended hand, but he does not release it. "And I will see you in the morning," I say, and he lets go of the paper.

He leans over and kisses my nose before seeing me to the door. "*Bonne nuit.*"

There are nearly as many Manets to know as there are Victorines.

When I arrive at the studio the next afternoon, Manet is hard at work on the background. I quietly change into my costume.

Some relationships are surprisingly hardy, as this one proves to be. This painting, too, is over, and I am sad as I am at all endings.

We stare together at the finished painting, as is our habit now.

He doesn't put his arm around me, but his voice.

"You still give music lessons?"

"I did. Lately I have been modeling." I grin.

"I've always wanted to learn to play something other than the piano."

"I don't need charity, thank you."

"And I don't need to give it."

He pulls his left shoulder back. I thrust my head into the air.

"I just don't know how it would work out." Such close quarters, side by side, standing behind him. No.

He softens. "I thought . . . I'm not ready for another painting, and I know you depend on your fee. If you have other job offers . . . perhaps Stevens?"

I bow my head.

I have misunderstood him, assuming that every man wants to bed me. I remind myself that I am pretty, not beautiful. Not that it matters—it's not my looks that men want—it's the "sexual vibrancy" that I am told emanates from me.

Maybe I don't need charity, but I do require rent money. Concerts earn more for my vanity than my wallet.

"Violin or guitar?"

He smiles. "You choose."

"Guitar it is."

We'll start with a guitar version of "La Marseillaise." I hope he notices the irony.

When Manet enters my humble room, his presence lends grandeur and light.

In the absence of a chair he reluctantly sits on my lumpy bed (there is no spark between us whatsoever; there isn't) and I teach him a D chord.

"Like this, eh *Crevette*?" he asks, and I laugh widely, openly.

"Almost." I reposition his hands, staggering the three middle fingers. "Now press down. It's a shape, a triangle, and then you bring the color out by applying pressure." I know he seeks to diminish me by using my nickname, and it tells me how much this means to him, how it is embarrassing him.

He tries. Nothing.

"Don't forget to strum."

He can't manage them at the same time. We laugh at how awkward his normally capable hands are, and I take the instrument and play a simple scale.

His eyes close as I play. "How do you do that?"

"Practice. Lots of practice." Sometimes at night I play, but no one can hear me because of the noise in the bar below. I don't mind the din. If I get lonely, I need only go downstairs for company, but I haven't been downstairs yet.

Loneliness is for those with no imagination.

I hand back the guitar and crawl behind him on the bed while he attempts to make his fingers conform to the shape I have requested. "Hang on—press down a bit harder." I breathe in the foreign scents of lemongrass, oil. His hair shines. I put my arms around him and press my fingers on top of his. I push my chest into his back, control his arms, his fingers.

"Now strum."

I can feel the tension in his right hand as he clumsily wields the plectrum.

"Loosen your grip." He looks at his hand and the pick falls into the sound hole of the guitar. I take it from him and shake it upside down repeatedly until the triangle falls out.

"Again," I say, returning both with the tone he uses if I let my pose go lax, which I seldom do unless I am in pain. He sits straight and clasps the guitar to him as if he is dancing with a woman.

"Good. Now, firm pressure with the left hand; moderate pressure with the right." His chord does not sound, and I get behind him again to guide him. I smell leather, and I remember the nights now I have been alone in this bed. By choice, I remind myself. His forearms flex as he strums; his thigh contracts beneath his pants as he squeezes the chord.

My throat tightens. Perhaps I have been too blithe about loneliness. To wake to a man like this in my bed every morning, a well-heeled man, one with groomed fingernails and no hair growing from unwanted places.

My heart aches. Suppose I scale this Manet? Suppose I clamber atop him and then climb higher and higher? What would be beneath me but men with pointy heel marks gouged into them. And when I ascend to the top, what then? A pile of men, the carnage like *La Balsa de la Medusa* by Théodore Géricault in the Louvre.

The painting made Théodore Géricault. *He* climbed atop the disaster of those men to achieve his own triumph. The argument could be made that he was memorializing them. I don't think so. I know a calculated composition when I see one.

Still, how many survived? If I were on the raft, I'd be the one with my foot on the barrel, waving "onward." I'd be the one standing, not the seated one who waits for death.

His face glows with satisfaction as the D chord sounds throatily. "Yes."

After he plays through the song once, I take the guitar from him. "Enough. Very good." I smile at him, and he returns it. We will never be friends, Manet and I. Never. And yet we entirely understand and admire one another.

I hand him a cluster of grapes well clear of the wood and give him a glass of wine. "It's like we're having a picnic," I say. I attempt to cover my legs bared by my twisted, dun-colored dress.

"It doesn't seem fair that your legs are showing and mine are not."

I laugh. "What do you propose—taking off your trousers?" My eyes half close. So do his. His warmth beside me makes me nearly forget myself, who he is, who I am not. But what am I thinking? I wouldn't wake to him in my bed because he would not stay the night. He would stay long enough to slake his thirst and then return to his bovine mistress.

He rises slowly and touches my leg, though it's not really his hand that touches it, but his inner eye. "Meet me at the studio in the morning. And bring your courage," he says.

After all that he has already painted me as, I can't imagine what he means. I can't wait to find out.

SIX

The Picnic (Le Déjeuner sur l'herbe)

Y OU CAN'T ask that of me." I pace Manet's studio, pick up a cigarette, but toss it on the floor at his scowl. He bends to retrieve it, straightens.

"You're no innocent." His eyes tell me that he knows the thoughts I was having about him last night.

Hands on my hips, I turn toward that blank canvas, the promise of creation, of the birth of something beautiful or thought provoking. Didn't I promise art that I would be in service to it? Here it is, stretched long and wide before us, representing days, weeks, possibly months, something so large. It's a sea of starched cotton.

"How can you bear to approach something so big?"

He laughs. "It's only turning it sideways that makes it seem so huge. I would paint the sky if I could, dear Victorine."

Someday I will be bones and dirt. My remains will be tucked into a grave, a rented one, no doubt, and when the lease is gone, they will remove my bones or just heave fresh ones on top of mine. This empty space promises something more. How am I to resist?

"It will make you," he says.

"You mean it will make *you*," but there is no heat in my voice.

He comes behind me and clamps a warm hand onto my shoulder. "We are making one another." He is a physically demonstrative man; his touch means nothing.

My mother will hate me even more if I agree to this. My father will just pick at his stained fingernails, no doubt.

"Indeed, I am no innocent." I turn to show him just how correct he is, but he is readying his palette.

It's to be a group painting of sorts: two clothed men and an unclothed woman having a picnic, while a woman bathes in the background. In truth it is to be an artist's studio and the model in the foreground is the same one who has posed for the background, but for some reason she is nude and having lunch, when in the background she is not nude. He never adequately explains that part, and I'm not sure everyone who views it understands the duality of what they're seeing.

"My brother will pose as one of the men, and Suzanne's brother-in-law for the other."

The first day he paints me alone. When I undress, he inspects me. He measures my legs, my chest. If I look bored on the canvas, it's because I am in real life.

I pose for him as the woman in the background, too, not sure what he wants. He has tried explaining it to me, but I don't understand. "Is that how you would naturally pose if I weren't painting you?"

I have posed for dozens of young men at the art school, not to mention all of those photographs.

"It's not my sitting, Manet. It's that you don't know what you want." It slips out, but there it is.

My father knew what he was trying to capture, and so did I. How easy to still my young legs, to gaze out the window at the dreams he wanted me to have while I ignored his.

During a break, I frown and shake my head at Manet's canvas. "That's not what my arm is like." I run his hand across it. "Feel it." He does.

He has done two previous paintings of me, of course, but they are not nudes. I breathe deeply, release it. I shake my head to ready myself for what must come now, if his paintings of me are to improve.

"Feel." I place his hand on my calf, and the smoothness of his hand, accustomed to balm, pleases. He hesitates before grasping my leg and following it from calf to knee, then inching up, grasping the muscle above it greedily, a blind man given sight; he squeezes before rising quickly.

He returns to the easel before tossing aside his brush. I leave my position and come back to him.

"Here," I say. I put his fingertips to my left cheek, and then my right. He touches the length of my ears firmly with his index finger and thumb. He grasps my arm and lifts it above my head, seems to remember he is supposed to be making love to me, and he brings his face so close his beard brushes my chin.

He picks me up and carries me to the couch and puts me down, sits beside me. "*La Crevette*," he whispers.

I will my eyes to open and remain so. He holds my face in his hands and gently kisses me. I feel his slightly crooked nose against mine, and I laugh. Nothing is demanded of me this time, but to lie here and allow him to explore.

My white thighs are carefully parted, and he touches my left one as if he is weighing it. Then he strokes it. He touches my stomach, lifts my breasts, motions for me to turn over so he can assess the rest of me.

"Good," he says, and I turn back over, much as if I have been examined by a doctor. He kisses me again, and I motion for him to lie down. I mount him, and I know he is measuring my interior. I am aroused and amused and am delighted to find he knows as much about pleasing a woman as he does about painting, and in just as unexpected ways.

Afterwards, I lean over and kiss him—we are not lovers; it is a sign of respect and the seed of universal love one automatically has for great artists. I kiss him once more, but the feeling wilts.

He goes to the washbasin. After dressing, he picks up his paintbrush.

Now we are not Meurent and Manet, but a combination—something more like Manette. I laugh and say it aloud. "Manette."

He frowns. "Do you mean the play?"

"No. Us. You might say we are one artist today."

He stares furiously at me and throws the brush to the floor. "Out. Get out." He says.

"What did I . . . ?"

"I AM NOT MANETTE," he yells at the top of his lungs. I quickly throw my dress over my head, grab my shoes, and run. The fury in his voice follows me, causes me to doubt everything. As my arms and legs gain momentum like a train, I hear the repetition: I, Am, Not, Manette. Underneath it I hear the refrain that keeps me awake some nights: *I am not anything.*

I run to the tavern, up the back staircase before anyone can ask me anything, and I begin to pack. The bed lends no padding beneath me as I sit, my trembling legs refusing to stand. My rent is paid through the week. Where would I go? This is my space. Mine. I smooth the covers that not long before have hosted the great Manet. I touch my lips that have kissed him as if he were statuary, and still, through all of this, he is holy, and I am not, and I fear what my life will be without him.

I have violated his very soul, have taken credit (fairly so, I must believe) for what he feels is the fruit of his mind. It is only partly so. A man does not like to think he has not created everything himself, I am sure. I have ruined what would have been his finest painting to date; he will not finish it without me.

Worse, maybe he will finish it, painting over my head, erasing me as surely as my parents have done. As my mind calms, anger replaces sorrow. How can he not see what I have brought to the paintings? Why am I to have no credit? I'm well shed of him.

I unpack my bag and walk the chilly city, wishing for my shawl. Paris is beautiful, even in her current state of disarray. She is faithful, one that makes one not want so much to want to be immortal, because she will always be here.

I breathe deeply of the air that has peopled my lungs from my first cry.

Though I am far removed from it, I keep my eyes on Notre Dame as I stroll. Knowing where it is keeps me from wandering too far astray. The majestic towers, the block upon block speak to my soul. I am nearest the northern entrance, La Porte Rouge, with its surrounding wooden pickets to keep us from the construction site. Always, always they labor at it, although why is it that an ancient building only becomes more esteemed with age, while a woman does not?

And why is the upper portion of the entrance protected by metal bars? I know, in the hopes of keeping the windows from being destroyed by yet another war, but it does seem to make God just that much more inhospitable. No matter—he does have a lovely home.

We are of the same make, this building and I. Should I never be known by those who come after, my interior is as grand as those flying buttresses, and my soul flies just as high and is quite as strong. What perfect arrogance we humans have to suppose our worth lies in what others remember of us, as if we carry our value in others' memories. Yet I do believe that part of who we are and why we are here as artists is because of what we create.

Manet must accept me back. I have to convince him that he must without explaining the truth: He needs me to help him see. Out from under his fury, I see now that I was partially correct: We do make the paintings together, Manet and I. What was wrong was my saying so.

Haussmann's ruins accuse me as if I have wrecked the buildings demolished to allow "progress." We are all about progress, we of the city that scoops up its ancient ruins and wheels them away, we who specially decorate an already lovely cathedral for an emperor's wedding. If beauty cannot save us, what will?

After three days I begin to inquire about music students, and I easily regain two. It's not enough, but it allows me to eat the cheapest of baguettes and drink the lowest of wines. I crave cheese: *Camembert*, some nice *chèvre*. Even at our poorest, we eat good cheese when we can. Better no cheese than the inferior stuff.

Will my parents wonder at not receiving the bundle of coins they have "inherited" from my father's cousin? I had Manet write up the letter. He was unwilling to do so at first, until I explained that my parents would be homeless without it. So my father received a portion of the money by messenger every week. What will they do without it? I simply have not enough to share and survive.

I revisit the cafés of my friends. I play all of the songs I have always played, but I can't feel them, not now, not with art blooming in my head, behind my eyes. The lyrics seem low and cheap and common. They don't speak to the things in me that Manet has been sounding.

At the Café Guerbois, the lunch crowd gathers out of the weather, those who either don't have jobs (and hence no money) or have so much money they can be here during the day. They don't listen to my music, not really, but I play on. Manet is absent.

A coin bounces into my upturned hat, and I glance up to see Alfred Stevens.

"Why are you here instead of modeling for Manet's magnificent painting?" he asks.

No one even notices that I have stopped playing in the middle of a song.

I shrug warily. "Ask him."

"He won't tell me. He just asks if I have seen you."

I tune a string. "He knows where I live."

"No one can figure out why he stopped the painting. Pity, because it was fine. Rumor has it that he's about to paint over it."

I grab my hat and put it on, barely stopped to retrieve the coins that rain around my feet. He stoops to help me, and I feel his eyes on me as he hands the coins over. Only later will I recall the smile on his face. Only then will I be grateful.

When I burst into his studio, Manet is painting his brother-in-law.

"Over there," he says by way of greeting. "No clothes."

I close my eyes before moving behind the curtain.

I sit obediently, silently, though his brother-in-law gapes at my naked body. I pull the dress beneath me up and about my middle. "Must we pose together?"

Manet dismisses him and repositions me. He drapes the blue dress I am sitting on across my left leg, then takes my left hand in his and places mine around my chin.

My father, arranging my limbs.

Must art ever be both blissful and sorrowful for me?

I can't resist pointing out during a break that the face on the bather is too serene, and I am pleased when Manet daubs at it with white.

As he paints *The Picnic*, we speak of his reluctance to do a full-on nude, despite pressure to do so. The men in the café, the painters, the critics, the writers, they all tell him that if he is to be taken seriously, he must do a nude.

"You are not afraid of a little flesh," I ask him one day as I pull my clothing on. As many times as he has seen me do this, and after what we shared, he still turns away from my body if he is not painting.

"No, I am not. In fact, I have been thinking of Titian's *Venus*."

I know the painting, though only from a photo.

He does not speak but looks off into the distance. He sits on the sofa and puts his elbows to his knees and cradles his face in his hands.

"It is not that one, though, I think of the most. There is one that reminds me of your shoulders in this painting. Your hair, in fact, is pinned remarkably like the painting I am thinking of."

"I noticed the effort you took with my hair. I just didn't know what you were after."

He turns his head until his fingers cover his lips, inhales, and then speaks.

"*The Rokeby Venus* by Velázquez."

I laugh. "Velázquez. Of course."

His eyes widen. "You know it?"

"I don't, but I know your fascination with him."

"His painting is of Venus turned from the viewer."

"From?"

"Yes. Her back is to us, and Cupid holds a mirror for her. She appears to look at us, but her face is blurry."

"So we don't see who she really is?"

"As she would have it."

I mull this. "What do we see?"

He stands, rummages through his books until he comes to one on Velázquez. "Here's a sketch of the painting. My uncle told me of the painting and on my trip to Italy, I decided to take a detour to England to locate it. It was in a private residence, but with luck, I was able to see it." He stands, "I have never ceased thinking of it. But it's something that one is not supposed to know about."

"Why not?"

"Men use that painting for . . . their secret purposes," he bites out, looking at the floor. For one so sophisticated, this gap surprises me. This dear, confused man, deflowered, no doubt, by the island women on his maritime journeys as a youth, his first and only real relationship, I suppose, with his former piano teacher who has clearly borne him a son that he cannot acknowledge, he still does not know what to think of women.

"Not such secret purposes, Manet. But let me see the painting."

The book shows a grainy photograph, and I am quickly again as mesmerized as Manet by the woman. She reclines upon a couch with, yes, her back turned to us. But her posture says she knows we are watching; one does not keep such tension and awareness in one's shoulders and thighs when one is alone. Cupid holds the mirror—love holds up the mirror, and Venus looks with that love back at the viewer, only to realize that he—that we—are not even looking at her face. Her body is the only thing of interest.

"I'd like to turn her around. I'd like her to face her viewer, make him realize she knows he is watching her body, the way she watches him now, but more directly. I want her gaze to be sure and clear."

"You want her to condemn the public, Manet?" I smile. He is so unaware of what he really wants: to condemn himself. That child that is said to be his either truly is or could have been, of this much I am convinced. But doesn't the woman live with him? Isn't he financially supporting the child? What more could be done?

The painting he wants to do would ask that. But would it answer it?

Art is so personal, yet so universal all at once. *Vive l'art.*

He sits again and puts his face in his hands. "But what am I to make of his source?"

"His source?"

He turns the pages again, showing a photo of a bronze woman reclining very similarly to *The Rokeby Venus*. "This is a copy he asked to be made of an ancient Roman statue, *The Borghese Hermaphrodite.*"

"The Borghese what?"

He flips the page, revealing first the curvaceous, feminine backside of the woman, and then another page reveals the front: a penis greets me, and I can't help but throw back my head and laugh. Soon he joins me, and we can't stop.

"So you want to paint a woman who condemns the men who want her, when in reality, what they want is a male, that is, themselves, the painters? They are merely having sex with one another's works of art?"

He cocks his head. "Victorine, where do you get these preposterous notions?" He claps the book shut and puts it back on the desk.

My eyebrow goes up and I wonder just who made that Roman statue. Odds are, it wasn't a woman.

Manet's mind seems elsewhere while he paints *The Picnic.* I see that indeed my shoulders in this painting come to resemble *The Rokeby Venus*, and my hair does as well, down to the color. Is this why he has favored me for so long, wanting to slowly inch toward this nude that he has been so loathe to do?

I may be naked in this painting, but I am not entirely nude.

The Venus in his beloved Velázquez, how does she compare with Titian's? I find myself wondering this as I sit. Titian's woman is friendly and open, spoiled and classist. Velázquez's is a real woman one might meet on the street, though thinner than I am. Her buttocks so solid and firm, mine will never match that. I don't mind, because I can't see behind and I live to please myself, not men anyway.

I enjoy thinking about her body, her curves, and how she invites me to look at it, while also asking me to see her face, her soul. She uses her body as an access point to more of herself, and I pity that she does not know better, but I love her for knowing there is more to her.

I don't like that insipid Cupid. It never makes sense to me that we must have these heavy-handed symbols, as if we can't make our art speak loudly enough without being overly clear. Manet does not do this, and yet sometimes he over-uses symbols because he knows others will easily recognize them. When I confront him about this he rolls his eyes.

"One would think you are a painter, Meurent, with all of your endless criticism. What if I tried to speak to you but I spoke in Italian instead of French?"

"I wouldn't understand you unless I knew Italian."

"Exactly, Meurent."

I think on this for a very long time. When Zola comes in, I ask him, "Zola, you write in French. Others write in French. How is what you write different from what others write?"

He smiles with a puzzled, pleased expression: "What a wonderful question. Well, our building blocks are the same, of course. The difference is in how we fit them together."

"But how can you be original and yet write in a way that is intelligible?"

"Why do you ask?"

He looks from me to Manet, who is cleaning a brush that does not need it.

Zola sighs. "I suppose it's how I say things differently while using the familiar. I make a word fresh by putting it beside something unexpected."

Manet smiles smugly.

Perhaps he wins this round, after all.

Anticipation builds in us both. This painting will be special, no doubt. It will build on the old, on work people are familiar with, and then it will destroy their preconceived ideas as they begin to trace the painting from one end to the other, from one diagonal to the next.

◈

Another sitting for *The Picnic*: "I understand why you want me unclothed and the men wearing clothes. Have you ever gone bathing and encountered a neighbor? Then you see that same neighbor at market? What if the neighbor were wearing a bathing suit at the market? It would be all wrong. That's why it's more disturbing if the men are clothed."

"It also suggests you and the woman in the water are prostitutes."

I lower my eyes and smile. I don't say that the greater condemnation would be on the men. I don't have to.

Gradually I find myself stopping by Willie's more frequently. It's just physical, I tell myself by way of excuse. He has forgiven me. But why then do I stay all night sometimes and why do we go about our days as if we had never been apart until he says or does something small, something shortsighted and I itch to get away from him, if it's just about the sex?

"Did you ever sleep with that artist?" Willie asks. "The one who paints women like they're ghosts."

"Manet? He does not paint that way. And he has a mistress," I say. Willie is appeased, but it is just this easy appeasement that irks me about him.

Willie frowns at the cigarette in my hand. He doesn't smoke and doesn't like anyone smoking near him because of his boxing. He claims it slows him down. I toss it from me and step on it. But I find myself wanting just one more puff, and when he falls asleep, I go outdoors and pull on a cigarette as if I can extract life from it.

When I go to Willie's fights, nothing has changed. He charges on. Nothing at all has changed. I vow not to sneak out in the middle of the fight, but I do. My own room seems like a haven after the crowded theater, after his frowsy bed.

There's a knock at my door at two in the morning, and I'm surprised to see Willie because of the time, not because he comes to see me. He hates to be alone after fights.

Willie staggers, though he seldom drinks. "Let me in," he says. He swoops past me and lands on my bed.

"I told you I love you," he says. "I told you I want to marry you. Don't tell me you'd rather live here in this little hole all alone than marry me?"

"As if your place is nicer."

"It's larger," he says, drunkenly indicating his crotch as he says so.

"Don't be crude." I shut the door.

"Crude? From what I've been hearing lately, you are nothing but crude. How come you pretend to be so much better than me? You should hear the stories they tell me about you. If half of them are true." He looks up at the ceiling, and for the first time I am ashamed.

"They say you posed nude for photos that every man in Paris saw. That you used to sleep with anything that moved, and that you are doing the same now, just with higher society artists." He breathes deeply and sits up. Ah. My working for Manet has caused people to dig for gossip.

"Is that what it is, Victorine? Am I not high society enough for you? Just give me a few more years. I think this British boxing will take off soon here, and then, well, you can do anything." Disgust fills his eyes. Willie is disgusted with me?

"Are they still alive, those who said those things against me? Tell me, Willie, how many men did it take to pull you off them? Surely you didn't let them say those things about the woman you 'love' without stopping them, not after what you did to my nose."

He throws his hands in the air. "There you go again about that nose as if you had the best goddamned one in the whole world before I hit you. Actually, it was just a little crooked anyway."

I curse but he grabs my hands and talks over top of me.

"Look, I love you, no matter what. I thought maybe you'd prefer it if you knew I knew so you could stop pretending."

I call him every dirty word I have ever heard. I tell him to leave, leave immediately, but he doesn't listen.

I sit on the floor. "What bothers you the most, Willie? You seemed happy to sleep with me repeatedly even after you knew I wasn't a virgin. Tell me, what's your body count? Seriously, what's your number? Do you even know it? I see how those women want you after a fight. Isn't that part of your payment? How many just since we got together?"

He sits silently.

"I told you I don't love you. That being the case, I owe you no further explanation. If you don't like what I do, there's no need for you to talk to me anymore."

Willie comes and sits by me on the floor. "Marry me," he insists.

So I do.

As 1862 has bled into 1863, so beauty has blended with truth in Manet's art. I willingly sit until I am sore; I would do this and so much more for art.

Slowly, *The Picnic* (*Le Dejeuner sur l'herbe*) completely emerges from the secret land in which paintings dwell until summoned stroke by stroke. I am always discovering another detail in this one. My eye starts in the right-hand back corner: A rowboat is covered by a pillar of brown fire. This same pale cloud frames the bather, and a deeper tone of it is found right behind the man reclining and pointing.

The women in it are paler even than the wan men. Behind the redhead is a wood, deep and dark. It is without a path, and it invites even more so because of that. The grass is a smooth carpet framed by trees. The eye wanders beyond those trees, wanting to know what's down that path, or who has perhaps recently been there. It's not a pretty painting; it's not a pretty scenario.

There is artifice and nature. He reveals vulnerability in my face, intelligence. Now he knows me. Again my head is uncovered, but my hair is back. He wanted me to wear my black necklace, but I persuaded him I would not have worn it in the water, and so it lies on the ground with my clothes, barely visible. Truth be told, I am beginning to feel fettered by that damn shoelace and am glad to have convinced him it must go.

We make a wave, the party of us. Starting at the lower-left hand corner one sees a tantalizing trail of clothing, beginning with a lovely blue gown, a pleasurably colored length of silk, a straw hat carefully put atop so as not to be flattened, bedecked with a navy ribbon topped with a sky blue one.

We have eaten our fill, I suppose, because our basket is toppled (innocence spoiled?). Fecundity, plenty, is suggested by the fruits that spill: grapes, cherries, plums, possibly peaches. Their indistinct red identities hint. Then there is the field of blue just behind the fruit, followed by an invitingly lumpy *boule de pain*.

Manet has seated me on an equally blue shade of material. A swatch of white lies directly behind the basket. Is this what I (she) took off when she stopped modeling? For regardless of what the viewers see, this is indeed a painting of a woman modeling for a painting, this same woman relaxing with the artist and another male in the studio during lunch. *The Picnic* is before the painting. The scene is artificial. I am stunned at its message and am not even sure I have it right. I refuse to ask Manet if I am correct.

I am uncertain who the man closest me is meant to be—I suspect Manet has doubled himself—he has had his brothers interchangeably sit for the man on the right, hinting that their individual identity is not important. Suzanne's brother sits as the other man. I try to feel Manet out on this painting, but it is as if he is not sure what he means, and he will not answer me. Maybe he cannot.

The man reclining across from the couple must be the artist, with that know-it-all wagging finger, the cane. His finger points at me as if directing me even during break. The man so close beside me that he might be my lover, or my protector, is bored or displeased.

The artist's face is nearly obscured by a thick beard (a device, dear Manet, and not a clever one) which makes it nearly impossible to read him, and undoubtedly makes it easier for Manet to use two men for the same model. There is a crescent of face, a triangle of nose, a reverse half-moon of neck.

Why does he paint us as if we were outdoors for this painting? I stand before it every break rubbing my neck, my aching shoulders. I wear a dressing gown then, but it seems pointless.

Indeed, her nakedness suggests that she might be a prostitute, if the painting is read as a story. Since the painter is included in the painting, perhaps it is a condemnation of the model as commodity. He knows he uses me, but he doesn't know how else to get at his vision, not without a tool. I hope he sees this, anyway.

Just behind my buttocks in the picture peeks the hand of the man behind me. It's a creepy thing, as if it either emerges from my body or as if it's about to secretly touch me. The man wears white trousers, echoed by the bather in the background and that same costume by the spilled basket—spilled innocence, again the prostitute and sexual images.

Why the dark foliage above me? Because that is the dark place that the artist's mind goes to. He doesn't like using us (we are twinned there), and he is the man on the ground. His anxiety over his art emerges.

This is a criticism of the males of our time, how well-to-do men will buy a woman for the day, row her to some quiet spot and take turns leading her down that dark path, come back and they remain clothed but she is naked in their eyes: They cannot see her ever again in her beautiful blue gown or her innocent straw hat. To them she will ever be a whore, though she did them the service they craved. And the wisdom on her face says she knows this. The evenness with which she stares (my God, I stare—I am accusing him) shows that she accepts the world as it is. She is much more at ease with her nudity than they are in their clothes. She keeps her foot upturned in the manner recognized by viewers: "I am a whore."

Though their moment of ecstasy is over, she remains nearly entwined with them: Her foot is between the artist's legs (with a small movement she could arouse him), and her body leans so close to the "second" man (*her* double is behind them, bending, with darker hair as she must serve the artist as so many, many different people) that he must feel the warmth of her body.

The men linger over her the way they do dessert. She is just another kind of food. He has called the painting alternately *The Picnic* and *Le Bain*—The Bath. I'm not at all sure which name he has settled upon, and it shows his dual nature. To picnic is to consume—this woman is being eaten. But a bath means to be immersed. It can be either a baptism to wash away the sins or imply being steeped in something as if it's not one's fault. I trust his paintbrush will eventually decide the work's title.

The three characters are a triangle, a *ménage a trois*. Just who is Manet trying most to indict? That he would even consider showing at the Salon answers my question when he won't.

Though I admire what he has done, childishly I silently decry the muddy colors. It is not a happy painting, and I do not feel honored by it. That is not the point of it, of course, and perhaps it's more because I must share the spotlight. I am not used to being a part instead of the whole message, and I wonder if this means he finds me lacking.

One painting of me by Manet becomes another. At times we take a break so he can work on something (or paint someone) else, but I am in the studio anyway, a talking prop. His fingers bloom flowers, mature fruits with touches of sepia brown and washes of black. We discuss color and texture, strokes, and shape. Today, I put out my fingers for his brush, as one might for a drag of a cigarette, a sip of a drink, but his left hand grabs mine; his look quails me as few things do. My eyes say *Fuck you*. In Paris, one does not dabble. One either is a painter or is not. My hand remains outstretched; his fingernails dig into my skin. Hard.

I could make him yield. I could.

"Have you thought any more about art school?" he asks coolly.

I will my hand closer to that brush; all my life I have been willing myself closer to it. My hand shakes. His fingernails do not release me.

I withdraw my hand, refusing to look at the reddened skin. He has no idea just how much pain I can take. Something about his eyes, though, makes me think he knows I have let him win.

That afternoon I leave early, stop by an art shop, and buy supplies. "For Monsieur Manet?" I am asked.

"Of course," I say, though I buy cheaper paints and brushes than he would. When I ask for the bill, the shopkeeper waves. "I will put it on his account." I grin. "I forgot a few things," I say, and I shop as if I am indeed buying for Manet.

Tomorrow, perhaps I will pay him for the supplies. But today, with the flesh of my hand throbbing, I'm not so inclined.

At home, I spread the wealth onto my bed. I stare at the blank canvas I have propped against the wall—it has cost more than I can afford, but I do not care. I will just do away with the wine for a few days. No, maybe I'd better keep the wine and do without the bread.

I pick up the palette and put my thumb through the hole. I toss it onto the bed.

Next week I will bend to retrieve a shoe and will find the materials under the bed, untouched, the canvas leaned against a wall.

Willie asks when I will start painting, and I shrug. "Sometime." My parents have relented, now that Willie and I are married. Still, it rankles, knowing that our standing in front of a priest (after a civil ceremony, of course) somehow makes me a decent enough person for my mother. We seldom visit, but I'm happy that I can again drop in on my father on occasion. Willie and I even had dinner with my parents right after we married. My mother made roast beef and asked about Willie's French mother. She asked if we wanted children and before Willie could say anything, I said a resounding no.

Our finances are not much improved, but Willie dreams of sending me to art school. I know we cannot afford it, yet it's a beautiful dream that we share, and the dream is almost as wonderful as I imagine the reality would be. Almost. We still send part of the money I get for modeling to my parents. I have discovered that even during those weeks I did not work for Manet, they received payments. When I attempt to thank Manet, he acts as if he has no clue what I am talking about.

Manet seemed more amused than anything at my marriage, congratulating me heartily and insisting on giving us a wedding gift: A small watercolor by Monet. Manet has been helping support the young man by buying his paintings, though Monet doesn't know who his benefactor is. It's a muddy swirl of vibrant colors, and I hardly know what to make of it. I take it to my father who is entranced as he tries to figure out what the man's aim is.

"Keep it," I say, and he hangs it in his shop where customers ask about it nearly every day, although more often they look at it and ask what it is, rather than admiring it.

For all of the fuss over *The Picnic*, after it is completed Manet puts it aside until time to submit it to the Salon, too. I am glad to be out of the company of Manet's brother-in-law. His brother was fine, but that other one . . . I am relieved the painting is over.

"It's been refused," Manet says, waving an envelope at me as I enter his studio.

"*Merde*," I breathe.

I know he means *The Picnic*.

Artist friends are gathered here as if at a wake—Degas, Monet, Stevens, Renoir, and several others. Drink flows.

Zola enters. "I have just heard the news. I will write the most scathing article that will convince them otherwise or will at least have the public swarming to your studio. You weren't the only artist to be snubbed. It's an outrage."

Zola is stout, opinionated, and waves his arms incessantly. His eyebrows need taming, as does his tongue. I want to tell him to shut up, that he is not going to be able to change anything, but maybe he can. Still, I wish he weren't so sure of himself, and that I were more so.

"It may be the end of my painting," Manet says, bowing his head. I cannot abide seeing a man feel sorry for himself.

"Cheer up," I say to Manet, suddenly furious at the attention they pay him as if this "disaster" will ruin him. "Maybe you can sell some of your work on the street so that your family may eat." They all know I speak of Renoir, of Monet, and the table quiets.

I stand, pressing my palms into the table. "You know nothing about hunger, about deprivation. Manet, if I didn't know that painting was more than a hobby to you, I would despise you."

Manet puts on his hat, picks up his walking stick, and puts some money on the table. "I am disappointed in you, Meurent," he says. "I thought you believed as I do that all artists are brothers. It is the one thing that transcends money."

My face reddens. "It does transcend money and sex. But you act as if this minor disappointment will ruin you, while others paint on, and it *is* ruining them."

He rises. "Then perhaps they aren't doing it right. Perhaps they need another occupation."

A hiss rises from the room.

"Do you know what a tube of paint costs? What about a loaf of bread? Do you ever have to choose between the two? Does your family go without so that the world will see what is in your heart?"

"Mlle. Meurent, let's continue this discussion when you are accepted by the Salon, shall we?" He turns his back on me, then whirls around and returns. "As much as," his eyes fill, "as I love art, I would never permit Suzanne or Léon to suffer for it. You will find they are amply," he rounds his hands wider than even Suzanne's hips are, "amply, I say, provided for."

His raised eyebrows tell me that he remembers that he has helped care for my parents, and his eyes sweep to and quickly away from Monet as well. I am ashamed to be made to feel so small, and yet rightly so. I don't care.

I stand on my chair and shout, "I will be accepted by the Salon, Manet. I will." When he turns away, I fling myself onto his back and beat at it. The roar of hilarity around us brings me to my senses and I slide off him. I sink back into my seat and try not to see the pitying glances of those around me, the

shocked look on Manet's face. While we have been in much more compromis-
ing positions privately, Manet's deportment in public is typically flawless. By
shaming him, I have shamed myself. His insult still burns, but a tiny part of me
thinks that what I have just done proves to him, to them, that I am uncivilized
and that they may dismiss me and any work I or my kind may do. I want to
berate them for their snobbery, but I fear I have a touch of it myself. Though
perhaps I am only playing the part they expect of me.

I make an excuse and leave, though Willie will have already left for the theater. Perhaps alone is what I most need to be right now.

Again I expect to be ostracized by Manet. Again, I am wrong. Manet can afford to be an artist because he has inherited money from his father. Why do
I fault him for his birth? It is no more his fault than it is mine that I was born
to my parents.

No matter how I try to condemn him, Manet is a decent man.

Before all is said and done, Napoleon III asks to see the refused paintings because of the sheer number of refusals and says there must be a *Salon des Refusés*
to appease those who were turned down. Some artists will have no part of it,
seeing it as admitting failure. When Manet learns about the *Salon des Refusés*, he
at first refuses to consider it as well.

"The Salon turned away over half of the five thousand paintings submitted.
Everyone will see your work in the secondary show and when they do, they will
know you were wronged," I say.

"They don't know what it is to work months on something, sometimes
years, because you plan it in your head for so long, and then to be dismissed,
to be offered merely a place among those who are rejected. It's too much. I
cannot accept."

"It must be seen. I thought you didn't care what they thought. . . ." I touch
his hand lightly.

He bows his head, sighs seemingly from the pit of himself.

"I will show it."

The beauty of *The Picnic* is found mostly in the still life, and the figures are
all strange (except perhaps for the nude woman). The public won't find much
to admire there. But if they listen to his condemnation of using young women

this way, that will be a step forward for our excess-steeped nation. When our art seeks to stop us, it is a sad commentary on our condition.

Manet reads the reviews, though I beg him not to. "Not one detail has attained its exact and final form," says critic Jules-Antoine Castagnary of the painting. He criticizes Manet's anatomical skills and accuses him of not having conviction or sincerity.

But Castagnary also says Manet's pictures have "a certain verve in the colors, a certain freedom of touch which are in no way commonplace."

One critic says Manet "will triumph one day, we do not doubt, over all the obstacles which he encounters, and we will be the first to applaud his success." It does not soothe him.

Manet paces his studio and finally puts on his hat. We follow him to the Café Guerbois like a flock of concerned birds.

"I lack conviction? I lack sincerity? Accuse my lines, doubt my colors, but never my conviction and certainly not my sincerity. It's too harsh. I will just quit."

I tell Manet that the critics are fickle, but he is too wounded to hear me. I grab those ridiculous papers from him and thrust them into the fireplace.

He quaffs a glass of wine, and then another. "What other reason is there to paint except sincerity? If a man wants to make money, there are easier ways. If he wants to be remembered, he would have a better chance if he assassinated the emperor. Art is fickle. No. Art is not. Critics are."

"I don't really understand what the critics are for," I say.

Zola puffs his chest and widens his eyes. As always, he has something to say. "Why, critics are to help the public understand what they are not educated to see. For instance, if they were to look at, say Monet's water scenes they might see a few strips of color laid down like so much ribbon pretending to be a river when it means so much more. They need someone to explain to them what to look for."

I shake my head. "Are you telling me that the art cannot stand on its own? That one needs educating in art?"

He laughs. "Of course it can stand on its own. But only once one understands sight."

"If a viewer needs someone to tell them what it means, then the artist has not done a good enough job."

Manet moans and covers his face.

Zola looks impatiently at me. "The artist creates because he cannot say what these things are that lie within. It stands to reason that unless he has done a very good job indeed, the viewer is not going to understand any better (nor is he likely to) unless someone trained to see explains it."

Although his loyalty to Manet moves me, I am not entirely convinced. While his defense of Manet is admirable, he ought to leave the critiquing to others and get back to writing fiction.

When Zola speaks of literature, I could watch the plump cherry red of the inside of his lips form words forever, puffing in and out with passion and indignation. Not only are the syllables life, but they paint almost as well as a brush. Why is it artists always want to borrow another's palette? Manet said he once desired to write a story but failed so miserably he picked up a brush and never put it down again. Thank God, I say.

After several drinks, Manet and I leave the others and walk the streets until night has overtaken the city. The streetlamps light our way. We know these streets, these cobblestones. Though each dip might be a bit different, it is our city and our feet groove these pavers. Together, all of humanity etches our lives and the weight of our beings into what seems impervious. The record is made.

We do not speak, unless to make our path known. I feel his art hover in the air, and I long to protect it, to see it reattach itself to him. All of the paintings that will light our country, the world, that must come from him, must come.

A rebellious thought: What of all of the paintings that must come from me? Who is there to protect them? Not Manet. Not Zola. Only myself. I square my shoulders.

Our shoes are dusty when we return to the studio. He sits and begins a sketch as if he has forgotten that I am there. I watch as quickly my face tops a uniform; an instrument blooms from my mouth. I needn't have worried. He doesn't seem to have put art aside yet.

He yawns and pauses for a long time and I circle the sofa.

"It's beautiful," I say of the drawing.

He is asleep. I gently take the sketchpad from him, lay him on his side. I lie down beside him on the sofa and put my arm around him, stroke his forehead. Poor Édouard. When he wakes, I must be gone.

◈

I hurriedly kiss Willie goodbye as I rush off to the opening of an art gallery.

"Give me a minute and I'll come with you," he says, tidying his hair.

"No need. It's just boring people complaining about boring paintings."

His hand stops raking through his hair. "Then why do you want to go?"

"Really, you don't need to do this."

"But you come to all of my fights."

I laugh lightly. "Yes, but these aren't my paintings."

He raises his hands. "Do you love me?"

How can such a simple man put so much meaning into one sentence? He asks every day, and I always give him the same answer.

"I married you, didn't I?"

I am beginning to think the only thing I really love is art.

My eyes roll involuntarily, though at him or myself, I'm not sure. "Let's go."

The gallery is owned by Paul Durand-Ruel, a well-known patron in the city who buys and sells the art of many local artists, from the most respected to the beginners. Room after room of paintings threaten to overwhelm. I turn around and around, delighted at the plentitude. My head teems.

"It's a forest of paintings," I exclaim, but my shoulder meets the middle of what I assume is a back and I turn.

"Pardon me," I say, but I really feel interrupted.

"Ah, *Crevette*," says Couture as he stops my spin, puts his hand on the top of my skull familiarly.

"Thomas," I say. It is the first time I have called him by his given name, and I blink as I do.

"My classroom misses you."

"And I it, sometimes."

He observes me closely, and a smile forms. I quickly introduce him to Willie, which delights Couture and he takes a faux swing at Willie before turning to me.

"You are lovelier than ever. There's something very different, almost taller about you, *Crevette*. I have seen much of your modeling." He looks embarrassed and I do too as I wonder if he means the postcards. Then I raise my head.

"There's only one thing missing from your studio, Thomas."

"And what is that?"

"Women artists."

His face freezes. "The truth is, I have been thinking of opening a studio for women. Some are saying that is the way to go."

"What do you say?"

He sighs and parts his hands, shrugs. "I have but one small studio with a few well-known alumni. Even if I did open it to women, would it make a difference?"

"It would make all of the difference," I say and press my lips firmly together.

"Yes, well, pardon me. I see someone I need to speak with. It's been good seeing you, Victorine, and meeting you, Willie," he says as he gazes off into the crowd. I don't watch him pretend his way across the room.

The show focuses on the work of one of the Academy's "finest," Gustave Courbet. Accused of being a "realist," I see a bit of him in Manet's work. Courbet's paintings aren't attractive. They show life as it is. One whole wall is taken up by *A Burial at Ornans*, the subject of which is the interment of Courbet's uncle. The "models" are the townspeople who were actually at the event. It seems not much more than a painted photo, and yet it touches me.

"Who allowed this vulgar painting in here?" asks a woman with high hair and a nose to match. She thumps her parasol on the floor. "It's ugly and prosaic. Why would anyone paint on such a large scale the funeral of an ordinary man?" she complains.

In the corner a man blushes, and I can only assume he is Courbet. When Manet goes forward to shake his hand and says his name, this is confirmed.

I quickly assess Courbet's work: He does not romanticize anything; he simply paints what he sees, obviously. That he does not manufacture false beauty or ugliness honors our true lives.

Willie walks along with me, looking at the ceiling with as much attention as he does the paintings.

I nod at the painters who huddle before canvases, chins in hands, arms crossed.

Finally Willie seems to find what he's searching for: refreshments. With his hands and attention full I am free to wander.

Bazille comes alongside me and, blushing, clutching at his high lapels, asks if he may accompany me about the room to get my opinion.

"I would be happy to, if you would first introduce me to the artist," I ask.

"I hardly know him, but I will make what acquaintance for you that I can."

Courbet is stout, with a long black and gray beard. His eyes are so dark they seem lined with kohl. Bazille scarcely has to open his mouth before Courbet is enthusiastically clasping my hand.

"Victorine Meurent. I see why Manet calls you his favorite model. If I were one who needed models, I'd steal you in a second," he says warmly.

"And I'd let you," I say, instantly taking to him. Quickly we begin a conversation about *The Burial*, the colors he used, the size of the canvas. Its reception. He speaks frankly of his aims and his disappointment at the general feeling about the painting.

In the corner is a delightful painting of two bored looking young ladies beneath a tree. They are neither pretty nor prim. The olive greens look familiar. "Has Manet been studying your paintings?" I whisper, and he releases a great bark that makes everyone turn our way.

It is with difficulty that Bazille manages to break me away from the fascinating man, and it's only through his effort that I realize he must have some reason to speak with me.

We have finished walking the room, and Willie waves something that looks like a piece of cheese at me. I nod back but Bazille indicates the entry to the next room.

"It would be a pity to miss Durand-Ruel's newest acquisitions," he says, motioning for me to go ahead of him.

I look back at Willie and shrug, and he frowns and makes as if he will head toward us, but as I pass into the room, a backward glance shows me he is closing in on someone circulating with a tray of desserts. I laugh and nearly turn to join him.

As we gaze at a pink nightmare before us, Bazille takes my hand. "I am thinking of doing a painting," he says. He swallows and I try to shake free my hand but cannot. "I was wondering if you would consider modeling for me. It would be outdoors, completely. Have you worked outdoors?" His face says things I don't think he realizes it is saying, and the sad, sweet way he says it makes me want to kiss him, though he does not at all appeal otherwise.

I succeed in retrieving my hand. "I have not modeled outdoors, no. But perhaps I should ask my husband if he minds if I pose. I suppose I would be nude?" I ask innocently. *Oh, Victorine, don't play this game,* and yet I do.

The young man flinches.

"I apologize. No one told me you had married."

I laugh. "It wasn't a society affair or anything. And don't worry—if I choose to sit for you, Willie wouldn't be able to stop me. I just had to let you know that I'm married." Why? I don't know.

The poor boy has no idea what to say, what to do. When Willie enters the room, I smile and let him lead me out, ignoring his angry countenance and the uncharacteristic glare he shoots at Bazille.

That is all Bazille ever mentions of painting me, though he does speak pleasantly to me whenever we meet. If only I were capable of wanting someone other than Willie right now. With the ache of being pregnant with art, I only half want him.

Art is everywhere. I cannot escape it. I paint in my dreams. When I eat, my spoon makes art in my porridge. The sky is a sketch. It invigorates me; it enervates me. It's as if I am at a feast and no one invites me to eat.

My stomach is full of others' work, but my own hides within my cells.

Willie can do nothing right. He cooks for me but I'm not hungry. He holds me at night, but I draw away. If only I were a man.

Between modeling jobs I return to my father's shop where we talk, of course, of art. He does not understand this modern style.

"They use many of the techniques of Hals, Velázquez, and Rubens, but all at once," I say eagerly. "They don't care what the brush strokes look like close up—it's the overall impression of the piece that they care about."

"Yes. I've noticed that they don't generally even mix their colors unless they need a color that doesn't come straight from a tube," my father says.

"And their favorite colors are those new ones, aren't they? They love their . . ."

"Cerulean blue."

We laugh.

"And their cobalt blue, viridian, cadmium yellow," I add.

"Future generations will think we were a very gay society, with all of this color, won't they?"

My father looks thoughtful. "It seems to me as if they must put wet paint over wet, because it looks so soft."

"You're exactly right. And they don't varnish the paint anymore either." The traditionalists do, of course.

"Their backgrounds are so light."

I touch my father's hand. "You have the right to paint, you know. She can't take that from you." I can't quit trying.

"My posters should be dry by now," he says, rising.

"I'll help you with them."

At least he will allow me to do this much.

After his disappointment over *The Picnic*'s reception, Manet takes a few days before he sends a note around, but he does, and by now I expect him to. He sprawls his name proudly across it with an excited, monolithic "M" at the beginning of his surname. Perhaps his talk with Courbet has encouraged him, though Manet did tell me at the showing that he found *Burial* a bit too café-colored.

When Willie sees Manet's note, he grunts.

"Do you not want me to go?" I ask. He will not win this war, but I can pretend.

"I've rented a second theater on the other side of the city. There will be fights going on there too, so I should be making more money soon."

"Why didn't you tell me?" I hug him.

He shrugs. "Do you really need to work now?"

It surprises me to realize that I do not think of modeling as work, per se. I've been apprenticing, it feels like, and that is why art is nearly formed in me. A lesson or two, I imagine, on perspective. A tweak or two at my brushstrokes, perhaps. Drawing, well, I know I'm not so good at shading yet. But all of this can be learned, and much of it lies within me already. I feel it ripening.

"I do need to model," I say. "And if there is any extra money, perhaps I can. . . ."

"Put it away for art school?" he asks bitterly. "Go on. Go."

Why the change? He was fine until he went with me to Courbet's exhibition. Somehow, he hasn't been happy about my association with the art world since. I would give up many things for Willie, but not this.

"He doesn't need me until tomorrow," I say, putting my arms about Willie. There is one thing I can offer Willie, and I do it willingly, knowing I will benefit from it just as much as he.

I wish I could explain to him the horror at having discovered that all I love is art. I want to care more for a human being than I do lines and colors on canvas, but art has been there longer, will be here longer. Art has never rejected or disappointed me, even at its worst.

SEVEN

Olympia

MANET GREETS me impatiently. He strides about his studio setting up props: a high divan, green curtains. He adjusts and readjusts them.

"At first, it will just be you. Well, most of the time it will be."

I am to arrive the next day, no wardrobe.

"Just tell me what your idea is," I ask. I lay my hand atop his, but when I feel his squirm beneath mine, I quickly remove it.

Manet and Suzanne are newly married. So far, their marriage has done nothing to our relationship. I hear she is very plain. We have not yet met, though they have been together for so long.

It was odd how they left the country quietly to be married in her hometown, not telling anyone until they returned. He still has not mentioned his nuptials to me—I heard only when his friends teased him.

That's how I learned that she plays piano, and I assume that is how they have come to be a couple. Manet does not talk about his personal life. Painting is his personal life; it is all I need of him.

He explains his idea for the painting, speaking in fits and starts between sentences. "It's like the *Venus di Urbino*." I have only seen the painting in books, but he says he has seen the real thing in Florence. And I already know what his inspiration for this is.

"Such beauty. Such vividness. And what that naughty young woman is doing that everyone is too polite to speak of," he murmurs. I know he is also thinking of Velázquez.

"You will be her, but to make it clear, you will be a courtesan refusing flowers from her latest client."

I am shocked but intrigued. He is calling Titian out, implying that Venus is a bored, oversexed, newly-married woman playing with the hair on her pudenda, not protecting it. Her petting is an invitation—her husband's away, and she has already "sold" her sex into marriage.

Manet's cheeks redden with excitement.

He sits on the edge of a sofa, motions for me to sit with him. He gestures to the awaiting canvas.

"Instead of the puppy there will be a black cat at her feet," he says.

I laugh, "With an arched back?"

He nods. "As in . . ."

"*The Ray*," we say at the same time, laughing, gasping to imagine what the Salon will say. He explains the rest.

"There's no way you will get it in," I say.

He stares at me steadily. "I don't care. Because of that, I will, you know."

I grab his face and search for his tongue with my teeth, pull at it as if I could summon the painting from him. I let go without concern when he doesn't re-spond and turn to the field of newly stretched canvas before him.

Suzanne. Willie. I forgot for a moment.

He cannot really want his bovine wife, if she is as ugly as they say, and yet she seems to feed that animal need in him in a way that does not spoil his passion for painting. She's gruel, and enough of it to stave off hunger, but not satisfying enough that he doesn't need more.

That more is art.

While I understand this, I cannot agree. If I can stir such art in him, what would happen if he allowed me to touch him in every way? I will do for art what I will not for myself.

Flesh is not enough for me. Never has been. But sometimes it is a conduit. Only sometimes.

Our feet nearly touch; our heads bent towards one another as we stare at the possibility across from us.

"How did you feel the first time you faced a canvas?" I ask.

He moves his hands apart and leans back. "My eye saw so many things, but when I looked more closely, one section cried louder, one color, one shadow. An image is like a woman. It has shape, curves, angles, lines. It has color—some pleasant, some jarring. It can excite or calm. I see paintings everywhere I go."

As do I. I remember my eye learning to see, my father teaching it to:

"Victorine, what shapes is this made of?" he asked when he took me to the park to look at the lake.

"Shapes?" He had insisted I learn them before, my mother says, my letters. "Triangles and circles?"

"Yes. Keep looking."

"Squares?"

"Good. Everything is based on shapes. If you want to make art, first see shapes, then color. The rest will come to your hand." I still see the shape of a thing before its color.

Manet says, "Though this painting will be after the *Venus*, she will have a different name."

He watches my face as he says: "Her name is Olympia."

"Absolutely not," I say. "No." I pace the studio's length, my yells echoing. "I. Will. Not." The name implies a more overt prostitute than I had imagined I would be posing as: It's a name often used generically for women who sell themselves. It will be supposed I am one.

Manet supplies me with a book with the photo of the Venus painting to study. In the background of *Venus* there is this odd, white-clad figure digging through a hope chest as if to retrieve something of her ladyship's, and yet the impression is of a child in white searching through a toy chest. Moreover, the small servant girl is kneeling in a way that seems like prayer with a woman looming over top of her. What is Titian saying? What will Manet say? Why must we women be defined by men?

Isn't that the only thing that makes me know who I am, though? I know best who I am when someone paints me. I saw myself on canvas grow from a young girl to what I am today. Can I see myself flung against another canvas, this time as an openly avowed prostitute? Would I dare? That it means daring ensures I will do it, naturally.

He waves his hand toward the left side of the canvas when I reluctantly rejoin him. "Olympia's head will be here. She reclines on a couch, under a luxurious shawl. She is naked except for symbols of the trade—a flower behind her ear, dirty-heeled shoes—and a necklace.

"The cat is here at the feet." He begins sketching. "Just about where the dog is with our Venus." The dog: a symbol of fidelity. Ah, a cat suits me better . . . sometimes I like to scratch.

His energy, ours, fills the room. His fingers fly across the pad.

"And the background?"

He sketches it in. Truly, his drawing skills are even better than his painting abilities.

Sit, critique, drink, sleep, repeat. Day after day we tunnel into this painting. Throughout the sessions, I am tired. It takes longer than the rest; he seems unsure at times.

Willie fights at night, sleeps while I model. We don't have much to say to one another.

"Paint me as ugly," I say finally to Manet. "A prostitute need not be beautiful to give a man what he needs. Besides, you do women more honor to show that we are perfectly imperfect," I say, thinking of Courbet. He hesitates. He has already painted me as ugly in *The Picnic* (not that he believes he has), but he painted me at such a distance no one really noticed it, not even himself.

I grab his sketchpad and begin doodling. "My stomach is not flat," I say as I draw an inflated version of my abdomen. "And neither is Venus's." He approaches this with too much reverence.

He indicts himself as much as anyone with the painting, as he always does. So often his paintings are studies of self-loathing.

"If you please," he asks, extending his hand.

Carefully attending to my comfort, he adds pillows behind my back, making small talk.

I love the acres of my body, given the largest voice of all, speaking for women, knowing, if done properly, this will change not just art but how women are perceived. Or will it? People have been looking at *Venus* for centuries now, yet no one talks about what Manet aims to discuss.

I stare at the sketch of it in Manet's art book, and then back at what he is doing. "You must lie exactly so," he says, demonstrating on the divan. I giggle to see him faux swoon.

He pulls his arm back, forms a triangle; his left is to cover his pubis. He motions for me to take up the pose.

There is no denying the comparisons between this intended painting and *Venus*: the swag of green curtain behind both of us, the sharp division into two. At the foot of her bed is a sweet puppy. At the foot of mine is to be a cat, an echo of the euphemism for that which my left hand covers.

"Isn't the addition of the actual cat in your painting too obvious?" Even though we spoke of the *The Ray* earlier, I wonder.

He frowns.

"The obvious elements lead those who do not know how to read a painting otherwise."

I lose my pose.

"You're right, but I hadn't thought to put it in those terms." I can accept from him what I cannot from Zola.

After that, I hold my pose a bit tighter, imagining someone standing before the painting years hence trying to decipher it.

In the background of *Venus*, two servants rummage through a chest for their mistress's clothes. "My" servant (black, as is the cat) brings an impressive array of flowers that I ignore.

The model, Laure, is a nursemaid Manet found at the Tuileries garden leading her young charges. He's painted her before. I can't help but notice while I've been given the red curtained side of the painting, she's got the green. Nature? That Laure and the cat are both black in this painting is no coincidence: the tiresome idea of temptation as a color.

Worth, that clever designer, challenges this idea of black (cat or woman) as an agent for bad or black as only for mourning by popularizing black dresses. As rapidly as he gets them entrenched into Parisians's closets, though, he yanks them out again for shocks of mauve and turquoise. Apparently, he believes Paris wants sheaths of flowers. With these colors, it may have them.

Venus's flowers are in her right hand, and she carelessly crumples them. One (her maidenhood?) has fallen upon the rich red of the bed.

We both share nearly identical thick bracelets like shackles, our legs are identically crossed.

"Should you paint me with the shoes?" I ask. "They will think I am a common whore, not a courtesan as you said you wanted to portray."

"It is the easiest way to show it."

"Is the easiest the best?" He listens, but not enough. So I find myself sketching my ideas for his paintings later.

Venus gets a window with a vista. I get more oppressive curtains and the sense that I am imprisoned. The dirty shoes belie that. I have been out. It is a willing confinement.

We two recline upon our crisp, inviting white sheets. I also have the reddish pillows, but he has turned mine the color of dried blood, as well as my half of the background. She is a fresh woman preparing for her groom. I am a prostitute getting ready for another customer.

Another triangle emerges: the revealed red pillows beneath our arms—a glimpse of inner delights.

"What will I hold in my hand?" I ask.

"Not flowers."

I can stay still no longer. I run to the end of the room. "Maybe a flowered shawl?" I throw a beige one with flowers and gold tassels into the air.

"Yes," he says, trying to grab it from me. I don't give it up and we wrestle. He pins me to the wall and grabs onto the material, rolls me in it.

Breathing heavily with the effort we stand face to face. "I love you," I say gently. I say it because I do, but not as a woman loves a man. I love the decent and caring man he has turned out to be. I admire the artist he is, and I have never believed in hiding what I feel.

It doesn't occur to me until later that this is the first time I have ever said those words to anyone. Then I will be sad that I have not given them to Willie, when it is such a small thing for him to want. Words cost so little, but the truth behind them is the real gift, and I will not give a false one.

Manet gazes so deeply into me that I am even more naked than the body I am housed in, and I uncross my soul's arms so he can see. Art requires all. Just when I think he will never return, he clutches me to him and kisses the top of my head.

"*Crevette*," he says. "So small and yet so mighty."

"As is the paintbrush," I quip, pulling away, my hands running across the thick hair below his rolled sleeves as I do. I pick up my guitar case and hug the black coffin to me.

I don't love him any more than I love Willie. Manet is a paintbrush, the tool with which I am created. I love simply what he can do, how he immortalizes me; that's surely the source of this groundswell of affection.

"Venus is an innocent with a sleeping dog," I say, not believing it.
Let sleeping dogs lie, Victorine, I say to myself. You have *le chat*.
"But she is not so innocent; that is the point of my painting."
"*One* of your points." I laugh uneasily and step away from Manet.

Manet takes weeks to create *Olympia*. When we are in the middle of a sitting, it alone is real. Time away is only time before we return to that world, and when it's finished, it's as real an end as death.

Willie is so busy with both venues he barely notices I am away so much. With our new marriages, you would think neither Manet nor I would be able to afford to be so busy, and yet we are.

I compare *Olympia* with the illustration of *Venus* in his art book, as it's so completely a companion piece: Venus wears a pinky ring. I get a necklace to go along with the bracelet. The bracelet is his mother's and contains a locket of his hair as a child. What does that mean?

While Venus's left hand plays with the hair she is covering, mine frankly covers my sex as if to say, "closed for business." What my latest lover did to deserve being exiled is unclear. What is clear is that Olympia will be in charge of her sexuality.

Venus's hair flows over her right shoulder. The upper portion is braided into a crown. From her left ear dangles an earring and she turns her head as if inviting someone to nibble on that ear. Her nipples are erect. Her right knee (though her legs are crossed) is lying a bit open, as if to suggest that she will welcome her husband. This is echoed in her candid, open look. If it *is* her husband she is waiting for.

Olympia's nipples are flaccid. She does not desire sex. Her (my) gaze is frank and appears to confront the viewer, but if one studies it closely enough, she is peering past the viewer. She does not care what the viewer wants or thinks. She is busy with her own affairs.

The curtains to the right of her (me) are barely parted. There is an escape there, albeit a small one. I could leave if I chose. The draping quality of the sheet makes it also seem a bit like a shroud.

The cat in my painting is not asleep. In fact, his eyes are wide and alarmed. My servant's eyes are just as wide. She seems afraid of me.

One of my shoes is off. One is on. I am ambivalent about staying or going, letting him in or refusing. I am very aware of the flowers, though I ignore them. This time, mercifully, it is the servant's head that is covered, not mine: I am in charge of the painting, and myself.

Laure and I aren't usually at Manet's studio at the same time. I love her huge, pink gown, but I don't like the easy way Manet converses with her. I admire the glow of her skin and her charming smile, and I like her, though I do fear her place in Manet's life. She's modeled for him previously; his admiration of her is undisguisable.

One afternoon, we pose together, and Manet claims he wants to see if he has captured the contrast of our skin.

"Why don't we have someone go get dessert?" I ask, anything to remove the sheen of concentration on Manet's brow.

"Sure," Laure says, looking questioningly at Manet.

Manet shakes his head. "Careful, Meurent. You're being painted right now. Sweets are not your friend."

It is the first time he has mentioned what I already have: that my body type is not ideal. It's ideal to me—(How could it not be? It is the one I have)—but not to fashion. The way men swathe us in material and froth in real life, does it really matter what our natural shape is? Still, I blush.

I shrug, though my eyes narrow. "It would take eating pastries for weeks to match Venus's cherubic body. Besides, isn't that the point, to show me as I am? Courbet would be so disappointed in you."

I mind the way Manet's eyes feast upon her rich brown skin and her round black eyes. Her loveliness makes me feel diminished. I remind myself that it's my body that takes up acres of the painting, and yet I'm not at all keen about sharing even a patch of my garden. Ah, but Adam was not Eve's true lover. God created her. He made a woman He wanted, I am quite sure of it.

Creating art imitates a love affair in many ways, and I do feel jealous. Perhaps the art requires it. How Laure grasps the bouquet, how she talks Manet into giving the flowers to her!

When he does: "I'm not feeling well," I snap, rise, and clothe myself.

That evening, a bouquet of flowers arrives for me, and I decide I won't trample them until they're good and dead, but then I will, for sure. It's not as if he would know if I did, anyway. At any rate, I don't thank him for them.

◈

We are about halfway through the painting, and Manet has asked me to sit again on Monday. Instead, I have Willie tell him that I am not well. Willie grumbles that I am sitting for Manet at all in the nude, because he can't believe a woman can be naked before a man and he not want her. If he saw Manet with Laure, he would realize which of us the man wants.

I sit in a robe, a hand on my stomach, when I hear someone at the door. Willie has gone to the theater to coax the Frenchmen into shape. He claims they simply do not want to give up their French style boxing, but he insists. I can't imagine Willie trying to convince anyone of anything, and I'd rather like to see him try, but I truly do not feel well.

I go to the door and ask hesitantly who is there. I cannot answer it dressed as I am.

It's Manet.

I lean against the door.

When I open it, holding my dressing gown securely about me, he turns his head from me.

"May I come in?"

"I'm not feeling well. I'm sorry I couldn't come, but I did send word this time." No matter how long we have been working together, the fear of that missed session and his threat lingers, but at a flip of his wrist I know he received the message.

He walks about the living room that also serves as a bedroom. The bed is, naturally, unmade since I have just left it. I quickly throw the cover over it. The room is smallish and barren. In one corner is a sketch I have made of him at his easel in profile.

"When did you do this?"

I smile. "Look at the canvas you are working on and you will know."

"Ah, yes. There's something right and yet redundant about being captured trying to capture something."

"There is indeed."

He moves close to the drawing as if he will touch it with his eyes. It is the way I have seen him examine works that he respects; I don't believe he even knows he does it.

Inhale, exhale, I remind myself.

"Do you have any more?" he asks.

"No," I say, but he has already seen and seized my sketchbook. In it are alternate sketches of the paintings he has done of me, takes on them he has not considered. He sits in a chair and pores over them one by one.

"In the first painting I did of you then you wanted me to add background?" he asks. He looks around as if he will see the painting that is almost a portrait. Of course it's not here.

"It is at my parents', and yes, I thought contextualizing me would have created a more interesting composition." I hold my stomach.

"What do your parents say of it? Your father seems to have a bit of an eye. I enjoy seeing his posters about town—I know his work when I see it."

I can't help but smile. "As do I." I sit back. "My family does not talk of art together."

He waits for an explanation.

I shift on the bed.

"My parents disagreed about whether or not my father should paint. So he does not and while he and I discuss art passionately, we never mention it in front of my mother."

He nods, but it's clear he doesn't understand.

"My father would like to put your painting in his shop, I believe, but he has said he fears it being left alone overnight."

It is Manet's turn to smile. "If only my work should be so valued. Or is he afraid it will be vandalized?"

"Perhaps he thinks someone will come alone and slit the poor painted one's eyes." I grin sadly.

He flips idly through my sketchbook until we come to my alternate *Street Singer*.

"She's quite different from mine."

She is. Buoyed from the concert, she smiles gaily and eats the cherries that she holds as if they are a bouquet given by the young men who follow her out the door. She holds her guitar over her shoulder, and she looks back, the hand holding the guitar making a half wave to her audience.

Around her neck she wears a cloth bag that bulges with coins.

"I do like your singer," he says. "Though there's nothing more street about her than mine."

"When I do a concert, it's like drinking the best absinthe in the world. I don't mind seeing and being seen, as your paintings seem to suggest. I enjoy it. Though the coins are a dream, really."

He nods carefully.

At my version of *The Picnic* he pauses. He turns the drawing sideways, then upside down, and then to the other side.

I have drawn a recognizable canvas in the background with the woman leaning over. The artist is identifiable because he sits, naked, with a brush in his hand. The naked young woman eats casually and offers him some cherries which he declines with his other hand. There is no second man.

"Intriguing," he says quietly, glancing at me as if seeing something about me he has not seen yet.

"But those are nothing," I say. "Better give them to me."

"No, wait. Have you a vision for *Olympia*?"

My gaze falls. He will turn that page and then so must we. I put out my hand. He watches it, watches me drop it onto the bed.

The page whispers as he turns it. Repeatedly I hear the whisk of paper. He says nothing; I do not look at him.

"This is not my vision," he says raggedly finally.

"I know." I who am braver than anyone I know cannot look at him. My sketches owe much to *The Rokeby Venus*.

I wipe my fingers across my eyes.

The sun intrudes and the shadow it makes of his face allows me to say, "But it is just one thought."

"There are pages of it."

I pray the sun will slice between us longer, but a cloud refuses my prayer, dammit.

"Why did you not come sit today?" he asks gently.

My heart speeds.

"I am ill."

He stands and comes over to me, sits on the floor, and holds my hand.

"Why did you not come sit today?" he asks again, even more gently.

I want to beg him to get up—he shouldn't be kneeling before me. It's beneath him, above me. What is this new respect for me in his eye?

"I am indisposed," I say quietly, clutching my stomach, all of the hint he needs.

His face screws up, despite what I believe to be an effort on his part not to.

"I see. And when will you be able to paint again?"

"I would say it will be safe to assume that I will return by Wednesday."

"Wednesday is quite soon enough. Or Thursday, if need be." He stands and begins backing away.

"We will talk more of these sketches then." Somehow I doubt it, but before I can say so, he is gone. I am right; we never speak of them again. But something of them creeps into his painting, anyway.

When Willie returns home, I wrap myself about him and don't let go, even while he sleeps.

After Manet painted *Olympia*, something indeed changed. Report after report comes to me then of Manet with willing women. It loosened something inside of him that I don't for one moment think he knew needed loosening.

"Good for him," I think, and yet I'm angry, too. I may have to paint my own painting to figure that one out.

One by one they trickle into his studio, Manet's friends, on the day the letters are to be sent for which paintings will be accepted by the Academy for the Salon of 1865. Though some of them are surely waiting for their own letters to come or not, they have all watched with great interest *Olympia* arriving on the canvas.

Writers and painters, friends of the family—his studio becomes warm quite early, though I am there by nine. Manet quietly said at our last session that "we" would be waiting today for the letter. I should hope so.

A servant rearranges the food and drink she brought quite early, filling in the gaps between the grapes with plump purple fruits and red round cherries, of course. My eyes graze the contrast between the colors of the fruit as we sit in chairs, on stools, on boxes. The floor.

Coughing men, fidgeting men. Scratching men. Manet's servant and I are the only women present. I do not ask about Laure; I am just grateful that she is not here. I am fairly sure I smelled her perfume in the air an afternoon last week when I stopped in at Manet's studio. I don't want to know why she was there.

As quickly as the food is replenished, it disappears. Urns of café and water empty swiftly. The servant pushes her hair out of her face as she piles pastries onto a platter. I want to help her, because she works alone, but I will not, not in front of the men.

Our chairs are turned toward the door. Every time someone else arrives, conversation and movement stop for a breath.

"Surely it will get in on its daring alone," says Zola.

Baudelaire, Manet's dearest friend and often fellow *flâneur*, laughs. The man has been ill, so we haven't seen much of him lately. "Of course that alone nearly damns it. Manet, you never listen to what I say. But what do I know—I'm merely a writer."

Manet puffs on a cigar awkwardly. "You know how very much I value your opinion, Charles, but really, I had to do it."

Monet, the poor, young painter shakes his head. "Yes, but ah, did you have to do it quite that way, one might ask."

I lean back. Surely Monet has not forgotten his and Manet's tempestuous beginning.

"Did you enter anything?" Manet asks, moving the cigar from one hand to the other.

"I did. Of course I did. Not that it will be accepted. I'm to die a poor, paint-stained artist you know. It's what I was born to."

"Perhaps you ought to wait at home for your own letter then," I snap before Manet can get out whatever unpleasantness he is working up.

The men seem to notice me for the first time.

"I think we are all quite anxious about this Salon," says Stevens smoothly.

"And why not some music?" says Bazille to me. "Can you truly play that guitar that you hold in *The Street Singer*?"

Manet's teeth clamp onto his cigar.

"Of course." I hold up the case I have reflexively brought with me.

"Please, allow me to accompany you." Bazille rises to go to the piano when the boy in the cap arrives, winded. He waves the letter about.

"Manet?" he asks Bazille.

"Give it to me, you silly boy," says Zola. He absent-mindedly hands the boy some change. The boy, noticing the crowd's excitement, lingers.

Manet drags on his cigar.

"Be my guest," Manet says to his friend, waving smoke. I make my way behind Zola and around to Manet. Either way, I want to be the first one to him.

Zola breaks the seal. Carefully he opens the missive.

"Get on with it," someone cries, and I'm surprised it's not me.

"Yes, here it is then. Well, it appears your work has indeed been accepted for the Salon."

A whoop goes up, a deafening shout. Manet is pulled to his feet. I put out my hands to him, but he is surrounded on all sides by men clapping him on the back, shaking his arm, embracing him.

Not once does anyone, not even Manet, look at me.

I make my way over to the servant. "The time for café is over. Better bring out the alcohol," I say. She nods and smiles, but I solemnly make for the door, my hand trailing over the pile of pastries, watching them all tumble in their mind-numbing sameness to the floor.

As if he senses he will need a talisman, Manet has chosen his friend Zachurie Astruc's poem for the exhibition brochure for *Olympia*:

"When tired of dreaming, Olympia awakens / Spring enters on the arms of the mild black messenger / She is the slave who, like the amorous night / Comes to adorn with flowers the day beautiful to behold / The august young woman in whom ardor is ever wakeful."

We argue about this, too. "You know that isn't what you meant," I say. I have returned to his studio, but only after he sent for me three times. I will speak my mind even more so now, knowing he thinks me no more than a prop. Then let this prop speak. "I don't care if he is your friend. It's horrible poetry and even worse sentiment, Manet."

Such liberties I take. Being so close to art has convinced me I am as educated as any of them. Art is its own education, and my eyes need to learn no more.

He doesn't reply.

Panderer. Weakling. He had an opportunity to speak of the oppression of Laure's people, but he makes her instead a cheerful florist, almost. An agent of nature. A servant.

At first when Manet asks me to come with him for the opening of the Salon, I say no. He asks twice more, and I give him the same reply.

"Is it modesty that prevents you?" he asks, surprised.

I laugh. "Wasn't I at the *Salon de Refusés* for *The Picnic*?"

"Ah, but you weren't frontally nude in that one," he says. "I suppose it might be daunting to be seen featured in a nude painting in front of so many people."

"I wouldn't be the one without clothes on. That would be you."

At the sagging of his face, I hastily agree to be there with him.

Room M is easily enough found. I have begged Willie to stay home, and reluctantly, he agreed. We would both be uncomfortable there, considering the subject of the painting.

"My name begins with an 'M' too, Manet. This is where my work will hang."

He has been walking the length of the portrait, back and forth, but now he stops.

"What?"

"I said this is the room where my paintings will be, too."

"Oh, M for Meurent; I see your joke."

I rear back. "It is not a joke. You said you would really listen to my criticism the day I have my work accepted by the Salon."

He continues his pacing.

I stalk him as he walks in one direction, then the other. He turns his head from me each time I get near.

"But you never took me seriously, did you? I will go to art school, you know."

"Go outside for a bit."

"I will not."

Sweat shines atop his head.

"I demand you tell me: You've seen my sketches—do you think me incapable of painting?"

His nostrils flare. "You have raw ability, yes. You know that. But if the Salon were to accept you and your, your *renderings*, I would not want to be accepted by it."

He wipes at his forehead with a white handkerchief. My painted body looms behind him.

"Dear Meurent, your take on life makes paintings that are much too personal. They are mere journal entries wrought with lines."

I thrust my hand in the direction of *Olympia*. "Better than hearkening back to ages hence, rather than acknowledging now. That's cowardice." That's not entirely true of his paintings, but. . . .

"And your way will never belong to the ages."

"Is that all you want, Manet?"

He picks a spot on the floor and jabs his walking stick at it repeatedly.

"It most assuredly is not all I want. But that's a great part of it. Else why would I do it?"

I'd like to speak of being moved, of wanting to share a vision, but it would be in vain.

"Perhaps these are things better talked of at another time."

"Quite."

He paces before *Olympia* as he waits for people to file by his painting at the Salon on opening night, and they do, horrified, scandalized. A woman nods at Manet, looks at the painting, and goes rigid. "And what does Suzanne say of this?" she asks crisply. Clearly, she is a woman of their acquaintance.

"If she's anything but a fool she will say how daring the painting is," I say.

The woman raises her parasol as if she will hit me with it, but my eyes tell her to just do it. I'd like nothing better than to unleash my fury.

Room M gets louder and louder. People point and yell, telling Manet that he is perverted, as is his art. They call me names. We stand and endure it for a time, hoping it will change.

Though many people merely avert their eyes and hurry on, on occasion a man will try to beat the painting with a cane. Someone throws a shoe at the wall, barely missing the painting, and I stoop and grab the expensive footwear, knowing the absence of it from the owner's foot will tell me who threw it. When I meet the gaze of the man searching for the shoe, he looks away without asking for it back. Someone will have to limp out into the gravel, and I will not be sorry.

It also comes in handy for wielding more than once in my defense throughout the evening.

Spit flies from one man in an effort to sully the painting, and that leads to more of the same from others. Though they try, their spittle does not reach the canvas, but their aim at me is truer. They hiss, an expectorating flock of birds. I allow the liquid to drip down my face so they can watch their work.

I glance over and see Manet wiping his beard.

Within an hour the painting is roped off so that people can't get to it, and us, so easily.

"Why don't you leave?" a guard says, but Manet merely shakes his head vigorously, face white. He removes his jacket and rolls up his sleeves.

Women pretend to faint before *Olympia*, and even with the rope they have to add security guards to protect the painting from men's canes. People lead pregnant women away from it as if it will cause them to miscarry.

"As soon as my parents arrive, I will leave," I say, as Manet tries, not for the first time, to get me to go. I wish I had allowed Willie to come; they wouldn't have dared do this with him here.

"Let's go," Manet says after I have wiped my brow for the third time, and after he has pushed yet another man who makes a noise at me.

"Not yet." I must see my father see this.

They just keep coming, the gawking hordes. The men look from the painting to me and back, their heads swiveling. The women raise their heads in the air.

Finally, my parents approach. I smile, reach my hands out nervously. I have purposely not told them what to expect.

They stop before the painting and my father examines it as closely as he can. I watch him take in the outline, the colors. He nods at the composition, the cat, the servant. Then he sees the painted me and seems puzzled. The story of the painting does not bother him at all, nor does it seem to sink in.

"Why did you paint her propped on her side?" he asks over the din. "Because it gives her more authority? *Venus*," he says, his face lighting up as he sees the connection. "And that wonderful servant." He is the only one who has even mentioned Laure here. Is it my nakedness or her color that makes her so invisible? As jealous as I may be, I can't help but feel defensive for her, too.

Manet has to lean forward to hear him, asks him to repeat himself. Before Manet can answer my mother has dragged my father away, her face beyond sour, though my father continues glancing at the painting.

"Whore," a man yells at me. I see my father flinch at that, but my mother tugs at his arm.

Manet jumps out from behind the barrier and takes after the man who runs out the door. When he returns, I gratefully agree to leave. I don't want to wear the hood to disguise my hair so I may safely leave, but I do. Just until the furor dies down.

As we exit, the man who threw the shoe earlier hobbles by. I open my purse and take out the shoe, hand it to him. He smiles sheepishly and I have him lean against me as he puts it on.

Manet takes my arm and after we escape the exhibit's perimeter, he sighs.

We say nothing. Absolutely nothing.

When we reach my and Willie's quarters, Manet takes his leave of me quietly. Before he can truly go, I ask: "When shall I return to your studio?"

He shakes his head. "Not yet, Victorine."

"But when one is most discouraged, that is the time to begin again. I have seen it repeatedly in artists."

When he says nothing, I say, "I will be there three days from now. And Manet? Do not read the reviews." He won't listen. They never do.

I crawl into Willie's arms that night, not saying a word when he asks how it went, just nestling under his arm.

Come dawn, I am still awake. I dress quietly and go out to buy groceries.

Just outside Les Halles a tank of shrimp in a shop window arrests me, and I am again a child before the glass. Two of the dogged crustaceans fight over a clump of food; I push my hair back to better see.

One of the iridescent, stalk-eyed creatures shimmers now greenish, now white, now pink. It uses its long, muscular tail to swat at its enemy. The two fall off the piece of wood on which they battle, the first still holding the food in its maw, flicking its lengthy whiskers, employing its secondary swimmerets to fend off the would-be thief.

They war until the one without food succeeds in prying a piece of nourishment from the other. Both quickly forget the fight and begin to eat until the larger one finishes its food and heads again for the other one, but too late: It's already moving upwards, paddling, using its hair-like projections to rise above the petty quarrel already satisfied.

I wave as always to the woman in the butcher's shop named Blanche with horrid breath and wretched teeth.

She points her knife at me, shouts something behind her and comes out. Before I can say anything, she grabs me by my collar and pledges to teach me a lesson. She is quickly joined by a sea of women in blood-stained aprons. They pull me behind the shops where they splash a barrel of offal onto my head. For a moment I think I will drown in this baptism of guts and blood, but I shake my head as much to rid myself of that thought as to rid myself of the offal. As I clear fluid from my face, I look down and think how beautifully the sun shines upon the vibrant blood.

"Get out of here, Olympia," they mock, this comment and the like. I am breathless from the quickness of the attack, from the cold of the contents of that barrel, and from the horror that women should do this to another woman. I have not even had time to fight back.

The one who led this madness puts her forehead to mine, and that breath, so foul it is a person of its own, propels my head backward.

"Suzanne says no," she says. Then I am released and alone as they scamper away as quickly as they have come. It's then I realize why they've gone: An officer of the law on his rounds approaches.

"What is this?" he asks. He holds his nose as he comes closer, and I laugh, although it's not funny, no, not at all.

"If you please, officer, I was just about to go take a bath."

He glances around and sees the upturned barrel, and a second one. "Here's some rainwater. Let me duck into this shop and borrow a pitcher." So he returns soon with a vessel borrowed from the very women who did this to me. I stand still while he pours container after container of water over my head. Then he peers closely at me.

"Aren't you . . ." he stops as my face falls. This is too much.

"I'll see if I can find you a towel." As he walks away, I run down the alley and around the block. When Willie asks what happened, I am at a loss. His arms are so big and covered with red.

I sit quietly with Manet while he waits for the reviews of *Olympia*, and it is not long until they arrive. While most are unfavorable, some are neutral or even nearly complimentary. Zola supports him, as always.

Others criticize his technique, the black outlining my body, the flower in my hair for being too limp, call my hands those of a frog, my body gorilla-like.

If only the consequences for me were confined to the written word. I can't play in cafés any more—when I tried, the men groped me. I had expected the painting to be attacked, but not myself. The last concert I tried to play, people booed me out of the café. The owner said I need to wait awhile before I try to play again. I think I would be reviled less if I were an actual prostitute. Society will accept many things, but it will not accept being publicly condemned. More than that, Manet and I flouted all of art's rules. That Paris will not tolerate.

Increasingly I prefer to be alone in our room, away from Les Halles, certainly. At night, always, the promise that fades with either the extinguishing of the candle or the coming of dawn. Ah, yes, dawn comes and rescues me from restless sleep.

I have nightmares of slashing *Olympia*, of making it disappear. When I wake, I know I would never want it to go away.

What of that young woman who modeled for Titian's *Venus*? What became of her after she posed? Was she spat upon? Of course not. She was given the name of a goddess, not a woman, in the painting. I wish I knew something of her, but when I ask Manet, he says he knows nothing.

No one decent will speak to me now except the lowest of my painter friends and the most liberal. Men offer me money, ask me to show them my chest. Every day I hear Manet's complaints about his treatment, never telling him what I have endured.

"Do you know that men who have known me for years cross the street so they don't have to speak to me? It's unconscionable when all I did was paint a painting. Why, it's getting so I hate even going out," says Manet.

"What are you going to paint next?" I ask.

"Yesterday the grocer wouldn't sell me a pound of sugar Suzanne asked me to get. He said he didn't have any, when I could see a five-pound jar of it right behind him. I just left the store. Didn't know what else to do."

"Maybe if you tried painting a still life again."

He shakes his head and sits heavily on the sofa. "I had no idea it would be so bad. All of these reviews." He cuts off his words, turns his face from me. "They don't understand."

Breath, barrel, blood.

At the end of the day he squares his shoulders and bids me to come sit again after the weekend.

A vicious part of me longs to tell him of my experiences, but I won't.

"Let me stay until dark," I say as he opens the door.

"You may stay as long as you like. Just shut the door behind you," and he leaves the studio. When it's good and dark, I wrap my shawl well around myself and leave.

The entire weekend I brood, attempting to read, fingering chords that just won't make up a song. Willie keeps asking me what's wrong until he goes to a match and comes back. Then his somberness tells me he knows.

It's a relief for both of us when the weekend is over and I head to Manet's studio. I don't get in: There's a note on the door saying he has gone to Spain. I take my spleen out on his door, but all I have to show for it is aching fists. The wooden slab shows no signs of perturbation at all.

When I return to the apartment, our things are in our suitcases and on top is a letter requesting that we vacate the premises immediately.

When I argue our case with the landlord, she leans in close and whispers "Suzanne says no." That cow. And I had thought her helpless. If I must go speak with her, I will. Ah, but they are in Spain, aren't they? I cannot then, clever woman.

The landlady says she will give us until midnight to remove our things. "Fine," I yell as I lock the door behind me. I just need time to think before Willie gets home. He's done nothing to deserve this.

If only I hadn't allowed Manet to talk me into sitting for that painting. If only he hadn't been such a coward, taking off that way.

"May your Spain-bound hands suffer misfortune. May your fingers not be spared." I pick up the candle and fling it across the room. I shred the note from the landlady and feed it to the fireplace.

Willie isn't at all worried when he comes home. "We can stay at the theater for now," he says. He picks up our suitcases and leads the way. For now. The police have been harassing him. They are closing down anything that they consider unseemly. They haven't managed to close him yet, but Willie says business is not good. He doubts he will be able to rent the second theater for more than a month. The police returned, after the Salon opened, but he remains unconcerned.

Every artist should only marry other non-artists. It's the only way to peace.

◈

Stevens sends a message to my father's shop, who brings it to Willie's theater, though my father will not come in and will barely look at me. I take the scrap of paper and hug him, and he looks at me for an instant with sorrow and repentance before shaking me from him. My mother has convinced him, then, that he must stay away from me again. I watch his back recede.

Stevens asks, as I suspect, if I am available to sit. Who knew such a walrus could be braver than Manet? I quickly assent and am working again within a day. I need to work—running away is not a luxury *I* can afford.

From time to time after that I stop into my father's shop to check on my parents. I know my mother won't allow me to visit home. Sometimes at night when I walk by, I see her through the window, hat and needle in hand, and I watch, wondering if she has eaten since breakfast and if she and my father are talking or if they are silent. Is my father lonely? These are the things I dare not think about.

I have modeled for Stevens for nearly a week when he overhears a man on the street call me Olympia and proposition me. The language the Belgian uses amuses me, though he pauses to beg my pardon after every naughty word. The man flees after Stevens begins employing his umbrella to emphasize each curse.

Grabbing the stout man's elbow, I lead him to a bench so he may regain his breath. "How often does that happen?" he asks indignantly.

I shrug.

"Well, at the very least let me see you home," he asks.

I shake my head. He is a kind man, this I have already figured out. "Stevens, don't worry about it. Do you really think Olympia can't fend for herself?" I kiss him on the cheek and walk away.

The next afternoon I follow my mother to the market (this is one disadvantage for her, I'm sure, to my being gone: She has to run errands that my father cannot) and cross in front of her, though she pretends not to see me.

"Maman," I plead, but there is no reply, not even when I stand right before her.

How is it that a painting has made me both more visible than before and less so as well? But then I've been mostly invisible to my mother forever.

It's Tuesday afternoon, and it's "Absinthe Hour," five o'clock. If Manet does not appear at the Café Guerbois today, he will be nowhere, for Stevens casually told me that Manet is back from Spain. I constantly look from my wine (no absinthe for me, not if I might encounter Manet) to the door. Stevens, Degas, Renoir, and Zola lounge about the place. Zola glances at his watch more than once.

"I'm not waiting for him much longer," he says. "I have a plot to unravel that's more cluttered than the Le Bon Marché Ladies Department."

I grin. "Have you ever thought about writing a story based on the department store? I used to work there, you know. It would make quite a novel."

"Indeed," he says thoughtfully. "Well, right now I have the plots for my next three novels lined up. It will have to wait, though it's not a bad idea. But tell me, do they really make you live there as well as work there, as if you are their prisoner?"

"Well, most women must. Not me, of course."

Everyone at the table laughs. Manet's paintings of me have become the accepted version of who I am, and in ways I find myself growing into the woman he increasingly imagines me: strong, respected, powerful.

As I tell them of a narrow escape when I worked there involving a coal chute and a misplaced blow with a shovel, I feel his presence. I pretend I don't see Manet and I continue my story, embroidering it with everything I believe will appeal to the men.

Eventually, Manet takes off his hat and slides into a chair at the table, waves toward the bar for a drink. I rise and silently make to leave the table, until I feel a hand on my arm. "A word, please," Manet says quietly.

He rises and we go outdoors, away from the out-of-tune piano being banged by someone who clearly doesn't know how to play.

"How was Spain?" I ask bitterly.

"Velázquez's work was just as wonderful as I remember it. Those muted colors and triangles."

"And those thick, black lines?"

"Always those." We walk on.

"Before I left, I thought I might never paint again. *Olympia* was such a wonderful idea. Everyone insisted I must do a nude, and it was such an irresistible scenario. I knew your calm arrogance was just right for it." His eyes fill and he blinks. "Velázquez's work convinced me all over again that I have done exactly right."

I walk on.

"My friends wrote to tell me that the things they said and did to me were nothing compared to what they did to you. I never imagined they'd treat you that way just because you were in a painting."

I shrug.

He grasps my upper arms and the scent of alcohol wafts toward me. "Please know how sorry I am."

"I've had worse said and done to me," I say wearily, though anger churns, thick and hot. "Your wife seems to have the most trouble of all with me."

He moves his walking stick forward and back again uncertainly, then forward before saying, not addressing at all what I have said about his wife. "Perhaps the worst of it is, I'd like to ask you to pose again. You will want to say no."

Spain. He left me here to do battle on my own.

"I'd like to, but I have so much on my mind right now."

He cocks his head. "Indeed? Such as?"

"Willie is having business troubles."

"Oh is that right?" asks Manet, tut tutting, knowing I am about to ask for something.

"Yes, well, the police have begun shutting down anything even remotely like fighting. First wrestling, and they haven't said he must shut yet, but they have managed to scare away some of his clientele."

"Ah, yes, the poor man."

"I'm sure if he had more decent, respectable people in attendance the police chief would be a bit less critical."

"Boxing. I haven't been to a match in quite some time." He strokes his beard and walks back into the bar. I follow.

"*Tiens*," he says, raising his voice to his table of friends. "We are going to a boxing match—tomorrow night?" he questions me. I nod. "Yes, tomorrow night. Let's meet here first. Please feel free to bring others."

Then, more quietly, "We'll start my—our—next painting on Tuesday. And in the meantime, I will speak with Suzanne."

"I wish you would," I say, although really I'd prefer to speak with her myself. Whatever he says, however, she must take to heart, because it's the last of her messages I receive. Which is less satisfactory to me than a proper confrontation would have been. Still, whenever anything bad happens to me, I stop and wonder if she had anything to do with it.

I hope Stevens has time to finish the portrait he is doing of me by Tuesday, because previous commitments be damned, nothing can keep me from working with Manet.

EIGHT

The Guitar Player

MANET WATCHES me pose for Stevens. I am, as always in Stevens's paintings, looking wistfully beyond my beautifully appointed surroundings toward something unattainable or unknown. Longing, that's what he paints better than anyone. I suppose men respond to it so well because they imagine they can fulfill that longing, or even that it suggests that perhaps women want more than just the trappings (literally) of a good life. Women respond to the "pretty" yet sad paintings because they so often feel the yearning that those women feel.

I would not want a life without longing. It would suggest that there was nothing more to want. There will always be something to want, something to create. There must be. And yet something about the way Stevens paints the longing of these women makes their wishes seem trivial, the product of a too-pampered life. It trivializes their feelings, and that angers me. Perhaps it angers me too that their dreams are not those of us who must literally sing for our supper. No, I'm being unfair. I saw the misery on the faces of the well-heeled patrons in the department store in which I worked. It gnaws at me, then, the fear that nothing, no nothing, can stop the holes. Except art. I breathe, deeply.

"I'd like to do a painting, Victorine, of you sitting with your guitar," Manet says quietly, as if he's the one painting. "That is, whenever you can spare her," he says to Stevens. Manet cocks his head and narrows his eyes at the white that Stevens is whisking onto the painting. I only know this because I saw the brush Stevens chose: He loads his brushes individually with colors, unlike Manet, who uses a color completely before moving on to the next.

◈

I'm both flattered at being asked to portray myself in such a strong position, holding a guitar, by Manet and extremely annoyed at being treated, again, as a possession.

Stevens tells Manet that I will be available the next day, should Manet require me so soon. I smile and hope he will. I don't even pretend that I am not eager to sit for him. For me, anger is a ball that I toss and never catch again; once an issue is discussed, I'm through. But wariness is a different matter entirely. This *Olympia* business gives me pause, as it should.

Stevens will give up an idea for the sake of painting a beautiful or pathetic scene; Manet will give up beauty for the idea. Guess which I prefer?

In *The Guitar Player*, my back is to Manet because we have been quarreling about his insistence on asking Stevens's permission for me, about the simple painting he wishes to create, me in a white dress, no shape, no lines, no color, just clutching my guitar.

We don't argue aloud again about his flight to Spain.

"You love texture and textiles. Why would you choose to paint me this way?"

"Haven't you had enough of color and shine, of dresses fancy enough for an empress?" His hand paints even strokes. A length of blue ribbon wraps around my head but mercifully has not been fastened into a bow, as have the dress ties knotted behind me.

In this painting, Manet finds my face's softness as I make music for myself. I shelter my guitar, my long-necked child.

Absentmindedly my left hand flits to my hair, attempting to cover my ear but Manet's glare stops me.

It turns out that this is my favorite painting he does of me, because he simply reports: He allows me to create myself. Or he comes as close to it as one can.

This is how he apologizes to me. That and his and his friends' new pastime: boxing.

The bamboo chair in the painting echoes the exoticism of the wild parrot, the spirit of music that plumes from my guitar. Passion parts my lips; the parrot flies. The guitar strap curves sharply on my lap. Instead of looping the protective strap over my head, I trust my arms, my hands. They will hold it, no matter what. The music is the parrot, not the instrument. My guitar is my fifth limb.

"You need a necklace," he says, and he motions for me to turn, ties something about my throat. When I put my hands up, I immediately recognize the shoelace I had thought lost. I cannot think how he got it. "This is yours," he says. It's the very same one. I confirm this by feeling the knots.

I pat the string affectionately and my eyes fill.

"Turn your head," he requests. I pretend he is not using my tears to add a glaze to my painted eyes.

Blackground surrounds me. Naturally.

As he paints me, I play a tune I have created. He nods rhythmically at my song, and later I fancy I see my notes in the stutter of his brushstrokes.

There are so many, many things Manet does not know he knows, God love him. That, I suppose, is what I am doing here.

But what does it mean that he never tries to exhibit this painting?

NINE

The Fifer

AFTER THE *Guitar Player* I sit for *The Fifer*, but so does Léon, the supposed brother of Suzanne. The boy is quite as thick and dull as his mother, who I have now had a few occasions to meet, however briefly. Her silent glare when I first officially met her at the studio told me that Manet has indeed spoken with her about me. She's ruddy faced and pudgy, with an unintelligent brow. But her wrists are fine, and her fingers appear supple; perhaps she does play piano as well as all that. And the way she watched Manet, without meaning to watch him, shows me that she cares for him.

Léon does not enjoy sitting and does not seem to admire art, either. I wonder how Manet endures this, if this child is, indeed, his. I admire his art. Why does he need anyone else to?

Yet Manet is slowly replacing my features with others' features. I try not to think about what this might mean while I watch him paint. Perhaps he doesn't know he does it.

Meeting his family at last frees me to ask questions I find myself belatedly wanting answers to.

"If no one in your family was an artist, how did you end up at Couture's?" I ask.

He tells me he was supposed to go into the military but that he couldn't pass the test. He had adventures at sea and learned he could paint when the captain asked him to paint cheeses that had molded so they could be sold. Perhaps it's because Léon is here today, but he reveals little else. I tell myself that I will pry further when we are alone, but I never do, and I like him all the more for not knowing. It leaves my imagination wide open; perhaps he is a unique breed of person called artist with distinctly artistic traits that I need to discover, or so I'd like to think.

I twist my black necklace and smile at this child he now paints who bites at a dirty fingernail and when he isn't so employed, just stares. I can understand why Manet feels compelled to paint this boy, but it's a misguided plan that results in fidgeting and sighs from the trapped boy. I sympathize. Sitting for my father was different, though: I cared about the result. I cared about being with my father in the pink-orange mornings. I adored the fresh mirror his painting was. Almost now I feel I am as I am because he painted me so. His strokes bade me to rebel against my mother, against school, against a society that would not allow him to be an artist. But, then, who am I?

Beholding this young man with his bored calf's face enrages me. He has a father (I presume) who could make him an artist, if he wanted, who is immortalizing him so that generations that don't even know his name will know his face, and Léon could care less. When Manet speaks to me, it interrupts my hatching intention to chide the lad who would merely not understand and how could I fault him? But I do.

"It took much convincing, but finally my father relented and agreed that I should go to art school. Couture was recommended by my uncle."

He sits heavily on the stool he has to use now and again as he paints, sticks a leg out, and rubs it. Clearly, he has been thinking about my questions.

I do not like modeling for *The Fifer* because I know I am not to be the ultimate face of it: I wear the clothes, I give it the eyebrows, the eyes, and perhaps the cheeks, but it has become our surrogate son as he blends the face of Léon with that of mine. I am saddened by this parentage by proxy, especially to so ungrateful a young man. Manet is revealing something he has kept from me: He loves me, but again, not in a fervent, romantic manner. Though he denies that parts of us have merged, he shows it clearly here.

I don't have names for those parts. They are not hands and arms. They are not even nether parts. But they mean more, and they are inextricably bound forever. I shiver at the immortality he lends me. I don't care what anyone says—if anything I know of the world is true, these paintings will last, will become beloved. He paints truths of this city. No. More. He paints truths of life, and though such truths may not at first be welcome, eventually they will be acknowledged because that is what they are. I wish I could say that to him. I suppose I do—with my modeling.

It's because of his temperament and not because of his abilities that I beg him to give the critics something they're more accustomed to. He's not a man who can handle rejection.

I have worn the outfit of the fifer uncomfortably, when it was my turn, all except the spats, which I like and take to wearing a set of outside of the studio at times as well. I am numb to stares and comments from the public. As long as they don't physically touch me, nothing else affects me.

In another act of fashion rebellion, I have hacked off the bottom of my skirts so I can show Manet's cast-off boots that I retrieved from his trash and stuffed with wads of fabric. And I don't always lace my bodice tightly—I like to feel the sun against my skin. For years I have done without hats. After *Olympia,* I find myself either wearing too much makeup or none at all, depending on who I want to be for the day. My face without color bores me, unless I am highly emotional, in which case there is more than enough color to my countenance. Most days I soothe myself with the knowledge that I cannot see myself, unless I look in a mirror.

"Do you know what the job of the fifer is?" Manet asks as he makes a generous-length stroke at the background.

I shrug, but his glare reminds me to remain still. "Don't they march with the soldiers as part of the band?"

He smiles. "Indeed they do. But did you know that their instrument can be heard even above the sounds of the battle? In fact, the flute often signals to the troops changes in formation and tells them what they are to do next."

Manet, signaling to the art community, telling them what must come next.

He paints a sideways bird's beak hat. The fifer tells a tale. Manet is trying to say something as coded yet loud as a fife might. I wonder if Manet's guilt at not legitimizing Léon is oozing from his brush. Why then has he made me both his child and his child's "mother?"

My mind hears now the high squeal of the fife, its incessantly fingered notes, the shrill persistence of such an instrument, and yes, that is just what Manet's art, what his message, is.

The jacket in the painting is dark with shiny gold buttons, echoed in the case for the flute, in the trim on the hat, the ring on the belt. The background is the gray he is beginning to favor ever since reacquainting himself with the Spanish painters, and it is at least a lighter shade of his blackground.

I do not have patience for this painting that will only open me up to a yearning for a child. *I don't need to be a part of this, Manet.* He has dalliances. He is an artist, and though he loves his wife, it is clear; he feels the need for more. I refuse to be that more. I'm already Willie's more. No, Willie does not need or have a "more."

The pants in the painting bloom generously, large-legged, and look as if they are the reddened bits that lie beneath a woman's skirt. I don't know what to make of it or the belt that swaddles the boy as if he is newly born. With music in his mouth. Oh, Manet, how your hands leak what you will not say. This is your son. This is.

"Léon," Manet says, "hold it straight." I feel for the boy.

"Don't be so hard on him," I urge Manet. "It's difficult to stand so with something in your hand. Have you ever tried it?"

"I have not," he said, "If I did try it, I would do it better than anyone else." No doubt he would.

Léon, lips trembling as he pouts them out as if he is blowing into the instrument, asks to be released so he may go out and play, but Manet shakes his head. "And what would Suzanne say if she heard you ask that?"

The boy studies his fingernails. "Never mind," Manet says. "Go on." He motions for Léon to change clothes and give them to me. I roll my eyes. I will be glad when this painting is through. I don't like feeling as if I am half a model, sweet sentiment or not.

"What do you think of our boy?" he asks as I pose.

"Pardon me?"

"The painting. What do you think of it?"

"Oh. He will please."

"He will please . . . ?"

"The Academy will like him, of course. An historical subject, a young boy, mostly traditionally rendered, though you might want to tone down that thick black outline . . . You don't have to circle an object for people to see it, you know."

His cheeks redden, but I continue. "And I do wonder why it is that you only show shadow at his feet, and precious little . . . is he not real? While I'm at it, his buttons are painted rather untidily, but you know what? I like that. It hints at the natural untidiness of a child, even though we don't think of buttons as being mutable." Even as I say it, enthusiasm rises in me for this painting that I didn't know was there. "Brilliant, that."

I circle the painting, come back to it. The dust comes in the window with the sun. "He's a shadow himself, isn't he? Because as young as fifers are, they might die in war. That's why the background is so light this time, yes?"

Manet is not here now, not to me, as I fall into the painting. "Oh, how you fear for the boy, don't you? Not because he will ever be a soldier, of course not. But because of what they say. . . ." I stop myself just in time. He would not welcome what almost came next.

"His foot is forward to show motion, and he leans a bit. I'm afraid you have given him my hips, poor boy."

His hands clench and unclench, and he breathes heavily.

"Forgive me, Manet, but you need not worry. Your name will protect him, you know, whatever the truth may be." I am inside the painting now, and whatever it costs, I must comfort him.

His cheeks bellow and he charges at me, but as I close my eyes I feel his arms about me, squeezing me as if I can right all that he has made wrong.

"Your paintings will protect him, your name, and your marriage. Your wealth. He is safe now," I whisper into his ear as he softly weeps. "You have paid enough."

He leans heavily against me. His leg. . . "Let's sit," I suggest, guiding him to that sofa where we have watched so many paintings grow.

"Forgive me," he says as he wipes at his face. "I have been in some physical discomfort. I fear it has affected me."

"It's a lovely painting," I say, stroking his face. "You have given him your ears." This is the way we should speak, cloaked. It is safest for us, and for art's sake. But without meaning to, I find myself crying. We look at one another's tearstained faces and laugh as if we will never stop. When we are through, we wipe our eyes, compose ourselves, and stare at, as he said, our boy. Ours.

Oh, how I wish something really could belong to just me, and not to the world. I resent it suddenly, that I am to have nothing of my own: no child, no painting from my hands. Why can't I say what I want to say? Why do I have to think about the wider scope, instead of my own hopes and desires? Isn't this just another way to distance and remove myself from the things that hurt? No. I do have someone: Willie.

Manet rises, signs the painting unsteadily in the bottom right-hand corner, his name sloping downwards, and viewing the letters of his name I think again how he has given the boy his name surreptitiously, since Léon's surname has not changed, not even with the marriage. I wish I didn't despise Manet's cowardice, because I understand it: Having wealth and a name means that you cannot afford to cast it aside. I'm suddenly grateful that I have nothing to lose.

Stevens immediately claims me for another painting, and while I like the sweet man, I cannot help but compare my time with Manet to that with Stevens. He paints fluffy, unimportant portraits of women in stunning clothing. So many false-faced women pretending from paintings, so much fabric and shine. His studio is a forest of emerald sheen, sapphire sparkle. Rows of silk, velvet, and toile dresses, lace veils. Hat boxes to rival my mother's stacks line one wall, as if women are folded and stored in them, ready to be painted at a moment's notice.

A plush tapestry-like carpet covers gleaming wooden floors, china elephants, and dragons litter tables, along with tall Ming-style vases of various colors containing fresh bouquets of flowers: carnations, *fleurs-de-lis*, and more, small flowers crowded out by large ones. Blues and oranges, yellows and reds. Too much. Europeanized Japonisme, I recognize it as.

Wealth is nice, but not necessary, as art is. His studio is overwrought and ornate, gilded. I feel as if I am in a showroom.

In the painting he does of me, my arm grieves toward the picture above my head, carefully placing the palm branch. I am dressed in a glamorous though soberly colored gown, the neck and wrists banded with white. A pretty painting, and thankfully not quite as mundane as those I see before me.

Clever Stevens goes just to the right of the critics' approval and now I will see to it that he goes to the left of propriety. Ultimately, that will be the difference in the painters: Manet will paint what he is compelled to and tell them he does not care while caring deeply, while Stevens has their approbation which enables him to steep the patriarchal frog gently in the pot. Or so I suppose, so I hope; so I will encourage. This is why I can bear to sit for this painter of dolls and froth, because I can see hints of what he is trying to say, even if he might not know he is saying it. I have followed (and shaped, I like to think) the intentions of painters since Couture's studio.

When I modeled at Couture's, I knew the virgins by their painting style: the earnest young men who painted me as a classical beauty (which I am not), rounding my curves into pleasant ones rather than folds of flesh, who shied away from painting too clearly the area between my thighs, those were the ones I stalked at break, took back to their rooms at night, made men for free. No need for them to go to a prostitute, to spend their hard-earned money at one of the dozens of licensed brothels when we both wanted the same thing.

I taught them with my hands and body the things their minds needed for uninhibited art.

Afterwards, their paintings of me always shifted. The young men became cocky and knowing. My skin took on an absinthe glow; my secret smile became a smirk. They hated me more for giving them what they wanted than they loved me for it. I went from being every virgin to every whore practically overnight to them. As a seasoned teacher might watch a new class of students, knowing exactly what was to come, I observed them from my modeling post. Soon they would no longer hate me. They would realize that sex was just another hunger, and they would seek me out. I was very particular then.

Palm Sunday, Stevens calls the painting he is doing of me with the palm branch.

"Something about the way you are watched when you go out reminds me of the occasion. How the young men watch you openly, the younger women with envy, the older women with scorn and hidden envy as well. The older men with veiled desire, present only in the wells of their eyes lest their women see it."

He puts a hand on my shoulders.

"You are triumphant right now, as was Jesus, *that* Sunday." Stevens says.

His brow gathers in concern that is sweet, but patronizing, too. We both think but do not say that Jesus' triumph was followed a week later by something much worse.

"You're riding high, now—the top. Everyone knows your name and face. It is unprecedented, this model being known as much as the painting."

"They revile me."

He smiles. "Not everyone."

It is true. In the midst of my angst over the hypocritical reactions I have scarcely admitted my triumph. I am widely known as Manet's favorite model. His friends have asked me to sit for them as well, as if something of his creativity will rub off on them. I do, when I can find the time, but I find these experiences forgettable and their paintings even more so. Except for Stevens's. There is something that is both an accomplishment and a failing in his creations.

I know how to mine painters, but as I listen to his heavy breath, I'm not sure I want to. He repulses me. What repulses me most is how he plucked me from Manet only after I had become well known as a model. I am a commodity to him, I fear, when I want to be something else entirely, though what? And yet he has seemed so kind. Here is a figure I don't know how to feel about. When he tells me that I am awfully quiet, I try to smile and fail.

I leave Stevens's studio for the day, set to head to Manet's after lunch with Willie. But someone calls my name on the street, and I turn, expecting another young woman with a necklace to show me or, holding an autograph album for me to sign. Instead, it's Bernice, a face I haven't seen in years. *Counters of fabric, her face above them, me getting fired because of her,* flash through my head. I nearly trip on a cobblestone. "Yes?"

A sizzle sounds on the nearby wood stove of a street vendor. My head heats and I must look aflame.

"Victorine?" she asks and as she touches my arm, in my mind I am again fourteen and working at Le Bon Marché. Without hesitation, I shove her with all of my might, as I should have that fateful day. She lands on the bricks, hard, on her backside and the shock melts her pretend kindness and she calls me names. I sit on my haunches over her. "Yes?" I ask.

She spits in my face and I take her by the hand, lift her.

"I only wanted to congratulate you," she hisses.

"We need our enemies to remain just that," I snap. "It's what spurs us on."

She leans against the wall and brushes at her dark hair, looking as lost as she did that day. Those who have stopped on the street to watch move on.

"Come with me," I say. She hesitates but I see curiosity win. Her new clothes, her precious jewelry, shout that she is doing fine. The pleading still in her eyes, though, says exactly what it used to: "Free me." I want to say that I cannot, but perhaps I can now in ways I could not then. Her money and breeding have not given her whatever it is she wants.

I pull her into the nearest alley and grab both sides of her head. I peer at the fear and longing in her yes, catch the nearly imperceptible lift of her chin. I pretend, and I pretend convincingly, that I can lift her ennui.

Instead of the crushing kiss she desires, I tenderly place my lips upon hers. I kiss the arrows of skin beside her eyes. I gently pat both wet eyes with my lips. Even though I have hated her for so long, I also want to give her, us, hope.

I place my fingers under her chin and kiss her lips more fully, more stirringly. She surprises me by leaping toward me, her lips insisting, and I know that even if I satisfy her here in this alley I will not give her what she really wants. She wants too much, more than anyone can give. Holey, she is, beyond filling. I recognize that. We must learn to fill ourselves, by whatever means makes most sense. Art will not move her; it is all I have to offer, besides my tongue that I run about her mouth, touching every tooth I can reach. I do her more harm than good by this, for all she thinks she wants me. And she does want me, wants my body, but only as a portal to my soul. Poor fool.

"Is that an apology?" I ask.

"I've been following you for three days," she whispers desperately. "Someone told me you were sitting for Stevens. I saw *Olympia* and knew she was you."

I used to want to brush her shiny brown hair when she came parading into the store. Or, I wanted to kiss her. Failing that, I wanted to destroy her, but she beat me to it by attempting to destroy me.

I push her again up against the wall. "Smile," I say. She does, uncertainly. "If you want me, you have to smile at me just the way you used to smile at the clerks behind the counters when you were trying to get a discount."

Her shoulders straighten, and she throws her hair over her shoulder, curls her lips purposely. I kiss that smile, pretending it really is for me.

She puts her knee between mine, catching my interest. We alternate touches. She does not touch as one who has been with a woman, but it's apparent she has been with a man—her husband, naturally—since I saw her last by the way she grinds her pelvis into mine, as if I will grow for her.

I disappear under her dress and, with some wiggling, gain access to all that she has hidden there. I touch her soft hair and she gasps. Soon she slides down the wall and I follow. "Someone's headed this way," she says, beating at my head.

"So?" I mutter through her dress.

She sits back and moans even as I hear boots pass behind me.

"Go away," she yells, and I hear something. A rock? She writhes, stills, and I crawl back out from under the circus tent.

She leans against the wall, her hair askew, face red, eyes newly alive. Now how will I ever get rid of her?

"Better come with me," I say. "You know you're not supposed to be on the street alone." She's not of the class that can afford that and keep their good name. I glance at the nearest clock and realize I only have an hour before I'm due at Manet's. He and Stevens are "splitting" my time for the moment. I take her to a quiet bar I do not normally frequent. We occupy a table in a dark corner and order two glasses of absinthe.

She glances around as if she has never been to a place like this, and I know it is so.

"What do you want with me?" I ask her. We both know. That moment in the dressing room at the store, the moment she got me fired because I unintentionally sparked something in her, something she has been carrying with her until now.

"How was it? Was it what you have been imagining" I ask her as she hides her flushed face in her drink.

She takes a second sip of the absinthe and as she sputters over it, I take it from her and down it. I order her a glass of wine and she holds it daintily and doesn't answer me.

"We shouldn't be here," she says.

"I agree." I rise, but she pulls me back down.

"I'm married," she whispers.

"I know. I saw your name in the paper."

She clutches her gloves in one hand, throws them back and forth.

"How did you . . ." she whispers, stops.

"How did I do for you what your husband cannot?" I smile. "I shouldn't answer you. You don't deserve an answer. But . . . first of all, I'm a woman. I should hope I would know what moves a woman. Also, if your husband does not please you, perhaps you are of the sort who only likes women. I don't happen to be one of those, but I know some who are."

"But I'm *married*," she says.

She tosses the gloves down.

I touch her hand under the table. "Only you can say how you truly feel."

"But . . ."

"Husbands take lovers all the time. If you feel the need to remain married, simply take a lover. Try an experienced man; if he does not satisfy you, try a woman. It seems more likely to me, though, that you simply confused yourself by desiring me when you were younger. In truth, I think you just wanted to be me: You supposed I was free to do as I pleased."

Her face flushes, and she's quite attractive. I still don't want her, even though I have just done what I have done.

"I'm married too," I tell her, and I know it in a new way. I know that no matter how I might enjoy pleasuring others, helping to cast from them the inhibitions that keep them from getting in touch with their art, their soul—my body only wants Willie, no matter how it reacts to simple, physical pleasure. That is a force-feeding; my meal of choice is Willie's irreverent passion.

I tell her to go home, not offering to accompany her. When she asks where I live, I am vague. I can only hope I'll never see her again, now that my rage is gone.

I walk briskly along the cobblestones, finally on my way to dine with Willie, stopping at an outdoor faucet to rinse my hands, raising my hem as if I were a lady, though it doesn't need raising. I smirk and wave triumphantly at the young women who lift their black shoelace necklaces for me to examine. I stick out a foot and show off Manet's boots laced with thick black laces. It's too bad that fame (well, perhaps it's more notoriety, in my case) does not necessarily bring money. Now I suppose I can't be entirely furious about *Olympia*. But it doesn't earn one the notice, necessarily, of those whom one most wants to impress.

Willie and I eat in peaceful silence, though food does not matter to me, just this moment with him. I squeeze his hand, smile at him when he looks up innocently at me. I don't feel I've betrayed him—he is impossible to betray, because he does not understand betrayal—he does not think he possesses, and possession is a necessary ingredient for one to feel betrayed. The only way I can love him is to know I do not "belong" to him. I squirm as I think of how I feel at Stevens's studio.

I eye my watch. I refuse to be late to Manet's, though I'm a bit sad to leave Willie to his preparations for the evening. I almost imagine he looks at me with knowing eyes as I ready myself, but when I turn from the mirror, the expression is gone. How could he possibly know about Bernice? He couldn't. I check my dress in the mirror again and pluck a long brown hair off my chest, glance at Willie, who doesn't look back.

Manet arranges his props in a trance. His eyes have not sensed me at the door. He stares at the empty white space as he moves about a bench, a guitar, a book. He frowns, shakes his head, and mutters to himself. He pulls out banners of material, drapes them over the chair—red, then green. No. Gold. Puts them all away. He turns the chair three quarters and then pauses as he sees me.

"Not today," he says.

"Excuse me? You asked me to be here."

"An artist friend, Berthe Morisot, will model for this." He doesn't look at me. Does he realize he gilds her name with his voice?

"What's the subject?" I ask, sitting abruptly. I've heard the name, heard the admiration in his voice when he mentions her, but I haven't met her.

"It's a portrait."

"She's hired you to do her portrait?"

He glances up, then away. "No. She'll be here soon, so if you'll excuse me . . ."

I pretend I don't understand until he comes out with it: "She prefers to be painted alone."

He smooths the back of his hair, straightens his tie as he glances at the doorway, then frowns at me.

I don't move, at least not at once. My face, again replaced. I smirk at him and slowly rise.

"What will you do, lock the door to keep your other friends out?"

"She is a friend, and a painter at that. Her sister will accompany her."

I can't help but jab again: "Women are disgusted by eagerness in a man, you know," I say as I head to the door. I hate this woman I have not met, especially since she paints.

"Can't you tell me anything about her?" I ask Stevens, whose studio I have dropped in on. Stevens will say nothing about the Morisots. The less he says, the more convinced I am that he knows something.

"What is there to tell? She and her sister paint. In fact, her tutor warned their mother when they were younger that if she wasn't careful the girls would turn out to be painters, it is rumored." He laughs.

"I don't find that funny."

He busies himself with a tube of paint.

After Manet's depictions of me, I am bored by Stevens' placid painting of me. I am impatient with posing for him. He never speaks of anything that interests me. His work is trite. Although I do rather like how he sees me, I can't see myself that way, but I am mollified a bit by his pity for me in his painting. It's sweet but infuriating.

His studio is too bright, too large. I feel suffocated in this wealthy drawing room.

It occurs to me that the painting might say something about me, more than being something he desires to capture. Probably both, but, "Are you worried for me?" I ask as I study it carefully.

He sighs, comes over and puts his hands on my shoulders, looks at me.

"You may hate me for saying so, but you pretend you need no one. Yes, there are some who see you as the very essence of *La Parisienne*, but you are still a young girl. You should be living with your parents, not married to a violent boxer, not doing who knows what for who knows how many painters. At the very least you should be learning a respectable trade. Don't you sometimes help your father? Why can't you do that instead?"

I wrap my shawl about me, cross my arms. This reminds me of my argument with Manet about why I believe I am the embodiment of the modern Parisian, and his refusal to see me that way. It's almost as if he'd have to use me for more "decent" paintings if he acknowledged my place in society, a place he and I see very differently.

"You speak as if you care about me, but you use me as your tool. If I weren't a model, if none of us were, Stevens, you painters would be stuck with real women, wealthy ones, and you wouldn't be able to guide them how you'd like because it wouldn't be 'respectable' for them to look and sit the way I do. I fulfill your unattainable dreams." We both know I am not now speaking of *Palm Sunday*.

Though he has been too much of a gentleman to say so yet, he wants me. For all of his efforts at making me a lady in the painting, claiming I should protect myself, I think what he means is he would like to protect me.

Why do we insist on using our bodies to explore the differences? Why can't our minds and words suffice? Why can't he be the kindly, wheezing, avuncular figure I wish him to be? They say beauty is a commodity. I find my near beauty to be nothing but trouble, and a part of me wishes my nose were still crooked.

I sweep out of the studio, coming back long enough to get my guitar. It takes an entire afternoon on a park bench complete with appreciative glances and catcalls before the world feels mine again.

A girl of about twelve stands before me and smiles, fingering her shoelace necklace from which dangles a heart-shaped charm. "You're Olympia," she says.

"No, I'm not." I smile back at her and I wonder who is making all of this marvelous profit from the shoelace necklaces that abound now.

Her mother quickly attempts to rush her away.

"But you are. I remember your hair color." The girl rocks forward and backwards and holds her hands to her mouth.

"I posed for *Olympia*, but I am not Olympia," I say.

"Please, we really must go," the mother, whose expensive clothing and neat shoes declare her respectable, says. While it was quite all right for the girl to see the painting of me and to wear a necklace like I wear in the painting, to fraternize with me is obviously forbidden.

The girl is sweet, nearly a woman but not yet. Her mother leads her away from me as if I were a gaping hole in the ground.

My heart burns as I think of all of those other young girls who have seen and will see the paintings I am in. Is it enough that I am affecting the painters, if I am not myself painting what the world is and what it can, should, be?

I think again of those paintings my father did of me and my stomach clenches as I watch the girl's braid bounce as her mother marches her away from me. Art can do so much good; art can do so much harm.

Willie and I dine *al fresco* at a café two streets from his theater on a rare night he has off. People recognize me, take off their hats, bow to us. "I had no idea," he says. It's hard to tell which of us is getting the attention. We stroll after we eat and enjoy the attention given us. Somehow between my posing and the rising popularity in his sport, we are becoming well known.

"Great fight last night," men say to him, pretending to pummel him. He laughs good naturedly; he is never bothered by being stopped, but neither does he court attention.

The men dare not say anything to me, although they obviously know who I am, and their gaze lingers approvingly. The postcard reproductions of the paintings have not, I am sure, lessened the attraction for them. Those too dense to get the real meaning will surely just "enjoy" the postcard. Those who understand the condemnation will not purchase one to begin with. But I imagine many of them memorize the image.

These are happy days and nights. I allow myself to forget that Manet is painting Morisot; I do not visit his studio as often because I cannot bear to see her mouse eyes on his canvases. Instead, I enjoy Willie's company and bask in the belated, sporadic approval that I do not understand from others.

When Willie is with me those who are so unpleasant as to spit upon me dare not. What they don't know is that they dare not even if I am by myself, not any more.

Whether it's due to our talk about models and art I'm not sure, but Stevens gives me a luxury I treasure in the second version he paints of *Palm Sunday*: I do not have to face the viewer. I kneel on a colorful chair in an attitude of everyday holiness. Another palm branch lies on the orange floral-patterned chair. My face is controlled, not overly sad.

Perhaps I do change how men paint. I was told this at Couture's school where I modeled for twenty-five francs a month, very different from the nineteen francs a week male models receive. When I was told I affected painting, I asked why I wasn't given the same amount that the men were given for posing. Couture sputtered but did not answer, and I could not demand one, not if I wanted my twenty-five francs.

Stevens paints with a fine-tipped brush, carefully covering his brushstrokes, smoothing his tracks as if he has committed a crime needing covering. This process is just as beautiful to me as the actual painting. In his second *Palm Sunday*, my face is only handsome. The nose and chin seem to melt a bit in sadness; my ear is vulnerably, partially exposed, my hair (mercifully painted a shade lighter) secured in a clip at the back of my head. My painted self is in deep grief, but he does not sentimentalize it with tears. My sadness is allowed me. In fact, I know this is why he wanted to paint me.

This sweet man seeks to redeem me, he sees it, from what Manet has portrayed me as.

"Shall I gaze just above the woman's head?" I ask.

"And not at her portrait?"

"Good idea," I say, though he wasn't approving my idea.

"The woman I am portraying can't bear to see it," I add.

He strokes his handlebar mustache. "Yes."

Stevens "Call me Alfred" (no, sir, I will not, not yet) is wonderful with his young son who routinely stops by, running in to kiss his father and twist his mustache. His wife comes as well, and she is cordial but only in a polite way. Has she seen *Olympia*?

Later Stevens tells me that she was from an outrageously wealthy family, and that she barely consented to marry him. "I had to buy her the most ridiculously priced Indian shawl for a dowry," he says, hunting at his desk until he produces the paint-stained receipt. I whistle at the price.

"What's worse, she never wears it. It's in a trunk at the foot of our bed."

I laugh at his indignation. His affection for his wife is apparent.

"Perhaps she likes just knowing it's there if she wants it," I say. I am jealous, though, that a man would love a woman so much that he would buy her an expensive shawl for the privilege of marrying her.

I haven't asked Willie for gifts, and he has given me none. That's the sort of gift I like best of all.

Though I am supposed to be decorating for *Palm Sunday*, the air of the painting is one of mourning. He understands that my "celebrity" has caused more sorrow than not.

Having gotten beyond Stevens' mustache, I am able to see that the nearly forty-year-old man is handsome, even if he is rather widely made. Not fat, mind, just broad, dandily dressed, even in the studio. This world that I am a part of yet apart from is nearly maddening. It is new, it is fresh, and when I am painted as a lady by Stevens, I pretend for just a moment that perhaps that is who I was born to be, until I look closer and see that I am but a prop.

I am no lady. I am Victorine Louise Meurent, and I am so much better than a lady. I am a woman who does what she pleases, who comes and goes as she wishes. No shawl can buy that, no pedigree. Not even a princess's dress.

I arrange my arms as he wants.

After the days of sitting, or, actually, standing for the portrait, I am invited back to see the completed painting. In it, there is a *white* cat. He has earned the kiss I readily bestow upon his reddened cheek.

"Why, Stevens," I say.

There's something impossibly sweet about a man who seeks to redeem you from society, from yourself, while trying to redeem himself. Even if you don't know if you want redeeming.

TEN

Young Lady of 1866

THOUGH MANET is enthralled with Morisot, to my surprise it doesn't prevent him from calling me back to work with him.

"Is the title meant to be ironic?" I ask Manet when he tells me what he will call this latest, static painting of me in pink: *Young Lady of 1866*. No one would accuse me of being a lady at twenty-two, and certainly not him, though my age doesn't have much to do with it.

"Even an actress can be a queen upon the stage."

"You don't have to be nasty," I hiss. "I never said I wanted to be a lady." The only ladies I ever knew were the snobby women who came into the store when I worked there and acted as if they were in charge. I was made to feel my place, but I paid them back in subtle ways. Sometimes their items arrived a day late, or wrinkled, courtesy of me.

Bernice was one of those who came into the store regularly with her mother. Every time she came in, she insisted on having me help her. She went from counter to counter picking up and putting down items: gloves, hairpins, jewelry. More than once I saw her secret a necklace in her blouse, but I never told on her, mostly because I thought she wanted me to.

On a particular Tuesday, I had been running from counter to counter all morning, especially the fabric counter. While it wasn't "my" counter—I was a floater—they did like me there. They said I had a good eye for color, and that customers liked it when I helped them pick out material for their dresses. It was true, and more than once they tried to put me working on the fabric counter permanently, but I didn't want that. My mind ran too fast to stay so stationary. I much preferred my status as someone who was free to run from floor to floor. I stayed busy, but if I saw a particularly quarrelsome customer come in, I could disappear. Except for Bernice, who insisted on asking for me. Because she and her mother were such good customers, the staff always hunted until they found me.

Bernice had that lovely brown hair and gray eyes. She was buxom and curvaceous—not so much now. There was absolutely no reason she ought to call for me. From the moment we saw one another we had that mutual hatred of two dogs in the street. I did not like the way she assumed I worked for her; she knew I had seen her take the jewelry and worried I would tell. The very air with which she carried herself annoyed me. She, meanwhile, seemed to sense how I felt about her, and so insisted on my waiting on her.

On the day I lost my job, she swept into the store, one hand lifting her skirts slightly as if our floor was unspeakably filthy. She marched over to me and snatched a fan from the counter, snapped it open with a crack.

"May I help Mademoiselle?" I ask disdainfully.

"Yes. I want a new dress made up by Thursday."

"But that's only two days from now. I'm afraid that's quite impossible."

"Figure it out," she said, waving her hand dismissively. She walked away and then returned. "Come with me," she said.

I obliged, but along the way I managed to step on her purple silk skirt three times, the last time separating the trim at the bottom from the skirt proper. I smirked because she clearly didn't notice.

We ended up in the underwear department, and she disappeared into the dressing room with a corset. "I can't get this on without help," she called.

The last thing I want is to be trapped in a small area with a half-naked Bernice. I shudder and walk briskly away. Why can't she be one of those overly modest women who won't even try on an undergarment in a store, much less ask for help?

"Please fetch Victorine," she calls imperiously. The head of the department, Madame Blanchard, crosses to me and implores me to go help the girl.

I reluctantly enter the small space where Bernice stands with her breasts unsheathed, an ivory statue, her hands behind her back as if reveling in the unfamiliar release in such a public place. The sun shines upon her from the small window opposite her, and I long for a block of marble and a chisel. My lips curve at the statue I would make.

"Are you making fun of me?" she asks, wrapping her arms around herself. A heart-shaped charm that I have recently seen at the jewelry counter falls to the floor.

My eyes go from it to her and back. I bend to retrieve just as she does, and her soft breast brushes my hand. She closes her eyes and leans into me, pressing her chest against me. I pull away, and her face whitens.

"Madame Blanchard," she calls, grabbing the charm from my hand. "She was trying to steal this. I saw her about to put it down her dress."

Of course Bernice is believed. Of course I am dismissed.

I get her address from one of the clerks, a friend of mine, before I leave the store. I send an itemized list to her mother of all of the things I have seen her steal, and if she asks to see the invoices, she will realize her daughter has not bought many of the things she possesses. It occurs to me that this may exonerate me, and I hope it does not: I have tired of this store, of this frivolous lady art substitute. Bernice has unwittingly done me a favor. I want a block of marble, no, that more forgiving paintbrush, and I will have it. But how?

Despite the fact that I work increasingly with Stevens, Manet asserts his "ownership," paints me as *Young Lady of 1866*, in response, some whisper, to Courbet's *Woman with a Parrot*. He can think what he likes—I only sit for those for whom it pleases me to sit.

In this painting Manet gives me a flowing pink peignoir, a blue ribbon in a bow (despite my objections) topping my middle-parted, pulled back hair. My left arm is down, my right raised so that I may smell the tiny bouquet of exquisite violets in my right hand. I do adore how he paints the flowers.

"If I knew I could have your violets, I wouldn't be too sorry if all of the rest of the paintings of them in the world were lost," I tell him, sighing happily.

He grins but raises his eyebrow as he stipples his brush along the canvas. "What of real ones?"

"The memory of their scent is connected strongly with their image, and you have captured it so completely that I feel sure I will always smell them when I see your homage to them."

"Still now," he says intently, and I stare as I have been at the bunch of flowers newly purchased this morning, now slightly limp but I am nearly cross-eyed with pleasure knowing he is painting them. There is a trueness and honesty to his flowers that he does not allow himself otherwise. He doesn't make them say anything.

While I can imagine what that look on Manet's face means and what dashes of color my worship brings from him, if I could see him painting, I would know better how to aid him. Perhaps a large mirror behind him? The image would reverse, but I could get an idea of the shapes and how he would prefer me to pose, how my body needs to turn to compose the painting in a more pleasing manner.

When he signals that I may break, I eagerly move to his canvas, and as I stretch, I admire his work while he pretends to clean a brush, his eyes never leaving the canvas.

From under my painted gown, a black shoe shyly peeps.

I wear the ever-present shoelace at my throat, but a different charm hangs from it this time. The shape of my eye matches the shape of my friend, the parrot's, eye. We are linked, as parrots are with women, with romance. Good companions because they can speak. On command.

My eyebrow crooks challengingly, and something about my gaze seems almost as scholarly as it is knowing. Always I wonder if perhaps a painter is painting something of me that I haven't seen before, and with each painting, I do discover something new about myself. I can't say yet what this one tells me, but it does say something I am trying to understand.

Around my wrists are cuffs of white fur, bright shiny blurs. Delightfully large buttons descend my nightgown, and a V of white satin interrupts the pink. He has certainly not flattered my figure with the shapeless gown, but I don't mind.

The gray parrot, a favorite pet, perches on an ornately carved wooden stand. The base of the sand-filled stand is littered with a ripped-opened orange, part of it rolled onto the floor. Ruined. I pray Manet does not see me as his parrot, the one who speaks for him in limited tones. Does he believe me to be ruined fruit?

With sinking heart, I keep scanning this painting for its rhythm, replaying it as I might a chord I am just learning.

This painting with the gray background is to redeem me to Parisian society, or so he said, and it might, but for the monocle in my left hand: lesbianism.

I am no longer condemned as just a prostitute, but as something "worse." At the very least I will be seen as a woman dandling her lover's monocle in her boudoir. Thanks be, though, that he didn't give me a tiresome lorgnette.

Why has Manet pictured me with a parrot twice? Is he saying I only repeat him? A parrot is also thought to belong—my head whirls towards him as I think on it—to courtesans.

"*Mon Dieu*, Manet. A courtesan again? Or did you mean for me to be a lesbian?"

He looks down. "What makes you say that?"

I walk to the canvas and scratch a line across the wet, gray parrot. "That."

"Leave the smudging—and the parrots—to me, will you?" he asks as he reloads his brush and begins dabbing at it, between frowning at me. He looks so fierce I laugh aloud. The gray paint dries under my fingernail. Now the painting and I are truly one.

Victorine Meurent is no lady. Why should it hurt so that he is not really picturing me as such? Isn't it a condemnation of what ladies are thought to be? Isn't it a way of explaining that ladies are really no better than me? Isn't telling the truth the way to set someone, even a society, free?

Manet doesn't know he says this. Should I tell him? If I do not, the art world will. Surely he must see it. I try again.

"Why am I dressed in pink?" I ask. Although pink flatters my skin and hair, I don't like wearing it. When I worked at the department store, I favored wearing pink bows and dresses. I am not fourteen anymore.

He shrugs. "It matches your hair."

"Ha. It matches Stevens's paintings of me, you mean."

His cheeks fairly glow, and he works his mouth silently. He scratches at the painting with the handle of his brush. I wait for it, not telling him I could just as easily compare his work with Courbet's.

It's delicious to feel the tension build, know the roaring fire is stoking itself and that it will find an outlet. I half close my eyes in anticipation because, in Manet, it's hard to say what form the storm will take. Any form will do.

His lips tighten as he bends over the canvas.

Silence.

Oh Manet, there is so much more I could tell you about this painting that would condemn it to your fireplace, but no.

"Where do your ideas come from?" I ask. In one sense, it is a ridiculous question: The eye continually creates paintings. But how does one decide which to paint?

He shrugs. "Sometimes I overhear something that inspires me. Sometimes I see something. Sometimes I just play about and see what happens."

"Which is it this time?"

I raise my head, and just as quickly lower it. The thing about endings is you don't always know they are endings. This time, I know.

Zola writes: "In *The Young Woman with Parrot* I find the personification of the native elegance that Manet has deep within him." I could say the same of myself: that Manet seems to find elegance in me that I do not.

That refinement kept him from lashing out at me, but his pride will prevent him from using me again, now that I have compared his work with Stevens's.

I shrug it off with drinking and sex. And there's Stevens, of course.

There are things about myself I like better in Stevens's paintings of me than in Manet's, though I know Manet sees me better than Stevens ever could. With Stevens, I take on a juvenile innocence that both infuriates me and makes me long for a time when surely I had once been that way.

My painted face is fuller in Stevens's work. He has me holding a figurine that is nearly a doll in *The Lady in Pink* (pink again). I am surrounded by privilege, as if things are more important to me than anything else. I hold *objets d'art* from around the world as if I am craving anything but the safe, sanitized life I have. The intricately wrought lace on the dress would suit a doll better.

Stevens paints gorgeously, but his work tends toward the treacly. One of his paintings of me he calls *A Study of Victorine Meurent*, and it seems so appropriate. I like that he names me; it shows a regard for me as a person rather than an object. Ah, but Manet named me first.

Stevens is not asking me to play a role in this painting. He asks me to hold my bare breast as if I am holding an infant. That my sexuality can still be treated so tenderly after all of my experience surprises me—in this painting, he reminds me of my youth. He allows me to bow my head, cast down my eyes. My features are not, for once, sensual. They are pretty and even: full lips, a decidedly Parisian nose (I will never take that for granted again) and eyes that are gently closed. I don't have to look at anyone this time.

He also uses the dark blackish brown background as Manet typically does for me, but he lends a range of hues to the spectrum. Stevens, an even greater master of painting fabric than Manet, cannot resist creating a glowing peach-colored dressing gown on me. He makes my erect nipple shine as if I am a childless Madonna, eager to breastfeed.

Though Manet sought to redeem me, it is Stevens who does so.

I cannot stare at this painting of me enough. It makes me forgive myself for all I have done and half of what I am about to do. It determines me to take M. Stevens a bit more seriously.

The painters, writers, and musicians make boxing their newest salon of sorts, in that fevered way something catches on until it burns out, which I am not worried about, not yet.

The men place bets on the fights. I have even heard them trying to bribe Willie into fixing them. Willie doesn't often get angry, but I have seen him ball-fisted at their suggestions. That's when I realize that his fighting is as much an art form for him as painting is for us. Respect peeks out of my heart's soil, a tender plant. So many shoots there are coming up for Willie, all so young and fragile.

The fights are a place of aggressions spent. Fights happen in the audience nearly as often as they do in the ring.

Periodically, the police show up, breaking up trouble or checking on supposed reports of violence. They haven't permanently shut things down, but they have tried, despite the moneyed who attend. The police bar the doors, empty the house some nights. They come in saying that they have had reports of riots and clear the place. It has gotten so that Willie does not know when a full night's activities will be allowed.

Things get so bad that Willie says there is no safe venue, no place to escape from the police, and he threatens to return to London.

"I know the perfect spot for boxing," I say. Anything but London, but life without Willie.

When the audience discovers the bouts are to take place in the catacombs, the crowds swell. Willie takes in more money than God, and he hands me a wad of it: "Towards art school," he says. Though he is surrounded by fans, I kiss him firmly on his lips before secreting the cash in my bodice.

The police will not reach us here. They are only interested in what happens above ground. Down here, we are our own species.

Perhaps because the fights take place in the catacombs, I am not surprised to run across Alphonse one night. My lip curls and I turn my back on him, but he seeks my attention anyway.

"So, Olympia, I was right about you," he says as he grabs my shoulder.

I wrench away with an oath. I can't believe I gave myself so willingly to him.

"As was I about you." I turn away again, but he grabs my arm, whirls me about.

"I'm the one who got your career started."

"Is that so?" I put my hands on my hips and rise up on my toes, put my face as close to his as I can get it, seeing as how I am shorter than he is by at least six inches.

"Perhaps what everyone would really like to hear is how you took advantage of a virgin for your own gain."

"You didn't seem to complain," he says. He lights a cigarette and I take it from him.

"I'm not speaking of the sex—I was curious about that. I mean that you took all of those photos of me and spread them around."

I drag on the cigarette.

"I miss you," he says.

"Funny, I haven't even thought of you since . . ." I hand him back the now-reddened-with-my-lipstick cigarette. Since I met Willie. It is such a comfort knowing I can call on a man to come pound this lump of human excrement at any moment. Even more comforting to know that I don't need him to.

I walk away, not even finishing my sentence, grateful when the odor of that pomade leaves my nose.

Underground, the artists lose their civility. Jackets come off; shirt sleeves get rolled. Language denigrates as the alcohol flows. When they're not fighting or watching the fight, they are slipping off into the shadows with crimson-lipped, hard-faced women. When I watch the men I respect disappear into the darkness to feed on these women, it is as if art loses its luster. How could they need anything but their art, and yet it seems they do.

A woman with braided coils of hair atop her head circles Manet. He has found a place close to the action, and he doesn't see her vying for his attention.

I'm not naïve. I've heard the stories about him.

He yells lustily at the opposite fighter to "fight, dammit," his fist in the air. I grin at his rare display of enthusiasm.

The woman pulls out a cigarette and apparently asks him for a light. He distractedly hands her a box of matches and goes back to shouting. When she pretends to fumble with the match, I approach her, take the box.

"Allow me," I say as I light her cigarette. She smirks but moves away. Manet has seen nothing.

We go above ground in the early morning hours, Willie's arm about me. I am grateful to the welcoming sun. For a moment I had feared that we might have become moles.

Still, my heart warms with my hands in the sun. It is something not to be taken lightly. I wrap my arms firmly about Willie's sweaty body. I am too young yet to know that this moment cannot possibly last, but I revel in it.

Stevens comes more often to the fights now, although he seems quite uncomfortable at them. Every time he sees me, he asks me to pose for him, though Manet has been using me. I agree, but only when Manet doesn't need me. Though I want to sit for Stevens, I cannot resist sitting for Manet; I know what Stevens will say with his paint, but not Manet.

Tonight, Stevens has a man with silvery gray hair with him.

"Manet, I'd like you to meet the writer, M. Gonzalès," Stevens says. As if he doesn't know of the fascination that Spain and everything relating to it has for Manet.

"He has a quite attractive daughter who is also a painter," says Stevens. I can't hear what else he says, but Manet reacts viscerally, as do I. I don't need to know what is being said to know I don't like it.

Is that smugness I see playing about Stevens' mouth? How intriguing. There may be even more to the painter than I suspected. Playing fair is not something artists do well, because art is above such pettiness.

In the ensuing weeks, Stevens calls for me to model more, and it gradually occurs to me that I have become increasingly available to him. While I'm grateful for the employment, I begin to wonder just why I am so free to sit. It dawns on me that this is the parting I have feared. However gradual, I feel it. If I know Manet, he is painting. But who is he painting?

I want to blame Morisot. Her name is still tightly linked with his, but as I have heard she has been out of town lately, I suspect M. Gonzalès's daughter might have more to do with it.

I drop in on Manet after a morning's session with Stevens. He doesn't meet my eyes, but he nods. A young woman stands with an easel beside his. Without introducing us, Manet shows her how to round a cherry with the wooden tip of her paintbrush.

My heart and legs move in concert.

There is a pile of the fruit on the table before them, and without a word I go to it and pick up a handful, start eating them.

"We're painting those." Manet says, glancing at me and quickly away.

I eat another. "Who's this?"

"Eva Gonzalès, this is . . ."

She interrupts. "Victorine Meurent, of course. Nice to meet you." Her smile is genuine, and her teeth straight.

I continue eating the cherries as if this is why I am here, but there are too many for even my appetite.

"I will just buy more," Manet says as I childishly stuff my mouth, but his eyes run between my mouth and my hand, hungrily scanning my lips. He wants to paint me eating these, I can see.

"I don't care." My cheeks are swollen with the fruit, and juice runs out the side of my mouth. I spit it onto the floor, just to watch the young woman flinch. Cherries, a guitar. A street singer.

Who *is* this woman?

"Eva is my pupil. Her father is a writer."

"Of course. Stevens introduced the two of you. Needing cash, Manet? You should have asked. Stevens is paying me quite well."

His face flushes. "She is a good student, and she's already had some training. I'm just helping her refine her skills."

"Ah. Refine away." I sit behind them and continue to eat handfuls of cherries, but there's another bunch of them to the side and I am quickly getting full.

He shows her to add white to the cherry for shine in just a spot. He recommends she add a black outline, but I make a noise and when she looks at me, I shake my head no.

"Did you need something?" Manet asks.

It's not until then that I see the portrait he's been painting of her. It's huge and lovely and in it, she's seated in the same chair he put me in for *The Guitar Player*. The bastard. It decides me.

"I just wanted to tell you I am going to be tied up with Stevens quite a bit in the coming months so I am afraid I will not be available."

"Best of luck," he says. He returns to advising her, standing close.

I stride over to the girl-woman and wrench the brush from her hand. I paint out her cherries, streak her background, which she is already blackening like Manet.

"Perhaps you'd better leave the painting of cherries to Monsieur Manet, as he is so fond of them," I say as I leave the studio, brush in hand.

I fling the brush onto the gravel outside Manet's studio, but the memory of the worn spot on the side makes me pick it up again just as quickly. My fingers flick that groove repeatedly. His always wear so. He has let her paint with his brush.

Without warning, I bend over and watch the cherries, only half chewed anyway, reappear. I slide down the wall and sit, waiting for the nausea to pass. Bazille appears at my side, bending toward me: "Mlle. Meurent? Do you need help?"

"Desperately," I say, allowing him to pick me up.

"Your paintbrush," he says, holding it by its tip.

"Thank you."

"You are not well. Allow me to escort you back inside."

"No. Thank you. I would rather go home."

The young man's eyes are so concerned. Kindness undoes me, always.

"Go ahead and have your visit. I will be fine," I say, patting his face.

He stands up straight, startled.

This confounded flitting between classes . . .

"I beg your pardon," I say. "I'm not myself."

"Not at all. I," he says shyly, "I didn't mind."

"Well you should have. I'm a married woman."

"Of course. I didn't mean . . ."

He has attended some matches. He knows who Willie is now, though I don't use Willie's last name as mine because I am known by my maiden name in the art world.

"Manet and Gonzalès are inside. Please, do ask her how she likes outlining her cherries in black."

Though the nausea hasn't quite passed, I flee.

I want to stay away from Manet's studio, but we keep inventing what I can only think of as excuses for either one or the other of us to visit. This time I stop by because "My father wants to know when you will require that print he is making." My father has asked me to deliver no such message.

Manet is still painting Gonzalès, though I notice that the painting she is supposed to be working on in his painting is actually one of his.

"He's a self-centered monster. Look, he's pretending his painting is yours. Perhaps he thinks yours aren't good enough," I stage whisper, but she doesn't flinch.

"Is that all your father said?" Manet asks, loading his brush.

"No, that is, yes. Manet, I want to speak with you. Alone." I haven't planned on saying this, not today, but regardless of my rapid heartbeat, I find I must.

"Eva, perhaps you'd like a cup of *café*. Please ask Madame Duchene downstairs to accompany you across the street. I'll fetch you when I'm finished here," he says, flashing a look of annoyance at me.

She gathers her starchy dress in her hands and leaves.

"What is it, Victorine?" Manet asks. "If it's because I haven't painted you lately, I just don't need . . ."

"Why not me? Why didn't you want to teach me to paint? Why her?"

He sputters.

"Manet, you made it very clear that a woman should not paint."

"I said no such thing."

"Then why didn't you help me when I asked? Why did you wrestle your brush away from me?"

"Why, I told you: Eva has already been trained. I'm merely giving her pointers."

"That's not it, Manet. I just want to hear you admit it."

"Admit?"

"That it's because I'm not of her class. She has money, and her father has influence, maybe even with the Salon. They're not so rich that it's vulgar for her to paint. The problem is, why are you all trying to paint the poor as if you understand what that means? Why are you trying to romanticize our lives? To assuage your guilt? Wouldn't it be easier to make our lives better?"

"Did you ever stop to consider, Victorine, that maybe it's not women painters I'm prejudiced against but you?" He goes back to painting. "Now, go get Eva for me."

"No. Wait. Stop painting." I reach for his brush, but he expects it, so he merely holds it above his head.

"It is because I'm poor, Manet. I know it. You don't want to share your subclass of painter with the likes of me. No, it's not the poverty, but my class. And not because you don't like me, because you do, very much, but you dare not treat me as an equal."

"I have never been accused of such snobbery," he says, but he lowers his head.

"If you allow me to paint, I might paint from my class, I might show your idealisms to be wrong. You think if your lot paints us as tragic figures, then your responsibility has ended. You make us beautiful but ill or becoming dissolute in the paintings, but you pretend we are not to blame. Manet, anything that happens to us is our fault, even our poverty, if we can't figure a way out of it."

He stands still.

"Then why haven't you made your way out of it, *Crevette?*"

"I'm climbing the stairs, Manet. I just haven't yet reached your level. At the moment, I'm very happy about that, because where you are is nowhere I want to be. And I am anything but a *crevette* nowadays."

I turn away.

"I'll escort Gonzalès back over, if you think my presence is acceptable enough for that."

I don't bring her right back over, however. I sit at her table.

"So, Gonzalès. What do you know about Berthe Morisot?"

She clutches her teacup and looks around as if she's afraid to be seen with me. Her eyes are large, brown. Her hair is black, and she wears it up. Her clothing is chicly French.

I'm surprised by how high her voice is, almost as if she were a young girl.

"That Berthe is around all the time. She paints."

She rolls her eyes. "I think he's smitten with her."

"Is that so?" I have only heard of Morisot's visits from Stevens who, I must say, rather rubbed it in. Between these two women, I'm beginning to understand just why Manet is not sending for me more often.

"She's not pretty, not in the usual way, you know, but when he paints her you can't tell it. And they have these long talks about things I really don't understand." Her eyes are wide.

The young woman shrugs and takes a drink.

"Is he helping your work?"

"He is." Her face brightens. "I thought I was already doing well, but my previous teacher wouldn't let me try anything. Manet lets me do anything I want, and then he corrects me."

"And your father pays him?"

"He does. I'm not in a position to pay my own way, am I?"

"I suppose you're not. But why not go to a school?"

"My father recommended Manet, and isn't it better to have all of the attention of a teacher?"

"But how can he get on with his work if you are there all of the time?"

"I'm not there all of the time. Not when Berthe's there, not usually."

I laugh. "His studio used to be known for its collection of men. It sounds as if that's changing fast."

"Not at all. In fact, the men seem to like having Berthe and me around, and my sister Jeanne, when she comes. I just don't paint when Berthe's there."

"And why is that?"

Gonzalès lets out a whistle of air, blowing her hair to the side of her face. "Because she likes to tell me what to do. When I see her coming, I put my paints away."

"Does Berthe let Manet tell her what to paint?"

"Sometimes. Usually she tells him to go away, and he does. They just seem to like painting in the same room as one another."

"Do they paint the same things, then?"

"No. She has sketches with her, and she works from them." Gonzalès rises. "I should head back over—I assume he is ready for me?"

How does Manet inspire loyalty so easily?

◈

Though I know I should stay away, I can't. Even when Manet does not seek me to pose, seeing him create stirs my own hunger for art. So while Willie sleeps during the day, I often visit Manet's studio. Eva and I have become friends of a sort—she has asked me to call her by her first name, and I have agreed, hiding my smile at her evident pleasure in granting me the privilege.

"You draw really well," Eva says when I show her a caricature I have drawn of a furious Manet when he scolded her earlier. "This one is *très magnifique*. You should take some classes."

I scoff. "But you stopped taking classes with Chaplin, you said, because he wouldn't let you paint the way you wanted to paint. Why should I want that?" I won't tell her about my dream of attending art school. There is still not enough money.

"True. I did. He also wouldn't stop talking about my beauty in connection with my painting." She says it as if her looks are nothing more than a coat as she pulls her gloves off and on. She always wears gloves except when she is painting; she's so proper.

I don't have to ask if he made her uncomfortable with that, as her shoulders move restlessly when she says it and she adjusts a satin heel.

"As if your appearance is more important than your art?"

"As if my appearance were my art."

She puts down the brush, picks it up again. "Manet is no better about Morisot. He said it's too bad she is a woman."

I make a scornful noise. "I think we both know he'd like her much less if she weren't a woman."

Her sister, Jeanne, waits on the sofa, her chaperone of sorts. While her parents prefer a male escort for the sisters, they have allowed that the two of them together is certainly better than Eva going out by herself.

She idly applies a stroke of red very close to but not on top of a stripe of white.

"Why is the impression of a thing more important than a duplicate?" I ask quietly.

Jeanne, in a dress very like her sister's, answers: "Because we can never truly know something. What we think we see in a glance, that's all we are allowed."

Eva nods.

"That's what reflection and study are for, aren't they? Only when you take the time to get to know everything about a person can you presume to paint them," I say.

"What of sunlight?" Eva asks, touching at the skyline of her painting where a blur of yellow challenges a cloud and will undoubtedly win.

"Is that why you are painting this indoors?"

"Light is fleeting. I do not benefit by painting landscapes out of doors. Manet and Chaplin agree: I am better at depicting people."

She paints her sister with a stubborn frequency. It's as if she's trying to discover something about herself through every line, every angle, of her sister.

"So why paint what you are painting?"

She dabs at the lake beneath the sky with a brilliant blue, the color we wish it were on a day we are full of love.

"Because Manet has set me this task."

Jeanne stands and examines the painting, points out a stray line.

"This is a first pass," Eva says without irritation.

Out the window I spot small tomatoes in a pot on a narrow balcony across the street, and they mesmerize me. Just before I can point out the taut fruit, Manet passes, the sun shining on his forehead.

Jeanne is in the middle of questioning a shadow on Eva's painting.

The stairs creak as Manet mounts rapidly.

"Now," he says, putting his hands together, "That will be all for today. I need my studio."

"I want my own studio," Eva murmurs as she begins to put away her paints.

"I thought Chaplin told your father it is a good idea after all," Manet says, hand out.

"He did, but all Father can recall is that Chaplin told him my having an atelier would make it more difficult for me to get married."

Manet helps Eva put away her equipment. "Is that something you're considering, marriage?"

"Right now I am in training, Édouard. That is all I can think of. Perhaps later . . . I do not know."

"Meurent," he says, as if he has just noticed me, "Did I call for you? I am very sorry, but I will not need you today."

"I came here merely to say hello to the Mlles. Gonzalès."

"Ah, yes, well I won't keep the three of you." He opens the door. Eva has not had time to even clean her brushes.

"I'll tend to them," he says as she looks back.

We meet Morisot and Bazille on the stairs and, after bearing her frosty greeting, lift our eyebrows at one another when she climbs the stairs. He murmurs an embarrassed hello, takes off his hat.

It occurs to me to stay nearby. "Would you like to gossip with me at the Café Guerbois?" I ask.

The sisters demur, noting the time. I have forgotten that they, as "respectable" women, do not frequent such rough places.

I bid them adieu and try not to glance back as they stroll away arm in arm. That is a painting I would like to make.

I don't go to the café either. Instead, I linger outside Manet's building. Within ten minutes Bazille leaves. Alone. He doesn't see me. Why do I feel like picking up rocks and hurling them at Manet's studio windows?

I could paint better than her. I could dress better, had I the same amount of money, and if I cared. I don't. Why should I?

Art slips further from me.

After a night of walking the streets, raging, and wearing myself out, I decide I really, truly must let go of Manet. But how?

Eva's father finally agrees to her having a studio, after Manet tells her father it would be good for her, that she doesn't need more lessons from him, or so she reports and she tells me I must visit it, and I do. Here is a place without that smug Morisot or even the interfering Manet.

While she paints her sister, I sketch her painting her.

Her delicate manner is also slyly aggressive. Her colors refuse to hint, even as she softens them just enough to show the shadow of her sister, of herself.

In this painting she shows Jeanne in profile, not enough of the young woman to really see what she looks like beyond that half turn of her head. The background is gray—dark, but not too.

Curls hang down Jeanne's back, over her shoulder. Her dress is an unassuming gray, not at all what she typically wears. This is a housedress, not a going-out one. She looks shy, unassuming. Her chin is rounded and youthful.

The interest in this painting for me lies in wondering why her sister wants to hide Jeanne. What advantage, that? Perhaps after painting her so many times Eva desires to keep something of herself in reserve. She is feeling, perhaps, protective of her sister. The vulnerability of the girl—yes, for so she seems here—is undeniable. I want to protect that feather of a shoulder myself.

The girl looks weary or wary. Her eyebrow is untamed—I cannot imagine Jeanne will approve of being portrayed in this way.

Overall, I would say this is decidedly not how I would expect a Mademoiselle Gonzalès to appear. For that, I like the painting. The colors, however, do not appeal. They are not bright enough, and yet they are not dull enough to make a statement themselves, either.

Perhaps I should not fault them for this, but I do. And thus I fault Eva.

Still, she is not the one-noted wonder I would have thought. She is not the imitating monkey of Manet that I took her to be, either.

"My father doesn't approve of my being an artist. My mother—a pianist—doesn't mind at all. I envy you, Victorine. You make your living with art. Not like me. You can go where you please."

"I don't want to model—I want to create art myself."

"Why can't you?" she asks as she generously applies expensive paint to even more expensive canvas in her clothing provided by her father.

"Money," I say, rolling my eyes, trying not to despise her. It's not her fault that she doesn't know.

"But we're not so different besides that, Victorine, are we? I mean maybe you've slept with more men than I have."

I raise my eyebrow.

"Fine. I've never known a man, but only because my sister is with me so often."

"I know a man or two who would quite enjoy introducing you to the pleasures of the flesh, if your virginity weren't part of your dowry."

She laughs. "What do you know of dowries? My not having sex has very little to do with marriage and much to do with no opportunity."

"But you have kissed a man?"

"Must we speak about everything all in one day?"

Of course she hasn't.

Though she temporarily looks dejected, soon enough her smile leaps back upon her face. "Oh, Victorine, I have the best idea. Lend me your clothes for the day."

"My clothes?" I wear a striped gown of dubious cleanliness. It was clean last week, but laundering my own clothing is not my first priority right now. The hat upon my head speaks of my mother's mastery of the craft. The velvet affair sports a cockade. Because she bade me, I agreed to wear it. She believes Eva and her set will become enamored of her hats if they see them upon me.

"The hat is quite nice, I agree. My mother made this," I say, since Eva has shown interest.

"Yes, but the gown as well. Where did you get it?"

"Le Bon Marché. On sale."

"Of course. It's last year's, isn't it?"

I shrug. More like four seasons ago. Surely she knows that.

"Hurry. Switch with me."

At first I refuse, but then I agree. Her dress is rose-colored, quite sheer in spots. Shots of silver thread only reveal themselves in the right light.

When I take off my warm, heavy dress I stand in my undergarments for a moment, face upturned. The breeze through the window feels lovely after a day of modeling.

I close my eyes and sing. Eva yelps.

"Hello, Stevens," I say, leisurely pulling on Eva's gown. She is struggling to find the armholes of mine after hastily pulling it over her head. He and Manet have appeared in the studio doorway.

"Bonjour. We seem to have come at an importune time," Stevens says. His back faces us, but his yearning troubles the air.

"Not at all. We are ready to say hello," and we are, though Eva's cheeks are red.

"Very good," he says, slowly turning.

Eva busies herself with her paints, enabling her to have a reason to turn her back to us. I go lean out the window, knowing Stevens will follow.

Has the studio become a dressing room?

"She fancies a little noble peasant play. I think we are meant to go out in the street and see how we are treated differently."

"And will you be, just because you swapped dresses?" he asks.

"Why do you not paint anyone in humble dresses?"

A smile of understanding comes upon his face.

"Your cheeks make that dress earn its color. Perhaps you should never wear anything but rose."

I scoff. "Blue suits me much better."

The feathers upon the hat that my mother made quiver in front of the easel. I turn back to the window.

Stevens leans so close to me that I must lean in as well to understand him: "Yes, blue. Awash in blue. I'd like to paint you thus."

"We were just about to go for a stroll."

"What are you trying to prove?" Manet asks.

"That just as you have judged the dress and asked a painter to step away from her own canvas, so are we judged by our clothes."

"The two of you out and about? Not alone."

"I am permitted to be alone. Because she is in my clothes, so is she."

"However, I answer to her parents, and so I insist that she not be out unescorted."

"Then consider me her escort," I say. Does he truly answer to her parents, or does he take that responsibility upon himself? Neither would work if Eva did not permit it. I must speak with her about this.

We walk into the street. The slight breeze catches the hem of my dress, sets it swaying. Though I don't want to, I feel like a princess. I walk straighter, smile larger, nearly waving, as if I am in a parade.

Eva seems to disappear into herself. The dress (one I hadn't hated, not until now) seems plain, and heavy with grime—not because it hasn't been washed but because I haven't the facilities to maintain a costume properly. Washing a dress in a tub of lukewarm water doesn't do much for it.

Manet walks back and forth between us, as if unsure of which of us to dance attendance upon. He finally lights upon Eva, and I hate him a bit more, even as I admire him: breeding over fashion.

Stevens takes my arm. "Tell me, Victorine, where you learned of art."

His question is warm, genuine, and yet within it I feel his desire to distract me from the couple ahead of us.

"I was born in Paris."

"Yes, but I was not, so tell me what that means."

"Even with your accent, sometimes I forget that you are not Parisian, although I ought to know," I say, narrowing my eyes at Manet's back. He keeps his distance from Eva, for all that he has thrown his lot in with her. And his head is bowed, especially when we approach people I know he is acquainted with.

Stevens's eyes encourage me with their earnestness.

"It's a matter, I suppose, of art being everywhere and in everything. My father. . ." I can't decide whether or not I want to tell Stevens this, and I find I do, or at least part of it. "My father was a painter when I was younger, and my first memory is of the scent of paint drying. He painted cabbages and flowers together. My mother hated it. She said he ought to paint either vegetables or flowers, but that everyone knows that you don't mix the two. Then he started going to the zoo and painting the animals. He would take me, and I far more enjoyed watching him than the elephants." I won't speak of his paintings of me.

"Your mother is a painter as well?"

I laugh. "No." I think of her gnarled hands stroking velvet. "But she has an eye."

"In Paris, everyone is an artist. That is why I adore this city. I could never leave it, you know. It is truly my home."

"I know."

We stride on, and I am entirely content to be arm in arm with this kind, compassionate man in public, no one looking twice at us.

Manet and Eva, however, get quite a few puzzled looks and scowls. We round the corner to the Tuileries and we are safe within the trees and bushes, the lush gardens, and the fountain.

"So art came to you when you were very young," Stevens says.

"I don't remember a moment without it." I speak, but my attention is captured by a bird I can't identify drinking as deeply from a red bloom as Stevens seeks to drink from me. We watch its pulsing wings. I wave it away from the flower and peer closely inside. From my vantage point, I cannot see what there is to want from its hollow.

"What do you see?" Stevens asks gently.

I pluck the flower and crush it between my fingers. Regret courses through me.

"What are Eva and Manet up to?" I ask, strolling quickly ahead. Stevens follows.

Back at the studio, we four talk at once, Manet begging Eva to take "that ridiculous costume" off; me saying how famished I am, Eva noticing the time, and Stevens saying we should do it again.

No one listens to anyone else with attention. Eva goes behind the screen to change. At her excessive modesty, I nonchalantly take off her dress before them all and hand it over the screen. She snatches it so quickly over the wood that I hate my old dress that needs starching even more.

I head to the props at the back of the room and sort through them madly until I find a simple white dress. I slip it on and gather my bag and guitar.

"I'll return the dress tomorrow," I say.

"Don't bother," Eva says. "It suits you." She holds out my dress. I pretend I don't see and take my leave.

The next morning two boxes appear on my doorstep: one containing my dress, freshly laundered and sweetly folded. The second holds a shiny yellow dress I had admired in a shop window yesterday, when I walked on Stevens's arm. No one else could have heard me mention it.

Though I want so badly to give this dress back, I will not. And I must confess, yesterday's dress looks much better freshly washed. I will keep it after all.

The painters quickly grow comfortable at the fights, shedding their outerwear as easily as their manners. Oaths once "beg pardoned" of me are now streaming out, fists waving, cigarettes burning. The men stay so long they smell of sweat, of too much alcohol smuggled in by young men by the bottle, sold for double its worth. The catacombs cocoon the violence.

The society men pass the bottle back and forth, lips second-handedly kissing one another. But then isn't that what they do anyway when they mimic one another's paintings?

Stevens turns to pass the bottle to me, realizes what he has done and withdraws it. I grab the bottle and empty it. The men nearest me cheer, and I mock them.

Soon my sight blurs.

Stevens leads me outside when I clutch at his arm.

"That is no place for you," he says.

"Because I am a woman?" I slur.

"That, but because you are more."

I laugh. "There is no more than that, Stevens. That's what I've been trying to tell you. Art is just one more drug. I wish it were more than that, but there it is. At least down there," I wish my words were straighter, "is more honest. It is vile and base and beastly."

"What do you mean?" he asks as he studies the shadow the lamp makes on the wall opposite.

"In there, men do as they would do every day had they the opportunity. Instead of polite words, fists; instead of moderation and glasses, upturned bottles. Instead of women, only men."

"Now hold on," he said.

I wave my hand. "I don't mean sexually, although there may be a bit of that, too. I mean no women allowed. Because we are too delicate to see."

"You were there."

"Ah, but I am no longer a woman to any of you, am I? And it is my husband's business, so I am under his 'protection.'"

"Am I to be made to feel guilty for everything I enjoy?" He rubs his slowly growing paunch, a pocket where he seems to be storing secrets for later.

"No." I stand on the wall, trying to put one foot in front of the other. "That's what I'm trying to say." I tumble onto the grass behind the wall. For a moment, I can't breathe. My back aches. "Why is being above ground considered so much better than being under?"

He puts out his hand and helps me up. I lean against him gratefully.

"You know, Stevens, you are so likeable." His stomach stands between us, and I press in until my pelvis meets his stomach so that I am able to put my arms about him. Then I touch the side of his face.

"Thank you," he says, smiling.

"I wasn't finished." I dig in, just a bit, with my fingernail, but not so much that I draw blood. "I was going to say that you're so likeable that I despise you."

He pulls my hand from his face. "You've had too much to drink."

"There is no such thing as too much of anything."

He helps me sit on the wall and puts his arm about my shoulder. "Say what you will, but I think you like me more than you care to admit."

"I might," I giggle. "But you shouldn't make too much of it. I only like you the way I like that big stuffed animal Willie won me at the fair." I make as if I will tickle him, and though I am drunk, I know to stop myself. From here it is only a spiral of laughter that will turn to tears. I don't want anyone, especially Willie, to see me like this.

"It will be ages before everyone leaves. Can't you take me to my house?" The moon shines.

"I would like nothing better," he says. He puts his hat on his head and offers me his arm at the same time I grab hold. "Wait. Let me go leave a message for your husband."

Friendly yellow lights shine from cozy windows. Evening sounds, too faint to make out, fill the air. For once I don't feel as if I am missing out.

We are silent all the way to my and Willie's room. Once outside, I find myself reluctant to let him leave. We watch the clouds float by the moon.

"You'd like to paint that, wouldn't you?" I ask.

He shrugs. "Yes, but who would pay for that?"

"But if you took a nice wide brush and made a filthy circle . . ."

"A filthy circle. Why, it's certainly not that, Victorine. It's a reminder of day, a place holder, the way I sometimes paint something that I don't mean onto my canvas just to remind myself that something belongs there, even if I don't know what. The image will be so strange that I will know immediately that that is the spot that needs something new."

"Now that I'd like to see you paint."

I reach my face up and kiss his cheek.

I go inside, peeking out to watch him leave. It's several minutes before he does. Instead, he stands with his face upturned, staring, I presume, at the moon.

When he leaves, I hope he hasn't taken the moon with him.

I watch Willie in the ring, practicing with a hairy-chested Frenchman. The man nearly brings up his leg again. When I ask Willie what he will do when he is too old to fight, he looks blankly at me.

"No. You cannot use the legs," Willie shouts. "That is not English boxing."

When the boxer has been felled by Willie twice, the man leaves the ring, saying he is going home.

"Teach me," I ask. This sweat, the ugly pain of it all. Knowing you are going to be attacked and that you will get the chance to reciprocate.

"Lace up," he says, tossing me a pair of gloves.

The gloves are thin leather affairs, and I want to pull the prophylactic clothing off, but Willie shakes his head, so I keep them on.

I step into the ring, surprised at its hollow-floored feeling, noting its similarity to a display window. Men are exhibited then, too, just in a different way.

I want to be seen in every possible way, be remembered in every possible manner. I won't have children. How else am I to be immortal?

The best way to be remembered is by remembering so vividly, so clearly, that others cannot ignore you. That's what my painting will do, as, yes, as Manet's does. I will paint with women's eyes. Surely we see differently than men do. I'd rather see with human eyes, but I'm not sure anyone has such unbiased sight.

"Raise your fists," Willie calls.

I crouch slightly as he does, then I circle him, hands ready.

He cuffs me lightly before I can even see his hands.

I swing my arm and hit him in the head.

"Use your fists, not your arm," he says, touching his head lightly.

He sneaks in another punch.

"Dammit." My vision wavers.

"If someone throws a punch or sneaks up on you, you have to be ready." He sounds serious, and I want to laugh, because he's never serious. Yet we have to be. The Salon has lasted weeks. Mercifully, it is concluding, but I cannot say when the public's outrage will still.

I throw myself at him and pound away all of the rage at *Olympia*, at life, at death. When I am finished, my heart beats quickly and my chest rises and falls.

I run to him and kiss him, and he attempts to pick me up.

"No. Here, in the ring." His willingness to please is highly appreciated, and he pleases me twice.

The moments when Eva and I are alone are like the beautiful pink, white, and gold tissue paper woven between chocolates in a box. When a cold keeps her away from her studio for a week, I realize I miss her. Only then does it occur to me that what we have is friendship, a kinship, for all her money and position. I wonder if she would agree.

I am delighted, then, to catch her at Manet's studio the following week. As always, we speak of art.

"Our parents," she says (and notably Jeanne is not with her), "believe we not only have the right to be educated, but that we have the obligation to be."

She dabs at a section of yellow on the dress sleeve she is painting.

"I should like to meet your progressively-minded parents." Indeed I should. I murmur to her that her paint is rather thick there, and just there, and she gently pulls at it with her brush.

"I think it comes in part from my mother being a pianist," she says.

Manet has returned. "Oh, is she? Suzanne is quite an accomplished one herself. Your mother must come over some evening. Perhaps the two could play a duet."

"It seems to me I heard that she was in your family's employ as your piano teacher some years ago, was she not, Manet?" I ask.

"That will do for today, thank you." He turns so quickly his heels snap on the floor.

"But I'm not here as a model today. I'm here conversing with Eva."

"Mademoiselle Gonzalès, however, is here as a pupil and as such needs to be left to her work." Why she continues to take lessons from the likes of him when she has her own studio is a mystery to me.

I want to hate Eva as much as I despise Suzanne, but when Eva looks over her shoulder at me with such apology, how can I?

I do, however, pull on both sides of the inside of my mouth with my fingers and wiggle my tongue, pretending to be Manet who is now lecturing her sonorously.

When she giggles, I turn promptly and walk out the door, narrowly avoiding the slipper Manet has tossed at me.

"*Ouah, ouah.*" I call back, as if I am a dog.

As I lie beside Willie that night, I imagine the dinner party Suzanne would put on for the Gonzalès family. Though I have never been to the Manets' home, I have met his sour mother a couple of times. She would be sure to be there, now that they have given up their flat to care for her. Or that is the tale. They moved in with her when Manet insisted on building that monstrosity of a monolith to himself during the World Exhibition. Rather than even attempt to have his work included, he made a huge exhibit hall just for his own work, nearly bankrupting not only him, but his mother as well.

His father hadn't been dead so very long. His two other brothers were of no effect in begging her not to give in. Why, by the time he asked for her help, rumor has it, the thing was half done. Alas, he lost most of his investment, as few came to see his work. Better had he rented out a gallery than build his own semi-permanent one. I visited it but had little else to say. His face said by then that he knew what a mistake he had made.

I toss and turn; Willie puts his arm over me, shushes me as if I am a fussy child. I get up and pace.

Suzanne would make Manet's company a feast. No, she would not. She has help who would. Maman Manet would, no doubt, tell her exactly what to order at the butcher's. What does a Dutch piano teacher know of dinner parties?

I give up on sleep and pace, staring out the window finally at what I can see of the stars. There would sit Manet in all of his glory, surrounded by all three of the women who adore him, no doubt quickly making a conquest of Eva's poor mother who is closer to his age than Eva.

There would sit his mother, literally the goddaughter to the crown prince of Sweden, feeling as if she were royalty herself.

I can't find a single star, so I slide outdoors quietly, stopping only long enough to slip on my shoes. Then, disgusted at my weakness, I tug them off and throw them in a corner.

The streets are dusty, unyielding.

My nightdress is thin, but it is quite late—or early. I stretch my arms as high as I can.

Suzanne was nothing more than a hired woman in their house, one who, rumor has it, won at least the loins of her worthy charge, if not his heart. Now she sits as his wife, having no clue of how that is done. She would give the guests the vilest of drink, the commonest of treats and think herself doing them a service. She would lend no worthwhile conversation and would misunderstand half of what was said by others.

Arms wrap a blanket about me.

"Come inside; you're sleepwalking."

I beat against Willie's arms and I cry. "No, no, no," but he insists and so I am back inside the cell that threatens to suffocate my dreams and he makes me take a drink but it's not water at all and it burns and I don't even ask what it is, just hold out my glass for more and he gives it and then he leads me back to the bed and there he holds me and too, too soon he is asleep and I am left wondering why, oh why no matter how I try I cannot seem to be what I know I can, must be. As surely as I know I'm a woman, I know I'm a painter. There must be a way. I question the sun as to how I might become one when it rises, but it tells me its magnificence is enough for the day. I pretend to believe it.

Bazille comes more often to Manet's.

"Here is your beau," Manet says to me, spying him out the window. The pair of painters stands before their canvases, brushes launched. He cocks his thumb through the wooden palette, but Eva holds hers as if she cradles a kitten. She has absolutely no idea of who she is apart from her sister, but other than that, she's quite the woman. It's too bad the sisters are root bound. One only need marry off either of the sisters to see them bloom, strong flowers.

"My husband won't thank you for saying so," I answer.

Eva grins. "Nonetheless, Édouard is right. See how he straightens his tie in the street, how he combs his hair."

"He's a lovely boy but I think I will keep Willie, thank you very much."

Manet's sleeves are rolled, and he asks me to open a window.

Bazille greets us all formally, saving me for last. He sits upon the plump sofa beside me and we watch the two work. I have been called in because Manet has not decided what he is doing today. I am more or less to be always on call, he says, unless Stevens is using me. I get paid more, of course, if I stay to actually be painted, but most days after an hour or so he tells me I may go.

This happens increasingly often.

"And what are you currently painting, Bazille?" I ask the uncomfortable-looking youth.

"Why do you never call me Frédéric?"

I hesitate. Manet and Eva trade amused glances; I glare at them.

"Frédéric it is, then."

He is a wealthy man, quite generous with his painter friends. Of course as with most of the painters his wealth comes from his family and not from his own hands.

Eva rolls her eyes and makes a noise. I make as if to throttle her behind Bazille's back.

"As to your question, I'm painting my family."

Look this way while I capture the light on your face, Louise. Is the sun in your eyes, Louise? My father was the only one who called me Louise, my middle name. I asked him about it once, and he hesitated before telling me that Louise had been an old friend of my mother's. "Don't tell her I said that."

"And do you often paint your family?" I ask Bazille.

He shrugs, rolls his hat in his hands, staring at them, then up at me. "A bit."

"It's been my experience that families painting one another can be a bad business."

Manet laughs. "I paint my family all the time."

"Especially Léon," I say. As if any of us have forgotten that Léon both is and is not considered Manet's actual "family."

"You know, I don't think I will need you this afternoon after all," Manet says.

"Banished again?" I ask. He hates it when I say things he doesn't want said, no matter how true.

"But Édouard, Victorine and I were going to have a walk at lunch today," Eva says.

"What would your mother say if she knew you were out with a, with Victorine?" he asks.

Bazille stands to his feet. "Manet, explain yourself."

I put a hand on Bazille's arm. "It's quite all right, Frédéric. Don't you see— this frees me up so that you can paint me this afternoon."

He flushes and his eyes flutter.

"That is, if you want to."

"Of course. I've been wondering how to ask."

"Tomorrow morning, Victorine?" Manet asks, an apology in his goddamned voice again.

Every part of me wants to curse him like the cur he is, but I will just have to repent later. I don't kid myself: I am in service to his painting.

"If Bazille, that is, Frédéric, does not require me, then I will be here." I will make sure Bazille does not require me, but I don't tell either of them that.

As I leave, I hear Eva scold Manet: "She's a model, not a. . ." but then Bazille says something and I cannot hear the rest. He storms out and joins me.

Manet, of all people, knows what I am and what I am not.

Thankfully, so do I.

Fuck Manet. And fuck Bazille. That afternoon, I do. Alas, he never gets around to painting me.

Bazille haunts Manet's studio, and we all pretend it is Jeanne he is here to see. When she is not here, we tease him and tell him he will have to come back another time. He is kind but so naïve that I fear to talk with him, afraid he will take to heart something I say that he shouldn't.

I wear the yellow dress the next day because Stevens is supposed to come to the studio, and I want to thank him. I cannot thank him aloud, but my wearing it will be thanks enough. It is Bazille who shows, however, and not Stevens. He hands me a tulip that he "happened upon."

"We spoke of tulips once," he says.

"We did?"

His crestfallen face makes me giggle and I think he then suspects that I remember very well our discussion. Which I do.

Manet says he is not going to paint me, and I prepare myself to leave, but Bazille asks me to stay.

"I cannot."

"Just until lunch," he says. "I will pay what Manet would have."

"There's a name for such women, Bazille, and though I am a model, I am not that," I fume and turn to leave. His lovemaking that one time was so reverential that I felt filthy. I made it abundantly clear that it would not happen again. I tell myself that is reason enough not to tell Willie.

Manet laughs.

Eva smiles at me, but she has said little since the day before. I long to pull her aside and see what it is that keeps her to herself, so I make up my mind to stay, but not for Bazille.

I ask, "Eva, what are you painting today?"

She and Manet, side by side, paint a platter of fruit.

"Shade it so," he says, forcing her to see the black line about his apple.

Her brush follows his command, and yet it does not. Somehow the apple is an oval instead of a circle, and I giggle.

Her eyes flash and she hands me her brush. I shrug and take it, stand before the canvas, and paint another circle, this one perfectly round.

"You must see it on the canvas before you paint it. It's already there, just waiting to be observed," I say.

Manet stills his brush. "*Mon Dieu*," he says, waving the implement in his hand.

The truth of what I have said echoes within. But I only know bits and pieces. I have merely the canvas of my mind and the bristles of thought that flow in and out.

Bazille stands beside me. "No, Manet, she has something."

"Mere thought. How can one teach such a concept? It sounds intriguing, Bazille, but it does no earthly good."

"Don't you see what you are going to paint first?" Bazille asks.

Manet raises his palette and lowers it repeatedly as he speaks: "I may see a bit, but if I were to see the whole thing, then what would be the point of painting at all? Where the discovery?"

"You don't believe, then, that the painting already exists and that you are merely calling it forth?" Bazille asks.

"I would be nothing more than a paintbrush if that were true," Manet says.

"He has a point," I say. "Perhaps the truth of it is more that I see the shape right before I put it there, and my eye casts that image onto the canvas just where it ought to go. But the truth is, I believe it is there and I only need transcribe it."

Manet nods, seems disgusted that we have even had this conversation.

"I like what you said first best," Bazille says softly. Almost I think I feel a hand on my hair. I choose to believe I do not.

We group about Eva's painting and she steps away from it, hands up. "I just paint," she says.

"Perhaps that is the best way after all," I say.

Every time it seems art becomes clear to me, it becomes just a bit murky. Which is why I adore it.

The bells chime. "Willie." When I am around art, I forget he even exists. But then I am in his dear presence, and all becomes focused again. He is food and warmth; he is comfort and hope. Art is necessity, but Willie is joy and vivid rushes of life.

"You bought a new dress," Willie says. "I like the color."

"Thank you." I spin. He catches me and holds me close, keeps me from falling.

"Coming tonight?" Willie asks.

Suddenly I am weary of art, weary of these pretentious painters, weary of trying to sound as if I am one of them. I am heartily glad that I am Willie's wife.

"I wouldn't miss it." I hope that other lot does, though.

ELEVEN

Le Sphinx Parisien

IN AUGUST of 1870, a rumor flits about the cafés and restaurants. It infects the streets: The Prussians are coming. Stores are quickly emptied of cheeses and loaves. The fashionable raid the department stores as if afraid they will have to do without their frippery. Store windows are constantly filled and emptied until only indifferent material drapes the mannequins.

Soon, however, the newspapers report that the Prussians have turned away, and we breathe easily. Of course we know the war is *out there*, the Prussian-Franco War, but what has that to do with Paris?

The young men, however, are spoiling for a fight. They seem disappointed. I must say, I am, too.

Willie says one evening that the men are beginning to leave his employ, joining the war. Some are venturing outside of Paris, some with the home guard. With war right on our doorstep, fewer people are coming to the matches. It's only a matter of time, he believes.

"I have been warned by more than one person that now is the time to leave. Victorine, we have to get out of here." Though I am twenty-six, I don't want to leave the city of my birth.

Surely he doesn't mean it. "Leave Paris? Why would I do that?"

The laundry is stiff from hanging about our room, but at least it's dry. I awkwardly fold a rough beige pillowcase and wonder why I haven't thought to at least embroider our initials on the pair we use. I do know how to wield a needle, and the stained ivory color would be much improved with a splash of silk thread.

"The boxers and audience are all about to get a taste of real fighting. There will be no one at the matches. We will have no money."

"I still model," I snap. We both know that's not enough.

I pull a sheet from the stretched rope that serves as our laundry line. The sheet is plain, its hem ragged. Had I noticed it before it would have been the matter of a few minute's work to fix it.

He reaches for an end of the sheet and helps me fold it.

"Everyone is trying to *get* to Paris. Why would I leave?"

"And why would I stay?"

I let go of the sheet, and it hangs from his hands before he finishes folding it crisply, far neater than I could have. He puts it carefully at the foot of the bed and I pat it.

This argument is one, I imagine, that we will tell our friends after the war, sitting around a table with absinthe.

"Willie, how did you get that sheet so square?" I ask, sheepishly handing him the tablecloth I have plucked from the line that looks as if I have pretty much just wadded it up instead of folding it. He takes it from me, and, in no time, it's neatly folded as well. I smile and put it in the trunk at the foot of our bed with the spare sheet and pillowcases.

My mother always says that even those who are poor ought to have nice tablecloths. That is something on which we can agree.

I have been able to convince Willie of many things, but I cannot convince him to stay. He pleads with me to leave with him.

His packing doesn't take long. He never cared for things.

I cannot leave Paris, I cannot. Art, my parents.

"If I could, Willie."

"But you can."

I put my forehead up against his. My throat will not let me say anything more.

He briskly hands his box to the porter, turns, and kisses me.

"I'll be back after the war," he says. "They'll be ready for some entertainment then."

As he leaves, it comes to me with the chug of the train; I chase it as he puts down the window. I yell: "I love you, Willie. I love you."

"Yes, you do," he says, patting the window frame.

Trains that leave also return. Surely the war won't last long. He is not wrong to leave. I am not wrong to stay.

When Willie sends money, I toss it aside and read his letters over and over.

Funny, although I knew he had parents and a younger sister, Annabelle, they never seemed real to me until he began writing about them. Every time he writes he asks for updates on the war, on whether or not Paris is suffering. I believe perhaps he cares for her a bit more than he pretends. He comes to life differently to me on paper.

"We are still waiting," I write. "Though there is talk of building a barricade." Committing my thoughts and feelings to paper disconcerts me, and not for the first time I regret giving up my schooling: I have to ask those about me more than once how to spell a word whenever I do write, though I try to ask different people each time so they won't realize how pitiful my spelling really is.

Besides bringing Willie too vividly to mind, the ink on paper (however plain the sheets) reminds me of the mystery of how paint transforms canvas. The two acts are not dissimilar. On a blank piece, one creates worlds. Both use liquid to transform a solid to something spiritual. That is true transubstantiation, I would argue to Father Vigee, the priest at the church my mother used to take me to, if he would listen.

In September, the rumors of war in Paris become fact as the Prussians slowly surround us. On September nineteenth, our city is fully encircled. French soldiers in red and blue flood every public place. The Bois de Boulogne holds seas of sheep and cattle, so many I cannot count them, to feed the military. The newspaper says there are tens of thousands there. The army troops in their red *kepis* paired with red trousers and the People's Army in blue, they of the *Garde nationale*, the *Garde mobile*, number nearly as many as they cluster about the Arc de Triomphe and line the Champs-Élysées.

At first, our streets are like a nightly festival. The weather is mild, and we stroll with pleasure, admiring the fine-looking soldiers in uniform and the strong wall surrounding our city.

In no time, it seems, we are told that the soldiers suffer from exhaustion and hunger. I sneak as close to the fence as I can, and I climb until my upper half hangs over. Below, I see a guard. It's nearly dark, so I can't see clearly if it is one of ours or theirs. Just in case, I fling the cloth bag so that it lands just beyond the man. Puzzled, he looks up immediately. I wave, and he frowns as he bends to retrieve it, opens it to reveal the round of *pain bis*. Then he smiles and bows. "Merci," he mouths, and then he motions for me to get down. I don't, not immediately. Instead, I survey what there is to see, things I can see better from atop one of our buildings and yet cannot get a true sense of: tents and cots, empty crates, cannons. I take in the leaves slowly changing color beyond the city, inhale deeply though they have not yet begun smelling of decay, and I wonder if I will be allowed to walk among them this year. Will we be able to go to the orchards and choose our own fruit? Just how long will this war last?

I imagine I can see London from here and that with a bit more of a tip of my torso, I might topple over and go to Willie. Of course I do not, would not. I have had my chance.

I enjoy writing of my love for him, saying things I would be too embarrassed to say in person. This love is a third person in our relationship, and we nourish it as if it were a child.

Again, the French guard motions for me to get down and reluctantly I do. But I am back the next night, and the next, with bread or fruit, anything I can afford to give. Most times, he is the one on duty and he allows me to peer over the fence towards Willie.

Who would have dreamed so many cannons existed in our city? The cacophony seems constant. I do not know where they get the cannonballs and powder for them, but it seems that day and night our conversations are punctuated with the whistles of war as we try to scare away the Prussians. There has not been firing upon our city, not yet. Rumor has it that they want to starve us out, rather than shell us. Surely they would not dare harm Paris. The world is watching.

The newspapers tell us not to worry, that with such fine weather and the high walls surrounding us, not to mention the circle of sixteen fortresses, Paris is safe.

Except for my missing Willie, the first weeks of the war continue pleasantly. For the most part, people are helpful and friendly, save to the Germans who have done the dirty, underpaid jobs we have no desire to do: housekeeping, nursing, building our fires. They have been mistreated, jailed, sometimes even shot. The American Ambassador, Elihu Washburne, has tried to get as many to safety as possible. Those he couldn't he cares for; a hundred of them, it's said, he shelters and feeds himself.

When my mother learns of this, she makes the Germans hats for just the price of the material. My father and I both take her to task for this, because they can ill afford it, but she stubbornly refuses to cease. "These people are not responsible for what their country is doing. Why should they suffer for decisions they have not made? They have lived peaceably among us all of their lives. At any rate," she says as she fits together scraps, "Why should they have cold heads? And if I don't make these, who knows what horrible relief hats will be dreamed up by women's societies? Best we ward off that ugliness now."

The war means she has allowed me to visit them in their home again. I guess I have one thing to thank it for.

I drink my tea, not wanting her to see that I remember how she talked about the stately and handsome American when he gave a speech last year, how she talked of his great swoop of hair that gesticulated when he spoke. I'm sure the Germans will thank her for her beautiful hats, whatever the reason she makes them.

"How can I help?" I ask with a heavy sigh, praying I am not beginning something I will regret.

She hands me a box full of hats. "Deliver these." I stroke one topped with pink feathers. "You're giving those away?" She had been so proud of finding them on one of her rare flea market trips; they have remained wrapped in the tissue paper in which she brought them home. My mother's generosity towards those outside of our home has always been laudable.

"Probably best I deliver them myself," she snaps, and I smile again to think of her devotion to handsomeness.

When my birthday comes in just a few weeks, I am surprised to receive the pink-topped hat from my mother, and I find it suits my complexion so nicely that I deign to wear it, even if the season for feathers has passed and despite my distaste for things that keep my head and face from the joys of the elements. It will not take much moisture to bedraggle the feathers, though, and so I find myself covering it with a scarf at even a whisper of rain until I arrive at my destination, which makes those about me laugh and me, too.

❖

As we so love to do, we French build barricades with old furniture, dead tree limbs, stained mattresses, wagon wheels, three-legged chairs, warped window shutters and store doors. Within no time, piles clutter the street, carted in by old women, by barefooted children, by men too ancient to wield guns. It does not seem to occur to us that a single spark could quickly eliminate this false comfort. Eventually, the police come and make those about move the material out of the streets, and the crowds protest because their participation has been cut short.

Sundays find Parisians promenading as usual. Slowly, what previously made up our lives begins to fade, even as we try holding onto what was. First, it is the luxuries that go; we don't mind giving up having every gaslight lit. They light every other, and then it becomes every sixth. People cannot find enough wood to heat and take to stripping the streets of trees at night. Buildings are ransacked of all usable wood. The poor burn their furniture in the extreme cold. Those of us with gas in our homes have it no longer. Water is rationed, provided only from eight until eleven each day. We are asked to limit our baths, something I feel our city cannot afford. I take to carrying my *mouchoir* and holding it to my mouth.

I watch one night as a young woman takes an ax to a small tree outside my window. The tree, one which sometimes lodges sparrows, doesn't yield easily. Without putting on my shoes, I run outdoors. "Don't," I beg, but she can't anyway. The ax glances off. She collapses at the foot of the tree, sobbing. The tree is deeply gashed.

I hold her lantern. "Stand back," I say.

She scoots away.

"Hold this."

By the light she holds I am able to fell the tree by hacking into its wound. When it lands, I throw the ax from me and go inside. It's a small enough tree— she can drag it home. I wish a cloud would hide the newly naked space, but the moon shines anyway.

This is the first act that really reveals to me how pervasive the war is. The next morning I open my eyes, walk outdoors, and behold the lonely, treeless space. I now see what I had not upon the streets: The thin and gray people hunched over as if to defend themselves from the cold, the deprivation. The wagons full of our wounded brought into the city and deposited into the hospitals.

◈

Our formerly small room grows in Willie's absence. At night, I sleep with a shirt of his that I hid under my pillow before he left. It's one he wore in the ring.

A red hair clings to his pillow, and I wrap it in tissue and fold it into my journal, which is filling rapidly.

I sketch Willie in my journal, too, but I find myself wondering whether or not his lips really were so large or if my love for him has exaggerated their desirability. I regret that I have no photos of him. The next letter I write, I ask him to have one made for me.

Often, no mail gets in for long stretches at a time now. And though I am grateful to see his blotted handwriting, his letters do not indicate that he understands how changed I am by his absence, by my discovery of what that means to me. He is well, missing me, he says, and I find myself hating the pale word *missing*. I want to hear that he longs for me, that he can't eat, can't sleep. Instead, he says he fights regularly and is trying to learn new techniques to bring back to France once the war is over.

Willie mentions no women, and I do not ask.

Still, when I imagine him touching one of those pale-skinned English women in their pastel dresses, I ache just a bit. I want him to touch me, not touch one of them with their voices stuck up their noses.

Missing someone is like being the worst kind of homesick.

When I don't hear from him for a week, I don't worry. The war.

The second week, I become concerned. The mail is unpredictable, we all tell one another as we wait.

I still sit, and as I model for Stevens one afternoon, I know I am not being anything more than a body. Watching Stevens wrinkle his brow, he feels something is off, too.

Why did it take the war for me to realize that love, my love for Willie, can be a wonderful accompaniment to art?

I'm at the Guerbois when my father pokes his head in and enters solemnly when he sees me. He stands at the door.

"What is it?" I ask as I cross to him.

"Let's sit down," he says. I lead him to a table off to the side. A group of men shoot a game of billiards at the back of the room.

He wipes his brow and takes something from his pocket, hands a crumpled envelope to me.

"They tried to take it to your rooms, but since you weren't there, they brought it to my shop."

Maybe I won't open the soiled thing. I don't recognize the handwriting. It could be anything, anything at all.

But it's not.

The letter, from Willie's mother, tells me that Willie has died in the ring breaking up a particularly ugly fight. It wasn't even his bout.

Numbness more profound than a night of drinking absinthe keeps me upright as I shake the envelope, hoping something besides this news falls out, and it does: a wrinkled photo of Willie.

I collapse upon my father when I see Willie's smile.

Père hands me a drink, but I refuse until his shaking hand holds it up to my mouth, his other hand holding the back of my head steady the way he did when I was ill as a child. I gulp the whisky and hand him the letter, though he's already guessed most of it. The bartender brings over another.

My father holds my hand awkwardly, and I crush his with mine.

What can be worse than a death when there's nothing to be done for or about it? No details to attend to, no service.

I'm crying, dammit, in front of everyone and I beg for another drink and someone brings it, but is it Bazille? I think so, and oh God, thank God Willie will never know about that. Slowly my mind loosens with the drink.

My father offers to take me home, but I refuse. To be alone in that space that has become so small, to be made to confront his pillow and his scent, which will die its own slow death, tormenting me until it does and yet leaving me longing for it when it is gone, seems quite impossible.

"You could pull together his friends, his boxers, and have a memorial," my father says. His eyes are so large and earnest that I laugh.

He still holds my hand and I want to throw it off but he's all I have.

"They are all safely away at war."

A concerned contingent about our table passes the letter around. Silence falls.

"A round," calls Manet, "In Willie's honor."

I will not cry again; I cannot.

"All he wanted was to fight," Manet says, and I glance sharply at him. How has he known my secret fear? That Willie loved boxing more than me. I do cry now, making the sound of a wounded bird.

"He *had* to fight," I manage to gasp as my father pats me on the back. I twist my shoulders. "Boxing was his art."

Inevitably, this turns us back to art, though slowly, or so it seems to me as my head tries to grasp the news.

"Indeed, I agree," Manet says to something my father has said about David.

As my father makes to leave well into the night, Manet claps him on his shoulder and asks him to come again. My father's happiness comes at my cost. Again. I insist on stumbling my own way home, though when I look back once or twice, I see someone in the shadows.

The streets are dusty and uncared for. They are like a widow in her bed, I think, as I wake long enough to peek out the window for the first time in weeks, it seems. Without the villagers who used to come inside the city and care for the streets, papers and bottles litter our city. I close the curtain and hide back under the covers, but someone is at my door.

It is Stevens. I tie the belt to my robe, try to tame my hair, and quickly give up.

"I haven't seen you in quite some time," he says gently as I let him in. I have taken to sleeping late, not eating much. There's nothing outdoors but war and death anyway.

My father has come to see me just twice; my mother, not at all. I have depleted my bit of art school money to survive once again. I don't care. I can't.

"You shouldn't be here."

He scoffs. "My friends would be delighted to have a reason to gossip right now."

"But your wife . . ."

"I have sent her and the children to Dieppe for safety. I hear Gonzalès has also decamped there."

"Yes. So she said, but I haven't heard from her since."

"I'm sure she will write soon." He sinks into a chair without asking.

"You seem tired, Stevens. Are you quite all right?"

A cannon sounds and he starts. "I think we're all rather tired just now, aren't we?" His fingers pluck at the arms of the chair.

He puts his hands on his knees and rubs his pants. "Victorine, I need a model and I was wondering if you would be willing to sit for me?"

This is the first I've been asked since Willie's death. Manet has made himself scarce, although the war surely has as much to do with it as his squeamishness at my loss. I do not despise him for this weakness, although I am hurt.

I want to say no, but Stevens looks unwell, and then there's the meager money in my purse.

He startles whenever a gun sounds—which is constantly. Still, the idea of getting up every day, going about my life as if Willie can. . . .

"The war has given me an idea, and I think you would be perfect for it," he says wearily.

The bombing continues, although we can see people still walking outside as if off for a day of shopping.

"That is, I was hoping to work at all hours of the night—what I mean to say is, is it possible you could move to a place closer to my studio?"

Though I am tired, his meaning begins to sink in. "I'm afraid I wouldn't be able to afford a place in that part of town." Am I really negotiating for what I think I am? I must consider. I hunt for my cigarette case.

"I would be willing to take care of your rent in return for your cooperation."

"My cooperation?" I light a cigarette, stalling.

"I could protect you there, now that you are—and I am so sorry that you are—a widow."

"Stevens, are you trying to say that you are lonely without your wife?"

His hands move from his knees and cross themselves on his stomach.

"This war. . ." his hands busy themselves touching each other. "Perhaps I am. I thought maybe you might be, too."

I smoke purposefully. "I believe I am to sit for Manet soon." I have only hopes of that, or less than that, a wish.

Stevens shakes his head. "I've spoken with him. He says I may have you as long as I like."

"But I owe him a painting. We started one before Willie, and he . . ." I struggle.

"It's okay; I gave him my finest bottle of wine for this favor. He said he will let me know if he really needs you."

For a moment my anger sparks at his presumption, but it gives way to desperation. Though I have not often made it out of this bed, I have imagined that if anything, art will resurrect me. Art with Manet.

"He says he is busy with Morisot."

"Is he?" My eyes feel like flames. "Then I accept."

So I move into a beautiful apartment provided by Stevens, and I quit sitting for Manet, who has sold me for a bottle of wine. Now my mother may make all of the accusations she wants, for they are true, I suppose. What does it matter who I live with, who I give my body to? There is no one I want to share it with, not now, and so anyone will do. I want to hate Manet. I imagine storming into his studio and giving him hell, but the war gives us all hell before I ever work up the energy.

The apartment is on the fourth floor of the building, but it has gloriously large windows. Light from them begins to penetrate my soul when I move my laughably meager belongings into it. We rent it entirely furnished, which suits me. When it is time to leave, I will not have to deal with the lot.

Two large bedrooms show me again how thoughtful Stevens is: He knows as well as I do that men and women seldom want to sleep in the same bed after making love. Except with Willie. When it came to him, beds were never small enough for me.

From the parlor to the bedrooms, each is trimmed with ornately scrolled woodwork. The herringbone floors gleam throughout, except where oriental rugs cover them. The walls are all suitably white. Though I know my mother would disapprove, I wish I could at least show her and my father this grand place. Perhaps she'd think twice about how she sees me.

I listen dully as the men talk of the war at cafés, which close at nine and sometimes randomly as the government insists. I almost don't care what happens to this city now. Too late I know there is, no, was, something I loved more than it. But more than art?

Our government at the beginning of the war was overthrown, that I knew, by the Republic. But then an outcry grew over them. Unrest from within and without. I don't care to follow it, though I know I should. The artists argue, but I don't take a side. I just want this fall that dares become winter over. I have no idea what I have asked.

◇

Though some artists—Manet, Bazille, Renoir and Degas—have joined the cause, of course Alfred Stevens, a Belgian, is not expected to fight. Still he joins the *Garde nationale*, and I am proud of him and a little relieved to have him out from under my feet some.

When Alfred is not on duty, he paints. At first, I feel guilty in front of the canvas, as if I have robbed Willie of his life by sending him away and staying for something as insubstantial as this. And yet it feels right, posing. I begin to awaken as I ask my body to cooperate with Alfred's eyes.

He asks me to pose in the bath; I say I don't mind, not thinking about all of the hours I will actually end up spending in the tub. There is nothing erotic about water-pruned skin.

The tub is large by Parisian standards, but I can't stretch my legs out in its cold zinc. He asks me to wear my underclothes in the water, and to hold two roses.

"You are a young woman who is spending an afternoon in the tub, reading, dreaming. . . ."

"Why am I in my clothes?" I ask.

He sputters. "Haven't you had enough of nudity?"

"A real woman bathing wouldn't wear clothes."

He looks startled. "No, but did you like how they treated you when Manet painted you?"

"Of course not." But Stevens has painted me partially nude as well.

I don't roll my eyes outwardly at his silence. We both know he will not insult Manet's work. We also both know that Alfred's nude of me is sweet.

He makes my hair well-coiffed, and naturally I would not get it wet during the bath if I were a lady. I wear jewelry—bracelets, a ring. In the soap dish is a watch to remind me of the time. Am I eager for the coming appointment or am I dreading it?

The faucet is swan shaped.

He keeps shrinking the box or cage for a woman until now he shows it as a tub. His commentary in painting is unending, but perhaps unnoticed because of the sweet expression he asks me to wear. All around me is luxury; from the plush white dressing gown my book rests on to the faux-marbled walls. My hands are still reverent about this wealth.

After hours of posing, I reach for Alfred's hand so he can pull me from the tub, and instead I pull him in. He laughs as he is half in, half out of the tub. He gets all the way in and scrunches his knees to face me. "This is one small tub," he says. "And the water is not warm."

"It's *cold*." I lean forward and kiss him, but it's a kiss that comes from without me.

I stand leisurely and let the water trickle down my body. As the sound slows, I begin stripping my garments one by one. When my breasts are bare, I rub them dry with the fluffy white towel before lowering it gradually to my belly, between my legs. I thrust my head upwards as I dry.

I put my leg on the side of the tub and stroke it briskly with the towel. Then I turn and dry my back with a back-and-forth motion, allowing the towel to drop below my back and onto my hips before rubbing it in circles.

Climbing out of the tub, I look at him. He is breathing heavily.

I help him from the tub, and he undresses clumsily. I dry him slowly and thoroughly, and then bring him into the bedroom with me.

Alfred's moves are sweet and simple, and I feel as if having me is the equivalent of communion wine to him, when I like to think of myself as a heady merlot.

"You make love to me as if you are a man who loves his wife." Willie used to cup my head and look into my eyes. He would pause in the middle of making love and hug me as if delighted I were with him.

Alfred stops on top of me and dismounts. After he catches his breath, he looks at me more crossly than he ever has. "I do love my wife."

I light a cigarette. "Fine. Of course you should love your wife, but don't make love to me as if you do. You know how you made me look dreamy in the tub and as if being in cold water for hours was exactly where I wanted to be? Well, what I'm going to need from you is a little pretending. Pretend that you are with your lover, for God's sake, a woman you don't get to see every day, and you have been waiting for her. Your loins are bursting with longing, and you can't wait to touch her."

He looks hurt, almost. "Do women care about sex?" he asks.

I burst out laughing, and then I apologize. "Please, I'm sorry. Do I act as if I am a woman who merely tolerates sex?"

"My wife doesn't seem to care for it."

I drag on the cigarette. "See, that's where you're going wrong with your painting. You are painting women that make women think they should be like the women in the painting. If I were alone in a warm bath with a rose, I think I'd be tempted to see how the rose felt on . . . shall we say . . . certain parts of my lower anatomy."

He turns his head from me.

"It doesn't make me less of a decent woman, Alfred. Your wife probably would like sex if she let herself. If."

He flinches.

"Where's my nightgown?" I ask, casually getting to my feet.

The city begins casting cannon. The government doesn't pay for it—wealthy individuals do. A great beautiful cannon named Josephine becomes a city favorite. Some of them aren't even set off but are more for the feeling of protection having them brings.

Alfred and I go to Josephine's christening. The joy on these ill, gaunt, faces is luminous, and I long to paint the waning sunlight shining on them, on the cannon.

Dozens of Prussian shells come in daily, big black orbs that make a whistling sound before finding a target or, more frequently, not. They are still far enough outside that their guns are more nuisances than not. But each day they get closer.

Like a belt is this wall around our city, ever tightening. There are parts of the city forbidden to civilians, so we take river "cruises" while the weather is still nice. Up and down the Seine we go, trying to see beyond our city, but while boys fish on the far shore, what we see further off just discourages: villages and fields obliterated of all trees and houses that might shelter the enemy. Our city is bursting with the families who ran inside from surrounding villages before the city was shut off.

I stand in the boat on our run up and down the river and look beyond, then down into the water that gets colder each day. How long could a woman survive if she were to fall in?

I catch Alfred looking over the side as well, and I can only hope the expression there isn't a twin of mine, but I fear it is. Perhaps art will save us both. We can only try.

◈

"I will paint you as Paris, as a sphinx," Alfred says listlessly.

He paints and we tisk over the deprivations that continue as the painting blooms: first meat rations, then the disappearance of horses from the streets. We don't say where they go; we all know.

The food is terrible—rat is now considered a delicacy, but we remain strong. We can endure this. Especially since we are told that wine and chocolate should remain plentiful regardless of the length of the war. For a price, of course.

"Gutter rabbit" becomes one of our city's favorites. I never tell Alfred it's really cat; I hope he doesn't know. I've never cared for cats, so it doesn't really bother me. It tastes faintly like goat, another meat with which I've only recently become acquainted.

Though Manet has enlisted, he is able to come by some evenings to see us, to bring us things he can get that we can't: today some cigarettes, an egg that makes me squeal with joy—one jeweler exhibits eggs in his window where once he had precious stones.

At first, I treated him coolly, but when he asked me quietly how Alfred was doing, I realized he had sacrificed me for Alfred's wellbeing, not because he didn't want to paint me.

When he mentions having seen Berthe earlier today, and that the woman had painted a lovely bouquet, I pick up the egg and drop it on the floor. The men continue talking. I stand and dance a jig in the yellow mess.

"One does wonder why one tries," Manet says to Alfred, looking at me.

"Indeed one does."

Manet sighs heavily. "I can only hope, old man, that she's worth the effort."

"Scarcely," says Alfred, and I dance faster.

I slip off my shoes and paint a sun with the toes of my left foot using the yolk.

Manet says he is not painting much except for quick watercolor splashes, but that he is drawing. It's all he has time for, he says. Others say much the same when I ask.

"And what has become of your paintings?" I ask Manet. Though the bombing takes lives, more importantly, it might spoil art.

"I have sent the most important ones to a friend's home in the country. Don't worry—they are quite safe."

"The most important?"

He smiles. "Indeed. Especially the controversial ones."

I relax then and drink more wine. The war is an ugly, ugly thing when it jeopardizes art.

Manet smokes a cigar with Alfred, and they talk of war strategy and things I do not care to hear about. His art is safe.

That evening when we go to bed Alfred asks me, "Don't you want to know where my art is?" He runs his fingers along my shoulder.

"Of course," I lie. Perhaps they will destroy it all. No. I don't really want that.

"Will you always think more of his work?" he asks. "You know others find my work charming."

"It is charming."

I can only hope he doesn't realize what scorn I feel for the word.

Alfred comes to me when he can, when he is not on watch, but I don't always know when to expect him. One such night I recline upon the pillows, allowing myself to enjoy the expertise of a woman I picked up at a bar when I hear a key in the lock. I stiffen but do not rise. When he comes into the bedroom, he exclaims and quickly turns to leave. After we are through, I dismiss the woman, see her out the door. Only then do I notice him sitting on the sofa.

"I wasn't expecting you," I say as I tie the sash on my dressing gown. I wonder if he heard my cries of pleasure and I hope that he did.

"We agreed this would not happen," he says stiffly.

"I agreed not to sleep with other men," I say.

He shakes his head. "Why on earth should you desire a woman?"

"Why on earth should I not? I have had plenty of you men," I say as I go into the bedroom, begin packing my things.

"Why isn't a man, why isn't *this* man, enough for you?" His mustache stays firm, but the rest of his face sags. His loneliness, his exhaustion from the war shows in everything from his wrinkled clothing to his just-going-on-too-long hair.

"Stevens, don't love me."

He comes to me and kisses me, takes the clothes from my hand, and leads me to the bed. I am sure he believes that the things he does to me (so tame, so calm) convince me that he is the only one for me. The dear, kind man.

"No one else is to get into this bed with you," he says firmly afterwards, taking my fist, kissing it.

I hesitate. If I agree to this, I will honor it.

"I am alone so many nights when you are on duty."

"Does nothing else please you?"

I glance at my guitar in the corner, at my neglected violin.

"You don't understand. The Arts stir up longings, they don't satisfy them."

He sighs, runs his hand through his thick hair, and exhales.

"I can't help my hungers."

"We all hunger. We eat and that is that."

"Hungers return." I turn from him, roll into a ball. I want a flannel night-gown and socks. I want a pile of covers, a mug of tea.

The more I feed my appetites, the more they increase.

"Fine. No women, either," I say.

"Tomorrow you shall have your shawl," he says.

And that is how I get it.

When he enters the apartment the next afternoon, he holds something behind his back. I lay down my violin, hoping he has not heard me play. After he brands me with a bad-breathed kiss, he holds out a brown paper parcel tied with string.

My pulse increases. If he has purchased an insignificant shawl, I will leave.

I open the package carefully, revealing thick cream tissue paper. I hesitate. I have never opened a gift so lavishly wrapped. Just outside of the tissue is a card advertising the store: *Hoschedé, Blément, and Co* in silver letters. One of the finest boutiques in Paris. It is true then that with enough money anything can still be had in Paris.s

"See what you think of it."

I pull back the crackly paper with one finger, rewarded by a flow of silk worthy in color of his painting. It cascades down my arm as I remove it from the package. It's light blue, with orange and gold flowers scattered about it. His love of Japonisme always shows itself. The shawl is the most elegant thing I have ever owned. I throw it on the chair and turn from him.

"You don't like it?"

"It's wonderful." Why is it that what I say I want is never what I really want?

"Bring it to the studio tomorrow?"

I pick it up, denying the thrill the material gives my rough fingers. The shawl is nothing more than another form of equity. It is not a declaration of his love. It is not a declaration of my worth. It is merely a bauble I asked for that he has found a way to capitalize on already.

He leaves the receipt on the table: twelve hundred francs, as much as the one he bought for his wife. If I returned the shawl and received the money, I could reclaim my independence. With a sum like that, more than a year's wages, I could do anything. Maybe I could even go to art school.

I run from the apartment, the shawl wrapped around my shoulders, barefooted, until I catch him.

"Thank you," I say. I want so badly to be able to tell him I love him as much I can see that he loves me. There is something comforting about his thick body, his broadness shielding my slightness. His weight anchors me.

If I could love a man besides Willie in that way, I would love him. My eyes say as much, and he kisses me tenderly before telling me to go indoors.

I sleep with the shawl that night, clinging to the silk, fearful of snagging it. I know now why women ask for gifts. It's not because they are greedy, but because they want tangible proof after their relationship is over, after their beauty has faded, that someone cared for them. That they were once worthy. I'm worthy without this shawl I wind so tightly around me, aren't I?

The next day at the studio Alfred hands me another package, similarly wrapped.

"No. You will ruin yourself."

"Not at all. Do you have any idea how much these paintings I am doing of you are selling for? Just remember that should you tire of me, I'd like these gifts back."

He means he would give them to his wife. I open the package with less ceremony, only to discover an ornate dressing gown of the same pattern as my shawl. "Alfred." It is all I can say. I pretend I have not understood him about returning the gifts. I also pretend that I have not heard that he is profiting by his artwork of me; I had thought I was his inspiration. Pretense is all we have sometimes.

I finger the material and shed my clothes before he even asks me to put it on. We break our rule of not making love in the studio as he lays me, wrapped in my dressing gown, on the rug covering the wooden floor. I am in love with my skin, with the whisper of this material. I begin to do things to him he usually does not allow, my head straying below his hips, he pushing my head away for only a minute before groaning acceptance. I am everything but the wearer of this dressing gown on the floor. I am vile Victorine, the coarse woman that Manet has painted as a courtesan.

I nibble at his shoulder, at his neck, as if I would consume him, as if I would warn him. He moans as I show him all of the things I know how to do, all of the things I have held back on, in our time together. Every kiss says, "Are you sure?"

I finish what I began. By his gasps I am fairly sure he has never had this done to him before, and that he likes it. I cannot raise my head to see his face.

After, I lie beside him for a time. His genteel self wrestles, his face contorts. Then he reaches for me, grabs me in a demanding way he has not before. He explores me. I submit as he does things that are decidedly ungentlemanly to me.

After he rests for a time, I know what he wants when he nudges me onto my side, and I rise and allow him to (so soon?) treat me from behind with the bitterness he really feels for me. His movements tell me that he despises the tasteful work he produces, that he is tired of the tasteful sex which is all he has allowed himself, on par with the elegant, boring meals served by his elegant, boring wife before the war.

After this, his painting changes too, and he is no longer kind in his portrayals of me. "It is not you I am trying to capture," he says. He admits I am his tool, and each painting catches something of me I did not know was there until I see it. Just as with Manet, if what he sees in me weren't there, try as he might, he would not be able to convey it, I am convinced.

The Siege produces cold, boring, frightening days and nights and little else.

When we are together (now it is most nights) Alfred feeds on me, uses me as his respectability and gentility fall away, revealing the need he has clothed so beautifully in wool trousers. I laugh secretly; I laugh openly.

"I do not love you," he tells me repeatedly as he ravishes me. His attempts at degradation are so amusing, and despite his efforts, so gentlemanly. His epithets are soft. Sometimes I shock him with filthy words.

Something more than respect but less than love is growing in me for him. At least this drives away his sadness and nervousness. It drives away my desire to leap into the river.

Every night for a week I wrap myself in the shawl. It's mine, all mine. But too soon I don't care, and I wrap it back in its tissue and bury it in my trunk.

Nearly every day he brings me trinkets: jewelry, jade figurines, chocolates, bottles of wine. There's nothing I want that he won't give me, and yet the more I get, the less I want any of it. He paints me as if I am just something else he has bought, and damn me but now it's true.

TWELVE

Like a Book

AS I VENT to Manet on one of the rare days he is at his studio, off from guarding the city for a day, he laughs at me, insisting on painting me if I am going to yell and complain for so very long. This is his way of painting me after our latest rift without appearing to give way. We are never through, Manet, never. Let the Evas and the Morisots come and go, Victorine and Manet are the pairing that will be most remembered.

I don't mention Alfred's Judas wine to him, but I come upon the bottle I know to be Alfred's favorite indulgence secreted on one of Manet's upper shelves; I open it and pour glass after glass, guarding the bottle until it is empty. Manet only rolls his eyes.

"I will never give my shawl to that brood mare." I slur.

He cackles at me. "My dear, every time I think it is impossible for you to stoop lower, you manage it."

"What do you mean?" I ask, breaking my placid expression to frown.

"When you took up with Stevens, I thought that admirable, because I knew you would break him from his petulant classical painting. Then you insisted on being given that shawl that is being spoken about by everyone—Stevens cannot hold his tongue after four drinks. He says he bought it at the very shop for the very same price of the one he gave his wife for a wedding present. No man buys a woman something so valuable, so comparable to what he has given his wife without it meaning, shall we say it, love?"

I lower the book he is painting me reading.

"He can't."

"He does," Manet laughs.

He gestures that I am to pick up the book again.

I stand, furious.

Manet moves his lips, then picks up his brush, begins (I know the movement of his hand even if I can't see him) pooling color in areas to show how shapes affect meaning. Even I can see that, though so many critics cannot. I love how he floods the planes, instead of stroking them into existence. I suspect that's how God created us, in bold flashes rather than carefully considered moves. Why else would we all be so flawed?

Without noticing that I do, I sit back down. I nearly cross myself until I remember that my mother is Catholic, and as long as she is, I have no desire to be. Well, one can't have all of life's comforts.

"I think your brush wants cleaning," I say as I notice during a break that the black appears smudgy-brown.

"It's perfectly fine," he says.

Manet keeps looking at the clock. When Morisot sweeps in, I know why he's been so keen on the time. Though she tries to be polite, clearly, she is not pleased that I am here. Neither am I. I don't want to see how the two of them try not to look at one another in that way, how Manet picks up and puts down his paintbrush nervously half a dozen times. The way she sits with such a straight back on the sofa, pretending to enjoy the portrait he is painting of me.

"What book is she reading?" Morisot asks politely.

"I am reading Zola, of course."

Morisot tilts her head and smiles at Manet. "When will you finish this? The blacks are a bit muddied, are they not?"

"Yes, I believe my brush is dirty." He smiles. "This can wait. I was just painting while we talked."

"You're not holding the book correctly," she scoffs at me. "Do you even enjoy reading?"

I slam the book shut and rise. "Who are you, my schoolteacher?" I stand before her, my hands in fists, longing to punch her snooty face.

"My dear Victorine . . ." she says.

"Meurent."

"Pardon?"

"You might suffer them to call you by your first name while the men call one another by their last, but if you've noticed, I do not. If you want to be equal with them, you must respect yourself, demand to be treated as they treat one another."

She laughs. "If I allow them to call me by my last name, I lose that extra benefit that they give. And I forgot: You're actually called *Crevette*, are you not?" she asks, rising and using her greater height to look down on me.

I frown. "And what is that benefit of which you speak?" My hands loosen, though, as I listen.

"If you do not appreciate being a woman, I do." She glances at my carelessly worn clothing, my barely respectable hair.

"I'd rather be appreciated for being a human than for being a woman. You will never be fully appreciated as an artist until the men see you as one of them."

Manet steps smoothly between us. "Is that how you see it, that we don't see you as an artist because you are a woman? But my dear, we don't see you as an artist because you are a model. If you created art, we would accept you."

"Is that so?"

He runs his hand along his struggling hairline.

When Manet's brother, Eugène, wanders in seeming at loose ends, I find a way to get him and Morisot to talk, hoping I can speak to Manet alone. Instead, I watch the pair. The man loves art but does not paint—I've spoken of it with him often at the makeshift hospital where I volunteer three days a week, where he appears, a roaming ghost. Soon Morisot is explaining her latest to him, the one she is now painting. She shows him the paint that has found its way onto her glove.

"My mother despairs of my ever keeping a clean glove," she says.

"Better a soiled glove and a good painting than the other way around," Eugène says.

Morisot beams. "Well said."

She seems easier with him than with Manet, and a plot worthy of Zola hatches in the back of my mind.

"I serve at one of the war hospitals downtown, Mlle. Morisot. I was wondering if you'd care to join me some time?" I ask. "M. Eugène Manet often finds himself there," I say.

Now that she has Eugène to focus on, she is less frosty with me. "I've been meaning to find something to do besides sit around with my sister. The war makes me feel so dull that I don't really want to paint some days. I'd be happy to help out."

"They could certainly use you there," Eugène says.

Though I go to the hospital nearly every day, Morisot's attendance is spotty. She gets woozy at the sight of blood, but she is the first one to lend a hand in surgery. I suspect she is thinking of painting a record of them, though no matter how determinedly she goes in, she comes out nearly bowed with nausea. Still, the soldiers like her.

Eugène has managed to find even more reasons to be sent to this particular hospital. Suddenly he has urgent messages and just-located supplies to bring on the days she is there. It becomes clear to me that my plan has a chance, a real chance, if Manet will allow it. Édouard, that is. I nearly hear a great spark.

The hospital smells, Morisot says. It does, but all I can see is the wounded there in all of their bandages, a tangle of missing limbs and dirty wounds. The musky scent of death lingers over the makeshift cots. I have seen death now often enough to paint it from memory, the blissful surrender. My sketchbook is full of drawings of those no longer suffering.

If only the evenings went as quickly as the days.

Alfred brings over some brushes, small canvases, paints, charcoal, and paper. Scarcely before I have washed the blood, shit, and vomit from the hospital off me of an evening does he fall upon me as if trying to capture the fleeting energy of death. After we have been together, he rushes to his art. I watch him mix his paint and am jealous of whatever it is I have done that takes him from my warm body to this cold paint. Isn't this what I wanted?

Now he only touches me, it seems, to cause himself to paint. Color bursts onto his canvas. As he mixes up that cursed blue, "Let me," I say as I grab the brush, move in front of the small canvas while holding a cigarette. I start painting from somewhere inside, somewhere untrained, and I have heard so much criticism I can recite it: "Monsieur, your colors are muddy. Take care to mix properly. Are you painting a woman's face or an ape's ass?" Couture is not kind to his students. I paint long swipes of blue, satisfied to see the color come from my hand, even if I am sick of the tone.

Alfred smiles. "Here. What are you aiming for?" He takes the brush, but I snatch it back. I continue to paint, mixing colors, fevered. Before I know it, shadows fall across the canvas. Alfred is gone. I look at the painting: It is not very good painting, but it is from my own hand. It is a soldier blue with death yet with a stiff smile. When it dries, I hide it in a closet.

The next time he comes over, he brings more supplies, and we paint together, although I am well aware of the lack in my compositions. I talk about modeling. "Painting is collaboration. You have a picture; you know what you want, but you can't have it unless the model complies. Tell her to sit straight, and if she doesn't want to, she will slouch, pulling all of your ideas down with her shoulders, with her sagging stomach. Best to let her know what you want and see if she agrees."

He is scandalized. "Am I not the painter? Isn't the model meant to do my bidding?"

"Yes, but you have to ask yourself why you chose the model you did: because she depicts something you want to capture. The only way to do that is with her cooperation."

Then he guides my hand, my eye, as I make my foolish, novice errors. "Start with this," he says as he can tell that I long to plunge into the color.

As I draw the objects he puts before me, we talk of my mother's hats, how she would make the flowers petal by petal, how they seemed more real than the ones in the Luxembourg Garden.

He tells me of his background, how his grandparents, his mother's parents owned Café de l'Amitié, in Brussels, where he was born, the café hosting the most current politicians, writers, and thinkers. He was raised at the feet of genius. Because his older brother, Joseph, was a painter, Alfred, too became a painter. His father owned a Delacroix, and more, Delacroix was a witness at Alfred and Marie's wedding. I hungrily listen as he tells me how, from an early age, he was party to country-changing conversations. When his brother came to Paris, Alfred soon followed.

I make him recount what the café had been like, attempted to smell the candles burning, the odor of alcohol. His words paint as prettily as his colors.

He listens as I speak of my childhood; he acts as if he wants to hear. He nods at points, bows his head when I have trouble forming my words as if to give me respite and space to frame them. That night, I cling to him. I only silently call him Willie.

◈

Next, he paints me knitting. He never paints as strong a jaw as I'd like, but childishly rounds it. He has me bend over "my" knitting as if nothing exists but it. An earring swings forward as if it would like to assist me. My eyes are closed, and my expression inscrutable.

The background of the painting is startlingly different than anything he has done of me before—it has an ethereal, golden glow strongly echoed in my angelic ivory gown. My outfit melts into the chair, and the wall, it, and I, are one. He is saying the woman is the house is the woman. After closely questioning him on this, he admits he is trying to say this in order to point out how ridiculous it is. Some will see this, and some will not.

"Does pointing it out condemn or perpetuate the attitude?" I ask. He doesn't answer. I don't know the answer either.

He ignores me as he straightens the upswept hairstyle he favors on me, moving pins and smoothing strands. Over and over again he uses this look on me, and so I begin to as well. He sees me so differently than Manet does. Who am I, really? When my hair is thus, I feel sophisticated, mature. I feel older, and as if I could settle into this pretend life he and I have, playing house during the war. He's not Willie, but this cage feels as if it could have been one into which I was meant to be born.

THIRTEEN

Our Father

A FEW WEEKS into The Siege there is a knock at my door on a Sunday afternoon. Upon opening it, I discover my mother, a large valise by her side.

"Come in," I say, though the scabs on her face cause my legs to tremble at what she might have to say.

She sighs deeply before she has her coat off.

"It was the smallpox. He didn't suffer long, though."

Everyone has heard of the rampant smallpox that has only increased week by week. We have stayed indoors when possible, until fear of death by ennui and stale air forced us outdoors.

My father.

I sit suddenly in the nearest chair while the water from my eyes tells me what my brain and heart will not acknowledge.

"When?"

"Two days ago. I had to find someone to take him away before I could come to you. I haven't been sick for a few days, so you should be fine."

"Where is he?" I rise.

"Père Lachaise."

"Where exactly did you put him?"

I've seen the death toll in the papers: hundreds dead a week of disease and more. We are running out of space.

Her face softens. "There are too many sick and dead for them to allow individual graves. I'm sorry." Her apology extends beyond the location of my father's grave.

I offer to make her tea as I wipe my tears, thinking it may be something she accepts rather than the hug I'd like to give her. She declines.

Numbness wraps me, and I cry in fits and starts. I am calm and then I sway, my throat tight, breath impossible.

Wails work their way up, but I shove them down. Not now, not in front of her.

I rise and make the tea anyway, but I end up dropping a cup, cutting my finger as I dispose of the shards, and when I try to stir in cream, my shaking hands will not hold the miniature spoon.

Life is loss; life is loss. It repeats in my head. I cannot grasp that I won't ever see my father again. That I will never ink a stone or wipe a smudge from his cheek. That I will never have his calm presence in which to speak my troubles while he works. That the city's poles will forever be without his posters.

My feet make for the door, to get the posters; some are still hanging now. I must go yank them from their nails, preserve them. Surely on the Champs-Élysées. . . .

"Sit," Maman says and I do as she makes the hot beverage, puts out a baguette with it.

We hold cups and stare at one another. Then I see the grief that runs along her cheeks, the dried scabs on her face and hands.

"But you were sick as well. Who cared for you?"

She shrugs. "I wasn't so sick."

"You should have sent for me." At the very least, I could have found a way to say goodbye: through a window, by note . . . something. I'm not surprised that she has deprived me of even this.

Typhoid, dysentery, smallpox, starvation, freezing, bombing, burning . . . so many, many ways to die during the war. Just now I'd take only, any, one.

"I found some of his paintings," she says shakily, "of you when you were young. Here."

My father, resurrected. "I thought you got rid of them." She cannot know that I knew where they were.

"These he had hidden under the floorboards of his shop."

She hands the case to me, and I open it to see a small stack of canvases of various sizes. I leaf through them quickly, remembering my family's front room, the cold floor, being naked, my father's penetrating gaze, my embarrassment, my ambiguous feelings, wanting, needing, him to pay attention. My mother's discovery, the shame.

None of the canvases in the case are of me naked.

What I see most in the paintings is talent. I see the unschooled painting by a man who could have learned. I weep, but not for me.

"He was talented," I say.

"Why you?" she asks. Her face screws up in pain. The question chasms as she asks.

"He needed a model."

She does not meet my eyes but rises.

I say what she has been waiting to hear. I can't keep it from her: "My father never touched me. Not like that. He simply needed a model." I am grateful that her back is to me.

I cross to her, stand between her and the door.

I reach out to embrace her, again. She stands stiffly as I hug her.

"Would you like to stay for dinner?"

"No, thank you. I must go. Madeline is coming over early in the morning for a hat." She spits the words.

Peach silk, white feather pillows. Madeline. My mother's plump hands weaving a needle in and out of the tender bloom of a rose. My father reading the paper. I ache. As my mother rises, I say it:

"I love you, Maman. Thank you for the paintings." Before she leaves, I stop her. I quickly dump some francs from my purse and force her to unclench her fist. Slowly she closes her fingers around them and walks away. The sound of her shoes echoes down the stairs.

I slowly walk to the bedroom and climb into bed. Sleep is a lovely friend.

Stevens and I are arguing once again about his paintings. "You have but three preoccupations," I shout. "Visiting, motherhood, and mirrors. You only paint *femme fragile* or *femme fatale*. Where are the women like me? I am not one of these."

"And what is so wrong with visiting, motherhood, and mirrors, Victorine?" he asks quietly.

"It's all so meaningless. These women are in these beautiful rooms that are like cages, surrounded by beautiful objects. Hell, Stevens, they, we, *are* objects."

This argument we are having is not new.

"And isn't that what I am trying to say?" he asks. "These women pursue boring pastimes in beautiful rooms in gorgeous clothes. The mirrors reflect back to the men what they have done from every side. We like it, Victorine, we men. We work hard to provide the cages that, unbelievably, some of you women even seek. Then we realize what we have done, but there is no recourse, and we do like having that stunning rose of a woman bear our children. We do enjoy how her dress matches the wallpaper. It doesn't have to mean that we don't love her for things other than that."

His very preoccupation with this tells me he knows how wrong it is.

"Perhaps," I say kindly, "women can teach one another that it is not wrong to want to be taken care of as long as it is not at the expense of the soul. Better, perhaps we can be given the ability to take care of ourselves."

"I love how she looks up against the sofa," he groans of his painting.

"You love the picture your family makes as you stroll through the park," I say, leaning in to kiss him, sliding my hands over his rounded buttocks, "and you adore it when I touch you."

"Is life always filled with these choices?" he asks.

"As you say, your wife enjoys her appearance when you come home. She fixes her hair just the way you like it because she knows your artist's eyes will notice everything. What's so wrong with that? Just because you also love . . ."

"I do love you," he says.

"What do you think of this pose?" I contort myself and stick out my tongue. He looks at me as if I have taken leave of my senses. I'm tired of arguing.

"Let's go skate upon the Seine . . . I hear it is frozen solid."

So we bundle up and rent skates riverside, joining the dozens on the ice. For a large man, he glides nicely.

Here on the ice we are all Parisians out on a winter's day, spinning gaily in our heaviest clothing that gets warmer by the minute. Our reddened cheeks and flashing smiles loosen for just a moment the constriction of war and we laugh and call out. Though we have had to travel though dusty, dirty, brick-strewn streets to get here, here we are, bricks of our city.

As I twirl myself dizzy, forms spin about me, young men and women, older ones who move carefully. I glimpse red and I try to stop and follow the color, just the color of Willie's hair, but I am spinning too quickly and there he is again, holding my hands, his face, his smile. But when I stop, he's gone. At least, the sight of him is. The feeling of having him beside me lingers deliciously, and the wound inside of me sews itself shut.

When my vision clears, I watch a mother and child, a son, skate together. She hugs the lad to her (he can't be above seven), and then, hands together, pushes him away. They twirl and laugh, and then she hugs him to her. The way she does so makes me believe that her husband is away at war.

"Are you ready to go?" Alfred asks. I say *yes*, but my feet refuse to move. I look over my shoulder at the pair as we leave.

We quit reading the papers.

Slowly melancholy creeps into Alfred's work.

The war grinds on and it grinds on us. I drink more, smoke more. I spend time at the Café Guerbois talking of art, drinking absinthe, and leering at women I cannot bring home. I drink deeply, gaily entering into contests. I dance wildly, lustily, but none of the men will make a pass at me. It is understood that if I am under Alfred's protection, no one else may touch me.

"Let's play a game," I suggest at the bar one evening as the cannons relentlessly volley. It's either that or hide under the tables. "Every time a cannon sounds, we take a drink. The one who passes out first must pay for them all." My game is met with cheers and it will work well, because I won't be the first one passing out, certainly not.

By the time the cannons quiet and Philippe, a lawyer who can well afford it, pays for everyone's night of drinking (or his wallet does, as the bartender has to fish the money out of the inert man's pocket), our ears can't even tell there is silence until we go outside. Smoke obscures the moon and stars in this hazy hell. I make my way only semi successfully over toppled bricks and list and pitch until I'm home.

War becomes another sort of weather system to endure, even permeating our dreams.

Once home, I take the basket of my father's paintings from its hiding place. I have never shown these to Alfred. I don't wish to hear either praise or damnation of my father's efforts.

Unrolling the top one reveals a little girl in a white dress with a pink sash.

She stares into the distance, her eyes too wide, and her expression trying to please. Her legs are crossed, her skirt riding slightly up the chubby thighs. Her hair is a rusted, braided crown.

I close my eyes and my father again takes the brush in his trembling hands, fussing with my hair, hushing me when I yelp at a tangle he tries to comb through. He sits behind me, picking up a handful of hair, and I feel a twisting motion, then another. A small bee seems to sting my scalp, and then another, as he jabs pins into my hair. One braid falls over my eye, and he gently picks it up.

When he finishes, I pose for as long as he wants, even after my body tires, even after his lingering gaze takes away the good feeling of the hair brushing. Even after I notice that my dress is too thin. I cross my arms.

"Are you cold, Louise?"

"No, Père."

That's when I learn to pretend, too.

I stare at the painting now, and I see how he made me. Though the child appears innocent, she only seems so to someone who does not look for the hardened edges of her mouth, at the pretending, knowing eyes that gaze at something to her left. She condemns the viewer, but only slightly, not the way Olympia did. My father made *Olympia* as surely as Manet.

These paintings touched parts of me that weren't meant to be touched. They explored the unformed areas, pointed out my flat chest, my shiny red hair, and my ruddy cheeks. They outlined the promise of the woman to come and spoiled for me the gradual dawning of womanhood. I knew that I was desirable before I understood desire. I knew that for all of the talk in church of the sacredness inside of me, it wasn't my "sacred" insides that were being sought, not by my father, not by Manet, and not by Alfred.

Better to yield what will be taken from you, anyway. Yet yielding a body is not yielding a heart, a soul. There are defenses that even the young automatically set.

The paintings (as I unroll another, similar, one of me in a pink dress) tell me clearly that sex, such a shamed appetite, is ever present and unrelenting. The child in the paintings knows this. Had he painted a clearer view of this knowledge, he would have condemned his twisted consumers, rather than titillated them just as Manet acknowledges his guilt and that of the viewers in *Olympia*.

My father's brush invaded me as much as his brown eyes, searching when he thought I didn't see, setting on fire my hair, my cheeks. I knew where those paintings were hidden all along, that finger my father laid to his lips when he parted the floorboards, the silent "shh."

When my mother brought them to me my first impulse was to burn them, but I couldn't. It would have been to burn his culpability, and mine. Somewhere out there are more of these paintings of my innocence taken, bought by men, maybe even women, the paintings that primed me to become the commodity that I became with Alphonse.

When is it art, and when is it something else? Ah, perhaps that's more of an individual's call to make, but I know it when I see it.

When I paint, I will paint life the way I perceive it, and not in that odd impressionistic manner that pretends to see things in a swoon. Just like a man. No wonder so few women want to become involved in it. This new style of painting is a man turning his head to catch a glimpse of a woman who will be the most beautiful woman he has ever seen because he hasn't seen her face. Just another attempt to reduce all women to one, and thus, less.

I have since seen similar portraits to the ones Père painted of me, in museums, and I know their purpose by the demure look in the girl's eyes, the far-off gaze that makes believe that no one is watching her. The dress is something very young looking, white or blue or pink, with a splash of color. She will hold a bouquet of flowers or maybe even a prayer book. Where is the "harm"? What is the appeal? A painting both a mother and a pervert can love, the mother none the wiser.

I pity these lurid gazers. My father's eyes told me that he hated how he felt, that he longed to hold me on his lap and not feel the stirrings of his body, and because of that he did not hold me on his lap, and he could not keep himself from thinking about it, the paintings said.

I knew (back then), although I can't say how, that this had much to do with the cold, hateful nature of my mother, of how she disapproved of nearly everything he did, and how she despised him, how he needed her to do so, how he needed me to love him in the way she would not. When she found out about the paintings, her disdain shifted from him to me. I put the paintings away and try to sleep. How can the world be so beautiful and so ugly all at once?

◈

Christmas during The Siege is miserably cold and gloomy. There is not much of a reason to make merry, but we try. Stevens takes me to a special dinner at a restaurant he knows. "Look at the menu," he whispers. It is extensive for wartime, although it is also revolting:

> *Consommé de cheval au millet.* (horse)
> *Brochettes de foie de chien à la maître d'hôtel.* (dog)
> *Emincé de râble de chat. Sauce mayonnaise.* (cat)
> *Épaules et filets de chien braisés. Sauce aux tomates.* (dog)
> *Civet de chat aux champignons.* (cat)
> *Côtelettes de chien aux petits pois.* (dog)
> *Salamis de rats. Sauce Robert.* (rats)
> *Gigots de chien flanqués de ratons. Sauce au poivre.* (dog, rats)
> *Bégonias au jus.* (flowers)
> *Plum-pudding au rhum et à la moelle de cheval.* (horse)

As adventurous as I am, I ask for just the begonias and a side of *pain bis*. The bread is black and flat, and it tastes of ash. As I attempt to bite into the hard mass, Alfred and I howl with laughter before things turn serious.

He grabs my hand. "I am creating something I would not have created before the war, before you. The city's gates will open soon and in will flood fresh produce and meat. Gone will be the rats for dinner. My family will return, and I will be happy to see them." He squeezes. "But I will always look upon this time as cutting the deepest impressions into my soul."

He straightens as our wine glasses are refilled.

"Had they wanted to win sooner, all they need have done was cut off our wine supply . . . every man and woman would have fought night and day," I say. I cannot tell him how his words have moved and terrified me.

We lift our glasses to one another and thank heaven that there is always enough wine and art.

Alfred has volunteered to guard on Christmas evening so that men with families can be with them. I tell him bravely to go on.

◈

I stop by my mother's, and when she won't answer the door, I leave a package on her doorstep. Inside is a box of chocolates and a pair of wool socks. I am an indifferent knitter, but I do like to imagine warming my mother's feet. I took up knitting scarves at the hospital. The soldiers love to tease me about how crooked my knitting is. It is, but I hope my mother will love the socks more and not less for this.

I knock at her neighbor's door, and they open it a mere crack to answer my questions. They have seen my mother just this morning. As far as they know, she is home. But they refuse to check on her for me because my father died of a contagious disease. I call them cowards and kick their door when they slam it.

"Merry Christmas to you! That brood you have could use a thinning!" I say vindictively, though I don't really mean it.

What is disease against the death I have already seen? Who else might be taken that I care about? Even as my heart asks it, uneasiness fills me. That's not a question to be asked, not something to dare.

Instead of thinking, I go to the Café Guerbois to find Manet and wish him a Merry Christmas, but he's not there; he has been sick, I am told. The whispered word hardly needs telling me: "syphilis." Manet has as many appetites as any other man, though he never overindulges and is extremely discreet. Still, in this city, a man with appetites is in danger. Before *Olympia*, I heard no whispers. Now, it is all I hear. His public position magnifies tales of his conquests.

I can't imagine he has even indulged in these minor repasts lately, not after seeing him with Morisot. She would not speak to me when I met her last at the hospital, as if I were beneath her. Perhaps she blames me for Manet's illness— she need not, else wouldn't I be sick too?

When I am tempted by a man with a thick hairline and burly forearms, I finish my drink.

A new poster on a light pole stops me; at first because I examine it carefully to see who has made it: with those tacky colors, certainly not (not ever again) my father. But what it says intrigues me: The *Théâtre de l'Athénée* will have a performance tonight of Hugo's *Les Châtiments* given by Marie Lurent. I stand outside of the venue and imagine going in, but it will be just more words of patriotism. I do not need them, not on Christmas.

Once home, I dig Willie's photo out of my journal and gaze at it. I have no photos of my father. The thrill of melancholy quickly grows into intolerable hollowness, if indulged. I tuck the photo—and my grief—away again. No wallowing. Christmas must be no exception.

Alfred is busy with a portrait of a still-wealthy patron, so I pick up an umbrella and head off to visit Manet. He's preparing a canvas. Apart from his limp, he seems to be feeling better. I say I have come to borrow a promised book, not that I am here to inquire after his health.

"I'm going to paint a balcony scene." He moves his hand crisply as if painting the canvas when he says it. "Here I will put a woman in a gown."

I'm not surprised he wants to do something so bourgeoisie. It reminds me of Morisot's work.

Pleasure flushes my face. "What shall I wear for it?" I ask. Though I have sat for Stevens so much lately, they both know I am Manet's model first.

Morisot comes from around the curtain.

"Oh is she to sit with me, Manet? I thought you asked Fanny to stop by." Manet mumbles.

Morisot smiles. "You didn't tell her about Fanny Claus?"

"The violinist?" I ask, looking at Manet who will not look at me.

"She's Suzanne's best friend." He shrugs.

"I see." I have been increasingly pushed out by Morisot who keeps encouraging Manet to go in a more acceptable, classical direction. She is still trying to get him to become respectable. Though aesthetically I don't disagree entirely, it will murder his art.

That, however, is not the immediate issue.

"Manet, what have I done to displease you? Why would you use someone with no experience and, pardon me, but probably no eye either?" I despise myself for saying this in front of her, but I never see him alone any more.

Manet raises his head. "Have you seen her work? She is better than I am, Victorine."

I reel. "I didn't mean her work. I meant Fanny as a model." I have lost, and because of that, so has Manet. He is besotted.

"Berthe?" he says, and she looks apologetic.

"Of course. If you'll excuse me, I have an errand to run." She rustles out of the room.

"You didn't have to ask her to leave on my account. I'm sure anything you are going to say she's already told you to say."

His nostrils flare. "How dare you. You know I have appreciated your services for all these years, but that's all they were. I did not choose you for this painting because you have been associated with, shall we say, baser matters in my paintings. Who would believe you as an aristocrat on a balcony after I have painted you as a, a . . . ?"

I fling my umbrella to the floor. "Are you trying to say that I am perceived by the public as a prostitute, as if it's not your doing, you who took a young girl and put her up for the world's scorn? I was spat on because of you and leered at. I couldn't walk about town without being propositioned as if I were a common whore. My parents disowned me in part because of my work. During the hottest moments of the *Olympia* controversy, you disappeared to Spain and left me to withstand the worst of it. I didn't even have clothes to hide behind—everyone knows what every part of me looks like. I did it not once but twice, and then I let you picture me as a lesbian, more or less, and then, as if you couldn't get enough of the theme, another prostitute. You know everyone has always assumed I was your mistress, and you and I know that is not so. I received all of the grief and none of the benefits, and when I got myself kicked out of my parents' house for Madeline, I didn't ask you for help. I have been passed back and forth between you and Alfred as if I were just another prop, and I did it for you, because I knew I could give you both what you wanted, what you needed."

He cleans his brushes as I talk on, my voice low and urgent. He will hear me, regardless of our stations.

"I moved in with Alfred because I needed a place to stay and because he was kind to me. I made your reputation, Manet. You wanted to be known, and if you had cared how you were known, you would never have painted the subject matter you did. You're like a child who wants to do something very naughty, but who doesn't want the adults to find out he did it willingly, so he blames another child. You blame me for the baser things you think and feel, and you think as long as you're with me you will be associated with those things. I get it; Morisot has opened different wants in you, but no matter how much you may love her, that doesn't mean you can get a divorce. You never would anyway. Sometimes we meet the right person too late, and we have to face that. You had your reasons for marrying Suzanne. Be happy with those."

When I finish, he crumbles onto the sofa, clutching a wet paintbrush as if he would snap it in two. I sink onto the sofa beside him. "She seems drawn to your brother, Eugène. Maybe that is a way to keep her close without being dishonorable."

He remains silent.

I sigh. "She's right, you know. This isn't my sort of painting, not for you. Stevens could pull it off, because he lies about me, but you've never been able to, Manet. The public would call it dishonest if you tried to put me in it."

"Aren't you ever lonely?" he asks.

"Suzanne's not a thinker, Manet; Suzanne is your comfort, and you must not give her up. Your class does not do what you are thinking of. Write Berthe letters, paint her if you must, hell, make love to her, but then let her go."

Just as he is letting me go, because of who he is with her.

"You would do whatever you wanted. You wouldn't let conventions stand in your way."

I dry my eyes, barely realizing I am crying with him.

Morisot pops her head back in. "Ready for me, Édouard?" she asks frostily. He sits up hastily.

I hate how she purses her lips when she talks, as if she's eating her own sharp-featured face.

I pick up my umbrella and head for the door, stop and look her up and down, inspect the white skirts trimmed with black braid. "Morisot? There's mud on your skirt."

◈

FOURTEEN

The Siege Continues

A LONG THE Boulonge-sur-Seine only three shops are open during the war: a hairdresser, a butcher, and a wine merchant. I smile as I think of our priorities. War numbs many emotions, but not all. The desire for beauty, for such food as is available, for drink to forget, are ever present.

I never use a hairdresser; I have never had the money until now, and Alfred is so practiced at fixing his models' hair that he enjoys styling mine, and so in these short, dark, loud days I let him play with the strands as much as he likes. There's nothing quite like the feel of boar's bristles gripping my scalp.

The rage of smallpox has just as quickly burned out, but people are still cautious of strangers on the street, not knowing if their families have been ill or not. It makes our resumed daily constitutionals less friendly. Does war spare nothing?

The Louvre is protected by sandbags, and the art is said to be crated and hidden. Let them burn our houses, cannon our buildings, but dear God, don't let them destroy our art.

The weeks that follow are a blur of hunger, shells, and misinformation. Soon my curiosity is satiated, and I don't really care what is going on, because there is no hope of stopping it. I have to go and ask for a ration card to buy my food: two servings of meat or four servings of other foodstuffs per day. Before they ration, we wipe the stores out of canned goods, we who used to pride ourselves on our fresh food bought daily. Those Americans among us have outsmarted us by weeks on that front, having long been accustomed to eating from tins. When I make a meal of canned goods, both Alfred and I make faces at the metallic taste of the peaches and the mushy peas.

Les Halles' seafood displays have quickly given way to horsemeat and dog. Rat is prized, though not as highly. Even the poor refuse to eat it unless they must. We are surprised to discover that animal grease can be substituted for butter. We mourn our white fluffy loaves of bread so quickly replaced with a much rougher sort. Later, the flour gets mixed with hay and sawdust. Full stomachs can be faked, to some degree.

The first time I bring home a pair of rats, I am amused though disgusted. I hope to be able to skin them without getting sick, and I manage it. But then I am bewildered when I think of how to prepare them. If I bake them whole, we will know even more what they are. Better that I mince them. I convince myself they are merely small lumps of beef and I cut them up matter-of-factly and stew them with some onions and cream. When Alfred asks what is for dinner, I tell him he may pretend it is anything he likes.

Rat, I discover, is quite edible, if one must eat it.

When I see the dreary colors with which Alfred paints these dull evenings, I realize that our food is affecting even our art, especially for someone like Alfred. Half of his pleasure from life seems to come from gustatory matters.

Alfred begins another, second painting of me that he also calls *The Parisian Sphinx*, as if the war merits a different rendition of the topic. He gives me a flowered summer dress to wear.

The man paints as if possessed: He hits my face with blush, smears pink lipstick across my lips. He spends the most time on a glorious up-do, the way my father used to when he painted me. By now my hair is past my waist, and he loves wrapping his hands in it while he sleeps.

He lifts it up from the sides and rolls it up and over before picking up a pair of scissors: "May I?" he asks. Before I can nod, he cuts bangs and I watch the clump of hair fall onto the floor.

I feel shorn, and when he asks next, "Put your hand up to your mouth as if you are startled," I do, only half pretending, my pinkie dropping nearly to my chin, and the finger beside it half opening my mouth.

"What are you aiming for?" I don't know how to look, and I am annoyed that he would snip my hair without my leave. I didn't have time to think. That's what all of these men have done, these painters, the photographer. They have given me no time and no choice.

"Just sit."

"I don't mind sitting, but what do you want me to do?"

"Nothing." He curses. "It's called *The Parisian Sphinx*. I do not want to tell the sphinx what to say."

So his first sphinx did not say what he wanted it to say. I feel the discord between the clothes and the makeup. It's as if I am some expensive whore who has had a night of it, yet my hair is not tousled.

And by the way, isn't a sphinx quiet?

As he paints, I am silent. The shelling continues, and my stomach rumbles along with it. One might as well try to make beauty.

He paints late into the night, and my eyes begin to close. "I'm rather tired," I say finally.

He nods and paints on. I have never seen him this way. "Alfred?" I say. He ignores me. "I must ask to stop." He looks up, then seems to register that I am talking. "Of course."

I stretch my back, my legs. Then I go to him, to the painting. I don't know what I expect, but it is not this woman who looks one part anxious to one part aloof. He uses Manet's blackground. Is there no way I can get away from that man defining me? I am angry; I am sad. I am worried; I am . . . I have no idea.

"Tell me about her, this sphinx." Sometimes with Alfred it is the only way to ease my disappointment at his work.

"She is Paris; she is you. Anxious about the future, yet proud. If you notice, she gazes into the distance—she is looking to the future, not to the troubles of now."

"And she is a sphinx?"

"She has a riddle for you, if only you will listen."

"Indeed." Every time I dismiss the man, he surprises me. Better I not write him off just yet. Instead, I ask him a riddle. He guesses correctly, and I reward him accordingly. Afterwards, I brush my hair with its newly trimmed bangs.

Me, as a child, my hair hanging loose, the brush in my hand. I had just read a story of a mother who took great pride in combing her daughter's hair one hundred times every night. I stood before the living room mirror and counted aloud as I moved the instrument down my back.

"*Un, deux,*" I counted aloud, my eyes not on the mirror but upon my mother who continued pushing her needle up, out, through. Her eyes softened as she gazed on the pink tulle in her hands.

I let my arms fall to my side, only to find my father staring at me with pity. "Here," he said as he crossed to me and took the brush. The tears in my eyes were reflected back to me, both in the mirror and in his eyes.

Slowly he dragged the brush from the roots of my hair to the ends, digging in just enough that I felt the pressure, but not so much that it hurt. I closed my eyes, wondering if I was meant to enjoy the moment. I did until I surmised hatred in my mother's eyes.

I put my hand up to still the brush. "I need to study my verbs," I said.

"Of course," my father said haltingly.

That night, I hacked at my long hair with my mother's sewing scissors, jagged bits falling about me. I gasped as I studied my chin-length hair in the mirror. My face looked stronger, my cheekbones more angular, and I grinned. I had lost nothing.

The next morning at breakfast my mother and father gaped. "You have disgraced me," she said, and she left the table. When I heard her exclaim upon opening the basket, I smiled, knowing she had found the coils of hair.

Was my being an only child more than just God's doing? My art comes from my father, but perhaps my passion comes from my mother's carefully buried longings which showed mostly in her passion for her belongings.

There was always something lusty playing about my mother's dark eyes and her generous lips that she made fuller when she spoke, thrusting out the red insides with each exaggerated word. French seemed ready made for her mouth. Her hands stroked material as if she would coax a reaction from it, and with her needle, she did, making rigid ones flaccid and slack ones taut with sizing and starch, and yet an unbearable iciness existed between my parents.

Maybe her coldness was but the closing of the morning glory at the end of the day. Perhaps she became a Venus fly trap because it did not benefit her to be a flower.

She had a dog, a tiny terrier that would sit beside her. If she had a client in, she would put the animal in her sewing basket to muffle his indignant barking. She fit Jup with a collar that she embroidered herself. She made him a fluffy bed of silk scraps and fed him special leftovers such as bits of nearly spoiled pâté by hand. Everything about the animal's life was luxury in miniature. He adored my mother, not letting me or my father get close to her without snapping his tiny teeth at us. The dog was just another thing my mother put in the way of our loving her, until he disappeared.

The day before, as my father bent to show my mother a story in the paper, Jup bit his finger. My mother said nothing, just continued looking at the paper. He cursed the dog and left the newspaper in my mother's hands as he went in search of a piece of cloth to bandage the bite.

I bent over mother's scrap box and retrieved a piece of linen. "Here," I said, bringing it to my father in the kitchen. I wrapped the cloth about his finger which dripped with blood, squeezing tightly. He winced. "I'm sorry," I said, letting go. "Be sure to keep pressure on it," I said.

"I need to go out," he said. He put on his jacket with the dangling hem and his hat.

My mother looked at the door as it closed.

"Your dog bit him," I said.

She said nothing, just pet the dog.

I left the room.

The next day, my mother woke me frantically, asking what I had done with her dog. I went into the living room where she alternately asked me and my father what we had done. Neither of us acknowledged having done anything, but I could have told her that the hateful dog had a new home with the circus.

I removed his rhinestone collar with its small bell and tucked it into my pocket, replaced it with a pink ribbon and told the man at the ticket booth that the dog was a gift for the child who performs on the trapeze. He seemed to know who I meant, though I did not. There is always a child who performs on the trapeze. The circus was to leave town that night, that much I knew. I wasn't concerned that the dog would bite a child; it only misbehaved because my mother allowed it.

My father never asked what happened to the dog, but the next week he bought me a dog charm for my bracelet. I wore it, but only when I was not at home.

My mother's even gloomier eyes after she lost the dog made me nearly instantly regret my actions. From that moment, I realized that though she maddened me, I must learn to love her because she was unable to love me. I spent the next day searching for the circus that had already gone, just as a measure of light had from her eyes.

Manet visits us after another night of guard duty. His leg is somewhat better he says, but he favors the opposite one.

I serve us up a typical siege meal: macaroni and herbs, carrots, and the main course, "steaks."

"And what is this hearty meat we are eating tonight?" Manet asks.

Alfred and I look at one another, and then away.

"Pollux was not spared," Alfred says.

"The elephant at the zoo?" Manet asks. "But I took Léon to see him just last spring."

"How are Suzanne and Léon?" Alfred asks as we all push the meat about our plates. At the woman's name I purposely stab the slab on my plate and, holding my fork aloft, gnaw at it.

"*Mon Dieu!*" Manet says as he covers his plate with his napkin. Alfred follows suit, but as Manet continues to talk of Suzanne, I reach over and fork Alfred's meat out from under his napkin.

The men shake their heads at one another, at me.

One wonders if Pollux could have been divided up so many times. If not, what are we really eating? Best we not ask. I know what it is to feel divided among many.

"No one saw fit to send me away, so I must get by any way I can," I say with a shrug. "Who is to say how long this will last and what lengths we will have to go to? This may be the least uncivilized we are."

(The meat is greasy and hangs in my throat as I force it down. I try not to think about feeding the beast peanuts when I was younger.)

Civilized behavior is for those who can afford it.

Manet still brings us better tobacco and cheese, but says food continues to diminish. This is weeks after Pollux, and I suspect none of us would complain about eating it now. Still, a fresh cigarette is welcome, though I do have to roll it myself. And the cheese he brings us needs only a bit of mold scraped from it to be good enough to eat, compared to our hunk that gets more questionably colored every day.

"What about your painting?" I ask Manet, worried that he isn't. He stops in to see us more often than I expected.

"I still really haven't been able to paint, just sketch. I'm storing the images in my mind for later." Just from the wagons of wounded I have seen come through, I can only imagine. Like uprooted trees the bodies mingle: mostly dead, a few pulled out for alive. Sheared limbs covered in copious blood. How could one paint such atrocities when confronted daily with them? The human heart can only take so much.

"I was on the corner with a friend last week, and gunfire broke out. We had to duck into a shop to escape. When we came out, a child lay in the street, victim to the battle. I found myself sketching him instead of checking his pulse," Manet says. "We are not living—this is a nightmare we are sharing."

Alfred nods and gets up. "I have something to show you."

While he goes to fetch it, Manet whispers: "How is he? He appears pale and worn."

"Not well. He screams in his sleep. He begs for his wife. He paints mud and death." I have not admitted this to anyone else. "I worry for him."

"Get him out more," Manet whispers as he returns.

I nod.

Alfred hands Manet a sketch of a bombed house just outside our window.

"It could have been us," Alfred says.

"You aren't expected to fight. What if a way out could be found for you?"

"You could join your wife. You know she needs you," I add, though of course this would make my place tentative at best.

"Leave Paris? Leave you?" he asks me.

"No one would fault you if your family needs you."

Hope flickers in his eyes, then flees. "There is no way. It is too late." I see now what Manet sees, what I have been avoiding: Alfred's face is white, his eyes red. He is stooped and drawn. Then he hears a cannon fire; he flinches.

"And how is our mutual friend Morisot?" asks Alfred after the sound has died down.

Manet flinches as if this question is just as taxing for him as the cannon was for Alfred. "She and her sister are well and still in town. They refuse to leave."

I know Manet has continued to paint Morisot, and they have even painted side by side on occasion as well, something I have learned from stopping in at his studio. I say I am needed at the hospital when I visit during those times, though when I leave them I roam the grimy back alleys that teem with wispy, homeless children who are nearly indistinguishable from the street filth until I get to know some of them. I bring what bread we can spare with me when I think of it, or when I go shopping, though I always wince a bit when Alfred asks later why I have not bought more bread. Obviously, I cannot tell him the truth.

"Many have refused to leave Paris," says Alfred to Manet.

He will not leave. I am worried; I am relieved.

Hunger becomes a matter of course as rations are reduced. We live now on wine, *café*, and inferior bread. Gone is even the shadow of a butter substitute. The vegetables disappear with the onset of winter. Manet is not able to bring us anything now, but I welcome his visits anyway as they come with talk of art now and art later. Of what's happening to the paintings from the past.

I like feeling hollow, but Alfred suffers from hunger and depression. My face thins, and my sides. I enjoy this new model of myself in the mirror, and I try to catch on paper the hungry look of her soul but fail.

Everything that the military needs is given precedence. Shops close as they can't get new wares or they are converted into hospitals, the wounded visible through the large windows like a new sort of white and red wrapped toy.

Gas is rationed so going out at night is unwise in the dark, as there are now no streetlights. We get no news of the outside world, although we are able to send postcards via hot air balloon. Alfred trusts that his family is safe but has no recent proof of it.

He finishes his painting of me, and I know it is a painting that could only have come when it did. I am grateful for the name he gives me in it, too. I have feared he thought me too simple, when I know I am a complex sphinx.

Alfred's mood does not improve, but neither does it worsen.

I read to Alfred by the faint light of a candle I bought at church and brought home to light—churches are allowed to have more than we, and I reasoned that, after all, I had paid for it. With a boom, plaster sifts down on us, but I continue reading Hugo until my throat hurts, trying to drown out the noise of war.

"Come to bed," Alfred says as I drop the book after the house rocks and screams sound too close by. He touches me as if I am a treasure, as if we can protect one another with our lovemaking. When he gets on top of me, he pauses to listen, but all is quiet. Instead of continuing, he climbs off.

I roll over and gently touch myself, provoking him to scold me in a shocked voice.

"You decided we were finished, not me," I say. It's not the pleasure I'm after, just the making of a point.

He leaps out of bed and flings open the window. The smell of fire comes to us, and I abandon my efforts and join him. Side by side we survey what used to be our city.

"Alfred," I say, putting my arm about his naked body. We were wrong to suppose sex could make these horrors disappear any more than a bottle of wine.

"Let's paint," I say.

"What?"

"Come. Now."

Deep into the morning he paints my naked body onto the canvas, but it is not me. It is the vulnerable city being destroyed right outside, us indoors hoping that brick and mortar can save us. We are the city, but the city is us first.

When he finishes, he picks me up and takes me back to the bed and before long we are both content, but too soon begins the anxiety of what to do next.

As the days slowly roll by with no regular routine outside of the house, we become irritable with one another. He rolls his eyes at my "complete and utter" lack of an education. I complain again about his frou-frou taste in fabric. More than once he storms out and to a café where he says later he met no one entertaining and drank piss. I don't want to join him because I've seen quite enough of him, but neither do I scold him for going. Instead, I spend more time at the makeshift hospitals.

Other nights, if we are lucky enough to have a bit of candle, I play my violin for him. He considers the guitar masculine, and so to humor him I play the violin, though I don't play it as well. It requires a pomposity and self-aggrandizement I don't possess, or a streak of emotionalism I am not prone to. I refuse to play for him the pieces I keep for myself.

I snatch moments when Alfred is away to draw something that sticks in my mind of the day, a sort of illustrated journal: the pale faces of malnourished soldiers being brought into town on carts, a child's sock in a shelled house, a book left open on a chair in an abandoned house. Death in a man's face at the hospital, a Sister sitting astride a wounded soldier to hold him down for treatment.

Alfred continues what I call "The Siege Paintings" of me. Besides *The Parisian Sphinx*, he paints one of me in a Japanese dressing gown, blue, covered in flowers, the same one he painted just after he gave me the shawl. He has me belt the shawl over it, and I wonder aloud why he always feels he has to add something to a garment.

I hold a fan in my right hand, but it is lowered, while I grasp the edge of a mirror with my left. He paints me looking into the mirror. My undergarment comes to the top of my breasts. I gaze expressionlessly into the mirror, staring into my own eyes.

Now he doesn't talk to me while he paints, and I am lost in a forest of troublesome thoughts, so I talk enough for us both, but he does not reciprocate. I reach for him because I am alone, because now I do not have Manet (as duties keep him away) or Willie or my mother, and because my father is gone, but Alfred loses himself in his painting, and I am just someone to pose for him. So I look into my own eyes in that painting and I wish I could see what the future holds for Paris, for me. My bravery wavers just a bit under a fresh deluge of shells. The mixture of hunger and fear cause me to become nervous, and I smoke constantly, even if the tobacco is thinned—with what I do not want to know.

I quiz him on any and every topic he used to like, offer him my body freely, which sometimes he takes, sometimes not. I am alone. His mind strays. I don't bother to speak with him about art now.

Another painting of me in a blue dressing gown with a gold belt at the waist, and this time a tiara. He has me hold a wilting plant in a black and gold enameled planter, but he magically paints flowers we only wish we had in it. I wear a gold necklace, glass earrings. If nothing else, I still enjoy dressing up. In this one I look solemnly at the plant as if wondering if it will survive, when in reality I am wondering if he will get by with this pretense of flowers. The background is soft brown velvet. When I ask him what this one means, he shrugs. I know now he is trying to out-paint the war, and I don't blame him, except I don't much like posing hour after hour with a silent man. He paints for fewer hours now and we sleep more. Though we are not malnourished yet, we eat even less, as does everyone. I am becoming slowly better acquainted with my skeleton as my bones emerge; Alfred has to wear suspenders.

Perhaps the most ghoulish—yet most interesting—of his war paintings pictures me in a negligee cradling a skull amid a desolate, rocky background. I don't ask where the skull came from. He leaves my hair flowing all about my face and has me look forward with my plump hand on my chin. It's hard to read my face. I don't look afraid. Is it a nightmare I am in? But my eyes are wide open. There are indistinct clouds and mountains in the background, so likely I am dreaming of death, but we all are, nowadays. Will we live or die? Though the casualties in the city are relatively few, they are real, and the reality of possible death is all about us. I have already lost the two men dearest to me—what else can the war do to me?

Alfred's brushstrokes are pencil-like in this painting. My hair is red, but the rest of the picture gives the impression of being black and white, with the merest hints of pink and blue. I shiver when I look at the painting. What it has taken to get Alfred's work so interesting seems nearly unbelievable. The war is an unanticipated school of art.

I sit repeatedly, losing track of just how many works of art he creates. In one, I slump in a chair hopelessly, and I think surely he is painting himself.

I escape to the hospital as often as possible, wanting to feel of some use to something besides tiresome art. Sometimes I eat the soup of a soldier who has drifted off to sleep without finishing. "How can I nurse anyone if I haven't the strength?" I argue with myself. For all of the argument's truth, it doesn't make me feel less guilty.

At the hospital that used to be a clothing shop, they are now using the fabric from dresses for bandages, and I laugh at how far we have fallen. I wrap wounds and wash soldiers, insensible to their nudity. I read stories, play guitar, and write letters. I pray with them, when they ask, feeling hollow as I do, but making the prayers as ornate as I can. The soldiers, so hopeless, do not hear my inherent doubt and anger, and I am glad.

One soldier, Jean, asks me to marry him. Something about him reminds of gentle Fredric Bazille with his soft and full whiskers, he newly fallen on the battlefield, mourned by us all. Now I am not sorry that I gave the boy that one sunny afternoon. I am sorry he never painted me.

I feed Jean spoonfuls of weak soup laced with cabbage. The ratio of water to vegetable does not rise to a density to merit being called cabbage soup. How can we expect our men to get better when there is nothing to feed them? He calls me darling and tries to squeeze my hand every time I tend to him.

"Marry me, please, Marie," he begs. "I should have asked before I left for war."

"Of course. Let me call for the priest now," I say.

I search until I find a sullen young man who has been tending the sick.

"I need you to pretend to be a priest and marry us."

He shrugs and follows me. "It's better than bandaging open sores," he says wearily.

With a surprisingly complete ceremony this doctor "marries" me to Jean, and for the next three days, my "husband" won't let me leave his side.

I sing to him, comb his beard, and try to feed him, but he won't eat. I force water down his throat, but it rolls back out the sides of his mouth.

While he dies, I write a letter to his parents and explain that he had wanted to marry Marie, whoever she was. I enclose a ring that Alfred has given me and tell them it's for Marie, from Jean. I hear his crossing-over breathing, and I long for it to be finished so I can go home and take a bath, drink some hot tea, smoke. I feel terrible about my thoughts, but they are only thoughts.

At last, he quits breathing, and I hold his hand until it turns cold; I run back to Alfred and never return to the hospital.

The Siege ends when Paris capitulates, but we celebrate prematurely, because it is immediately complicated by The Commune, a civil war of sorts that goes on for months more and ends in a mass shooting of the ringleaders, over three hundred, in Père Lachaise.

As the city starts to rebuild and repopulate itself, art is again in demand. France has lost not only Napoleon III (good riddance) but Alsace and part of Lorraine. The Prussian forces have been removed from all but the eastern part of the city, and they, too, will leave as soon as we pay back our indemnity. Where will five billion francs come from in a country that has been torn repeatedly by war and revolution?

We complain about this at night over candlelight in the cafés, but really, we are giddy at how much of our city has actually escaped damage and at how quickly our lives begin to feel normal again. If we don't count those who are gone forever.

Slowly the city refills with the artists who had fled. I rush to the café to hear what has befallen them.

"I was nearly shot," says Renoir, "Because the new French government took my painting style for spying, because nothing so ugly could be art to them," he says indignantly. "I was only barely saved because an officer at the barracks knew me."

"Well, that would have only meant your life; I stored my latest paintings at Pissarro's, but the Prussians used his home for butchery and his (and my) canvases as aprons and rags to smear the blood on," says Monet. We all groan in laughter and horror, but the two men drink deeply when we toast the war's end.

Because Bazille's father takes him home, naturally, to bury him, we are deprived of a formal way to remember him, but we do find a means, those of us still in the city, to commemorate him.

When we gather at Bazille's studio to honor his paintings, it's easy to see what we've lost. His style has shifted, and his genius emerges. It hurts more to see his paintings than it would to behold his corpse.

We each sketch one of his paintings so that we will remember them when his father comes to pack them up next month and take them away, as he has said he will. I even attempt sketching his copse of trees. I do a good job of capturing them, or so I think, but when Monet leans over my page, I clutch it to my chest.

We unite, then, artists and all, to talk of rebuilding art. Slowly the art museums are being set right. Pissarro, initially so forlorn, now seems hopeful. "It is a good thing, to lose all of my art. It forces me to begin again."

Manet groans. "Sometimes, my friend, I would give anything to lose all of my art."

Now why should that sting so very much?

"All of it?" I ask. "Even *The Balcony*?"

He blushes and drinks deeply from his glass. I laugh and tell those at the table that my glass is empty. That lack is quickly supplied thrice over.

FIFTEEN

Perennial Paris

THE GALLERY windows of the Champs-Élysèes bloom with postwar art. Flag-laden creations by Monet, Renoir, and more, battle scenes by Meissonier, the new style finally making sense to me with its smoky view of the war. It is all any of us has of the war—vague impressions of what it was like where we were. Soldiers cannot imagine our deprivation and terror; we cannot comprehend their abject exhaustion and inner losses.

After the war, one sees men missing limbs, coat sleeves flapping in the wind. Those who are "whole" belie that tale with their eyes. I find I cannot visit the hospital I formerly worked at after it once again becomes a store. Somehow it cheapens for me the lives of those I stayed with during their transition from life to death, from sickbed to sometimes a semblance of health.

I smile to see the art, old and new, in the windows until one of Alfred's interpretations of me stares back. I put my hand to the glass, proud of him, proud of me. We have survived, together, all that the war brought us. As always, his work remains popular, selling quickly. Somehow even his grimmer paintings find favor, perhaps because the public understands all too vividly what he paints.

Manet's work begins to sell too, all of a sudden, with Durand-Ruel ordering thousands of francs' worth in one order. Everyone is talking about it. Privately, opinions had been very split on him, but with sales climbing, his genius cannot be doubted. And still I stay away, except when seeing him cannot be avoided. Not seeing him is like holding my breath, like swallowing my art. Being around him, however, is too painful. Morisot has affected everything about his work, and I cannot forgive either of them for that. I certainly cannot forgive the way he has sold me, as it were, to Stevens.

I hear that the poet Stéphane Mallarmé will hold court at Manet's this evening, and this is one draw I cannot resist; I stop in sheepishly. I have met him briefly but have never really talked with him—he speaks carefully, as if he was afraid of being charged by the word.

After losing Willie I found poetry to actually mean something, finding refuge in verse, and now I am drawn to the man's work, hoping it might explain the mysteries I have not been able to puzzle out on my own but have felt, entire, in Baudelaire's work, as well as Mallarmé's.

Mallarmé is clearly charmed by Morisot's admirable, intelligent gaze. Her looks are not inconsiderable, if one is bewitched by dark eyes and a daring glance. She questions him about his group, *les Mardistes*, a group of men who gather at his home on Tuesdays to talk about literature and the like.

"I think I should dress as a man and show up," she laughs.

"There's no need to dress as a man—just show up," he says graciously, batting his eyelashes as if wondering if he really ought to be offering.

"I couldn't. I was only teasing, but thank you."

My eyes flash. "I could."

"Then you must come," he says stiffly.

I don't care if he means it or not. I'm going.

The very next Tuesday, I am there, waiting to enter in decidedly feminine clothes. I have asked Alfred to fix my hair, and he has.

The men enter the modest home on the rue de Rome, near the Gare Saint-Lazare, and I wait to cross the street. Until Manet, I did not like reading at all. They are sure to talk of people and books I have no idea about, but I want to know more about poetry. And I must go in. Not only because Berthe is too scared to, but because I am.

I boldly cross the street and knock at the door which is opened by a short maid who is astonished when I tell her my business. I don't think she much likes allowing me in.

The men sit about in a tangle of chairs smoking cigars, drinking whisky, and talking in small groups. I wander between them, avoiding the comfort of Manet, trying to latch onto a conversation. After their initial surprise at seeing me, they continue their talk, and I feel unseen. Here I am not even a model but a painting, there to be seen and forgotten.

A hush of men sits poring over a collection of poems. "Ah," one says. "Yes, mmm . . ." says another. Then I know: They don't know what they are doing with poetry any more than I do; they are here because it is the place to be. It is another excuse to drink and smoke and stay away from their wives. I am determined to throw aside my intimidation.

"Let me see," I say. I read the poem and laugh. "'With nothing of language but the beating of the sky . . .' what a madman, this poet. He seeks to take a fan and make it a poem. It can't be done, not with words. With a brush, yes." Yet I am intrigued by the words as well.

The men are grave and embarrassed, and it is then I see our handsome host behind them, guess that it is his poem.

"And what is there to object to in making a poem from a fan?"

My eyes tire.

"It's the same as making eternity out of a night with a woman."

They all gaze elsewhere.

"Ah, but some nights, isn't that how it feels?"

"With a woman? Yes. A fan? Is the sky out of stars?"

"I'm afraid so. It's time we make stars of fans."

"May I read the rest of the poem?" I ask. When I do, I repent as its meaning filters into my understanding. Not openly, but I repent. I am quiet for the rest of the evening. Manet slowly walks me home, even though I object. No one else offers to, and someone must, it is murmured.

On the way to my house I forget I am angry with him and ask Manet question after question—along with the thump of his cane. There are so many things I don't understand. Here is another hunger, that of the mind. How can humans exist with so many needs?

I find myself tasting the words of Mallarmé's poem repeatedly, tasting the syllables. "It's not just the meaning, is it?" I ask as I say them again.

Manet humors me. "It's not."

"The words seemed sort of, I don't know, arranged on the page." I know this from peering over the shoulders of the man holding the book with the poem in it.

"They are."

"How can you just want to paint when there are words, too?" Neither of us mentions that he once attempted to write, to no avail.

"How can I not paint when my painting can say just as much but with color?"

I shake my head because I am thinking the same thing. "Ah, but Manet, here is another sort of painting, but I don't know how to do it." I do know how to paint; I know I do, for all I haven't, not really. My soul knows that I know how, and I feel it growing in me. Yet words are something precious, too.

I am intoxicated by the night's show of intelligence, even if I do detect a performance behind much of it. My mind is full. "Oh how wonderful tonight was!" I have forgotten that the reason I have come is to show up Berthe Morisot; I cannot wait until next Tuesday.

"Will you come again next week?" I ask.

He shrugs. "Probably."

"Do you think I would be welcome?" Manet's salons are not so weighty, so meaty.

He laughs. "I would be surprised if Mallarmé doesn't come courting."

I am indignant. The man is married, and there's Alfred, of course. "Only if he gives me his wife's fan and writes a poem about me." Though we laugh, I would be flattered if he wrote a poem about me.

Life begins to layer again. At Mallarmé's, I meet Debussy and other musicians, and we are able to share our love of all things musical. I bring both my guitar and my violin, but my violin tells too much of me, so I don't use it there. For all of this, there is something lacking. At night there is still emptiness where Willie was, the pain reemerging as the war's terror recedes, and nothing can touch it. Nothing. So often I wake disappointed to find Alfred beside me instead of Willie.

I barely resist starting an affair with Mallarmé. It's not that I don't want him or that he doesn't want me. What stops me is the inevitability, after a time, of a lover becoming unlovely. I want to want him without guilt, without the threat of loss.

He would willingly be my new protector, and if the cooling of Alfred's ardor is any indication, he could without much resistance from Alfred. But I want Mallarmé's poetry to feed on, not his lips, and the older I become, the more I understand this. Why would a man with access to such heady wine for the mind want a mere body, anyway?

My eyes ask him this as he reads me another of his poems. His answer with the hooding of desire. Ah. Does he create poems in order to garner desire? No. I believe the poems create it in him.

At his sessions, I am quiet while the men speak of politics and war in a higher way than they do in the Guerbois or its like. My mind rises out of the shoulders of my emotions and longs for more. I admire so much in them; I despise just as much. I hate myself for being so uneducated. I would not have to sit at their feet if I knew more.

Within weeks, though, I realize that much in the same way that they don't really say anything about poetry, they say the same things, have the same arguments, every time, about "weightier" topics. They might insert different names, but I begin to know which hot head will complain and which man will keep his cool and seem rational. There is a rhythm to what they say, and I don't even have to know the issues to participate. I don't tell them this, because I still find it mildly intoxicating. After the isolation of the war, this is heavenly.

Sitting behind them, I watch the wave of their arms, the sway of their cigarettes. I can even calculate the cock of their hips as they make an impassioned point. The subjects are immaterial. It all comes down to pride and sex.

I insert myself, then, into their arena. I pull on a string here, one there. I compliment one, roll my eyes at another. Their politics shift; their opinions. I am sad to see the underside of their intellect, but glad, too. Why do they do it? Because they want to be accepted and respected. I provide that gratification far easier than the other men and more pleasantly, as I flirt, and they sway to my sun. At other times, I stand back and observe with pleasure.

I close my eyes tonight and hear the exotic words and concepts, and I am seduced all over again. When I open my eyes, Debussy stands by me. It's late, nearly midnight. They will stop soon.

"Like the sound?" he asks.

"What do you mean?" I frown, not pleased that this forward man has interrupted my reverie.

"What beautiful thoughts were you thinking?"

"Was it so evident?"

"Why do you think I come here? I can get all the politics I need in my local bar. This group is different."

"They are, but how?"

He closes his eyes. "Close your eyes again and try to pick them out, like you might pick out an instrument at a concert."

"How did you know I do that?"

He smiles.

I heard he gave up his big first break because the orchestra was only going to have time to play the opening of his symphony. He stole the music right off their stands because he said it wouldn't represent the whole piece. Some thought he had given up every chance he'd ever had by that, but they were so wrong. I have admired him from afar after hearing that story.

So when he asks me to close my eyes, I close my eyes again.

"What do you hear?" he whispers.

"Manet's easy to pick out," I say. His confident, soothing sound is mellow and steady, like a percussive instrument.

"Good. Now who's next?" He grabs my hand.

I nearly sniff the air, as if that would help. "Mallarmé's voice is the underlying bass. Then you can add Monet's mumbled praise about the snacks."

We giggle and look at one another. "He's very poor, you know."

"Great painters should never have to be poor." I shudder.

"What else?"

I listen. Tonight is a rare night, with many in attendance. In the corner is Rodin whose work I cannot bring myself to care for, and Degas has come over several times tonight to say hello, to make sure I am not feeling lonely. This isn't so very different from a bar, except that the men are better dressed, and the conversation dominates, rather than the alcohol. There is no music, except for their voices.

Whistler has put in an appearance. I am taken by his tangled mane. There is a man who could swallow me whole. I wouldn't mind if he did, at least not for a while. His frank sexuality speaks powerfully to me, but it's too obvious.

Debussy seems disappointed. "You are distracted by the artists."

"How could I not be?"

"You hear their music. No, I think you see it." His eyes widen.

"I do. I want . . ." I turn from him.

"What is it?"

I make my right hand into a fist and squeeze it as hard as I can. "I want to paint what I see, hear, taste, and feel."

He pats my arm. "That is what we are all trying to do, in our different ways."

I hate feeling as if I would have discovered something if he had left me alone to think my thoughts through. I excuse myself and join Monet at the buffet. Soon we are laughing about the extraordinary size of the night's shrimp. Inevitably, someone calls me by my old nickname: *La Crevette*. Nicknames are both comforting in their familiarity and limiting in their scope.

Right at midnight, I thank Mallarmé and bid adieu. He tries to get me to stay, but I protest.

"I am about to read a new poem," he says.

"Can you send a copy of it to me?" I am distracted by Whistler's everything.

How to express to them all that I would much rather have their thoughts than their bodies, than their money. This, too, is weariness. The war is gone, and so much has gone with it. What is left? Why do we try to dress up what is not worthy of doing so?

Eva comes home, along with her sister. I visit her studio as soon as I can, which I am thrilled to find reopened. Over cake, we gossip for hours about the war. She cuts thick slices from a crusty baguette, too, and smears it with butter, a luxury I shall never again take for granted, and I eat voraciously. Between the two of us, the loaf is gone within no time, even faster than the cake.

"Are you glad to be back in Paris?"

She shrugs. The skin around her eyes is dark, and she picks at her fingernails.

"What is it?"

"While we were away, it was decided: I will marry."

"Marry? Decided? Why?"

"My parents said it is time, and with the war, they fear eligible men will be few. Someone came to them and asked for my hand."

"Who?" My eyes narrow as candidates flit through my head, but I don't expect who she names: Henri Guérard. "He's an artist," she says, as if that helps.

"I know who he is. He's no more an artist than my father. Less, in fact. He uses that cursed aquatint method, rather than intaglio. They are both etching, but his method . . . my father hates it. He says—said—it is cheating."

Her face tells me that she has no idea what I'm talking of.

"He said? Did your father die?"

I ball my hand. "The war brought many losses to us all."

She hugs me.

"You are so thin, and have suffered so much. . . . Why didn't you write me?"

"Thank you for the card you sent when Willie died," I say against her shoulder.

After Willie, I couldn't bring myself to write anything except one short note to his mother.

She withdraws her arms, and we sit side by side, she holding my hand.

"Promise me you'll come and visit me," she says.

"What do you mean?"

Her eyes say they are about to deliver a blow. As she lifts them, I take in what she sees: She is not re-opening the studio, she is closing it.

"When? Where?"

"Monet and Courbet speak highly of Honfleur. You know they have both painted there, especially during the war. Henri's business takes him there so, of course, I must go. He says Paris will take too long to recover."

"Honfleur? But that's hours from here." It's on the west coast of France, not that I've ever been there.

"But there are summers. You could use some time away from here surely, once I'm married and, you know, settled in."

That feeling of having found a friend dries up and cracks like an autumn leaf underfoot.

"Please, do say you will visit me." Her voice trembles, and she changes topics. "Victorine, the way you talk about art . . . I haven't even heard Morisot speak of it in this way. You need to go to art school. You've spoken about it often enough."

I don't enjoy speaking about money with the wealthy, because poverty seems but a flimsy excuse to them to not do as you please.

"It is my goal," I say gently. "But I am not ready yet. As soon as I am. . ."

"Do you imagine the desire to be an artist grows in you like a sunflower?"

I draw myself upright. "I cannot imagine a taller sunflower than the one art is in me. Dear Eva, you make it so I must speak the truth: I have not the money. Several times I have come near having it, but circumstances have arisen. As soon as I am able, I will go to art school." I crush my left hand in my right.

She laughs heartily.

"I will help. Even if I weren't able to aide you, you have half a dozen artist friends who would."

"Friends? You think they are my friends? I am their model. I care about them, but because of my class, they do not, cannot, care about me." I will not mention that Alfred only wants me because I am not a painter, but a model with an extraordinary eye. Or that he withdraws from me incrementally with each note he receives from his wife.

Her eyes widen. "Then you do not believe I am your friend?" Tears show themselves in her eyes.

"I didn't mean you. You have always treated me as if I am quite as good as you are. I meant the others."

She rises and goes to her desk, coming back with her purse. "How much are classes?"

I touch her hand as I watch her remove a bundle of cash, imagine taking it gratefully from her, and just as quickly, I know I can't.

"Thank you, but no."

I can't express my feelings, because there is only the ache of having to say *no* to not only my dream for now, but to this generous offer from my beautiful-hearted friend.

She shakes her head and sips her tea. I find myself doing the same.

Before I know it, Eva is married, and Jeanne and I wait at the train station to see Eva and Henri off.

I agree to visit, even as I see myself painting over this scene on my mind's canvas, blotting her out from those who are close. Perhaps this is a better sort of friendship anyway, this distance.

Her sister weeps so to see her go that I fear for her health. Jeanne clutches to me.

"Aren't you to go to her after they return from their honeymoon?" I ask.

"Yes," she blubbers, "but that will be a month or more from now. We've never been apart so long."

Jeanne is to spend some time with them, ostensibly to help her sister set up house. I suspect they will also look for an eligible husband for Jeanne in Honfleur. I shudder and realize how I will miss Eva, how much I have missed her during the war. For a moment, I doubt art. My heart cracks a bit as I think of the value with which I have imbued it. What if even it is not enough? What if it is just another train out of our troubles that we board, one that loops back to where we began?

Life slowly returns to Paris. I sleep beside the antsy Alfred who writes his wife weekly to come home, though he thinks I don't know it. She claims her mother is too afraid for her to come back until we are sure that Paris is safe from war, and then she writes that her mother is too ill for her to leave.

Too soon for my liking, however, the word gets about: She is on her way back to Paris. Alfred does not mention it, but I notice his quietness, and he spends more time on his side of the bed. I try not to notice when his engraved toiletry set and his best cuff links disappear. When I walk by his house the next day, there is light in every room, and a servant beats a rug outside the back door.

I awaken to a persistent rapping at the door. I thump the bed, trying to get Alfred's attention, but the bed is empty. Did he not come home? Home. I smile at my thoughts through my sleep.

I stumble to the door, clutching my dressing gown closed. A filthy but adorable boy with brown curls and flushed cheeks holds out a note and wipes his nose. I scrounge around until I find some coins for him, dropping a couple in my haste to reach for the letter.

He waits as I open the envelope, watches me read it. He fetches me a chair as my knees sag. His eyes gauge me intelligently; even in my grief I see this.

"The bastard wants me to move out," I say. "Just like that. Because his wife is home."

He clucks his tongue and snorts up the moisture on his face. Absentmindedly I fetch my *mouchoir* from a table. With a reddening face he uses it, and then tries to hand it back to me.

I wave my hand as I read the note again.

"I'm to wait for a reply," he says, snorting.

"Well, I'm not sending one." I am too angry to cry, too hurt to do anything but curse the stupid war.

The boy pulls up a chair, too, and he looks longingly at the mound of bread on the table. I make sure to have too much of it, now that it's available again.

When it gets stale, I take it to the park and feed it to the ducks that quack with pleasure. After the deprivation, it feels extravagant and my due to waste food.

"Eat it, if it's not too stale," I say. He attacks the bread as if he were one of those hungry ducks. His zest reminds me of Willie's.

"I was going to say I have some jam as well, if you'd like," I laugh.

"Okay," he says, mouth full, eyes darting to see when and if the promised condiment will appear.

"I'm Victorine. Who are you?"

"Pug," he says through the wad of bread as I hand him the jar of jam.

As he eats, I pace. I try not to panic. I've taken care of myself before, so many times. But I have become used to this life, I am ashamed to say, accustomed to the comfort and beauty of this apartment, the ease (even during the war) of having my needs taken care of. If I must rent a place to live, there will go the small stockpile of money I've been able to save again towards art classes.

I walk those kitchen planks as if they are a jail cell, and I realize it is a sort of entrapment, this dependence I have formed. Stevens is doing me a favor. Yet why does it feel as if he has cut me off from more than this place? Shouldn't he owe me more for the comfort I gave him while his wife was away? Not monetarily necessarily, but loyalty? I am sure at least a fraction of him loves me. Has his wife learned of me?

"Fine, so I have to find a room, soon, one that isn't too dear. That shouldn't be too hard, should it?" I look at Pug.

He swallows and nods. "I know where there are places to rent, cheap." He surveys what he can see of the apartment. "Not like this, but. . ." He puts his finger in the jam, and places it in his mouth.

Somehow his confidence reassures me. I pick up a hunk of bread, sop it in the jam, and fill my mouth. I'm surprised to find that beneath the panic, excitement wells up at the thought of having my own space once again, of not being on call to anyone.

"I don't need it to be fancy, just clean." He looks doubtful. "Or capable of becoming clean." He looks at the floor.

I sigh. "Maybe you'd better just take me to see what you're talking about."

The shock of being thrown over is wearing off and seems inevitable now. I will feel better when I am no longer dependent on Alfred. I'm more hurt than anything. Of all of the men I have known, I would have sworn Alfred to be the kindest, the most reliable and loyal.

It's his loyalty that is causing him to reject me, but not loyalty towards me.

The dingy room that Pug leads me to is in a mostly burned-out section of town, one where the street lamps have not yet been mended. It's a scary, spooky place, but thankfully the landlady does not appear to recognize me and thinks that Pug is my son, which strangely warms my heart. I pound my chest to dislodge the unfamiliar feeling, but it won't go away so easily.

When she quotes a price, I open my mouth to accept, but Pug interjects and offers only half the amount. The woman's gray bun shakes with her head. She licks the corner of her mouth, her tongue almost touching a large mole just above her mouth, and I look away.

"Fine," she says. "But it's not big enough for more than the two of you, so you'd better not be sneaking a family of seven in here."

"I can assure you we will not," I say, putting my arm about Pug, who tries to squirm away but I clamp my arm tighter. Better she not yet know the truth.

"Let's go get lunch before we move our things in," I say as I tuck my arm through Pug's. He stiffly walks with me.

Although I know Alfred is not a "scene" person, I will make him speak to me. I send Pug back with a note later that day and tell him he is to wait for an answer. "If you bring me back a reply, I will buy you as much chocolate as you can eat today," I promise.

I have thrown a few things around uncertainly rather than packed when Pug finally returns with a scrap of paper. It says simply "Tomorrow. Two. Studio."

Pug is perhaps ten, maybe eleven and is nearly as tall as I am. His face is still war gaunt, I suppose. His eyes are always watchful, as if determined not to let an opportunity slip by.

We sit together in a confectionary shop and I watch him eat five, six, seven pieces of candy. I'm not surprised when he asks for more.

"Just don't make yourself sick," I say as I ask for five more pieces. He eats those nearly as quickly and asks for just three more. I buy five and I hand him the three he requested, and he eats them now at a more leisurely pace.

I grin at his grimy face with the cheeks plumped with candy. "You know how I like to eat them? First I force the back off with my teeth." I demonstrate before removing one from my mouth and showing him the remaining filled shell. "Then I scoop the insides out with my tongue." I demonstrate it and he laughs. "Lastly, I crunch right into that chocolate's carcass."

He smiles back at me and tries it with his remaining candy. His hair falls over his brow, and I sweep it back. His brow is quite handsome, though it does wrinkle indignantly too often.

"Why don't we buy some for you to take home?" I suggest.

His eyes glow, but he shakes his head. I order a box anyway and we walk slowly back to my new apartment. Somehow, although I think I should be devastated at this turning out (and a part of me is), instead, I feel as if I have been given the gift of this shaggy child. Impulsively I hug him to me, and he pulls away as if unaccustomed to affection. This makes me want to hug him again, but I refrain.

"If you need some work, I sure could use someone to help me paint those walls." I force the box of chocolates on him and he tucks it under his shirt.

He nods. "I'll come by tomorrow morning," he says. Then he ducks down an alley and is gone.

I look a long time after him, and I slowly go inside this place that has never really been mine and continue to attempt packing. But what is mine of the household and what is Alfred's? Are the clothes he bought for me mine? Which are gifts and which are props? Which am I? I long to lash out against this place, rip, tear, break, and stain everything in it, and yet that would be to make him seem more important to me than he really is, and so I won't.

The next morning Pug and I begin cleaning my new room in preparation for painting it. He instinctively knows what needs doing and does it without instruction.

As I flounder about, he points: "Throw that lot out and let's move the bed by the window." I am grateful for his help and his company, though I am determined to educate him about bathing as soon as I think I can get by with it.

It is with confidence that I leave the boy to work while I visit Alfred.

I arrive at Alfred's studio right on time, somehow wishing Pug were with me. I greet him frostily and avoid the kiss he tries to place upon my cheek.

He appears newly bereaved, and his whole body sags. I cannot be as angry as I want to be.

"Thank you, Stevens," I say, using his surname to aid us both in this separation, "for all you did for me during the war." I cannot hate him, seeing the depression and self-hatred that ravage him. It is just that tenderness towards those he loves that has drawn me to him.

"I have a new address; I will leave it at our old apartment for you. Just send around whatever is to be mine."

"Whatever is to be yours? Why, it's all yours. What need have I for cutlery and negligees?" The hurt gives temporary life to his eyes. His glance strolls up and down my body, and then he turns as if impatient with himself. "Take it all away with you, all except…"

He means that damn shawl, the one that has made him feel so guilty, perhaps the guiltiest of all. He was the one who sold his loyalty to his wife for a scarf. I feel the least bit guilty myself knowing that of all things, that was the one for which I should not have asked.

"Anything but that." Knowing what is right to do does not at all mean we will do it.

"I told you," he says, "That in the event . . ."

"Has she returned then?" I ask so that his face will turn from purple back to its normal color, not because I don't know.

"She has. The baby has grown so much. . . . I missed them."

He sobs then, his shoulders lurching, and I throw my arms about him as I have so many times before.

I take his face in my hands. "If only you understood that what you feel for me has nothing to do with her and never will. Then maybe, but no. Thank you for all you have done, though."

The cutting of this cord frees me; his wife will look after him now. The war is over. There is no one I must care for; money is not my first concern. My mother can be supported for very little now that she has rented out my old room to a woman just a few years younger than my mother. I am both relieved and jealous of the roommate whose chief function besides the rent she brings seems to be going to market and running mother's errands. It is the perfect solution.

I want to give him this one thing he asks of me, and yet it is the only proof I have of his true feelings and attentions toward me: "Alfred, I need the shawl."

He raises his head as if to fight. He's the one who chose to give me the equivalent of what he gave his wife. He must live with the guilt that plagues him surely more than any need for the money.

"She found a copy of the bank draft for it, you know, and she is livid because it's as much as I spent on hers. It was really unfair of me."

"I will return the dressing gown." I cannot spare the triumph that the scarf represents.

"Keep them. Keep them both," he says, appearing weary and old. "I will just have to explain it to her."

I go to the door and turn again. I run to him and throw my arms about his waist, and then I let go.

Before sundown, Pug and I have transferred everything that will fit from the apartment to the room. I give him the excess to sell for himself. When I wave goodbye to him, it's all I can do to go inside and shut the door.

Many a person has, I suppose, attempted to paint without the benefit of art school. Those people do not live in Paris. True, I have heard art instruction from painters most of my life. I have the advantage of having sat for painters, so I know more about the construction of a scene than perhaps they do, having been in many. I have had a small amount of encouragement from Alfred as to my use of color. But I cannot at all claim to truly know what I am doing.

When I dig out the art supplies buried in my trunk, my hands shake with eagerness.

I am my first subject. Carefully, I set out all of my materials, put on an old apron. I lay out cloths and brushes, paint. I bow my head, wishing there was someone I could pray to who would aid me, ease my fear. Just as quickly I raise my head and my hand.

When I study the canvas later, my painted head lists and my eyes are uneven. My hair is Medusa's rendered in copper. It is not at all what I had intended. The colors are all wrong. I tear the painting from the stand and with much effort, kick my boot through it. Why did I ever imagine I could do this?

So many streets have been emptied of their trees by The Siege's lack of fuel that in the spring Paris replants trees, despite how long it will be before we see them truly take root. Though it will take time, most everything can be replaced. Everything except Willie.

I plant flowers in a large pot outside my room, hoping to bring spring a bit closer to me. A carriage stops before my house, and out steps a man, leaning heavily upon a cane. Manet's face is white and drawn.

We briefly embrace; he kisses me upon both cheeks. "You did not come when I asked."

Seeing his pinched face, I repent instantly. "I will now."

"Finish your planting," he says, peering at my filthy hands, at the cab. "Tomorrow is soon enough. But Victorine? Please do come." He slowly climbs back into the conveyance.

The next morning I get ready slowly, luxuriously fixing my hair, thinking of how I used to sweep into his studio, now such a foreign place to me. I long to still be the brazen woman who confronted him so many times, for him to be the arrogant painter who needed it. Neither of us is who we were.

His studio feels hollow now; it's too large and too clean; someone has been rearranging it, and that someone is not Manet. He's not meant to create immaculate art. He motions for me to sit on a plush sofa, offers me a drink, which I refuse. We sit without saying anything.

"I have a painting in mind that I thought you might be perfect for."

I study the embroidered carpet. "I appreciate the offer, but I don't model anymore."

He flips his hand vaguely towards me. We have made an uneasy peace, and with his illness, how can I refuse him?

I stare at a portrait of a man smoking a pipe and drinking beer. It looks like a Hals, very nicely done. I like the custom artists have of displaying others' work in their studios. It helps lesser-known artists get a start.

"Whose is that?"

"It's not been sold yet."

I laugh. "No, I mean who painted it."

"You like it?"

I wonder if Eva or even Morisot painted it during one of their sessions with him once upon a time, and I hesitate to praise it, but I can't be so small. "It has very nice light and shadows, life-like features. It reminds me of The Masters."

"Thank you. I painted it when I got back from Holland."

"You? Are you going to exhibit it?" I ask, because I have to say something.

"That's the idea."

"They'd like it."

"You don't?"

I like it, but in the way I like something that has existed in a museum forever. "It's beautiful, Manet, but . . ."

He bristles. "What is wrong with it?"

"The tonalities, the values. The composition. This looks as if you've copied it in the Louvre."

He tosses his cigar into an ashtray. "Ask Bellot about that. I made him sit for me over sixty times."

"If it were anyone else's, I would love it." I touch his arm. "It's just not the Manet I know."

He presses his lips together, and they quiver. His eyes glisten. "The Manet you knew was young and arrogant. This Manet is ill and wants to be recognized, or the rest of my work will be forgotten, too."

I understand him, yet it still seems a compromise. "If you like it . . ."

"I'm going to submit it."

"It will be accepted."

He picks up his cigar. "I know. Now, let's talk about when we will start this painting."

"I really don't model anymore."

He blows smoke as if blowing away my protest. It works.

This time he pictures me with a young girl, at a railway station, the Gare Saint-Lazare. We do part of it in the backyard of his banker, and though I ask, he only mumbles when I ask whose child it is. It's entirely possible that he stopped her on the street and asked her guardian if he might paint her; A woman stands waiting for her in the corner—her mother?

He adds the railway to the painting later. It's a mix of plein air and studio painting. He's trying to get used to painting outdoors, but I don't think he really cares for it.

It feels right, sitting under his gaze. He has put me in the role of a mother, or a nanny, in this painting, but I'm not paying any attention to my charge, who is enthralled by the railway. I notice he has given me Morisot's fan, and I protest initially, but it's hard to deny this failing man anything.

Morisot is being courted by Manet's brother, so it is considered improper for her to pose for Édouard anymore. I try not to smile when he explains this when I ask.

"Thank you for adding the girl," I say of this painting. He acknowledges by this that I am grown, that I am capable of maternal feelings. Pug, my sweet friend, visits me often during the sitting, and I talk with him about my day with Manet. His is a face I trust implicitly.

Muriel, the young model, won't be still. So Manet paints her with her back to us. It relieves his need to paint her ever-shifting face. It also makes the statement he needs to make: He rejects me and what I have meant to his work thoroughly in this painting: I am the past, aging, unfashionable (the dress is three seasons old). The young girl is facing the train of the present, whereas I am unable to bear where things are going. He tells me he no longer needs me, but he does it with affection and kindness, with tired brushstrokes. It's difficult for me to be offended, because he scarcely needs art, and what am I beside that?

While I sit, he talks of another painting he is doing, his *La Parisienne*. Every painting he has done of me has been a way of refining his vision of just who she is. But he doesn't use me. I ask about his model, Ellen Andree, a statuesque woman not associated with the lowly works that I am. By asking about her, I ask why he did not choose me. He doesn't answer either question.

This is why I can't rely on a man, on anyone, to paint who I am. I'm the only one who will be able to do that.

On the days Pug visits Manet's studio, he talks with Muriel and quickly catches on to what is needed of her when she can't.

"Stand like this," he shows her. When she begins to wiggle, he bribes her to be still with chewing gum that she promptly gets stuck in her hair. Manet pretends to wait patiently for Pug to remove the clump.

The two children become, if not friends, then pleasant with one another, and one afternoon I have every reason to bless Muriel when she tells Pug she won't play with him during a break because he needs a bath. He stays away two days after that, but when he returns, he is cleaner than I have ever seen him, and he smells fresh.

I catch Pug one afternoon going through the dustbin just outside Manet's studio sorting out rags and bottles when the painting has moved indoors.

"What are you doing?" I whisper.

His face colors. "I was going to sell these. Do you think he would mind?"

"No, Pug. I don't think he would. But how much do you need?"

"Supper for seven," he says, not looking at me.

"Done," I say, digging coins out of my purse. "You can always ask me, Pug. I may not always have it to give, but if I do, I will give it to you. You don't have to go through the trash."

"Why wouldn't I—they're just throwing money away, and you have your own rent."

Muriel's caretaker, the woman who turns out to be, indeed, her mother, approaches, and I block Pug's pile with my skirts.

"*Bonne nuit,*" I say.

She nods back suspiciously as she goes indoors to collect her charge.

"Just tell me next time when you need something," I whisper as I kiss his forehead. He jerks away, but not before I see a hint of a smile.

I sell what household goods I can to a local pawnshop, one of those government places meant to aid those of us in need of money, and I give Pug what money I don't need for the week because I know he won't ask.

It feels good, letting go of the things from my old apartment with Stevens that are really too ornate and too unsafe to keep in my small, musty room at the top of a winding set of stairs. Though I give plenty to Pug, I kept more than I need. Even with its fresh coat of paint, this room is not a desirable lodging.

Letting go feels almost as good as acquiring. I enjoy the new space in my home. Just as not eating fueled me during the war, so giving what I can for Pug and his family fuels me. I don't know how else to show the child that I care.

While my mother at least receives me in her home now, as always, she does not require my companionship since she moved to a smaller apartment. I leave her a gift now and again, but I can see that with her boarder, she really has no need of me. Sentiment is not strong in either of us. I suppose I should be grateful for that, but it causes me to be all the more tender to Pug.

I actually bring Pug to her apartment once, but at the last minute I ask him to wait outside. I don't know that my mother will understand or approve. While I can handle that, I don't see why he should have to.

◈

Now Manet stands as much as possible while working on *The Railway* because his leg hurts. Then he tries sitting because his leg hurts, but no matter what, his leg just hurts.

This past and present business in the painting tells me that he is saying goodbye to me as a model and perhaps he is contemplating taking leave of even more. It's clear that his illness is progressing, though at what speed, I cannot determine. I have trouble sleeping some nights for fear of a world without Manet in it. As bleak as the world is without Willie, at least I fancy I see him in the things he loved. But Manet not here, not creating the world?

I square my shoulders. Am I not just as in charge of creating the art world as he?

This year Manet is rewarded, finally, by the Academy with a medal (though not for a painting of me). When I hear of it, I do not congratulate him—I do something else entirely.

SIXTEEN

Académie de Julian

W HEN I READ in the newspaper that Manet has been awarded a second-class medal for his stylized portrait of Henri Rochefort, it decides me.

I pack the shawl Alfred gave me (still swathed in its tissue) into the brown paper from which it originally came, tie it gently with the very string it came wound in, and retrieve the receipt from my box where I store my scant *bijoux* and a few *billets-doux*. I tell myself I cannot sell it, because there are some things for which there is no going back from selling, but as soon as I say it, I know I must. That does not prevent me from shedding more than a few tears.

Instinct guides me to dress in my best (a costume Alfred let me keep) when I go to the shop; modeling tells me how to pretend to be Alfred's wife out for a day's shopping in the fine fashionable shops lining these streets. I dab at my hem before I enter the store, then I shrug and go inside.

"May I help you?" a young man says over his pince-nez. My lips don't want to behave as I listen to his affectation. I turn my eyes from the mannequins in the shop window, gaze at the bolts of material spread over table after table, a garden of luxury.

"Yes. I have a purchase to return."

He takes the bundle from me, views the receipt I thrust haughtily at him.

"Madame, this is from some time ago. You cannot expect . . ."

"It is in impeccable condition, and it was used in one of Stevens's paintings," I say, straightening my shoulders.

He opens the package and surveys every inch of the fabric.

"We have never," he says, but then he pauses. "Alfred Stevens?" he asks. "One moment. I shall return presently."

"See that you do." I allow my elbows to rest on the marble counter while he is gone, sink my chin into my hands. I pluck at a corner of a light blue silk, listen to it hiss between my fingers as I let it drop.

When he comes back, he removes his eyeglasses, twists them in his hands. "Although I am afraid I cannot give you any money, I can provide you with the name of a shop that should be more than happy to take your item."

"Fine," I snap, picking up the card.

At the dingy pawn shop (although a better class than the ones I am used to in my neighborhood), I pretend not to watch the clerk count out the money as my heart races. I open my frog purse and tuck the money carefully inside, leave without saying goodbye.

When I am out the door and around the building, I beat the now-over-stuffed frog against a wall until its mouth gasps and money bounces onto the ground. I turn away, but then I grab it up again, just as an old man leans over.

"Here," I say, handing him some coins. On second thought, I empty the purse into my hand and give him the deflated frog. He tucks it into his jacket as if it's an important letter, nods conspiratorially.

To my surprise, I nearly skip as I walk away.

In less than a quarter of an hour I am at my destination at the Passage des Panoramas. I glance between the two doors and two staircases at the address and fling open the first door of Académie de Julian. "How much for classes?" I ask the woman who comes forward. She quotes me a price twice that of what the men pay at Thomas Couture's academy; I blink twice: "Sign me up." I dump most of the money I have into her hand, and as she juggles it and roots among a table full of tablets for a receipt book, she glances at the money and says it will do for the semester.

"And where will you get next semester's payment?"

She doesn't wear glasses, but if she did, she would be looking over them at me.

I glare: "What concern is that of yours right now?" I ignore the nervous feeling in my stomach. This school is one of the few that admits women, and the students produce quality art. Though the national academy, the École des

Beaux-Arts, may be denied me, if I can help it, this will not be. I have never felt the want of money more.

I must wait an interminably long month for a new round of classes to begin, No Glasses tells me. In that time, I secure a job as an usher in a theater. I have had quite enough of modeling, and this job promises tips as well.

My life is divided between art and work only artificially; to me, work is the thing that keeps me from art, but it allows me to create it by supplying my meager needs.

I admire the theater's architecture where I work, the *Théâtre de la Renaissance*, built by Charles de Lalande on the former site of the Deffieux restaurant that the Communards burned. It's a magnificent theater. That it is right beside the Porte Saint-Martin, which reminds me of a less grand version of the Arc de Triomphe, makes it seem even more elegant and certainly to scale.

The date it was built, 1872, is proudly etched in its upper parts; the inscription is held by a sculpted man and a woman. As I walk into it, I note the cherubic children holding instruments perched upon each of the windowsills as if to guard the magic within. Faux columns decorate the upper sections, and a quartet of laughing sisters with heads draped with shawls greets theatergoers. The top is ornamented with a harp, almost as if the building were a Christmas tree.

There is always something to admire about the building's exterior, as even the round windows are charming. Here is something of Haussmann of which I certainly approve.

The inside is even more glorious. For all that it does hold six hundred (not so large, not so small); there is something intimate about it, especially when the lights are doused. One, two, three, four levels, not to mention the ground level, are all red walled, trimmed in gold. The figures painted on the ceiling give one something at which to stare while waiting anxiously for a play to begin, as if everyone wearing their theater best isn't enough for the eyes.

I don't mind ushering, except that it isn't painting. I live on tips, so I am careful to be professional and kind, to keep my wit to a minimum. Occasionally a man who is alone asks me to share his box, and I am able to see the whole show with my manager's blessing. Then, I forget I am working and am carried away to foreign times and lands. While I enjoy the ballets, I enjoy the plays more.

Raised voices greet me today. I know immediately who is arguing as I watch the actors in their rehearsal positions. Hippolyte Hopstein is the director, but the playwright, Victor Koning, and he are always fighting. The actors listen to Hopstein, but when he leaves the stage, Koning tells them to do something else. Koning enjoys *opéras-bouffes*, while Hopstein says they are silly, airy things with no substance. He prefers plays by Zola. I must say, I see his point. He is in the middle of getting up a production of *Thérèse Raquin*, Zola's "scandalous" novel.

I stare wistfully at the poster advertising the play every time I come to work. While I am thrilled to see Zola's name written so large, my father could have done a better job with the poster. The figures in this poster look skeletal and spooky, not at all appealing. Who has convinced them to print it in black and white, when playbills cry out for color?

Still, watching *Thérèse Raquin* enthralls me. The story of the half orphan, forced to marry a cousin she does not love who then finds passion with a painter, is romantic. As with most true romances, it ends in tragedy. But what happiness before the fall. *Willie.* Romance is such a remote notion now.

I feel guilty when I accept money from the poorer patrons, and I wish I could charge those with money even more. The fancy loges are occupied by women wearing plunging black-and-white striped silk, opera glasses at the ready. The men sit beside or just behind them, leaning forward to address penetrating questions to the tops of the unsuspecting women's bosoms.

I adjust the already high top of my plain black dress. Art may cost many things, but haven't I paid enough?

At the theater, my eyes decode the ballets quickly, hungrily, aided by my friend Degas who frequents the theater with permission to have total access to all facilities backstage.

He has remained such a quiet yet steady presence at the cafés that he is seldom noticed. Though he may be gruff and a bit smelly, he does not hate women as some say. How his paintings can be so misinterpreted puzzles me. With the help of his commentary, muttered behind the scenes of the ballet to me, and his lightning-fast sketches, I quickly learn how unpleasant and unlovely a ballerina's life is, how determined he is to show what is. I quite believe it, if it's anything like how unglamorous a model's life is.

As the house lights are slowly doused one evening, I wait eagerly in my chair in the front row, just to the left of the stage, for the curtain to rise. Degas smiles at my excitement at the privileged spot he secured for me. As long as I return to my assigned post by intermission, I may stay here.

The dancers twirl: I lean forward. Their limbs exhibit a simultaneous, puppet-like control, striking diagonals and perpendiculars. They busy the space before our eyes, their limbs there, not there. Their whirling gauzy white skirts populate the scenery of *Coppélia*.

I glance quickly around before I give myself over to it. Here in the near dark, I indulge in what I know does not exist. Degas offers me his handkerchief. I hold the dingy square, but I wipe at my face with my sleeve.

He touches my arm as a dancer bends awkwardly to fix her shoe, her calf bulking. The rapid heaving of the groups' chests belies their grace. One of them looks pitifully thin, and I am glad when the performance is over. From then on, I decline offers to get closer.

Eventually, I am able to enjoy again the performances from the back of the room, but not without remembering what I am really looking at. When I meet some of the girls, I recognize the deadness in their eyes, and I flee from it as I have flown from it in my own.

I praise Degas's paintings while hating him for them. When I tell Degas that, he snorts. "You have been around Stevens's painting too long."

"But I do not enjoy Stevens's work."

He smiles in that sardonic way that makes others hate him, but I find him instructive. "Didn't you sit for him? Then you helped him create his work, did you not? Could you not have changed it?"

I cross my arms. I don't mention the war years or the painting with the skull. Though paintings may be public, not everything about them is. I am, however, shocked and pleased that Degas understands a model's influence on a painting.

Within two days, I am posing for Degas as a woman taking a bath in all of her awkward glory. He drags the pastels across the paper swiftly. When I see the unglamorous result, I don't blame him for wanting to rid his sight of me, for wanting to see beauty again. I don't ask him if he's seen the Stevens image of me bathing; it's obvious he has.

"I do look just this ungraceful while bathing, I'm sure. It is not at all what men usually see in a woman."

"They see it, but they pretend they don't, and so they paint you as you are not, both to please you and themselves."

"All except Manet."

Degas inclines his head. "That is what is so disconcerting about his paintings: He makes you neither entirely beautiful nor entirely ugly."

Realization sparks through me.

"Dear Degas, you have hit exactly upon it."

The next evening Degas approaches me, and I busy myself with a patron Eventually I look up, and he is engrossed in drawing short, broad strokes on thick paper. We seldom thank people for truth, especially when it's stark. I was right to say I do not want to model anymore. The time for that in my life is through.

I don't bring anything but lunch with me the first day of art school, because I don't know what we will need. I arrive early and smoke a cigarette on a bench while I wait for the school to come to life.

I have been told that I must choose between the stairs on the left which lead to a classroom with only clothed models, and the staircase on the right, where, "You'll no doubt be more comfortable," the class *messier* (I refuse to learn No Glasses's name) says.

"And do you remain on this side?" I ask her. That is, the left side.

"Of course," she says primly.

"Then the right it is."

How can they expect women to paint with passion when they cannot even see, much less touch, the male equipage? Perhaps it's good that I have been regarded much as a chair, rather than a woman. For it has enabled me to get to the heart of art and not only to polite society paintings.

Even when the doors open, I watch several young women of means in a rainbow of quality clothing enter the school without approaching the white door myself. Though their ages range from perhaps sixteen to thirty-five, I'd say the average is twenty. Though I'm not the oldest, I'm certainly not one of the youngest.

I amuse myself by guessing which flight of stairs they will mount. Sometimes girls who chatter together outdoors solemnly separate and wave as they climb into separate worlds.

I throw down my cigarette, step on it, push wide that door on the right, and as easily as that, I'm inside.

Because the women "must" be taught separately from the men, the class consists of a couple of dozen women crowded into this dimly lit room.

A woman to my left introduces herself as Annie, "from America," and I merely nod. She bristles at my lack of interest and shapes her tartan skirt about her fussy bustle. I'm aware of the prejudice shown in France to those who come here to pursue art, but that is not why I disdain her. She has an inherent arrogance upon her face; arrogance must be proven to be merited for me to pay it any mind.

After we group into the room, we jockey ourselves into position (I'm relegated to the middle of the pack, something I fully intend to remedy as soon as possible). We turn our attention to the front of the class when the teacher and founder of the school, Rodolphe Julian, enters and welcomes us "home" for the semester, and there is laughter, a bit of eye wiping. On the one hand this is true for me: My home is among art. On the other hand, I can already guess I will no more belong here than elsewhere.

We are to be here promptly at eight a.m. and regularly, the gray-haired man with a receding hairline says. He is lightly tanned, though his face is much covered by his curved mustache and wide beard. His waist is somewhat thick, but not in Stevens's friendly way: M. Julian thrusts out his vested abdomen in a frustrated manner whenever something displeases him.

"You are expected to know the rudiments of drawing. If you do not, please see me at break," he says, raising his chin in a way that thins his neck.

I am relieved that I have had some practice.

"In addition to painting techniques you will learn . . ." he goes on and on, walking about the room and distributing a brush and palette before each of us, advising us to pick up before tomorrow the supplies from the list he gives us.

Naturally, there are more expenses than I expected. Why couldn't my passion be writing, which requires only pen, paper, and ink?

Our actual lesson for the morning does not begin as I would have anticipated. Indeed, he orders us outdoors. Once there, "Hands in the air, raise them up high. Wiggle your fingers. Yes," says M. Julian. "Now bend from the waist and swing your head gently to and fro, circling around." I cannot watch those who try to do the exercises in their bustles and great crinolines. Annie's rear sways in so silly a manner I dare not look at her. They are instructed to scale down their clothing for tomorrow. I am proud that I in my art widow's weeds will not need to do so.

Once we are warmed up, as he calls it, he permits us to go indoors where we once again claim space in the smoky room. Though I am not a fan of painting outdoors, I'd rather, I believe, than attempt to breathe in this atmosphere. I quickly open all the windows, though I am glared at by M. Julian. Not only the air but the extra light is appreciated.

"Now we will learn how to hold the brush," he says, and I must wonder if he is trying our patience on purpose. My fingers clutch this wooden stick with pig bristles attached or some such, banded by metal, practicing the grips he exhibits and then calls out: baton grip—held from underneath with my thumb and index finger, or the over-the-hand grip for close work, and finally, the handwriting grip which, as it sounds, much resembles that of simply writing. While I've heard these before, I've never practiced them. Why practice what comes naturally?

I thirst for color on the tip of my brush, long to kiss the canvas with streaks of my soul. How can he expect me to learn these worse than rudiments—crudiments? I cross my arms and glare, then realize how ungrateful I am. Perhaps these others have not had the benefit of growing up with art.

My gratitude nearly deserts me when we are tediously taught how to use the palette (it doesn't take much more than sticking one's finger in and leaning it upon one's arm) and how to clean it to make room for more paint (a palette knife taken to the dried remains). How many times did I hear that sandpaper-like shuffling sound as the old made way for the new at Manet's? I silently sigh through this first lesson, eager to pop open a tube of paint.

He tells us that he will not be our teacher often. We will have a series of guest painters and lecturers to cover different topics. And he must divide his time between the studios—the two here and the ones he has for men elsewhere. A disappointed ripple goes through the crowd and he raises his hand. "I will be here weekly to check on your progress," he says. "Do not neglect to be here on Saturday mornings, as I can devote more time to you then."

Quiet whispers and the faint rustle of skirts as one woman leaves and soon returns are the only sounds in the room as we are allowed to begin testing the brush upon the canvas. I hold my breath to listen for the sound of the paint-brushes at work. From left to right, I see a symphony of wooden handles all playing their own score, and I secretly wipe my eyes.

The next four hours go exceedingly quickly.

After we are released for the day, I go to the shop I know Manet frequents with M. Julian's supply list, and just as I have done so many times for him, I hand the list to the shopkeeper, one I do not recognize but who recognizes me.

"For which painter is mademoiselle purchasing these? For whom are you sitting nowadays?" asks the presumptuous woman with the plentitude of skin tags on her neck.

"Madame is now attending Académie de Julian," I fume. I may be a widow, but in my heart I am still married. I enjoy the safety the title gives.

"Ah yes, of course. An excellent school." The woman, probably my age, scans me from head to toe, as if critiquing my appearance, the way my hair has dimmed and my skin sallowed just a bit from the cigarettes. I want to punish her for her impertinence, want to openly notice her pudgy neck and potato-like body, but I merely stare at her until she disappears into the back of the shop.

Instead, I tour the place, inhaling the scent of the convergence of all that I love. This is the Palace of Packaged Potential. My pulse charges.

She returns, breathing heavily, covering the counter with paint, leaves, brings back brushes, canvases, a mahl stick, palette, palette knife, shop rags, an apron, and more. When she carries out a portable easel I laugh.

"However will I transport all of these things?"

"Best let us deliver them to the school."

I promptly agree to the proposal.

She gazes over my head. "I wish I could go to art school."

"This is Paris! Surely your shop does a brisk trade," I encourage, letting go of my lingering resentment.

"It's not my shop. I only work here."

"Perhaps one day the École des Beaux-Arts will be open to us women as well and just as the men do, we will not have to pay anything to learn?"

"Or maybe one day I will get enough ahead to pay." She laughs. "I have three children whose father perished in the war. Of course this will never happen for me, but I draw at night when I can."

"One would not be a proper citizen of France without creating some sort of art," I say, patting the counter. "And you are bringing up three children who might be artists in their turn."

She rigidly rings my things up. I don't blame her—children be damned, I'd rather be an artist than pass it on as if it's eye color.

"I'll be taking this with me," I say, picking up the oak mahl stick, marching out into the street and waving the thing as if I'm leading a parade: I'm going to art school.

The Paris art scene is so incestuous that within hours everyone who hasn't already heard that I'm going to school will. But I must put my past place in art behind me. I am to be the eyes now, not the body. My sight sharpens at the thought.

We are allowed at school, finally, to take up the brush in preparation to attempt a still life instead of incessantly pretending, mixing colors, and painting nothing but lines and shapes. On all sides I am surrounded by women who wipe their faces and pull their collars away from their necks, all intently watching the brushes in their hands. I begin with the brush in my left hand, as I have been accustomed to doing.

Immediately my fingers squirm and approach the canvas, not wanting to wait. But when M. Julian raises his eyebrows at me, I quickly switch the instrument to my right. That, too, feels correct.

I switch the brush back and forth between my hands. Will the painting look different if I use one hand versus the other?

On the guitar, one has two hands doing quite different things: The left (for most) sets the foundation, the chord, of the tune, while the right hand brings forth the sound. Why do we artists use but one hand? Cannot the right and the left both learn to do their part? Perhaps they have different mysteries to utter. Does the heart know what the brain knows? Can it?

M. Julian approaches, and for a moment I can't remember which hand "should" be holding the brush. It's in the left again.

When I learned to write, my mother and my teacher constantly took the pen from my left hand and put it in my right. When they were not looking, I used my left. After a while, I was just as proficient with my right hand as my left, although I preferred using my left. It amazed me that I could get the same shapes from both hands, and yet when I wrote, it seemed as if my right hand spoke from the head, and the left from the heart.

They never said how once I would have been considered evil to have been left-handed, but I knew anyway by their fearful side glances and the way they insisted I not use it.

I switch my brush to my right hand and my teacher moves past me with a nod.

Manet once told me that Michelangelo, too, was ambidextrous, and seeing photos of his work, I don't doubt it. "Ambidextrous" reminds me of ambitious—both of his hands were ambitious, as are mine. I've been waiting so long for this that I'd prefer to use them both at once.

"As you can see, about the room are bowls of pears. I'd like you to study one," says our teacher.

Now I am not even as important to art as that bowl of pears that M. Julian asks me to capture, and yet it wounds me to have to, no, to be expected to paint them as if they are significant. What's unique and individual about fruit? This is asinine.

Painting still life never seemed a challenge to me anyway. "There is no breath to fruit or flowers," I argued with Manet once. "There's no need to capture it quickly or before it sneezes. It's too easy."

"That is why it is called still life, because it is still and there is a true art to painting it," he fumed. "It allows for the capture of detail and nuance, you pedantic ignoramus."

Though I am sure M. Julian will not agree with me either, I must ask. "Excuse me, but what do the pears mean? Why pears? Why am I not painting a person, an animal, something with spirit?"

"Still life is the beginning. You must conquer it before you can attempt something with movement and life. Because with movement and life, with something living, you will be required to stop it with your eyes, give it a death of sort, my dear. Fruit. Yes, start there."

"Who cares about fruit? I don't care about fruit, dead or alive. Do any of you?" I raise my eyes, sweep my hand. "When we are dead, will any of us look at a painting of a pear and say, 'Ah, yes, I miss that pear,' or 'I should like to have known that one'? It is the coward's way, dear teacher, and I do not wish to learn how to paint a pear when I could paint a dog waiting expectantly for her master or a woman who has just heard that her husband is coming home from war."

"Perhaps you can stay after class, Victorine, if you wish to talk further about what makes for a worthy subject. For now, the task is painting a pear, and if you feel this is beneath you, then I suggest," he says, whipping the air with his leather-capped mahl stick, "that you consider going home for the day. Unless you'd like to make it longer?"

My eyes war with his before I drop my gaze, shrug.

M. Julian nods, stands before a bowl of fruit and a small square of mounted canvas. He extends his stick and points, sticking out his full abdomen, puffing his rosy, rounded cheeks.

"And now we begin," he says.

Yesterday we learned about all of the colors and how some complement others and how some contrast. The truth is all colors belong together: It's merely a matter of proportions, in my opinion. We were taught how to mix them, but I know from watching other artists how easy it is to allow your eye to guide this process. Instinctively a good eye will know just which colors to blend, and then how much white to add to lighten it. Mixing is almost as satisfying as painting, to me, and while I'm doing so, I forget anyone but me leads the class. I delight in finding how easily yellow lightens from sunflower to lemon.

After I cover the background of the small canvas with burnt sienna, wiping it on and off with a rag, I realize the beauty of beginning with something so easy. The background is there, ready, waiting, and it's foolproof. I can look about and no one's work is "wrong." My background has areas of dark and light, and I nearly want to take it home because it is beautiful on its own.

Then we form the rough outline of the pears. Again, we are urged to make just the slightest hints of them, and to simply wipe away or paint over what does not serve. We will have ample time to round them later, we are told.

If only life were so forgiving. Perhaps it is.

My eyes, I discover, are more trained than my hands. I try not to be disappointed in what I produce, because I know that within me is the ability to paint. I just have to figure out how to get to it. And I will.

It is more than an exercise, this task. Soon we are adding highlights and shadows, and in no time, we are through. I feel myself now equal to creating any still life. Doing it once convinces me that I can do it again. It's not until I attempt a complicated flower that I realize the kindness he gave us in beginning with a simply-shaped fruit. My respect for Manet and his flowers doubles.

By the end, I am convinced I can do this. After the horror of attempting a self-portrait at home, this comforts me, though when M. Julian tours our work, I assume a bored face.

It hasn't been so long that women have been admitted to art schools at all in Paris. Though it was considered, at first, morally questionable for a woman to be a painter because she would be seeing the nude male form, soon it was accepted that this is the way women, too, must learn. M. Julian had started the Academy with men and women together, but due to protests he quickly separated the two. Not that Parisians cared; it was the English who complained, and he wanted to open his classes for all, or so he has informed us proudly. Which is why there are the separate classes for those who dare paint nudes.

After a few taps on the shoulders of those about us in the next few days accompanied by, sometimes, crying and the gathering of art supplies, storming out, we learn that if you are not talented, they will ask you to leave. In this way they are able to keep the class closer apace of one another. I see it as just another way to discourage women from painting. It does keep us all on our toes.

I crowd my easel closer, redrawing a white circle on the floor in chalk to claim my space closer to the platform as I have already seen the other women do. It means I have to erase half a circle of a girl who has just left the room, but I don't care. Art is not bred of politeness.

If they wore more sensible dresses, instead of these huge dresses with crinolines, we would fit better. These peacocks are clearly too wealthy for their own good. And yet I discover that while sometimes their love of art is a mere desire to become simply competent enough to be called accomplished, just as often these women are here to truly learn how to create. I discover again how unwise it is to judge people on the size of their purses.

Annie crowds closer up front and to me as well, determined, it seems, to be my friend.

"You've had practice, haven't you?" she asks.

"Not much, and you?"

She shakes her head and works on, the scent of her *eau de toilette* accentuating her movement. Somehow the way she holds her brush reveals that she prefers drawing. It's almost as if her fingers long to get closer to the canvas than the brush allows.

It is Saturday before we know it. We have not been told that M. Julian will critique us before the class, and a sound goes up from the students when he announces his intention.

"You. Bring what you're working on," he says. The girl blushes and nearly folds herself in half as if she can hide.

"Now, now, now," he says. She stumbles over the leg of an easel as she makes her way up front and hands him the canvas, which he puts on the empty easel before him.

"Fine colors, good tone, nice lines," he says. "Careful with the thickness of your pigment. You're doing nicely." He hands her back her painting and waves someone else up. As no one is yelled at or asked to leave, the tension seems to dissipate. Soon it is Annie's turn.

"Simple shapes, nearly but not quite sentimental tones. Lively subjects. Very good," he says. "Leave it up here for the moment." Annie, blushing and grinning, returns to her post near me, looks at my painting and sniffs.

I am next and after ascertaining that the paint is dry enough with a quick rub at it with my finger, I tuck it under my arm and saunter up, set it myself on the vacant easel.

"Look at that heavy outline. Are you working with Manet again?" he asks. Everyone titters. "This is supposed to be a young boy, isn't it, and not Olympia?" (We are now working at individual subjects and perfecting what we have done before.)

I haven't even used an outline, much less a black one, but my lifted chin says so for me.

When the judging is over, Annie is declared the week's winner and she is permitted to move her easel to the front of the class. I am just relieved to have her away from me; her alternating attempts at friendship and disdain are too dramatic for me.

Of more interest to me, Julian says that there will be monthly competitions. Some special competitions will be blind judged and all students, male and female, may enter.

At break the students buzz about me. "Is it true, is it true?" they ask.

"I am here to learn to paint properly, just as you are." They droop. I hate the instructor, who, not surprisingly, hates Manet's work and thus, me.

I am older than most of these spoiled rotten young women who paint mostly indifferently because they are here on a whim: Their parents have sponsored them, hoping they will get art out of their system and come home cultured and ready to settle down. Some of them do have a flare, as Annie does. She loves France so much, she says, she's going to make it her home.

"What was working with Manet like?" Annie asks. Her French is more than adequate, but she tends to linger over letters that we swallow.

"Modeling for him was pretty much like modeling for anyone else." I owe her nothing.

"What can you tell me about him, though? He painted so many naughty things. He must have been a naughty painter?" She widens her eyes, and my face hardens.

"That's the nice thing about art, you know—it's pretend."

She looks disbelieving. "Do you mean to tell me that you never . . ."

"I was a model, not a whore."

I am the first one to return to my easel from break, and I am disappointed to find that I have smudged my figure on the canvas after all.

"Where is our model?" our instructor of the week asks. "There was to be a young boy. Let us take a break while we locate one." Normally the stairs are draped with models looking for work in the morning, but we started today by listening to a lecture and so those seeking work have already gone home, despairing of the five francs they had hoped to earn for the day since the model for midmorning had been chosen, but he seems not to have appeared.

Instantly I think of Pug and of how good he was at helping Muriel pose.

"Excuse me? I know someone you can use."

"Go fetch him, and fast. The rest of you, sketch this vase."

It is worth the racing through the streets to avoid drawing the fussy object.

When I get to his apartment his mother answers, her stomach bloated with another baby. "Pug?" I ask, winded. He comes to the door, boots unlaced.

"Come with me." I don't give him time to tie his boots.

As we walk, I explain. At first, he balks, but when I tell him he will be paid for just standing still, he agrees.

Within half an hour Pug, wrapped in a loincloth for modesty's sake (because he is a child, not because our side requires this), climbs up on the platform. I argued with him before convincing him to change—he wanted to remain in his dirty gray slacks. He holds a long rod designed, I suppose, to keep him at attention, but he reminds me of an ancient picture of a shepherd.

Many women plunge in, brandishing paintbrushes. I carefully observe him, note his uneven haircut, his bored expression. I call out, "Pug. Can I get a smile?" which makes him scowl. Bravo.

Annie copies Pug's hand, I note from just behind her, capturing the anxious curve that I have not noticed, the tightening of his grip on the stick. She brings up my posing for Manet again over her shoulder while the *instructeur du jour* makes his rounds. His name is Stéphane, and he smells of a bright cologne that the room certainly does not need.

She asks again about my relationship with Manet. I again tell her I was nothing but his model.

"Still, I don't know. I don't think you can pose for something like that without . . ."

"Without what?"

She lowers her eyes. "It's all right. I have a boyfriend."

"Congratulations."

I circle the room to see our differing levels of progress. The room is dank and small, and it stinks of gas fumes and turpentine in addition to what Stéphane adds with his scent. The room is so poorly lit one would imagine windows had never been invented. I can't believe we are being charged so much extra when our working conditions are so much worse than the men's are. It is the price to pay for being a woman who paints, I suppose. *Mon dieu!* It is not fair.

I am close enough up front that I can talk to Pug, which gives me many of his expressions from which to choose, and none of them is boredom. I ask about school ("I ain't ever gone."), about the war ("Stupid men blowing one another to bits. Wish I could've fought.").

At break, I share my cheese and ham sandwich with Pug. He eats it incredibly slowly, and I hand him a hunk of chocolate I brought back with me which he wraps in a *mouchoir*, which I recognize, and puts in his cap that he places carefully on the floor behind him.

I sit again after break on the uncomfortable, backless stool that I usually eschew. My dress is severe, black, compared with the others', and my hair is all of a length, my bangs finally grown out, and the mass is pulled back tautly. I will not have them say I am just another former nude model. I dare them to think I am the frivolous, longing, skirt-wearer Alfred portrayed me as. I refuse to pose as some of these women do when the teacher comes around.

This palette of instructors is generally of the insincere kind. They applaud and praise a woman if they like how she looks, regardless of her art. Or, now that they have us thinned out to a "talented" class, they influence the students so that the women are afraid to begin a scene without significant input. One incline of the head and the young woman scrambles to adjust her vision to match that of the teacher.

If the teacher's work is known to her, or if he (always the instructors are men) brings in a work of his for us to copy, these weak women become his disciples, refusing to stray from his original. When I see the women this way, I understand the disdain with which we are greeted. I could hate us as a bunch myself were I to think this is all we are or all we are capable of being.

I mix my colors on my palette today without hesitation; because it is Pug, I know where to start: with the nose.

After a morning of painting in inferior light and smoke, my eyes are tired, but I see Pug put on his too-thin coat and pop his hat on his head, stop, take the block of candy from the hat, and stick it into a pocket.

"Want someone to walk with?" I ask.

He shrugs.

We exit the drafty building together. Pug sees me the whole way home. As we end up at my door, I say, "Here we are."

He nods grimly and starts to leave.

"Wait."

He stops.

"Come in for a minute?"

He nods again.

I scavenge for food.

"Want a sandwich? I'm starving."

"Sure."

I cut him a thick slice from the block of cheese, some salami, and two hunks of bread. His eyes thank me as he eats, this time quickly, as if to keep himself from stopping. Something about him reminds me of my younger self. Maybe it's his ferocity when he is, in truth, so vulnerable. Maybe it's that he tries so hard.

I slice a small piece of cheese for myself and light a cigarette. I lean over and brush at the right side of his face: God has visited me, and His face is covered with crumbs.

"Hold on," I say, and I grab a sketchpad.

Pug holds *le briquet* to his mouth, his eyes wide, so Pug wide. The pose reminds me of the one Manet had me and Léon hold for *The Fifer*.

I sketch quickly. Yes. The hat askew upon his head, the tufts of hair just below it. The eyebrows that unevenly frame the eyes. The purple circles under his eyes, first one, and then the other, as if my pointing out his hunger will prevent it in the future, appear on the canvas. Ah, but he and I are of the hungry class. We will never be completely full. It is what draws us together. It is what feeds us.

"Wait, Jup. Wait," my mother used to command as her terrier balanced the bread upon his snout. He wouldn't eat until she allowed him to. Afterwards, he would always lick her hand in thanks, as if she had been kind in letting him eat and not cruel in delaying his meal. Just another reason to despise the dog. Why didn't he hate her, too?

I motion for Pug to eat as I outline more impressions for the painting, only to realize his tender lips already suckle the hard bread, his hands clasp around the hefty slab in prayer.

Our father, who doesn't always give us bread, I think. Or love. It's left up to us to hustle for both, and yet we're supposed to give thanks for our self-provided meals? To whom?

I grab a dusty canvas from under the bed, brush it off, and set out my paints.

"There," I say eventually, having caught enough of him to build upon after he's gone. Though he's accustomed to modeling, I don't want to be yet another source of discomfort for this, to me, heroic child.

"You must sit for me every day until we are finished, *oui*?" My desire to capture his essence, because of my affection for him and my artistic ambition, wars with my concern for his well-being, and yet I don't want to abandon my painting. Because this record of my affection will last past the both of us, it's also a measure of my affection to paint him.

He nods, continuing to eat.

His slightly flattened nose reminds me of Willie's, and I make his hair a shade or two lighter than it actually is. If you squint, it could be said to be red.

My brush charitably lends his dirty white shirt a shimmer of color to exonerate it. I make a mental note to wash it for him when we're through.

But then what would he wear home? Nothing I own will do. Manet's studio is full of clothing and props, down to a pile of small Léon's discarded wardrobe. I don't have to ask if Manet still has it, the packrat.

When we've finished for the day, I write a note and ask Pug to deliver it to Manet, pretending I take no pleasure in having an excuse to write my friend.

"Wait for a reply," I say.

After my waif leaves, I stroke the painting's background with colors that always please me: purples, grays, light brown. A bit of black, but only a touch.

What are they speaking of, my mentor of sorts and my boy?

I use my finest brush to delineate his cuffs and color with a crispness they ought to have but do not, in reality. It's not as if I wear the best clothing either, but I am at least presentable. Our world, our city, makes much of what one wears. My poor boy.

The painting is my prayer for his future. That he will forever be allowed a secret innocence in those eyes, if even just a grain of it.

I run the color around his image's hands and wrists to echo their movement.

When initially settling him for the painting, I told him to look away from me, away from the world's prying eyes. Not for him the confrontational gaze Manet caught in me. I want Pug to remain the observed and not the observer. To be as apart as he can from the open-mouthed Parisian beast of art.

Pug returns wearing an immaculate, although too-large, shirt. He hands me a note, which I open a tad too eagerly for my pride, though he either doesn't notice or pretends not to as he raids my box of macarons, which he knows he has my perpetual blessing to do.

Manet asks after my welfare, says "the boy" may keep the shirt, and asks if he may paint Pug. I shred the note immediately, telling Pug only that the shirt is now his.

I put my arm around his slight shoulders and squeeze. When I receive a bundle of clothing from Manet later in the week, I give it to Pug, but I don't tell him where it's from.

Later, I critique my painting of Pug. I could have tidied it, although the looseness fits with his active spirit. The outline from Pug's jaw to his ear on the right is almost an unwitting homage to Manet's handiwork and I am tempted to smudge it, until I realize my work will always bear traces of his, whether I get rid of it or not.

Perhaps the hands are uneven. But even hands must earn their keep in a painting, and these do. The smaller, right one is plump and young. But the left one is powerful and conveys his strength. This boy will survive, I've no doubt. I'll see to it.

When the painting is finished, I hang it near my favorite chair so I can see it every day. It's good enough to exhibit, yet I don't. My boy has been exploited enough.

I call the painting *Le Briquet*, after the rectangular bread, which may seem unimaginative until you consider just what—or who—the brick is and what it symbolizes. Bricks are the building blocks of our homes.

At first, the brushes feel too fat and awkward. The bigger ones don't give me the control I desire, and the smaller ones take forever to fill in with. I begin to appreciate a bit better the painters I have sat for. They make the painting seem easy and the modeling hard. Now I know neither are easy tasks.

I dislike the new finish on the paintbrush handles. It seems the thick paint is a barrier between me and my idea, and I don't like that they are as smooth as the sides of a pencil. I scrape at my brush with a chisel I find on a windowsill in our studio until I uncover a chunk of natural wood. Then I carve a slight dip into it, and I want to toss it aside, yet it feels right. No harm if I take comfort in a brush that feels as if it is Manet's, is there?

"Let's play a game," M. Julian says on a Saturday morning after he has judged us for the month. As I suspected, Annie, a fast favorite of his, has won, and not only is her artwork hung at the front of the class, she has also received a medal.

But M. Julian has taken note of my work, of that I am sure. His comments, still barbed, are becoming more favorable, and though I understand that he is prejudiced against me, he would have to be blind not to see the progress even I notice in my work.

"I will tell you a tale, and then before you go home this morning, I want you to paint it."

Excitement whispers through the class.

"You are the Virgin Mary and the angel has come to you and told you that you are to give birth to God. I don't want the moment of the announcement. I don't want the moment before. I want the moment after the angel has left. Show me that moment. I must go next door to judge, and I will return to check on your progress. None of you may leave until I am satisfied with your work.

"They shouldn't have any trouble painting that next door," I mutter to myself, but Nicole hears me and bursts out laughing, and so the rest of the class insists on being told. We have a moment of happiness that fades as we all turn to our easels. How can we be friends when we are competitors? How can we support one another as women artists when there is only so much space for us both here and in the world? How indeed.

For a moment my brush sags, and I see that it is better for me to paint it in my mind before I attempt it with my hand anyway. Unconsciously, I switch the brush back to my left hand and Annie notes it, and I know she will tell when the teacher returns. I don't care.

For once, I am glad that I am not clear in the front. I allow the image to fully fog my mind before actually beginning. I circle the room once, twice, making sure everyone has begun before I quickly execute my take: the profile of a terrified young woman barely past puberty who stares off into a future filled with nothing but thunderous skies of lightning and rain.

The instructor asks me to remain after class. Creativity is appreciated, but some things are considered sacred, he says angrily.

"I have made the moment more sacred, for I have caught the probable reaction of one so young and scared."

"She would have known what an honor . . ."

"Yes, but God created us and so any reactions we have are sacred."

He thrusts his hands in the air. "Victorine, you have expressed to me your desire to have your work displayed publicly. You cannot slap the public and expect them to welcome it. Did you not learn this from Manet, from even Stevens?"

"Manet said anything he liked, the Academy be damned."

"Is that entirely true?" He tugs at the back of his hair as he has a habit of doing when talking with me.

He's right, of course: I have told myself repeatedly that I will paint what is expected of me and then change things gradually once I am accepted. Manet bounces back and forth and that is why he is alternately revered and castigated.

"But the brush says what it will."

"And who wields the brush?"

I bow my head, cross my arms tightly across my frame. "I do and yet I do not. Art has its own say, if it is allowed."

"Tell me what you believe our Virgin would like you to say."

I bristle. "That is not fair. I did not think of her as that when I painted her; I thought of her as myself, how I should feel if someone came to me and told me such a tale, how I would react if I believed it."

He raises his hand. "Stop. I am not a father. I am an instructor. I cannot tell you what to believe, just what you are expected by society and by the Academy to believe."

That's good, because I couldn't say myself what I believe anyway.

"Know your audience. If you are hired, heaven forbid, to paint a portrait, are you going to paint every blotch on a face, every gray hair?"

"Of course. Or at least as many as need painting to convey the feel."

He sighs. "Then you will never make a portrait painter."

"Who says I want to be one?"

Neither of us says anything more, because unless I want to sell tourist-level sketches in seaside towns, it is unlikely that I will create anything else for pay.

"Art that is paid to be created is poison and untrue," I say bitterly, collapsing onto a stool.

M. Julian pats my back. "Some of the world's, indeed the Church's, most spectacular sights were created by commission. Statues, paintings, altar pieces, tapestries, hymns . . . we owe much to commissioned work."

"True art cannot be. . . ."

"Perhaps one of the saddest things we must reconcile ourselves to as artists is that we are always being commissioned. Whether it's for money or for the good public opinion we want, our work is never pure."

"It's not the love of money that's the root of all evil then, but the need of it," I say bitterly.

"Michelangelo may have been paid to create the *David,* yet he looked at it as being given the time and marble to allow his own spirit to flow to future generations. Sometimes inspiration merely needs channeling, and it will bloom because of the guidance better than it would have if it had been left to meander."

I see what he means, but I don't want to.

"I knew you were a true artist, dear girl, but this solidifies it. Whatever you paint, you must use both your mind and heart. When you do, nothing can stand in the way of creating what is best both for you and for the world. For the future."

This is not a new conversation to me, just new with him. My chest feels heavy and my heart weary. He is right, he is, and yet there must be another way.

"The *David?*"

In my mind the statue, a giant in its own right, topples, breaks into tiny pieces, and is swept away. Now I imagine the world without it. Is it a better world? It is not. This is like wanting a kiss, loving the wanting, and yet loving the kiss itself and the ache of its absence.

He smiles sadly. "The *David.*"

"I shall not paint people as they wish but as they are or I will not paint at all," I say.

"Then you shall not paint at all, I'm afraid. It is a rare patron who wants to be reminded of mortality, of imperfection. Art is meant to hide those things from us, else it would be called something else."

Pulling a stool out, he sits in front of me and holds my trembling hands.

"You are discounting a very large thing. The artist. Whatever the artist does is art, if done with love, attention, and affection. Or sometimes even if not . . . art is in service of the artist, and not vice versa."

I gasp, though I know I am overreacting, but I'm not, either.

"You are in full control of your talent, if you have trained well, if you pay attention. With care and toil, you can create anything. What raises something to the level of masterpiece is simply diligence, patience, and a willingness to start again when necessary."

This, then, is the hardest learned lesson of my schooling. I try to learn it, but just as quickly, it seems I forget.

◈

In class I learn shading and perspective. I find I don't like these rules, that I enjoyed watching the art created without having to know the terms for what is being done. "It's a bit like watching a fine meal be made in the kitchen, isn't it? It takes all of the beauty out of it." I say to an instructor, who growls.

That is not to say I don't adore learning, I do, but I am eager to be done learning the terms and methods so I can go on to put my own thoughts on them. No more sieving my work.

I follow the rules carefully at first, because I am so unsure. Unlike Manet, the Salon will accept my work. As Alfred does, I will make my veiled statements, but I will perhaps nudge a bit harder. As in real life when you use double entendre and some people are too thick to pick up on it, so my meaning will be lost on some. Unlike Manet who is always confessing and unlike Alfred who is always trying to mean what he says, I *will* mean what I say. I gladly paint this young man before me, but the one I am most eager to successfully paint is myself.

At break time today we troop outdoors to get some light and air, and we re-mark about the ridiculous nature of being able to see so much better outdoors when we are supposed to be making art inside.

"Why do you paint?" I ask the four girls around me in an attempt to form some support among us. They laugh and swing their hair.

"Because men enjoy saying their wives paint."

"Because Maman desires it."

They give reason after reason, but no one says because they must. I know then they are not a threat, not any of them. Except Annie. She shrugs off my question, but I detect embarrassment beneath her contempt. This young woman does not want to appear to love art.

I preach the gospel of creating *we*, and they appear to listen intently, though Annie argues with me. "I paint so that men will take me seriously."

"Perhaps if you took yourself seriously, it wouldn't matter so much how they take you," I say, and only two of them laugh at my double meaning.

"Tell us why *you* paint," a quiet woman named Nicole asks, and I love her for this.

My eyes blaze but I say nothing. I will only sound pretentious if I speak now, and pearls before swine and all. . . .

"You modeled for Stevens, too?" Nicole asks as if she's been waiting to ask me about this. "I like his work."

"He's good and one of the kindest men I sat for." I don't say more.

Hearing how little they connect with art, even those like Annie who are actually talented, scares me. What if I fail? What if it turns out making art isn't magic, isn't a way to touch the soul, but is really only another trick? After all, I am paying a fortune to be taught how to paint like me, whatever that means. I'm trying to communicate, and yet I have to keep to myself if I am to succeed . . . this bewilders and discourages.

Is there a way women paint? Didn't men create the rules? What if there's a better way to see and create? Why am I paying to listen to a man teach me what men have been saying is the only right way? It's only because I want to beat them by their own rules that I tolerate it.

I will dedicate myself after that to seeing if there is a womanly way of painting—and I don't mean subject matter or technique, exactly, but what if the female soul expresses itself best differently? That is not to say that there aren't crossover areas, and it doesn't mean the sexes can't learn from one another, but why should a male tell me the right way to paint any more than I should tell him? For all I know, male and female eyes contain different parts as do their genitalia. I try to say these things to the women around me, but the words twist and tangle, and I don't half understand myself. When Annie laughs, I just shrug and go inside. It's probably preferable to the old Victorine who would have slapped her freckled face.

"We will also have an annual competition for best painting," says M. Julian. "The winner will receive a trophy and be allowed to learn with the men if she chooses for a week." We may use any of our class works for the contest.

When he announces this, my eyes dart over to Annie, who is a mere two easels from me.

She has a feeling for the paint, and a sweeping style that shows her arrogance to advantage. I'm not sure I can follow her in that, but no one can trump my eye for color. Competition only ever helps artists, as long as they strive for excellence in their own work on par with but not imitative of others.

Which is to say, I'm not intimidated.

◈

We are warned in advance that for our anatomy lessons a female cadaver will be dissected before us. Attendance is optional, and on the day of the lesson the room is not as full by half as usual.

We gather around on stools and in chairs as the man from the Sorbonne nonchalantly begins. He speaks about the anatomy in detail, and then he unzips the woman's chest with a scalpel, hacks harder to reveal more. I lean forward and am awed by how the glistening muscles attach to the bones, how the organs take up unsuspected amounts of space. So that is a heart. There is nothing beautiful about it.

A faint odor wafts to us, a mix of chemical preservative and natural decomposition. It is not overwhelming, but it is a reminder of this foreign-yet-familiar being before us, this used-to-be woman who, we are told, was—is—a fifty-year-old domestic.

While he roots among his tools, I turn over the woman's cold, calloused hand and trace the jagged scar I discover at her wrist. No need to tell us how she died. I fling her arm from me as the lecturer glares and rights the limb.

"No touching," he says as if he should have no need of saying so.

"Somehow I think she'd prefer my sort of touch," I say, earning myself another burning glare.

That evening, instead of going to work I remain at the studio and paint and paint the woman from my mind's eye until I can begin to dismiss the purple flesh, the blackened scar from my thoughts. The scene, we students gathered about the corpse, our teacher pontificating about us, reminded me much of Rembrandt's *The Anatomy Lesson of Dr. Nicholaes Tulp*. Manet has a copy he made of it, not much more than a painted sketch, but I love the emotion of his version which he fittingly gave to his doctor.

My painting mimics Rembrandt's, but of course with women instead of men. In the painted women's hands are brushes and palettes with which we circumscribe the dead woman ghoulishly. Above her is a mini scene in which she labors with a mop and a halo, below the examination of her is her funeral procession and the open grave with mourners about it.

I promptly put the canvas out with the trash.

I am grateful to have a clearer understanding of anatomy but suffer to think that my knowledge must come again at such a price to the unhappy woman. I try to tell myself that better some use come of her body, but I wish I could be sure she would see it that way.

The joy of painting becomes a part of me. At a break from class I wander into a group of students, both classes being on break at the same time. As some of the young women light cigarettes, I bite deeply into a *pomme verte* and stare contentedly at the white flesh my teeth reveal, try to ignore the rich scent of the brown tobacco reminding my nostrils of bistros and concerts, of a prop that never failed my fingers. I have given up smoking, for Pug's sake. The boy asked me if he might try it last week, and when I scolded him, he asked how come it was okay for me to smoke.

"It makes you smell like a grave anyway," he said.

I gave it up the next day. Though my fingers miss it, I easily enough fill them with a paintbrush, and it is more than enough. Since I have abstained, my sense of smell has brightened, and with it I almost believe my painting has gotten better. Most days I do fine without them.

I will take whatever help I can for my painting. Annie and I are, in my opinion, tied this month. We both hone at portraits—mine of Pug, me still stroking in his irresistible combination of innocence and experience—hers of a Sister brought in after Pug. The habit and wimple stand out lifelike from the grayish background, the face is round, rosy, and yet though the eyes are wide and serious, the smile is sweet. I wouldn't have had to meet the woman to know her. I complained that we had once again a clothed model when I wanted to paint a naked male. They seem to be leading up to this, and I will pester them until they follow through.

When M. Julian selects the winning painting, I am surprised to find that Annie wins again.

"You were a close second," my teacher tells me, "but you painted from love. That is a mistake. You cannot be entirely truthful, cannot focus objectively on facts when you care so much about your subject, unless you practice."

I understand what he means, but I want to curse. Annie does not openly mock me, but I feel it in everything she does, in the way she looks at me over her shoulder. Next month I must win.

I put my painting of Pug in the corner behind a stack of canvases. As I flip through them, I see the one I put in the trash. Who has found something worthy in it of saving? My eyes see again the woman's wrist, the scar, the scene in the background of her at work, alive, of her funeral in the bottom corner. There is perhaps something of beauty here, even if it is melodramatic.

M. Julian joins me. "Now that painting would have been a worthy contender. Whose is it? There is no signature." His eyes tell me that he recognizes my short, careful strokes.

"Some paintings are not meant for anyone else."

He scoffs. "There is no other reason to paint. If you want to keep your thoughts to yourself, write in a journal."

"I disagree."

"Victorine," he says, patting me on the back, "you do not need to be falsely modest. You are good, and you have an agenda. I know that you long to show those you have sat for that you, too, can paint. I know that you have been made to feel as if you are nothing but your body. Why do you think I will not allow you to easily win? Because you are one who must be challenged to greatness, and the more you are challenged, the better you will become. Just how good you become will rely upon how open you are willing to be."

"You don't know me. How dare you presume . . . ?"

"Perhaps you will sign this painting?" he asks, handing me the canvas. "There is always next month's competition."

I take the painting from him and sign it as the others crowd about me and ask what I have painted. I do not answer their questions, but I do submit it to M. Julian next month. He critiques it before the whole class and explains how bizarre it is that I should try to tell multiple stories of the same woman upon one canvas. He points out the good things about it but is just as harsh about the overly purple shadows and ignored midtones. However, he praises my updating a classic painting, saying that I both condemn the lecturer and venerate the subject at the same time.

"She has tried something original: She doesn't seek to capture the scene in which our heroine is felled, but her whole life. She doesn't glamorize the woman's toils or her self-destruction. For that, I choose this as the month's painting."

Though I proudly move my easel to the front of the line, I also feel uneasy. I don't know what I set out to do when I began that painting, but I do know that I have not succeeded.

After my win, my confidence grows. My eyes seek sights among the city to paint, and I see them everywhere. Montmartre is one of my favorite places to visit. The gentle, whirling *moulins*, the slopes, and the pastoral pocket found right on the other side of it comfort me.

A blond-haired child stands among her father's sheep, and I know she is to be my next painting. After some negotiations, her father agrees to let me quickly sketch her.

I begin by ducking into a nearby art shop and buy a tablet and charcoal, not even notifying the school that I will not be in.

She is maybe eight. Her hair blows about her face, and her thin dress presses against her legs. About her amble her four sheep. Her face is serene and strong, and she stands in the wind as if it were thirty degrees warmer. She does not have to gather the sheep; they come to her. One of them buries his triangular face in her knee, and her gentle smile is just for him.

The strength she shows isn't just against the wind—it's against my presence and my plea for her to stand still for just one more moment, just one. She does with no trace of impatience. When I stop, she accepts my small payment: all the coins in my pocket.

"Merci," I say as I leave them and walk down the hill. While I adore paint, almost I am tempted to use only chalk for this one. The circles of the sheep's wool, her lone shape against the blue sky, would lend themselves to the impressionistic material. No. Chalk is not permanent enough to suit me. I don't wish to think of all of the things that are not permanent, and so I quickly get to school, ignoring the indignant look of the week's instructor, an untalented simpleton who insists I take my stool at once and get to work. He can't paint, though his work is shown at the Salon. All he paints are animals and hunting parties, and poorly at that.

Instead of sketching the taxidermy fox he displays, I begin drawing the shepherdess on canvas. When M. Spittle comes around and indignantly asks why I am not copying his animal, I tell him impatiently that I am busy. He protests and I tell him quietly that I am paying more than I can afford for these classes and that today I need to do this study rather than draw the moth-eaten animal at the front of the room.

He stiffens and sputters, but he leaves me alone, which is all I ask for.

My painted shepherdess pleases me much, and when I am finished with it, I bring the initial sketch I made to her father, who thanks me repeatedly and promises to cherish it always. The child beams when she sees her face surrounded by her sheep. She seems certain that her life is as it should be. I envy her that. Certainty would feel almost as good as creating art, I think sometimes. But then I know that isn't true.

I do indeed win the month's prime placement in the classroom using Annie's common subject matter, which she can't help but notice and comment upon. A tiny piece of me feels ashamed. She has found what moves her, but I have had to borrow from others.

What I want to paint I am not yet ready to paint. I must be quite sure that I can successfully recreate myself before I attempt it again.

Back and forth Annie and I paint, war, win, lose. There are now about a dozen women left in the class, but for me and Annie, there is only one other. Clawing, fighting, we elevate one another by competing, though neither of us is foolish enough to say so, not to ourselves and certainly not to each other.

When Annie and her rich friends enter the theater where I work to see *La Petite Mariée*, an *opéra-bouffe* by Charles Lecocq, the others wave until Annie clasps her hand to her mouth and whispers, laughs. The next day at school they come up to me gravely and Annie apologizes if they embarrassed me. When I say of course not, they laugh again.

"I'm not ashamed of working. I couldn't afford to be at school if I didn't."

"I heard one of your 'painter friends' helped you get into school," Annie says. "I've never heard of prostituting yourself for art. You must really want this. Too bad your family can't afford to send you."

I knock my canvas from the easel and find myself running down the street.

"Wait." I hear Pug's voice and I wipe my face.

"I spit on her, you know," he says.

"Pug."

"Well, she's pure evil. I hate her."

I laugh. "Mostly evil, yes. Pure? I doubt there's anything pure about her."

I hug him to me, and his head lingers a moment too long upon my chest. I sigh and gently push him away.

"What were you doing there, anyway?" He hasn't sat for us for some time.

"I wanted to give you something I found." He hands me a book.

I sit on the steps of nearby St. Stephen's and look up at him as I hold the volume. The book's pages are browned and pungent. As I turn the pages, fine lithographs of pinks, purples, and blues fill my sight. Women in dresses, flowers. Scenes of court life.

"It's amazing," I whisper. "But Pug, you should return it. You have to."

"I found it, I told you. It was in a dustbin."

"Just what were you doing going through a dustbin again?" I close the book carefully.

"The one near the market has good food sometimes," he mutters.

"You could pawn this book, Pug," I say.

His face blanches.

"At least let me buy it." But my pockets are empty.

"Wait here," I say. I go back into the school. Annie looks innocently at me.

"Empty your pockets or I'll tell M. Julian what you said to me," I insist.

"I didn't . . ."

"Do it now. It's for Pug."

She reaches me a handful of change.

"Now your lunch."

"Surely he can buy . . ."

"Just hand it over. You could do without eating lunch for a few days." She sucks her cheeks in and gives me a flimsy canvas bag.

Pug and I lunch on sausages and pastries on the steps of the church. When I return to class that afternoon, I lick my lips in Annie's direction.

For a time, I spurn the company of artists except the unavoidable contact of those at the school. Every morning after copious amounts of tea with cream, I stand before the canvas with excitement and fear. It's easier if I have an ongoing project, because there's a place to start. If it's near completion, however, one has to be careful not to ruin a canvas by overpainting. A painting is both a novel and a postcard. I envy Zola, Flaubert. Words, words, words. They are allowed as much space as they need to tell the tale. Even my largest canvas confines me to one scene with layers of meaning, if my instructors are to be believed. This is why painters plan so carefully. That is not to say that writers do not plan, but they have more scope. Paper is not so expensive or so fragile. While I can repaint a face (and I have, many times), I cannot alter the scale or position of many things lest I ruin the composition. I would have an entirely different painting if I tried.

Composition is the skeleton of painting. Only on its bones may we add those pleasing objects. What seems hurriedly dashed is really the result of much care and study. Perspective is not something we often play with, either, because if one tries to paint from more than one angle, the viewer becomes confused. Confusion is not typically the intended message. These things and more I learn with my eyes and my hands in ways I did not as a model.

What, then, of those bodies that seem bloated or to float, disconnected from earth in art? Is this bad technique or a statement? Sometimes it's either, or both.

When I stand before that primed canvas, I often know exactly what I will paint. I have studies and drawings. Sometimes, however, I allow sheer emotion to suggest things to me. "A butterfly," I say, and then I realize a butterfly the size of the canvas would be quite frightening and so I must add in a bush, a park, and perhaps a boy crouching to see the butterfly. The boy is larger, but if he is not looking at it, we will be scared of a butterfly that is writ too large. In fact, we may be reminded of a certain English author who favors giants and tiny humans in order to express his disgust at politics.

My art classes involve more than technique: I also learn nearly as much about musculature and anatomy as a medical student. We behold dissected bodies for very different reasons than medical students, and we do so more than once. The women think I am ghoulish as I sketch gladly the muscles of a forearm. Funny, we painters seek to both hide and reveal, as flesh does the muscles.

Manet sends for me. I refuse to visit him. I don't want to be anywhere but inside this world of painting, immersing myself inside of this wet paint, these shapes forming before me, from me. As I fall asleep at night, they pattern my mind.

When I step inside the school the third day after I decline to see Manet, a circle of women is formed around someone. I move closer, though the voice I hear doesn't leave me much doubt as to the source of attraction.

Manet stands in the center in his padded, fitted redingote, now a bit out of date, to his delight, I am sure, though it is clearly an expensively crafted garment. His eyes meet mine.

I cross to the props table and pick up the violin there, fingering the purfling bound about its edges, knowing it allows the top of the instrument to be much more flexible than I will be with him. I scrounge around until I find a bow in the case under the table. After quickly tuning the instrument I stick it under my chin. The strings squeak as I saw the bow along them.

Quietly at first and then louder and louder I play. My torso sways with the instrument. My hair flies about my face, and I stamp my feet as everything I have been withholding from myself identifies itself. I don't have to open my squeezed-lidded eyes to know his nearness; his scent announces him.

Clack of a cane (the bow squeals), clop of his now-heavy legs (my bow sighs), and then nothing but the strings as they sing, sing, call. My fingers long to speak directly to the strings without the remove of the bow, to make the soul post inside the violin aid not only the bridge but me in transmitting what I have to say as well.

I toss the cheap violin, throw down the swan-bill headed bow, and open my eyes.

Manet looks intently at me. The room is otherwise empty now.

"I need your help," he says. He sits heavily on the prop table. "Julian showed me the painting you're working on."

It's a painting of the heads of three Greek statues. I have added a sunset and trees, and I am rather proud of the colors and that I appear to have intertwined the *en plein air* and still life in my study.

"I made it clear that I did not wish to be summoned; I have my own art to create."

He lowers the pitch of his voice. "I can see that you are making real progress. What a clever pairing. I don't think I've seen it done in quite that way by anyone."

"Did you see the yellow?"

"We'll have to talk about how you are getting those vivid colors. So many aren't mixing these days."

"Yes, but that means they are missing out on what these new colors can do."

M. Julian pops his head in just as I'm about to show Manet more of my work, and Manet nods.

"Victorine, I need you for this painting—it's a croquet scene. I'm going to attempt to capture it in the new style."

Croquet—the only sport men and women can participate in together publicly. "Manet. . . ."

"I know it's a lot to ask, but I'm trying something new."

As M. Julian again dances in the doorway, Manet touches my shoulder. "Why don't we go get a drink?"

My departure is not unnoticed by the other students.

I walk slowly so that Manet can keep up with me. He says it's just a touch of arthritis. Of course it is not.

On our journey, I curse the cobblestones for their unevenness as the poor man attempts to traverse them. I made him come to me. Still.

"Wait here and I will call you a carriage," I offer.

He puts his hand on my arm. "No, thank you. It's a fine day. Let's walk."

So we walk in silence. I have missed our walks, our silences. Every silence is unique, I know that suddenly, and ours is purple. Quiet walks with my father, Willie, Stevens, or even Pug all had their own shades.

"You can't expect me to pretend that I'm just a model anymore."

"Did you ever?"

We laugh.

It's not until we sit at the café that he tells me that the painting will be done at Stevens's house over the weekend.

"As his wife is out of town, chances are he will have company there."

"A mistress, you mean?"

Manet sighs at my bluntness. "Her name is Alice, and I thought perhaps she could sit in on the painting too. I've used her before."

I glare at him. "Why her?"

He shrugs, and I realize that he doesn't know why, just that the painting requires it. That I understand, even more so now.

He takes in my clothes. "But you won't wear that depressing dress, will you?"

"I don't much care what I wear these days, Manet."

"Tell me you aren't one of those dreary, pretentious artists who thinks fashion unimportant?"

"Is that why you're wearing that jacket, because it's fashionable?"

He pulls it closed.

"No. I happen to be one of those dreary, pretentious artists who thinks what I wear is so much less important than what my models wear. And this was a gift."

Two years ago, if what remains of my fashion eye is correct. Morisot, no doubt. She has been keeping company with Manet's brother for some time, but rumor has it that she refuses to marry until she feels her painting is established under her own name.

"I can't blame her as a painter for not wanting to share your last name."

"I don't want her to," Manet snaps. "That is, who do you mean?"

A laugh escapes me, and he laughs too. Apparently, age helps one take oneself a bit less seriously. Bitterness twists his lips. "You were right, you know. She and my brother seem to be perfectly paired."

"And isn't that better than not having her around at all?"

He clasps his hands together. "I don't know that I would say that."

I don't know that I would either, but I mean it of others.

"I didn't know you could play the violin like that." Even under his illness, I see longing for something just out of reach.

"Tell me more about this painting," I say briskly. I haven't got whatever it is he wants, but I want it, too.

SEVENTEEN

A Game of Croquet

LFRED'S ESTATE is flowered and vast. I haven't been to this new place of his just outside the city. Alice Lecouvé is introduced as "a model of Manet's" when she joins us. She is vaguely attractive with, interestingly enough, red hair. I hate her toothy smile and her propensity to giggle as if she understands everything when clearly, she understands nothing and certainly not Alfred.

Alfred greets me as if we are dear friends, kissing both my cheeks. When he pulls away, I see tears in his eyes.

"Let me show you to your room," he says as he picks up my bag. I follow him down the hall. The curtains are wonders of velvet and silk, the walls are wainscoted with dark brown wood below, topped with striped satin.

"Will your wife be joining us this weekend?"

"No. She is visiting her sister."

"That Alice seems nice." He turns to me but says nothing.

When we get inside the room, he puts my suitcase on the bed and embraces me.

"I'm here to model," I say, prying myself out of his grasp. "And I know about Alice."

His breath is heavy, from carrying the suitcase, now that he is even thicker, with graying hair. I don't want to despise him in this beautiful room full of exotic colors and his tiresome Japonisme, but a part of me does.

"Dinner will be served in an hour," he says and leaves the room. The door barely shuts. If it had been Manet, he would have shut it quietly, but not that quietly. A click would have told me he knew he had been rebuffed. Alfred has never known the things Manet knows.

◈

We stand in place in the back lawn for Manet as he tries to capture the sun's shifting, and he bobs his head as if he is dodging bullets. I don't care for Manet's *plein air*, "fuzzy" style of impressionism, though I don't tell him so. His attempts at this new art are unfortunate. Just because some critics have tried to cover him with that label doesn't mean he is obligated to try his hand at it. I try not to think that the illness creeping upon him might have something to do with his painting.

First of all, in *A Game of Croquet*, I can't tell it's me. I hold my mallet, and my right sleeve is rolled up as if I am a scullery maid. I am painted larger than usual and squat; my dress blurs with the ground. If he ever thought I was attractive, I certainly don't seem so now, though I do seem important, by my central placement. This time he paints my arm as he has so many times before, but he paints it with strength and power, acknowledging, I think, I hope, that I have become an artist. He covers my head with a scarf—a blur of blue. It reminds me of Alfred's scarf picture, and I suppose it reminds Manet of it, too. I still hate covering my head, though I have learned when to acquiesce to the necessity and inevitably of doing so.

In this painting, I am hunched, about to swing—about to submit my work. He gives me, as always, the most important place in the painting—I am the focal point. There's a watering can near me—he is saying that he has been the one to nurture my art, and he has. Behind me is Paul Roudier, a bland painter friend of Manet's.

In front of me are Alice and Alfred. I know nothing of Alice; she's a boring sort of woman content to merely be in the painting; she doesn't talk of herself. Alfred sits while I make my move. Seeing that both he and Alfred age, Manet is urging me on in my art.

We are situated diagonally, indicating space. That is not something Manet often considers, space. Is it the intervening years that he paints? The distance between him and me, between Alfred and me?

The weekend goes fast, between the sittings and the actual playing of cro-quet that we insist upon. Manet cannot play. He walks with his cane while I swing the mallet. He has given me something to lean on in the painting, or something to use as a tool. Or as a weapon.

I cannot deny that he has helped my painting. It is the last painting of his for which I will sit. I am very clear with him about this: I don't need anything more from him; he needs nothing from me. I don't think he would ask again, anyway. His eyes skim over my face as if it is yesterday's newspaper. When a fresh young maid serves dinner, his eyes follow her.

Ah, but he has given me a mallet—in this painting, echoes of his cane. Is art our crutch?

When Alfred comes to me in the night, I hold him, but nothing more. It feels, then, as if this would have been enough for him all along. Surprisingly, I discover I don't mind it either. I wake before dawn dreaming of cannons and Willie. Alfred puts his arm about me and we go back to sleep. I pack as soon as the sun is up.

I gratefully say goodbye both to Alfred, once again, and to my sitting for Manet. For good. I shudder as I think of those thick arms around me, and that thick paint of Manet's. The past is only worth revisiting in one's mind. The present is much more pliable. And this final painting of "me" by Manet? Dismal.

The weekend sends me plunging gratefully back into city life, back to school and Pug. He is a delightful diversion. I can count on him to be waiting for me, sometimes even after I get off work. He is a faithful companion, and he is not at all artistic. In my heart, though, he is my and Willie's son: something about how his hair flows over his brow reminds me incessantly of Willie.

"Go home, Pug," I say one snowy evening after work. I'm glad to see him; I've been worried for him, but I'm tired. Between art and work, I have had little time for him and even less time for my mother.

"I'd rather build a snow fort," he says as he bends down and quickly forms a snowball. I let him hit me with one, and then I scamper behind a tree.

We walk by the Luxembourg Gardens, and the place is blanketed in snow. The Medici Fountain sports icicles.

"Truce. I will help with your snow fort if you stop throwing snowballs."

Together, we scoop the snow into our gloved hands and pack. It takes a very long time without tools, but eventually, we are sitting in a fort.

"Why did you want a fort?" I ask as the quiet cold surrounds the cigarette smoke of our breath.

"So you and I would have a place to live," he says, ducking his head.

I put my hand on his chin and lift it, reach over, and kiss him on his cheek. It is the purest kiss I have ever given, and it feels like the only kiss I will ever want to give again.

"How are things at home?" I ask as I share a bit of chocolate with him.

He shrugs. "I need another job."

"Have you tried modeling for other schools?" I ask, but as I ask it, I feel uneasy. Not every school has the reputation of ours, and I fear for him.

"They don't want me," he says. "There are too many models."

"Could you sell newspapers?"

"Maybe." He throws the bit of paper from the chocolate into the snow.

"Hey you. No littering up our home." I ruffle his hair, and he grins, but it's a sad one. We're both pretending to be happier than we are.

I wish it were in my power to take him in, but how? I live in a dingy, tiny room that I frequently bring back women ushers to. Impossible. Like our friendship.

As late as he says goodbye, the next morning he is at my home to take me to school. It's rather like having a puppy. Or a son.

I don't try to run Pug off; it wouldn't do any good. Instead, I buy him a shirt and more food, always more food.

Not for the first time I ask him about his education and am horrified when he finally confesses that he does not know how to read. The next day I take him to a lending library where I set up an account so that he may borrow any books he likes, but only when he is ready.

"I can read some," he says at the library, and I make him show me using children's books that he scorns. I nod when he guesses a few words. For all of his scorn, how tenderly he turns the pages, how absorbed he is in the illustrations, and how his lips move as he struggles to read those simple words. I want to gather him in my arms, but I know better.

Though I don't have any idea how to teach a child to read, I was taught. Surely I can figure out how to teach him. What would appeal to someone that age? I think about the books I read as a child, and I settle on *Le Comte de Monte-Cristo* to read with him. When the weather is nicer, I take him to the gardens, and we sit on a bench where I read one page, and he the next. He learns quickly, and after no time, it seems, he begins checking out books.

"Keep them here?" he asks after yet another visit to the library as we take a load of books back to my place. He settles in, rather than getting ready to leave.

"Doesn't your mother need you to help with the younger ones?" I ask.

He rolls his eyes.

"Pug, they're your siblings."

"And how many brothers and sisters do you have?"

"Well, none." I pick up the top book from the stack and open its cover, close it.

"Then you can't possibly understand the smell and noise. As long as I bring money home, my time's my own."

I flip the book over, pretend to study it. Pug does not often speak about his family. "What became of your father?"

He scowls. "Never had one."

I want to hug him, smooth away that fierce look. "Do you have grandparents?"

"No. My mother works, when she's able," he says. "Between having babies."

I don't ask what sort of work she does. I already suspect.

"She's ready to have another one. I'm the only one working."

He kicks at the bench, rises. "I'd better be going."

I remember how he has pocketed my most recent treats rather than eating them.

"Pug, here." I hand him half my baguette money for the week. His mouth trembles; I look away. He tries to give the money back, but I won't let him.

I can't afford to keep a whole family in food; I must find some work for him, or better, some decent employment for his mother. Another baby. Oh my.

After he leaves, my room's quiet surrounds me. I think of how many years I may yet have to live without Willie. I leap out of bed and grab my sketchbook. Soon I forget how alone I am.

Not having seen Pug again for a few days, I search for him.

Finally I wait outside his place, ignoring the rancid odors and river of suspect mud. "I haven't seen much of you lately," I accuse. I have filled my pockets with all of the coins I can spare.

He grins as if pleased to have been missed. "I've been working. My mother still can't."

For all of his pride, I can't imagine a young man can support a family so large.

"Does your family have food for tonight?"

His foot destroys a small mound of dirt, and I give him the coins.

"Meet me after I get off work tonight, ok? I have nothing else or I would give it to you now." I could only pray the night's work will bring me enough for bread for a family, and for my upcoming tuition.

As if heaven answers, a man comes into the theater alone who asks me to share his theater box with him; he has asked before, and I have sat with him but with the utmost propriety.

Tonight, when he hints at loneliness, I nod. "Me too," I whisper.

When I come out of the theater on the man's arm, I wave my tips behind my back at Pug until I feel them taken. I am not sorry for what I am about to do.

Pug comes over the next day and I hand him some money and tell him it's for walking me back and forth to school so many times. I'm not, after all, selling myself: I'm just being polite to a man who needs it, and if he leaves me a gift that is his affair. I asked for nothing. When Pug tells me his mother is back to work, I fill my evenings with sketching, and even though I don't regret what I have done, I am relieved. Pug's face has rounded out again, and he doesn't stare hungrily into store windows. I don't worry that he will steal something and be hauled off to jail. No, there are many things to regret, but not what I have done.

At school the next morning I give No Glasses all of the money that I have, because she has been hounding me to pay.

"But you owe three times this amount. It must be paid by week's end or, I am afraid, your spot will be given away."

"I will have it by then. In the meantime, a receipt, please."

She scrawls freely and tears the receipt from the book.

"Merci," I say, meaning anything but.

I spend the week ushering, playing concerts, and pawning anything and everything at hand, and still I am short what I owe for my classes. I plead with Lucille, No Glasses, to give me another week. She refuses.

"We have a waiting list for these classes, a list full of those who *can* pay."

"You aren't an artist at all, are you?" I ask.

She smirks. "You will need to pay us the rest due or starting tomorrow, you cannot take any more classes."

I sweep past her and into the studio. Only when I am out of sight do I allow my shoulders to sag. While I'm supposed to be painting the generously endowed fellow up front, I'm trying instead to steady my hands all morning. At last we are allowed to paint a nude, and I cannot keep my mind upon the task.

"*Qu'est-ce que c'est?*" M. Julian asks as he stops in front of my easel.

"It's supposed to be him," I say, pointing to the fellow who seems quite proud of displaying his equipment for us.

"Ah. He would thank you for this," my instructor says, pointing to the oversized member I have given the man by accident.

"It's useless," I say. I rub at my forehead and discover I have just smeared wet paint onto it. "It won't matter much longer anyway; I won't be back after today," I confide. There is nothing else I can do.

"What do you mean?" He puts his hands on his waist.

"My funds are exhausted."

"Come with me," he insists.

After a long conference between Lucille and M. Julian, it is determined that I may pay as I can. When asked why I fell behind, I merely say, "family obligations," and am surprised to feel I have been entirely truthful. Pug is my family.

"While normally this method would not be available to most students, having you here is good for the reputation of our school. I don't need to remind you," M. Julian says to Lucille, "of the prestigious visitor we had recently."

"Merci, merci," I repeat. I want to hug someone, kiss someone, but I don't. Instead, I allow my eyes to speak.

"Class is not yet over," says M. Julian gently.

What if he hadn't been the instructor today? I would have disappeared and been forgotten.

Back in the studio, I smile smugly at Annie, who turns her head.

After class I approach her. "Let's go," I say. I'm in the mood to celebrate.

It takes a few glasses of wine at my place, but I discover I am right: She wants to be with me. She has never been with a woman, it is obvious, and it is equally obvious that she considers this a Parisian adventure, a libertine experience. The part of me that enjoys the art of seduction comes alive, and soon the American is convinced she is a lesbian for life, and I won't have to worry about her bothering me again. I don't tell her what would save her untold misery: Appetites are genderless. It is we who decide which attractions we will follow up on, and usually those are the ones that are more socially approved of.

Into the night we make love, she becoming better at receiving and giving before dawn. I normally don't care enough about sex any more to devote such time to it. She is younger, with long brown hair, black eyes, and cherry cheeks. She pretends to be good but wants to be allowed to be bad. I give her many opportunities to be both. She is still my enemy, my rival, but now she doesn't think she is, which is what I need.

I slip her out of the house with a lingering kiss, reminding her with my tongue what I have been doing all night long, and it isn't until I turn to go in that I see Pug.

"What are you doing here so early?" I hiss, pulling my dressing gown together, tying it.

He turns away at my rebuke.

I sigh. "Come in."

The room smells, and I quickly pull the duvet over the rumpled sheets.

"Make some toast if you want," I offer as I go behind the screen and quickly wash, change clothes, and comb my hair.

I hear him busying himself near the small table.

"I don't mind," he says.

I poke my head around the screen. "You don't mind what?"

"That you like girls. Do you get paid for having them stay over?"

"Paid for? You've got the wrong idea about me."

"I've heard of women who like women."

"I like both men and women," I say, walking to him, grabbing his face, making him look at me. "If I liked just women, I wouldn't care who knew it. Never forget, Pug, that you can't help who you love. You can help what you do about it, but feelings are just feelings." I release his chin, notice his upper lip is darkening. I suppose that happens. I have known him, after all, for over a year now. He is beginning to get taller, too.

"So you love her?"

A priest couldn't have made me feel guiltier.

"Time to go," I say briskly, tucking these thoughts away to examine more closely later.

I usher him out of the house, and we walk toward the academy.

Too soon it seems I am vaulted by graduation from my artsy nest. M. Julian gives a commencement speech worthy of a political figure. He also gives us all certificates of graduation and despite not wanting to, I am proud to hold mine.

My mother has deigned to attend the ceremony. She says nothing of the paintings that I show her. Maman does not say that she is proud of me, but she bestows upon me a gift: my father's painting supplies that I had thought long gone.

"Where were they?" I ask.

"Under the floorboards. With the paintings," she says.

I had never excavated under the boards. I had only seen a bit of canvas hanging out once and lifted a board enough to identify the bundle without looking further. Why would I need to see again what was etched into my mind?

The small, red wooden box containing my father's brushes closes with rusted hinges and crude edges. I remember it well, though I haven't seen it since I was small. I dare not open it until I get home, and when I do, a squall of grief blows in with the sweep of turpentine from the box. Then I am glad to be alone.

I hold onto my job at the theater while attempting to find clients to paint.

I allow myself to take on themes in my painting I would have normally considered too bourgeois, but I must paint them if I am to catch the Salon's attention and then subvert it.

My scant training has meant that though I have learned much, I feel that I am a novice. When people ask me to paint portraits, I do. It's a way to continue practicing while getting paid. I ask them before I paint them if they wish a true rendering or a flattering one. While sometimes they seem insulted, I find it best to ask. At times what they say they want is not. Then I alter the painting as we go; I try to ignore the part of me that feels singed by this. Those nights I drink until I fall asleep.

But I'm beginning to understand that what they really want is a portrait of how they see themselves, and I am doing them a service by that. We all desire to present our best selves, whether we do or not. There is nothing wrong with that; it's a human trait. Or at least that's what I tell myself after a glass or two of wine.

I suspect Manet and even Stevens are sending clients my way, but I can't prove it. I bring my card to the art shop where I always bought my supplies for class, and I thank the woman who sold me the first batch whose name I now know: Adele. For her kindness in also sending people my way, I paint her three children as a group.

The only portrait I have not yet completed is my own.

Gradually, I find that I am asked to do more portraits, and I am able to quit my ushering job. I miss the secret, dark evenings spent in a crowd of good-smelling, well-coiffed people, all of us enjoying music, ballet, or plays. I go on my own occasionally, but it's different to pay for a ticket and be seated without being able to move freely from one area to another while attending an event. Now I do not know the actors or the dancers. I do not get to watch them improve from performance to performance. There is only the one time, much like when people see my completed paintings.

Pug continues to appear magically at my elbow, sideburns forming on his face. His voice deepens in the coming months and as he gets taller, his eyebrows grow closer together. I find myself painting another portrait of him, as if to record the vanishing boy.

As I change clothes during this painting, after a session in which I have accidentally smeared entirely too much paint on myself because we have laughed so hard, Pug makes tea for us. Then we sit side by side on my bench, one of the few pieces of furniture in my room.

He has a cookie crumb just above his lip, and I wipe it away. He leans in and kisses me, awkwardly trying to force his tongue into my mouth. I freeze.

"Pug." I lean back. I feel as if the remainder of my innocence has just been taken from me.

"I'm sorry," he says.

I leap up and pace for a time before speaking.

"You're a growing boy. You have feelings you don't know what to do with.

You know I've had lots of sex. I do understand. But Pug, you are like my," I
can't say it, because it can't be true anymore, and he will always think it was his
fault and maybe it is best if he does. "We need to not see each other anymore."
There. I haven't meant to cut it off so definitively, but I have. It really is the
thing to do.

"I'm sorry," he repeats.

"I'm not blaming you, Pug, but people are beginning to talk."

Damn me for taking on portraits that require a reputation! Damn me for
this and more.

He stands and stumbles over his own feet, puts down his tea cup, and stares
back at me forlornly. I stand to hug him goodbye, but he is gone, leaving the
door open.

If only I had been able to tell him, though, that he is going to turn out to
be quite a kisser.

Why must I always be saying goodbye?

After several letters from Eva, I agree to visit her. She does not offer to pay
for the ticket, not out of rudeness, but because she does not have to think of
money. I can't afford to go, but I need to see a friendly face. As I buy the ticket,
it occurs to me that this could have fed Pug's family for two weeks. I quickly
ask for an upgrade, even though it severely depletes my funds. I will just paint
all the faster when I return.

My mother lends me several fashionable bonnets, insisting I must wear
them and instructs me to tell Eva that she can buy them if she wants them.
Of course I will say no such thing. But nevertheless, my trunk contains three
hat boxes.

"What is the good of having wealthy friends if you cannot ask them for
favors?" my mother asks.

"Not taking favors is what keeps us friends," I tell her.

The train trip promises to be many hours long, and I have never traveled so
far alone. I choose a seat near a window and pad the hard bench with my shawl.
Though the sun shines outside in the early spring, I rub my hands together.

I pull out Zola's latest novel, *Le Ventre de Paris*—the Belly of Paris, which is
about Les Halles and the working class. I am enthralled with his portrayal of
my people, but alas, the train arrives before I finish the book.

◈

At Honfleur, I am quickly bundled by a kissing Eva into a carriage and swift-ly carried to her home. It is a large brick affair with acres of land about it. Though it is nearly dark, I stand for a moment after we get out and admire the newly flowering view.

"You'll like it here," Eva says as she watches my eyes try to take it in. I've never been so far from Paris, never been so far in the country. My eyes quickly fill and refill with images and newness.

The next morning, I am up before anyone else and out the door. It's the same as sneaking out for a walk in Paris, and yet different too. Nature sleeps as surely as a city. Watching the sun rise, and the animals gently begin their nearly unseen murmur is much the same, I discover, as watching the city lights go out and the shop doors open.

"We'll go see the painters today," Eva says at breakfast, fully dressed and wearing a string of small pearls. Her hair is turned up and mightily pinned, I'm sure, because I know how heavy it is.

"There are plenty of painters in Paris," I answer.

"I think you'll soon understand why they love Honfleur so."

"And do you love it?" I ask, touching her sleeve.

"Jeanne does not visit as often as I like, and I miss my parents, but other than that . . ."

We visit her artist friends at Boudin's *pied-à-terre*. Monet is there, standing close to a painting of the sky that looks as if he has merely gazed upward and added in black and gold streaks.

"Would you say you are becoming one of them then, M. Boudin?" I ask as I look at his painting of lime trees that doesn't look in the least like Manet's work to me.

"Oh no, no. Don't get me wrong—I've agreed to exhibit with them, but . . ."

At this, Monet turns his head.

"Where will you have it?"

Boudin says, "We are still hunting for just the right place."

I tune out the rest of what they say. The scenery has much more to say to me.

◈

As I tramp with the men during the afternoon through the fields, even painting with them, I understand their attraction to the Honfleur light that flees at the speed of life.

"See just now it is and then it is not. If I do not paint briskly, I will not capture the glow on the side of the tree," Monet says.

"Perhaps you could use your imagination?" I ask.

He scoffs. "The imagination is no substitute for the eye."

How very like Manet he is in that, except Manet does not trust his eye enough to paint quickly. Not true. He paints quickly, but only after knowing what he wants to paint, and seldom does he allow something as changeable as the light affect his vision.

"You are saying much more with your painting than it appears," I tell Monet.

Eva smiles gently as she paints a black outline and floods it with color in a familiar way.

"You are not persuaded?" I ask her as I desultorily paint the sun as reflected from the nearby barn. I'm not yet convinced by this new method of painting, for all that I do understand it. Degas has also shown me what there is to admire in it, and yet. And yet.

"The men know how I feel."

In fact, this new style might be said to have been developed not in Paris but in the country. Nature surely lent a hand, and many of these painters take to the outdoors, their art subtly shaped by Paris's new architecture. That nudge outdoors has only aided them in discovery

As for myself, breathing country air, painting freely, anything I please, has caused me to feel that my art belongs now to myself alone. I experience freedom anew.

"Can't you stay longer?" Eva asks. We have giggled and walked, danced, and plotted, shared a bed like good sisters and told one another our deepest secrets while Henri returned to Paris on business. I found myself having to make up secrets for Eva because I don't keep anything from anyone but myself. Those are secrets I can't share because I don't know them.

In the lumpy bed we lie side by side in our heavy, ivory-colored gowns. I wear the one she insisted on giving me. I prefer to sleep unencumbered, but that will not do here. I don't habitually sleep naked to prove anything—if someone is seeing me sleep then they will have seen me nude already. I do it because I want to be able to move about freely in the bed. I want to experience my body as the animal it is and not the feathered bird others insist it be.

We talk for hours and I toss when I do try to sleep.

"What's wrong?"

I rise up on my elbow. "This is a beautiful gown, but I despise wearing it." I sit up and yank it over my head. She giggles as she stares at me in the faint light coming in the window from the moon. She, too, sits upright and takes off her gown. Her body is full and dark, lush.

She lies back down and smiles at me in a way I imagine she does not at her husband any longer, not after the things she has told me.

The moon shines brighter onto me, into me.

"Come on," I say. The girl in me stirs.

The moon beckons and I open the window. I insist we climb out it.

"But no one will hear if we go out the door," she whispers loudly.

I hike a naked leg over the first-floor windowsill, then the other.

"Come on, Eva." I don't know why I must escape this way but escape I must.

Her hair splays about her bare breasts, and she follows.

Once outside, I make my way to the pond.

"Victorine. No."

I grin and plunge in.

Pinpricks of cold chill me—spring has not yet fully warmed the water. I move my arms and legs, let them carry me as far from shore as the little pool will take me. A splash sounds behind me, and she swims towards me. Her shivering smile warms me, and she comes to me, puts her arms about me.

"Have you ever kissed a woman?" I ask scornfully as we stand together in the shallow water.

Water drips down her face. Her eyes, this close, seem offset.

"I can tell you want me," she says. "What's the harm?"

"You didn't answer my question."

"Of course not. I'm married."

I sigh. "I don't do that anymore, Eva."

"You don't do what?" She moves her body closer to mine, and her breasts are against mine.

"My paintings are my lovers."

"Not even for one night?" she asks.

"One night, is that all you want? Here I imagined you might fall madly in love with me and we might run off." I stride out of the water and sit on the bank.

"What did I say? I know you've been with plenty of women. Can't I kiss you?"

I put out my hand and almost touch her shoulder.

Then I do put my hand on her shoulder. "Why don't you paint me instead, friend?"

That night, she begins her first nude painting. I am her willing model, and we never again speak of her advances. She paints with those olive fingers; those thoughtful dark eyes, and I have to wonder if they see things mine cannot.

"What pose?" I ask before we begin.

"You choose."

I sit in a chair with my legs crossed. I smile in a friendly manner.

She frowns. "This is like no nude I've seen."

"Paint it."

She holds onto the ferrule of her brush, and then puts it down.

"Victorine, I don't understand your pose."

I laugh then and I think I will not stop. This is the first time I've been painted by a woman.

When Henri comes home, he walks in on her painting me. I don't flinch, but she rushes to cover me with my dressing gown.

"What are you doing?" Henri asks. His face is red. I wish I could teach him all the things I know that would satisfy his wife. One deserves satisfaction in all areas. Art and love may sometimes clash, but that is because both can be obsessions. When handled delicately, perhaps they can come together. Just not for me.

"You must get rid of this," he says.

"Why?"

"It's not decent for a woman to paint a nude."

"Is that just one more thing it's not decent for a woman to do?" I ask. But I stand and slowly put on the dressing gown Eva has thrown over me and leave when she inclines her head, asking me to. Later Eva tells me he made her get rid of the painting and I try not to hate him for it or her for letting him. How can he, an artist in his own right, not understand that a woman may paint anything she likes?

But in the evening—the day before I am to leave for Paris—I tell her quietly how to take care of her own yearnings. She both blushes and giggles. The smile she gives me the next morning at breakfast makes me believe she has followed my suggestion and found it most satisfactory. God help that selfish Henri.

In Paris, conversation heats at the café. The Anonymous Society of Painters, Sculptors, Printmakers, that new group of painters, begs Manet not just to join them but to take the lead.

"Display your work with ours," Monet pleads. Renoir, Degas chime in.

I have to crowd closer to hear all that is said.

"Forget the 1874 Salon—just exhibit with us."

"And be branded an Intransigent or an Independent as you have all been?" Manet asks, chewing at the tip of his cigar. His voice thunders and the lowering of his brow warns me—as it should them—to back off.

"Morisot is. . . ."

"What Berthe . . . Morisot does is her affair. The only way to break the Academy is to function within it."

My eyes (and my mind) go back and forth between the two sides. These artists do not know what I do: Morisot has revealed her forthcoming marriage to Eugène Manet. They are to be married just before Christmas, or so Manet told me.

The Anonymous (as I call them) get up their exhibition without Manet. It is to run a month, from April fifteen to May fifteen. They have, after much discussion, decided upon the photographer Nadar's former studio to hold their works, all of them for sale. I can't wait to see just how many do not sell.

Nearly thirty of the group exhibits, eschewing the Salon, although truth be told I believe the only reason they exhibit independently is because they are rejected by the Salon.

The building at number thirty-five Boulevard des Capucines encompasses the entire block. I go alone to this Manet-less exhibition because I know I will meet with plenty of my kind there. Eva and I have been in constant contact about this, though she declined traveling to the city for it. She has news, she says, from the doctor who says it is best she stays put for now. In this delicate way she means to say she is once again pregnant. I can only write back my prayers that the baby will be safely delivered this time. She has been married now without a child for some time, and although she is not convinced a child will not keep her from painting, she fears Henri wearies of her barrenness and that perhaps it is this that keeps him traveling so much.

I walk up the stairs into the rooms in my simple dress. I pay my franc at the door, giving it to some young man whose hair practically drips with oil. The slight drop of his jaw reveals he knows who I am; in art circles it is inevitable. I steel myself for more such encounters.

"Would you like a catalogue?" he stutters.

"Of course."

I pay the fifty centimes he says it costs, and I am permitted to enter the rooms only to discover that Nadar has bathed the walls in red. My eyes object immediately. Some photography equipment in a corner brings me back to my time with Alphonse. I shiver.

"And we are open from eight to ten in the evening as well," Renoir says to a woman who stops before the painting he straightens.

"Auguste," I say as I kiss his cheeks. One cannot call this dear "Renoir." "You look absolutely exhausted."

He points his hand at the painting he has just leveled. "Don't they look fantastic? My committee is in charge of the hanging. Truth be told, I've been here for three days and I've done the work mostly by myself."

I wonder if that's out of the other members' laziness or because he is such a perfectionist, but I say nothing.

"How many paintings are being shown?"

"One hundred and sixty-five. Seven of them are mine. Tell some of your friends that they are all for sale, will you?"

"I can't wait to see them."

"Yes, do take a turn, dear Victorine, and tell me what you think. You'll find that they hang no more than two deep, so that they are better seen."

"How wonderful." My eyes begin to take in the swirl before me, and I find myself drifting away from Renoir as my attention is pulled from canvas to canvas. At thirty years old and with an art-school-educated eye, I can finally view paintings and enjoy how they are made as much as what they look like on first glance.

Faces leap forward, colors charge me. Familiar places and people everywhere in paint, as if someone—lots of someones—love my Paris as much as I do. This is not the world of the Louvre. Here, everyday scenes and events are portrayed as if there is nothing insignificant about our lives, about ourselves.

I flow from room to room, as does the alphabetized artwork.

When Manet taps my arm with his cane, I turn and share my tears with the pinpricks in his eyes.

"Isn't it marvelous?" I ask, even though I know neither of us would ever want to be a part of this.

"It is," he says, but I notice his eyes follow Morisot who leans on his brother's arm before what are surely her contributions to the exhibit.

"I think you have chosen wisely," I say as I pat him.

"Perhaps not, Victorine. Perhaps not."

"Meurent, if you please."

He doesn't hear me. I wander away.

I plod through the rest of the rooms. The colors are garish, the technique slapdash. What pleases in the beginning is just repetitious at the end, for all that they claim they are very different in painting styles.

Yet something lingers from these canvases and I attempt to puzzle it out. I have to leave Manet's presence to do so. What is it about the man that I can't even have a proper artistic thought with him nearby?

That wouldn't be possible unless I allowed it, and yet I do, but I don't know why. All I know is that my life is so much duller when I stay away than when I do not.

Disgusted with myself, I slip out without saying goodbye to Renoir, also avoiding the just-entering Degas.

The pronouncement after the month's run is not dismal, but it's not great, according to Degas: "We had about thirty-five hundred visitors altogether. And we sold about ten paintings. That goes a long way towards making us legitimate."

"Did Morisot's paintings sell?" Manet's eyes betray his eagerness.

Degas shakes his head back and forth, raises his squeaky voice: "But then neither did mine. It wasn't the selling as much as the showing. I think that we had so many visitors shows how successful we were in exposing the public to our new way of painting."

I don't share my thoughts, because they are not charitable.

I wake one morning to a knock at my door. When I open the door, Pug stands in my doorway with a bloody nose, and I bring him in, minister to his nose and then give him hot chocolate and a croissant. Just as one should never trust the public to tell you what or how to paint, one should never allow anyone to tell you whom to love. He is the son I never had, and let anyone dare make something of that.

Now Pug comes in and out while I paint in my small room, one that I must make do. For all of the complaining of how much space one needs (and one can use much space if it is available), I find more painters who do not paint because they "don't have the space" or the money. One must have supplies, but space is optional. Don't we have all of outdoors if we must have more space? Artists have so many excuses ready, when only one needs saying that usually covers it all: "I lack courage." No matter what the result, I will not allow myself that vice.

I carefully peer into the mirror, trying to see my true self, not the Victorine that others painted and photographed. Sometimes she is right there, but sometimes she flits away, and I make my brush bring her back to me.

With the tip of my brush I add a spot of white to my painted eye's pupil. I darken the shadows about my nose, add another stripe of red to my hair.

So many thoughts can serve to distract while painting, and yet the process needs to be unconscious and conscious all at once. I smile at myself as I suspect the truth: All of this chatter in my head is to allow my mind to create without worry. When I look at the canvas, I realize I have finished: I have painted myself, Victorine.

Pug helps me wrap the painting in layers of brown paper and tie it with twine to get it safely to the jurors. Even the title of those who will decide, "juror," makes me feel judged. I suspect my reasoning for getting my canvas accepted is very different than others'. Perhaps that I have been a model will intrigue and influence them, but perhaps that I have modeled so often will do the opposite.

Pug insists on helping me carry the portrait. No one but myself will do to deliver it, and if it cuts me in half to hold it, still I will. As pilgrims to Mecca, we lug the canvas to the Palais de l'Industrie. When I am asked the title, the man taking the entries shows surprise at my reply: "*Victorine Meurent.*" It is cataloged and the entry information put upon the back. I am told I will be informed whether or not it has been accepted into the exhibition. There is nothing more to be done; I may now paint anything I like.

I start with *my* version of *Palm Sunday*.

As I paint *Palm Sunday*, I am tender with Pug's sister, Juliette, who sits for me. She is a couple of years younger than he is, and at first, I felt guilty painting her instead of him. But I needed a young girl to paint as I think Alfred meant to paint me, younger, innocent, and free of the worries and cares put upon me.

Sometimes when we were alone, he would say that art was meant to make life better, bearable. He said he worried that for me it simply laid bare my pain. He was both right and wrong. In this painting, I seek to paint myself aright.

I dig deeper into Juliette through conversation, and I learn that she wants to be a ballet dancer.

"Did you ever see Degas's paintings?" I ask.

"Yes. I want to be a dancer just like those girls in his paintings." She rises and does a half twirl.

"How carefully have you examined his paintings?"

She shrugs and sags back down. "I don't know."

Everything anyone needs to know about humanity is stamped on his faces, in the movement, in the tableaus of greedy backstage managers and the legs and arms that are separated in their thoughts from the rest of the person, in the silly grins on the faces of silly girls who are brought in for the pleasure of an audience, used, and then discarded. Dancers do not last.

The theater (I worked there long enough to discover) threw the girls on the street the moment someone more talented or younger and stronger came along. Degas drew pretty pastels with enough intensity to titillate and not scare braver girls and inobservant girls. I could hate him for that alone, for all that he is my friend, if I didn't know he is trying to say something that the less obser-vant aren't comprehending because he depicts the ugly and awkward alongside the graceful and colorful, and the latter distract from the former.

He is my friend, I say. Nothing more. He doesn't have liaisons with either men or women. Some whispered that he was a eunuch, some that he loved his work too much to give time for anything else.

"Why do you want to be a ballerina?" I try to conceal my scorn.

She smiles dreamily. "To dance under the lights, to move your body to music and create something that people will go home and dream about. To wear such beautiful costumes."

I can't argue with those dreams, and I wish she could see herself in ten years' time dancing, her legs aching and refusing to bend, her without an occupation, maybe even driven to being someone's mistress just to survive. I can't take this dream from her. If I could, though, I would take her into the city and have her talk to the older ballerinas. No. We shouldn't be deprived of our dreams, however ephemeral they prove to be.

Besides, dance holds a place in my heart. While it does not move me at all in the way painting and music do, it is there. Don't my fingers dance up and down the guitar's neck? Doesn't my violin move for me in ways that I cannot?

As I paint, gratitude for things with one syllable: sun, life, wind; and gratitude for other simple nouns—flowers, trees—rises in me. Verbs become less important, and nouns trebly so. I have always been a verb. No more. That thought saddens me, and I quickly move from it. Alfred is right: life is meant to feel good.

When Juliette leaves, I pull out a canvas to study. Something she said reminded me of my painting of Luxembourg Gardens, where the man sells food to feed the ducks, and a woman hawks balloons. I feel at one with the painting, a representation of the bourgeoisie on a Sunday afternoon, hurrying to weekend pleasures in high dress while those of the lower class melt into the background in their drab clothes. I felt a part of them while I painted the preliminary study of it from the balcony garden overlooking the duck pond. Painting the scene made me feel more than a part of it. It made me feel as if I were creating it, and I realized the world is mine, too. A classmate at art school said it reminded her of Manet's painting of the Tuileries. I would not disagree with that, and yet without me, those things I recorded would not exist, it seems.

◈

My mother's birthday approaches. She's not one for fripperies, and I'm not one for buying them. The motion she still makes, all these years after Jup has "run away" or been stolen—when she has a leftover crust of bread or a bit of cookie, yes, even now, her fingers flicking and she barely stops herself from letting go and sending a morsel to the floor, towards the invisible Jup—decides me on what to give her.

It will be what a painting always has the potential to be: a happy reminder, or a painful one. A study to pleasure the senses or to horrify. What it will mean to her will be partially set by my painting, but I can't decide for her what her reaction will be. I can, however, offer what I believe will move her, if only privately.

Meant to be an apology, I sneak the collar from her sewing basket which I know she has immortalized there, though I hardly need a reminder of its rhinestones, its small bell. I want to cut the shapes of the collar, the niches, into the painting with my brush.

From my box of important papers I unearth a crumpled poster of my father's: an image of a circus. In its corner, a small dog with a collar, and, faintly visible, a bell. Maman, so seldom one to go out, would not have seen this proof of his guilt at my crime. But I'm grateful for it now, as it serves as my model. Yes, his eyes were so, although I pose him as I often remember him: He would sit across from my mother, paws upon an ottoman, and watch her sew as if he were the guardian of the hats. His ears would cock when she spoke with him. When she was silent too long, or too still, he would bark to remind her he was there.

Sometimes I was tempted to take up barking.

As I paint, I add a glimmer to his eye, almost a smile to his face. His ears point like the wings of a nun's wimple. The shine of his fur on his ears, above his eyes, and the length of his nose I convey with white highlights. The fishbowl effect of his eyes I capture by extreme rounding, by pooling hazel at the bottom, the murky mark which reflects my feelings towards him.

I dot the eyes with a dab of white and pull the paint beneath it just a hint, for shape. More shine. Manet would do well to allow his figures to round and shimmer, as he does his fruit. Why does he refuse to idealize people in the same way he does a cherry, or even a flower? Is the man so frightened of his feelings? Idealizing people on canvas is another way of saying you love them, that they are even better than they imagine. That they are important to you.

Sure, maybe in real life they have a mole on their face, but that's okay. You won't notice it and you won't tell history about it, either.

Says the woman who paints for her mother a dog which she, the daughter, sold off the way Joseph was sold by his brothers, out of jealousy. Things turned out better for Joseph. Maybe Jup experienced the same?

Not that I care.

The background is unmistakably mine and not Manet's. Its light serves to allow the dog to be front and center. I resist the urge to add the pink and purple I typically do, and I add a cool mélange of beige instead, still within my preferred palate, while allowing his patches of fur (at least as I remember them) to be lighter.

Because I put Jup's name at the top, I am forced to sign it at the bottom instead. It feels strange to sign my name so formally when the painting is for my mother, but partly from habit, partly because all artists must, I think of a time when the painting is passed on. Sure, it ought to go to me, but if it doesn't? What if it wafts on the wind for a hundred years, say, or more, ending up in an attic. If I don't sign it, will anyone know it's my work?

Will they if I do?

With all of the art ranging up and down the halls at an exhibit (and those the chosen ones!), how do any of us expect to be remembered?

And if my painting is remembered, who will know about Maman's damn dog? Except her.

After I sold the pup, I sometimes imagined I heard it barking at night. My guilt mingled with my certainty that I had every right—responsibility—to rid our lives of that usurper.

My mother did away with my father's painting. What I did to her was much less cruel to her and kind to both my father and me.

Still, I have to wonder if her having something to love might have eventually done us all more good than my spiteful selling of her terrier. The cruel way I left the bejeweled leather collar with its tiny bell by the steps so that Maman would assume someone had stolen the dog haunts me. She simply put the collar into her sewing basket along with everything else she treasured, and that was that.

I wrap the painting in layers of paper left over from my father's shop and leave it on my mother's doorstep on her birthday, though my hands do hesitate to release it. It will be as much as admitting I am sorry, and I equally am and am not.

When I visit next, the painting is hanging on her wall much as Pug's portrait hangs on mine: close to her favorite chair. Where she can see it without moving.

I hope Jup enjoyed the circus. I can't help believe it was a more exciting life for him.

EIGHTEEN

Room M

FOR MY SELF-PORTRAIT, I wear a satin, sleeveless dress with a black bow up front, from Eva. In my painting, I'm not a street singer, not depicted as a prostitute. I'm a lady of society, *Le Parisienne* of the upper class, still free, but not depicted as the lower sort for once.

As a painter of myself, I'm freer than any of them have ever been.

The background is dark, brown and black, with highlights of anything else that pleases me, the better to showcase the vibrant yellow I overlay with ochre and hit with an even lighter shade. I'm pleased with the black lines I interject at just the right points to indicate folds. It works, especially from a distance.

No one dares compare my background to Manet's.

Sitting for oneself is immeasurably better than sitting for others, though it does require a balance between honesty and vanity.

I take breaks whenever I need. I choose the colors that feed me most. I decide to climb the social ladder several rungs simply by the dress I paint myself wearing. Yes, I thought myself a good enough model for all of the others. Maybe I was Manet's favorite model, as he so confidently told everyone, but I'm my favorite model as well.

Unlike his inclination to use me because I was fearless and helped him make better paintings than he would have without me, I am inclined to use myself as a model because I have earned the right.

Has too much been made of the relationship between light and dark already?

What has darkness to do with light? Ah, the utterer of that is surely no artist. Without one, you don't have the other.

My shoulders and neck rise from my dress. I'm proud of the triangular inlay to both pronounce my shoulder and create my collar bone. The eye can so easily pretend. Almost as easily as the heart.

A flower of hair, a hair of flower, the bloom blends so that it doesn't matter which it is and that is the point. If I must be technically correct, it is a flower, but I want it the color of my hair and so it is.

My shadows and shading have always been superior to Manet's. They are here, too. How little effort to create the hint of a bosom that we all know is beyond pleasing and yet it is mostly sheathed, after being bared for so many.

My nose I give a hint of a bump, all that remains after Bazille's excellent doctoring. How easy to paint it out, and yet I have not. I want to remember Willie in every way.

My ears are small and have been painted well by others, but never so well as by me. I paint me. I create me. Foolish men to think otherwise. Here I am.

With a ray of light, I highlight my white skin, of which I am proud.

The color of my eyes is not in dispute between my painting and those painted by others. But the expression in them may be. Between them and my clamped mouth, I am, as ever, issuing a warning to the viewer: Stop staring. And yet, if I want that so badly, why don't I simply quit painting, quit sitting for paintings, even my own?

This dress is a gift from Eva. I'm fashionable in it and covered. Decent. Elegant. I'm mostly neck and shoulders here.

It is only with self-control that I call it a self-portrait and not my version of *La Parisienne*. It is two years since Manet and Renoir painted versions of that painting (neither using me as their model, of course), and yet I still feel I am that woman more than either of the women they depicted. Maybe it's only pride that makes me want to call myself the universal French woman. Better to be myself, to represent myself, for once. How much better to be yourself, to show who you believe you are, than to be no more than a paintbrush in a jar jammed full of them.

I am painting a clump of violets when I hear the knock at the door; when I see the boy's postbag, I weep. I tip the boy generously as he hands me the envelope and I hug him. He laughs, disentangles himself, and speeds away on his bicycle, looking back with a wave.

My work will be in the 1876 Salon, or so says this note that bears the sum of my painterly dreams to me on nothing more remarkable than a piece of linen paper alive with ink.

My self-portrait has been accepted. More so than just wanting my work to be recognized, I want to be seen the way I see myself. At thirty-two, I have finally painted myself.

There are so many people I want to tell, but the first is Manet. No. He will find out. I want to tell my mother, but will she care? I want to tell Pug, of course, and I know I will have the opportunity to do so as soon as he is out of school for the afternoon. I have used the "spare" money I have now that I am out of art school to send him back to school. He lives with me, an arrangement his mother agreed to when I gave her some money from the first portrait I sold. She has a husband now, wonder of wonders, and her next-eldest son also works. So Pug is not missed as he might have been.

Painting portraits makes me feel useful. I don't command fortunes, but I am able to keep myself, give my mother some money, and now send Pug back to school. He complains and says he is older than the others in his form, but I know he is secretly pleased. He says he wants to be a sailor someday. "When the time comes," I tell him. I hope it never does. He likes my art, but he likes the pastries I buy him even better. That makes me smile, that he can't discern a difference in value between the two. Neither could Willie.

For the Salon, I wear a black dress, my hair combed carefully into a chignon. Once there, my mind whirls with the variety and number of paintings. Thousands of them line the hall, some placed so high in the room no one notices them. Mine is in a darkish corner, but at eye level. Shoes sound on the stone floor as the crowd files by, their eyes numbed by the enormous selection. The Palais stuns with music and banquets in the courtyard, vendors selling programs and popcorn. Opening night is one of the year's biggest social occasions, and I am waiting.

I tour Room M repeatedly, but there is no familiar black slash of a signature. My eyes, then, confirm the rumor: None of Manet's paintings have been included. Sorrow floods me, quickly replaced by smugness. I stand straighter. His money has bought him no space, nor his gender. I do not allow myself to wonder if I am here because I am his former model, the face and body in so many of his works. If it were a matter of being connected to him, *his* work would be here.

If only I were allowed to stay all night with my portrait. I'm in Room M, the place I've been looking to get into since, it seems, I was born. I have created myself. I will be seen.

Pug stands by me, looking at his shoes, bouncing a ball he has brought with him, turning in a circle. I send him out to get some air, and he gladly leaves.

I wish it mattered to me, all of the people who come by and tell me how much they enjoy my work, the ones who ask me about technique or subject matter. Later I will reflect and be grateful, but right now I am only waiting for one person. I have to see his reaction. Alfred will be supportive, of course, but what will Manet say? After all of this time, what he thinks means the most, even though I still have my private criticisms of his work. I don't deny that he is a master.

A large man in glasses stops and stares up and down at the painting and then at me as I stand in front of it, and I can't tell if it's my presence, as the artist, in front of her own work, that arrests him and the others or if they still recognize me as Olympia. The man nods at me and walks on. I'm both relieved and miffed.

I nervously turn my back to the never-ending flow of the crowd and stare at my painting as if I haven't seen it before.

The lift of this maturing woman's neck is proud, and she looks, as always, frankly at the viewer, a stance that is not so unusual now, but certainly echoes Manet's painting. Lines of loss show in her face. Most decidedly she does not wear a black shoelace at her neck.

She has properly proportioned features, handsome but not gorgeous, and the shadow hits the appropriate places on her face. There is something soft and inviting about her, even though there is something that is also tough and enduring and, perhaps, a bit endearing.

Occasionally someone will stop and say something pleasant about my work, and I smile and thank them. I wonder if they think me vain to be here, but I must, because he will come; he must. If it were not for the hope of an en-counter, I would go home and read the reviews, if any, later. With so many thousands of paintings, I haven't much hope of being singled out. So what? I didn't paint it to be reviewed. I painted it to set the record straight.

My former colleagues from the theater come to see me in pairs or in small groups, as if on a mission of mercy. I still do not enjoy the company of young women who talk of art as if it is another sort of dress one might buy, but I have learned to appreciate their fashion as a type of art. Stevens had that on me a long time ago.

I pace the short distance between my painting and the next. He will show up; Manet will show up, I tell myself. What will I say, though, considering his own work was rejected?

As I wait in uncomfortable shoes, I bounce on my heels. Alfred pokes his elegant head around the corner and smiles as if he knows I am watching for him. We embrace and his mustache pokes my cheek.

"How have you been?" he asks as he holds my elbows.

"Fine, just fine."

He nods and continues to survey me.

"I'm sorry about your wife," I say.

"Thank you. It was such a quick illness." He tears up and I pat his hand, feeling the loose skin.

"How are the children?" I ask.

He has seen my painting and does not reply as he studies it. "A great choice of dress, though a bit drabber than I'm used to seeing you wear."

I smile. "It was a dress I wore to art school."

"Art school," he says as if I am a child who has mentioned the circus.

"You have created a lovely composition, and I think you have captured you much better than I ever did."

I feel the truth in what he says, and I know it has taken a stripping of himself to say so.

"Thank you. That means a lot."

"You know I have started my own little art school. If only you had waited a bit longer."

I nod. "You're very patient. I'm sure they're lucky to have you." Neither of us really believes I could have studied under him. I miss him, it's true, but as one inevitably misses things one wishes one had appreciated more fully when one had the chance.

He hugs me, pats my back, and moves on. I watch him lumber away and I wipe at my eyes, remembering the comfort of his breathing beside me.

The air feels stale in this too-warm, cavernous place, and I run outside to get myself a drink and some popcorn. I am so nervous I can't eat it, but instead walk the grounds observing the sculptures and listening to the music. Ah, Paris.

For a time I forget that I have deserted my post as I watch the young men surreptitiously kiss the young women and the children chase one another, blurs of ribbon and linen, hats ducking in and out of the crowd. The elegant men and women assume cultured airs and stroll quietly, whispering to one another, stopping before statues. Those in thinner clothes show their sweat and their appreciation of the statues with whistles and loud tones. An occasional person reveals him or herself as an artist by the nervous way they listen to the remarks before their piece, by their inevitably worn-looking clothing and unfashionable hairstyles.

I nod and smile at so many people who appear to know me, although I am sure I do not know them. At least there is no spitting on me nowadays.

Every time I think I see his proud, half-bared forehead, every time I imagine I see Manet's shoulders, every time I see a man in a dark jacket and light trousers, my heart runs away with my breath.

Before long I find myself inside again, sure I have not missed him. He would never come so early; Manet would not. Besides, I feel sure I would have known if he had been there.

When I do finally spot Manet, I cannot speak. His face is drawn, and he leans heavily on his cane, as if soon it will not be enough. Pain lines his face, and his attractiveness is dulled by his paleness. The way his hair feathers out about his mound of scalp makes me want to smooth it. He reminds me of his father in the painting of his parents that he had first accepted by the Salon.

Tears fill my eyes as I watch him come round and view the thousands of paintings, his eyes scanning dully as if to say that none of them is his: not that one, or that, or that. As crowded as the room is, I know his forehead and his gait, for all that he does limp now. I wait for him by my portrait, and he does not disappoint me.

Then I am pleased and saddened that my work has been accepted and not his.

◈

Manet's gaze meets mine and stays with me as he advances. As he stops before me, I twist around, hunting for Pug, but he is still outside. I reach out for Manet's hand as he stares past me, not seeing my action.

"It is a good likeness," he says.

"Yes, but what do you think of the colors?"

His eyes follow the browns, the coral, the copper of my hair. His nose twitches at the yellow of my dress and his throat tightens visibly at the frankly dark background. Something softens and hardens in him.

He pats my hand absentmindedly. Then he is gone.

Rage fills me at his dismissal. I run after him, and it doesn't take long to catch up to him. In the next room he is leaning into a corner wiping his eyes.

I slowly walk back to my portrait. It doesn't actually feel good to surpass your teacher. I want to go to him, to breathe health into that ebbing body.

I go in search of Pug. There's no reason for me to be here now. I'll return tomorrow to study others' paintings.

On the way out, I see Manet seated in the middle of a group of painters in the courtyard, his friends from years before. They are laughing and chomping cigars, clutching drinks. I stand back and listen to him hold court. They are still fascinated by his commanding voice, still drawn to his passionate discourses on art, his dismissal of the nearby statues.

I stand in the shadow of the building in order to watch unseen. The cold bricks are against my back, and I rub against their roughness as I listen to the now-familiar arguments between the men.

"And what of your Olympia, now a painter herself? What of her work?" one of the men asks, a squat Frenchman with an overly ornamented hat.

I lean forward slightly. Manet cuts and lights another cigar, clutching it between his teeth. He breathes in deeply and exhales.

"Was her work here?" Manet asks blandly.

The men guffaw and I step out of the shadows.

"Perhaps you didn't recognize it because I wore clothing in the painting or because I wasn't posed in a way to give you pleasure," I say, coming into their circle.

"Which of you has ever had to pay the rent by posing nude? Which of you has ever had to be photographed for the illicit joys of men to afford supper?"

People are beginning to stop, to stare. Let them. Isn't that what I was born for, schooled in?

"I dare you, any of you, to come by my place tomorrow and let me paint you without your clothes and see what becomes of you. If you pose well, I might even give you time off for lunch. But you must supply your own food." I rise and spit my address at them over my shoulder. As if they would dare come, the damn bourgeoisie. As I glance backwards, I see regret on Manet's face. He's never been one to enjoy causing pain. I think of his tears earlier and of how much effort it must have taken him to even come today, and for an instant I am sorry.

After I leave, I remember that I was supposed to be courting their favor. Well, all the better to condemn them and myself for wanting their approval.

When the Salon is over, Pug and I retrieve my painting. We carry it back to our small apartment already cluttered with canvases; I unwrap it. I have no desire to sell any of them. When I paint portraits of others, I tell myself that I am creating gifts for them, and then I know with every stroke the painting is not mine. It's the only way I can part with my work.

Manet sends me flowers, along with a congratulatory note and a vaguely worded apology. Pleasure and grief, those always twin emotions accompanying my every interaction with the man, flood me.

After finding a vase for the spring mix of striped tiger lilies, delicate Queen Anne's lace, and soft yellow snapdragons, I turn to my self-portrait. I can't help but compare it to the portraits of me by my father now hanging on the walls. They sway slightly, when the wind blows through the loose windowpanes, re-animating my childhood self.

Without realizing I am about to, I take down my father's paintings and re-place them with my self-portrait. I trace its wooden frame with my finger: first the right side, then across the bottom, and up the left side, then across the top. *Bonjour*, Victorine. *Bonjour*.

NINETEEN

Trials and Errors

EVA WRITES to tell me that she is returning to Paris to give birth. She wants to be with her family during this time. After I read her letter, I dance and sing about my lodging. Then I look at myself in the mirror, touch my dry skin.

My hair is lank and unkempt, my fingernails jagged and dirty. My dress is limp and of cheap material. I don't care that I go about this way, but I wouldn't want my friend to see me like this. I sigh and heat some water as if she will be arriving today instead of in two weeks.

Though she tells me not to, I meet the train. Jeanne pouts and tells me I "need not" wait; I do anyway. The train pulls in and we wait, then wait some more until finally a head topped with a fanchon of pink peeks out, a hand waves, and it is the jolliest yet palest face I know, complemented by a puff of stomach at her waist.

After she kisses everyone in her family, she turns her dark eyes on me.

"Eva."

She hugs me and compliments the hat I have worn in her honor, one I borrowed from my mother. It's a large-brimmed affair topped with a dazzling display of pink and white ribbons that won't stay still—they bounce when I move my head. It's a foolish head covering but Eva makes over it, so that I'm not at all sorry that I have worn it.

Once we get her into the carriage something else becomes obvious: Her eyes, though they sparkle, are black beneath. Her forehead is wrinkled, and when she thinks no one is looking she slumps in apparent exhaustion.

She has failed to have a baby before now, and a selfish part of me wishes she weren't attempting it. Her crossed ankles are puffy, and we have to stop twice for her to vomit, though she is so far along. We continue the gay talk as if none of us notices, but it soon becomes apparent to me that she hasn't just come home to have her baby.

Jeanne and I sit on either side of Eva, at Eva's command.

Her parents speak of what the cook is making for lunch and Eva must stop once more to get out of the carriage.

"Oh, Eva," I say when she takes my hand.

Jeanne glances at me and takes her sister's other hand. I long to squeeze this hand until I transfer my own strength to it, but the limp weight in mine tells me this is a vain hope. What good is being strong if it's not transmittable?

Eva is only a month away from the time the doctor says she can expect the baby when she returns to Paris. I visit her when I can, tell her tales of my painting.

"And Manet? Do you ever see him?" she asks hungrily.

I glance compassionately at her. "No." We do not want to add to her burden by telling her the state of his health. He never goes out anymore, and he only paints in his studio and then infrequently. The gods of art seem to be demanding Eva and Manet at the same time. I cannot think on it, so I don't. Instead, I attempt to amuse Eva by swaggering like a particularly arrogant painter we both dislike. She tries to laugh but her gaze is so far away that I know she is only humoring me.

The following week I visit her home, only to be turned away by her husband who has since joined her. But the good news is that she has been safely delivered of a boy, he reports. That is the only news about her that I am given. The rest, I fear, is inevitable.

TWENTY

Manet's Funeral, May 5, 1883

T EVA'S I am admitted (with some maddening hesitation) by her tall, awkward husband.

"Don't go upsetting her," Henri whispers.

"How is she?"

"Not good."

Jeanne is at her bedside, forcing Eva to drink some water out of a pink glass. The glass magnifies the size of her lips and I wish I could paint her thus.

"Hello," I murmur to Jeanne as I take in the dark circles under Eva's eyes.

"Victorine. Thank you for coming. I've been so lonely today," says Eva. "I've wanted to speak with you about an idea I have for a new painting."

Jeanne frowns and tucks the yellow and pink flowered quilt, which covers her sister, under Eva's feet.

"Jeanne?" Eva says.

"You know you need your rest right now. I'm not at all sure you are up to company today." Jeanne looks at me.

"Jeanne," Eva repeats.

She hesitates. "I need to just go see to the baby and make sure Henri gets some dinner," she says.

The bedroom is full of light and flowers. A well-filled vase sits just beside her bedside on a small round table skirted with white.

The roundness of her pregnancy is accompanied by an unhealthy pallor and thinness.

She holds out her hands to me and kisses my cheeks when I approach. Her breath smells of imminent death.

"Did you see my darling baby yet?" she asks. "He's my best painting yet."

"No, I haven't seen him. I'm sure he's a handsome fellow." I adjust her pillow and ask if she wants me to draw the blinds.

"I like the sun," she says regretfully, and I know then that she knows she is dying, though she is only thirty-four. I am a mere five years older than she, and yet I feel maternal towards her. I tuck in her covers.

"My baby is not handsome you know, not yet. He's got Henri's nose and his fingers look like ghostly twigs, but he will be as handsome as his grandfather someday." It takes some effort for her to get the words out.

She indicates the chair by her bed. "Sit, please. You're the only visitor I've had all day, which is very odd. I haven't had a day like this since Édouard's surgery." Her hair is well coiffed, but a curl escapes and she wraps it about her finger, lets it go abruptly.

"Why are you dressed in black?" she asks.

"It's quite fashionable right now."

She scoffs. "But even when you wear black, you always have something colorful on—a scarf, a necklace. You are wearing unrelieved black and a mourning brooch; I want to know why." Her voice rises.

Her arms claw at her shoulders.

"The surgery didn't help, Eva. Manet is gone."

She sinks farther back into her pillows and says nothing. Her arms slowly fall.

"His funeral?"

"Later today."

Her eyes cling to the view outside the window.

Finally, "Can you help me sit up?" she asks. "And hand me all of the yellow flowers in that vase."

I shake the water from the daisies and lay a towel in her lap before placing the flowers in her arms. It takes her a silent half hour to weave them into a wreath as she chooses a flower, refuses it, picks up another, and intertwines them until her hands fall. She pauses, begins again.

I offer to help her; she refuses.

"For his grave," she says as she gives the flowers one last twist. "Please?" she asks, winded.

I hesitate. "Of course."

But she has fallen asleep. I lift the wreath off her chest and take it away with me, seeing myself out, turning back to get one last look at my friend.

I am grateful that the Church of Saint-Louis d'Antin is crowded. Though it holds five hundred, many stand in the back and the doorway is plugged with onlookers. I hand Eva's wreath to one of those aiding with the funeral. I whisper to him who it's from, and he whisks it up front and leans it against a standing flower arrangement, goes to the front row and leans over a woman who must be Suzanne. She turns as if she thinks she will see Eva.

The circle looks so small beside the other flowers, and yet it's twice as full of love.

I decide to remain at the back, and I view the funeral album, noting the names of those already here: Renoir, Degas, and Pissarro. It's obvious we are all painters as we slash our names theatrically across the page just as we desire to slash our way across time.

I push my hat back so I can better see where to sign, but I put the pen down without marking the book.

The church—so near to the fashionable store Printemps and the railway station Garde Sainte-Lazare, places dear to me—looks like a living painting, so many of his models (male and female) are here. Oh that I might capture this sight with my paint, the dome encircling all of these great painters and more. If the roof were to collapse now, how many lights would go out in our world? On the other hand, it might also extinguish some that do not burn so brightly.

Its arched sides distract me nicely as I try not to imagine Manet's body, robbed of a limb, up front. The story is that the surgery, performed just days ago, was a butchery that did more harm than good. In fact, rumor has it that his removed leg was tossed into the fireplace and temporarily forgotten. That I don't believe. The stench of a gangrened limb is something I well remember from the hospital.

I try not to think about the surgeries I aided with at the hospital, the blood, the pain, and worst of all, the sound of the saw cutting through what is not meant to be cut.

Manet so often stood contrapposto when he painted to take the weight off his sore leg, and he adored strolling the boulevards with Baudelaire. Better to have let him die with it, knowing what we know now: that it was all for naught.

I spot the back of Alfred's broad, graying head. The program says he will be putting the flag on the casket, along with other artists.

There are two boxes near the back, regular fixtures of the church, I assume. One is labeled "Confessions," the other "Deniers." I feel as if I should be putting something in both boxes, and yet what is there to confess? It is a mistake to regret, and confession is an expression of regret, in a sense. One does what one must. That is all. Still, I find myself tiptoeing over and sliding coins in the box. I notice Suzanne lean towards her son, and I add an extra coin.

Up front is that wooden ship that holds a man I have held, minus a leg. What tales he used to tell of his time at sea before he became an artist. Though he never expressed a desire to return, he was never sorry he went, either.

I can smell the flowers back here. Flowers overwhelmed his death room, I have heard. I sent around peonies as often as I could, knowing how he loved to paint them. I never signed the card, though.

The rows teem with familiar faces from the Salon.

Though I must strain to see her from where I am, my eyes locate again Suzanne and Léon up front with the other Manet family members. Suzanne says something to Eugène, pats Berthe, whose frame is rigid, and head bowed. If anyone has anything to confess, it is Berthe, not me.

Antonin Proust speaks on and on and I do not listen. Afterwards, we leave the church and wait for the coffin to come outside.

The pallbearers for Manet must, of course, also be well known. Émile Zola is one, as is Monet.

He is to be buried in Cimetière de Passy.

Stevens embraces me as we wait outside the church. After he releases me, he tugs at his suit jacket.

"Are you coming to the cemetery?"

"No. I prefer private displays of grief."

He shakes his head. "You know that if there's one thing he wouldn't have wanted, it is that."

"I'm afraid I haven't been in much of a position lately to know what he might have wanted."

Now everyone stands outside, his family, Morisot, who is crying as if she has lost herself. Suzanne, dazed, sees me and her face hardens.

Suzanne's arm is about a stoic Léon, who, I am pleased to see, has red eyes.

Suzanne, it occurs to me, is a Manet, yet I never think of her by that name. Her reddened peasant cheeks, her frumpy way of dressing, even today, do not reflect well on the family.

It won't matter. When there is an artist of Manet's caliber, history will remember only one Manet: Édouard. All others will necessarily have to add their first name and a description of who they are ever after. While he made the family's name, one might also say he has ruined it.

I can't help but be a bit pleased about this when I look at Suzanne, at Berthe who still uses her maiden name for painting.

Suzanne turns to watch the men carry her husband out, a man who has belonged to Paris more than to her, and the depth of her grief stuns me. Her eyes do not hide her loss, nor does her body, nor her limp clothes.

In that I see a hint of what Manet saw: her dogged devotion to him, her utter disregard for art, and her absolute rapture at him as a person.

Who wouldn't want that?

I hear my own broken gasps of grief: Willie. My life has been art for so long that love seems a distant song and one to which I no longer remember the words.

I sag against Alfred and hear a low moan that must be mine. I angrily wipe at my eyes.

They load the casket onto the carriage, which sinks under the weight, drape it appropriately with the French flag, and the horses' muffled clomps are the only noise that informs the world that Manet is taking his last ride.

Clusters follow the carriage by foot, and Alfred makes to lead me forward.

I shake free. He pats my arm and walks on.

Suzanne holds her son's arm and together they walk down the street. The declined angles of their bodies reveal that this is no everyday stroll. Pug offered to come with me, but I told him not to miss school.

Manet would have loved this long parade behind his body. He would have painted it.

When it's much too late for me to catch up unless I run, regret courses through me.

Manet used to tease me that the word for canvas came from the word "cannabis," another word for hemp. He knew of my early experiments with the other application of the plant and he said that perhaps my love of paintings came, in part, from that.

"But it's made from linen now, Victorine, so don't try to smoke it," he would say, laughing at his worldly cleverness. He loved to pretend to know about things that he had no experience with. Though he painted *The Absinthe Drinker*, he never drank it himself.

The weave of canvas is so simple: the weft and weave are one weft under one warp thread, and then under the following one. Waterproof.

Life's weave is neither so simple nor waterproof. That boat Manet is in will leak within days. Within months, I suppose, he will be unrecognizable. Soon nothing will be left but his skeleton and were we to dig him up, he would be indistinguishable from all other skeletons.

I can call art merely mangled plant material (canvas), repurposed animal hair (paintbrush bristles), ground rocks (paint). I can say he will rot and decay, but I cannot make it mean any less to me for all of that: Manet is dead.

But I am not, and even though his death threatens to overtake me, art revives me once again. As I imagine painting, I almost feel guilty about the smile that stretches across my face, the tingle in my fingers to touch a brush. Almost, but not quite.

Within the hour, I am at a blank canvas, brush loaded and raised. I look upwards, and then begin. Again.

Acknowledgments

Boundless thanks and affection to Barry Drudge, my favorite human and musician, and a formidable writer himself. Without your cheerleading, patience, support, sense of humor, and love, I daresay this novel would never have been finished. I'm so glad to be doing life with you.

To my and Barry's beloved children, Mia and Zack. You are adored.

Additional thanks and love to:

Lisa Gallagher, agent extraordinaire at DeFiore and Company. Your tireless efforts on *Victorine's* behalf are greatly appreciated. It's touching to know you care about her as much as I do.

Doctor Jonathan Watson of Manchester University for introducing me to the painting *Olympia* and the genre of art in fiction, the genesis of this novel. Thank you for the enthralling literature classes.

The Summer 2013 Spalding MFA novel writing workshop held in Ireland where I first presented a draft of *Victorine*. Many thanks to the group, which was led by our dearest Sena Jeter Naslund. To Cindy Lane, Rick Neumayer, Margery Gans, and Cherie Hamilton, thanks for your spot-on feedback and generous reading. Sena, for so many reasons, this novel is for you.

My Spalding mentors: Rachel Harper, Robin Lippincott, Roy Hoffman, and Julie Brickman. My heart is happy just thinking of you! To the Spalding mentor who got away due to scheduling conflicts: Eleanor Morse, I so wanted to work with you. And to the rest of my Spalding MFA in Creative Writing forever family, both staff, faculty, students, and alums, loads of gratitude, affection, and karaoke.

Kyle (K.C.) Kirkley for his scholarly lens and his intoxicating writing. Your use of language astonishes. Truly, you are an American treasure.

Shirley Jump for her long-ago writing group that she welcomed Barry and me into, for her absorbing fiction, and her continued friendship. Shirley, what an inspiration you've been.

James Tennyson Sizemore, my dearly departed uncle and writing mentor. How I wish you could have read this novel.

The Shepherd's Center book discussion group in North Manchester, Indiana. You continue to give me literary shelter. XOXO!

KenapocoMocha Coffee Shop's friendly staff for endless pots of tea and a lovely writing atmosphere. Amber, Becca, Reilly, Erin, Ashley, and Krista, thank you for the refills. Also a big thanks to the patrons of the shop who kindly ask how the writing is going and if my novel has been published yet. Here's your answer.

Steve Galiher, family friend and encourager, just because I'm glad you're on this planet. Whether hosting on TV or not, you are always admirably yourself.

Many thanks to Édouard Ambroselli for allowing us to use his photo of his painting, *Self-Portrait of Victorine Meurent, 1876*. What an honor to be able to share with readers what has long been supposed to be a lost painting.

And above all, thank you to my muse, Victorine Meurent, who set me on the journey of a lifetime. Much love and appreciation!

Works Consulted

I am indebted to the following books for ideas, facts, and/or inspiration:

Manet Manette by Carol Armstrong

Manet, Monet, and the Gare Saint-Lazare by Juliet Wilson Bareau

Édouard Manet: Rebel in a Frock Coat by Beth Archer Bombert

The Painting of Modern Life: Paris in the Art of Manet and his Followers by T.J. Clark

Manet's Modernism: or, the Face of Painting in the 1860s by Michael Fried

The Judgement of Paris: the Revolutionary Decade that Gave the World Impressionism by Ross King

Manet and the Painters of Contemporary Life by Alan Krell

Alias Olympia by Eunice Lipton

The Greater Journey: Americans in Paris by David McCullough

The Private Lives of the Impressionists by Sue Roe

About the Author

Drēma Drudge suffers from Stendhal's syndrome, the condition in which one becomes overwhelmed in the presence of great art. She attended Spalding University's MFA in Creative Writing Program where she learned to transform that intensity into fiction. Drēma has been writing in one capacity or another since she was nine, starting with terrible poems and graduating to melodramatic stories in junior high that her classmates passed around literature class. She and her husband, musician and writer Barry Drudge, live in Indiana where they record their biweekly podcast, *Writing All the Things*, when not traveling. Her first novel, *Victorine*, was literally written in six countries while she and her husband wandered the globe. The pair has two grown children. In addition to writing fiction, Drēma has served as a writing coach, freelance writer, and educator. She's represented by literary agent Lisa Gallagher of Defiore and Company. For more about her writing, art, and travels, please visit her website, dremadrudge.com, and sign up for her newsletter. She's always happy to connect with readers in her Facebook group, The Painted Word Salon, or on Instagram, Twitter, and LinkedIn.

About the Paintings

Readers interested in viewing paintings by Manet and other artists for whom Victorine was the model, as well as a sample of Victorine Meurent's own paintings, may do so at dremadrudge.com/victorine-visuals.

Fleur-de-Lis Press is named to celebrate the life

of Flora Lee Sims Jeter

(1901–1990)

CPSIA information can be obtained
at www.ICGtesting.com
Printed in the USA
FSHW021602270220
67479FS